I0725415

THE *HOLT FAMILY* SERIES

T.M. CROMER

ISBN: 978-0-9965720-2-6 (EPUB)
ISBN: 978-1-956941-31-9 (PRINT)

Cover Design: Deranged Doctor Designs
Edits: Trusted Accomplice

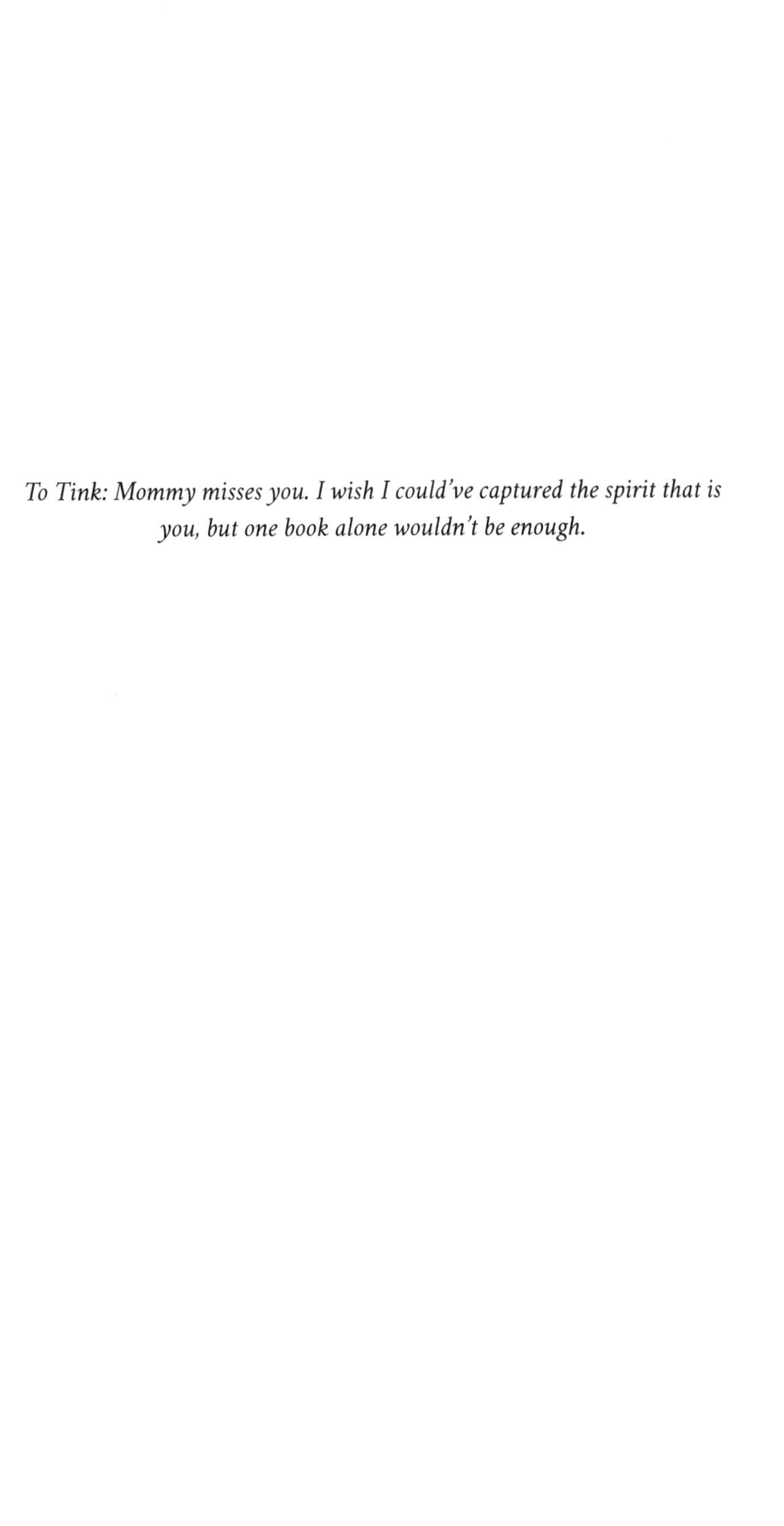

To Tink: Mommy misses you. I wish I could've captured the spirit that is you, but one book alone wouldn't be enough.

PART I

CHAPTER 1

She dove for a vacated seat at Gate 3.

The harried woman who'd gathered her case to leave said seat shot Annie Holt an irate glare. Offering a sickly grin, Annie slid in sideways and hugged the pet carrier closer to her chest. All she got for her troubles was a grunt when her computer bag connected with the passenger next to her. Okay, so she wasn't making any friends today.

Seriously, what did the woman expect? A fight for space was happening here. Even this podunk airport resembled a sardine can during the Christmas season. Only another hour remained until her flight, but she'd be damned if she moved from this spot.

A scarcely audible whine rose from the carrier she set at her feet.

Tink, her sweet puppy.

Annie unzipped the opening enough to insert her hand. With a gentle rub of her fingers on Tink's silky chest, she whispered, "Please don't have to pee. I just snagged this spot."

The poor wee thing eyed the throng of people hovering around them. An ant in the land of yetis. *Now* her anxiety made sense.

"I know, sweetie. Crowds make me nervous, too."

Rebelling against the airline's rules, Annie opened the top of the carrier.

Tink's blond head popped out to survey their surroundings.

"Not long now, and we'll be on our way to the Keys. You're going to love the beach, you know." In an attempt to soothe, Annie continued the stroking motion. "Those seagulls and sandpipers aren't going to stand a chance. You'll give them all what for."

Tink turned her goofy canine grin on Annie.

"I can see that makes you happy, you beastie."

The single sharp bark pulled a chuckle from her. Her fur baby never failed to make her laugh.

Pure love swelled inside her for the little blond fluff ball. They'd bonded over the last nine months—two lost souls in need of companionship. *Her fuzzy soulmate.* The only soulmate Annie was likely to have, if her history was any indication.

Lifting the soft-sided cage, she dropped a kiss on Tink's black-tipped nose, and in return, Tink's abnormally long tongue swiped her chin and ended on her mouth. Annie giggled and rubbed the spot with her shirtsleeve.

Right when she would've mock-scolded her pup about trying to slip her tongue, a tingling started at the base of her spine.

She was being watched.

Off to one side, resting his shoulder against a pillar and observing their interaction, was a lone man. The vast expanse of his chest was emphasized by his arms crossed in front. His pose screamed casual.

He was in no way casual.

His gaze sharpened, and he eased upright.

Caught by his intense spark, a shiver of awareness coursed through her.

His stare locked with hers.

Though travelers darted between them on their way to and fro, Annie was unable to break her odd connection with the stranger. Enthralled. It was the only possible excuse for her temporary paralysis.

Reality came crashing back in the form of a woman's booted heel connecting with the top of her foot, and Annie let out a muffled yelp.

Sonofabitch, that hurt!

She jerked and fumbled Tink's carrier, barely managing to keep it from falling off her lap.

Mindful of the increasing crowd, she placed her laptop and the soft-sided carrier between her feet, then scooted to the edge of the chair to hunch over, protecting her two most precious possessions. A shadow fell over her, and Annie threw her hands out, prepared to defend her pup from another accident-intent tourist.

But it was her newest obsession, and he squatted down on his haunches to point at Tink.

"What kind of dog is it?" His voice was deep with a whole heap of sin.

Every cell in Annie's body woke up and took note.

His questioning eyes were green with flecks of amber and brown, framed by thick, dark lashes that shouldn't have existed on someone with his light coloring. Tiny lines bracketed either side, indicating he smiled or laughed frequently.

Finding her wits was a chore, but she finally managed. "Morkie." His frown prompted her explanation. "A mix of Maltese and Yorkshire Terrier."

"Never heard of that breed."

The barest hint of a Southern drawl did strange things to Annie's internal wiring, short-circuiting the pathways between her brain and mouth. She gnawed her lip to contain a girly sigh.

"May I?" he asked with a half smile.

Hell, yes! Anything he wanted. Any *way* he wanted.

The tilt of his head and raised eyebrows suggested she'd taken too long to respond. What had he asked? Tink barked, and Annie was reminded of his initial question. She sighed, happy her bestie had her back.

"Of course." Did she gush? God, she hoped not. At thirty-three, gushing like a schoolgirl was frowned upon in at least one hundred and ninety of the one hundred and ninety-five countries of the world.

Strong, capable hands reached for Tink, and Annie shoved aside a twinge of jealousy. He found the perfect spot behind the pup's ear, and her ecstatic face had Annie longing to trade places with her.

Lucky dog.

The stranger had an artist's hands. Long, graceful fingers with calloused tips.

He played guitar and fairly frequently.

Annie knew a musician's hands when she saw them.

The man grinned up at her. A wide, generous smile with startlingly white teeth. The average Joe didn't have a mouth like that. Nor did the average Joe inspire a woman to write sonnets and draw hearts in place of the dots over her I's. But this man did.

Being in the presence of all that yumminess made her overly warm. That's when recognition hit and heart failure threatened.

"You're Quinn Jensen!"

All signs of friendliness abruptly disappeared. To see his open, animated face lose its heart-stopping smile was a crime against humanity. Fame had drawbacks. And as one of America's leading action stars, he must be recognized nearly everywhere.

The teen sprawled beside her had his earbuds jammed inside his ear canals and was preoccupied with an app on his phone.

She released a relieved breath and grabbed Quinn's forearm. A current of awareness shot through her.

This man would be important in her life.

He jerked as if she'd shocked him.

She damned well shocked herself, too.

His wary, cold expression screamed for her to back the hell off. She'd spooked him and not just with the thick current of energy that transferred between them, but more likely because he was a famous actor and some strange woman had latched onto him.

"I'm sorry. I..." How could she reassure him her blunder had been an accidental slip of the tongue? That she had no intention of announcing who he was to the whole airport?

A slight tip of his head acknowledged he got her message. Reaching into his duffle bag, he pulled a ball cap out and crammed it low on his head.

"I really am sorry," she whispered.

He opened his mouth to respond, but whatever he'd intended to say was cut off by the approach of a tall, leggy blonde.

CHAPTER 2

*C*rikey! The woman's legs had to be longer than Annie's entire body. Because her mother had always told her never to hate, she quelled that particular emotion. Instead, she settled on intense dislike.

Since the man was Quinn Jensen, the clinging vine had to be Hailey Newberry. They'd been linked as a couple for ages. As he moved away with Hailey attached to his arm, octopus-style, the woman whispered something in his ear. Quinn glanced back and gave Annie a long look before turning to Hailey with a comment that caused her to smirk triumphantly.

Their whole exit scene made Annie feel about three inches tall. She shifted her attention to Tink, and the pup's sympathetic expression made her downright irritable. Not for the first time, she wondered if the dog wasn't a human trapped in a canine body. An empath, like her, but covered in fur.

After the abrupt departure of Quinn's overpowering presence, she slowly counted to ten, sensing them move farther away, since she refused to look in their direction again. There was only so much humiliation a person could suffer.

To kill time and try her best *not* to appear pathetic, Annie pulled out her laptop and continued work on her newest client's ancestry chart. Delving into the past was always a good distraction. Genealogy had been her anchor for as long as she could remember. Because it was her job, she didn't have to feel guilty when she did a deep dive.

This time, however, her work couldn't provide the distraction she needed, and her thoughts returned to Quinn Jensen again and again. To the feeling she'd had that they were somehow connected on a weird, cosmic level.

Quinn.

That man had some incredible genetics. *Ugh!* Why did she have to go there? Maybe she needed to get laid. During the last two years of her marriage, her only choices had been to turn to her battery-operated boyfriend or go without. Christ, *that* should've told her something was off in her relationship. Who goes without sex for two years running?

Apparently not Charlie!

He'd been getting his rocks off—only not with Annie.

She'd always been a glutton for punishment and had stupidly ignored the warning signs. Her convoluted thinking made her believe she could reconnect and fix their marriage. She'd been wrong. Again.

Speaking of being a glutton for punishment...

Giving into the temptation to peek again, Annie lifted her gaze to the first man to stir her juices in what was tantamount to forever. He sat in the front row at the terminal next to hers, chatting with Hailey.

What she wouldn't give for one night with him!

Annie snorted. Half the women on the planet had probably thought the same thing.

Quinn chose that precise moment to look up. Whatever he saw —most likely her undeniable lust—caused him to pause mid-conversation. In spite of an embarrassed flush, no doubt making her appear like a boiled lobster, she wasn't able to break eye contact.

It seemed he couldn't, either.

For the longest moment, their gazes remained locked. There was a wealth of unspoken thoughts hidden behind the fact they were strangers and the politeness attached to it. If he'd been single, would he have approached her for her number? Probably not. He didn't seem the type, and he had his fame to consider. Would the average woman want the man or the celebrity?

For Annie, the answer was simple. She wanted the man. The status attached to him held no appeal.

Hailey put a stop to their staring contest when she snapped her fingers in front of his face.

Rude!

Quinn must have thought so too, based on the irritated look he gave her.

Kick that bitch to the curb, Annie mentally projected.

A dark frown formed, and he cast one last quizzical glance in her direction.

Prodded to wickedness by the devil on her shoulder, she grinned and winked.

Quinn's mouth fell open.

Why the hell she'd done *that* was beyond her. But damned if it wasn't funny. It took every ounce of willpower not to laugh aloud. Turning to check on Tink, she noted the look of approval. When Tink offered up a happy bark, Annie chuckled.

A quick check of her watch showed she still had roughly a half hour until boarding. Enough time to delve into a few online resources before they would announce her flight. Clicking open her three favorite websites, she struck a gold mine of information. Finding records for this particular client was going to be a piece of cake.

In the midst of creating a spreadsheet, an icy blast hit her. The hair on the nape of Annie's neck stood at attention, and everything within her stilled. Whipping her head up, it became apparent why the warning hit so fast and furiously. Dark-gray auras encapsulated a good ninety percent of the passengers around her.

Mouth desert dry, she surged to her feet, barely catching her laptop before it impacted the floor. She spun in a slow circle, trying to determine the threat, to see if something inside the building would capture her attention.

Nothing.

Another flash of premonition came and went.

Time was of the essence.

After tucking her laptop in her bag, she swung it over her shoulder and clutched the pet carrier to her chest. A third chill—this one of epic proportions—slammed into her, jerking her body.

A picture of the imminent disaster flashed in her mind.

"Run! *Run!*" She backed away, furiously working the zipper on Tink's carrier and continuing to scream. *"Get away from these gates!"*

Full-on panic hit, and she could scarcely inhale enough air to speak again.

The strangers around her were all going to die if they remained where they were. Yet there they sat, staring at her like she was batshit crazy. Perhaps on a normal day she might be, but not today. Right now, she needed to get everyone away from the oncoming danger.

Her gaze shot to Quinn.

"Move! Now!" she yelled at him.

Maybe it was the fact he'd seen her before she flipped out—when she'd been somewhat reserved—but he jumped up. He took three steps forward, only halting when two security agents rushed to restrain her.

"You have to *move*," she stressed to him, ignoring the manhandling agents. "It's going to crash into these gates."

She cast a desperate glance at Hailey, hoping to find support there. The other woman was frozen in place, staring at Annie like she was an escapee from an asylum for the criminally insane.

Frustration for their inaction choked her as rough hands grabbed either arm and the security staff attempted to usher her away. Annie fought like a madwoman. Tugging, pulling, and straining like hell to break their grasp.

"No! *No!* You have to listen!"

Gates 3 and 4 would bear the brunt of the impact. A good portion of the passengers took her warning seriously enough to grab their items and distance themselves from the terminal. Others sat, watching her like she was brainsick.

"Goddammit! Why won't you people *listen*? Please... *please!*"

As security became more aggressive, so did her dog. Not wanting to hurt Tink, who was snarling and snapping like she was rabid, Annie stopped fighting. As they led her away, she glanced back one last time.

Quinn had moved back to the seat he'd vacated, but he half turned to cast her a troubled look. She met his concerned eyes with a silent, mental plea. While his aura now appeared less gray in color than the others, she had no doubt he, too, was going to suffer a life-threatening injury or worse. Unable to see that beautiful star extinguished, she ducked and twisted her way to freedom.

Annie rushed toward Quinn, and he—for God only knew what reason—met her halfway. She dumped the carrier in his arms and forcefully pushed him toward the security team.

"Run!"

Then Annie, in a dumbass heroic move that should only be reserved for the big screen, rushed to save his girlfriend.

Too late.

The high-pitched whine of an engine signaled she was out of time. The small commuter plane she'd briefly glimpsed in her mind's eye was mere seconds from crashing through the northernmost wall.

When the other passengers finally registered their danger, chaos ensued.

Annie jerked Hailey by the arm and tried to flee, but the woman pulled away to go back for her bag. The tidal wave of people knocked Annie into Hailey, sending the two of them tumbling to the ground.

Dear God, what had she done?

She'd probably forfeited her own life to save a woman who

wouldn't do the same for her. Another flash of premonition hit, and she knew she had to protect Hailey for a very different reason.

They never managed to regain their feet, and Annie gator-rolled them closer to the row of chairs, sprawling across Hailey. A quick search for Quinn showed him struggling to get to them. A salmon battling his way upstream. And he no longer held Tink's carrier!

Annie's throat tightened.

Where was her baby? Being trampled to death?

Just over the pounding pulse in her ears and the deafening din of screaming passengers, she could discern a dog's anxious yelping. Her desire to find Tink and protect her from the stampeding crowd made her heartsick.

Unable to fight against the onslaught of people trying to make good their escape, Quinn was swept backward. No help was coming from his direction, and saving Hailey was all on Annie.

The floor-to-ceiling windows made a loud popping noise, shattering into millions of tiny shards as the plane created its own entrance into the airport. The craft's nose breaching the exterior of the building was the last thing Annie saw as a beam slammed into the back of her head just as she was scrambling up to get to her dog.

CHAPTER 3

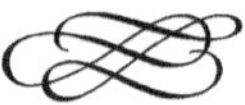

Trace Montgomery hovered by Annie Holt's bed and bore witness when she woke disoriented, with no little amount of anxiety. The monitor, with its already sharp beeping, pinged its annoying tones faster as her heartbeat escalated.

"Annie, I'm Dr. Montgomery. I need you to stay calm." He placed a hand on each of her shoulders, pinning her to the bed. "You were in an accident at the airport, but you're okay now."

"Tink! Where's Tink?"

Annie's blood pressure shot to stroke level, and Trace swore under his breath, hoping like hell Tink wasn't a nickname for a missing child. A panicked mother would be impossible to control.

"Who's Tink?" he asked soothingly.

"My dog," she croaked, then moaned. "I have to find her."

With little regard for those trying to help her, Annie tore at the leads attached to her, then fought him as he tried to restrain her. It hadn't yet registered with her that she was immobile from the waist down.

Trace hollered for assistance, taking a precious moment to press the call button.

Having dealt with irrational patients before, one of the night nurses rushed in and inserted a sedative into Annie's IV. Less than a minute later, sleepiness overtook her, and once again, she drifted toward forgetfulness, much to Trace's relief.

His own breathing was labored due to the tussle. Who knew such a little woman could fight like a warrior? Especially fresh out of surgery.

As he watched her a moment longer to ensure she was well and truly sedated, he noticed tears seep from the corner of her eyes. Her lips barely moved as she tried to speak.

He leaned closer.

"Tink, I'm so sorry. My baby. I'm so sorry." She repeated it like a mantra as her eyes shifted behind her lids.

Trace strongly suspected she wasn't going to rest until she had her pet back, and he heaved a tired sigh. The day had already been brutal, and it was about to get worse. He'd come in to see if she was awake and speak to her regarding her emergency procedures, and instead, he'd gotten one more thing added to his to-do list—find Tink.

Stuffing down his irritation, he strode to the nurses station and addressed the second-shift staffers.

"Will the three of you make some phone calls? See if anyone found a dog from the airport accident. The security office at the airport, the humane society, and the local emergency vets would be the best places to start." He ticked each potential location off on his fingers as he spoke. "Odds are if it was traveling in a carrier, it couldn't have been too large. Probably less than ten pounds."

The head of his team looked at him like he'd lost his mind, and he couldn't blame her. But luckily, Monica was trained well enough to not say a word. As she pivoted to go, he called her back.

"They found Annie Holt's computer bag close to her, and it's stored in her room. Check for a cellphone. She may have a picture of the dog. If it's an iPhone, bring it to me. We'll use her thumb or facial recognition to unlock it." He smiled to soften his request. "If it's not, one of you will need to tell me how to unlock the damned thing. If necessary, we'll create flyers."

Trace returned to Annie's room for one last check and, seeing she was no less agitated, patted her shoulder. "Don't worry. I have everyone making calls, Annie. We'll find Tink."

His words seemed to penetrate her medicated haze, and she calmed marginally. The tears stopped flowing as fast, and the frantic side-to-side motion of her eyes beneath her lids stilled. Her murmured "thank you" surprised him. She'd been given the equivalent of a horse tranquilizer, and she shouldn't have been coherent, in the least. But unexplainable circumstances happened every day in his chosen profession.

"You're welcome. Now, for your sake and mine, get some rest. Okay?"

Trace departed to follow up on the other victims. He wondered, not for the first time, how the hell a plane had crashed into the terminal of their small airport. Freak accidents like that didn't happen in Sagefield. In the end, he shook it off. Not his mystery to solve. He'd just pulled a double and was bone-weary. And right then, he had more pressing matters.

The movie star's girlfriend being a primary concern.

As he entered Hailey's room, Trace noticed Quinn Jensen dozing in the visitor's chair beside the bed. The actor was haggard looking, and his lips were tight as if he were struggling with pain. As hard as he tried, Trace couldn't wrap his mind around the fact the guy was here, in *his* hospital. One would assume celebrities of Quinn's caliber resided in Hollywood or somewhere other than a rural North Carolina town. His presence was bound to cause an uproar and be fodder for the gossip mill for months to come. Trace could only hope like hell it wouldn't interfere with the well-oiled machine that he'd created.

"Mr. Jensen," he called softly to wake him. When Quinn's lids fluttered open, Trace said, "I'm Dr. Montgomery, Chief of Surgery. We met earlier, but things were a bit chaotic in the trauma center."

"Yes, I remember. Have Hailey's test results come back yet?"

"The ER doctor ran a CT scan and had imaging take X-rays of her spine. We're waiting for the radiologist to make sure nothing was missed and there's no extensive damage. But the initial readings are normal." Quinn opened his mouth to protest, and Trace held up a hand. "Because her primary injury was to her head, I requested a neuro consult. I imagine Dr. Adams will want another round of scans if she doesn't wake soon."

As Quinn absorbed all the information, Trace absently watched him. The actor had the type of rugged good looks that appealed to most: strong jaw, thick blond hair, and piercing moss-green eyes. Quinn was also a man's man. The perfect action hero. And although Trace had seen more than one of his films and enjoyed them immensely, he was able to separate the person from the movie star. Right at the moment, the guy looked pretty fucking rough. He was a human being in need of care.

"You look exhausted, Mr. Jensen. Why don't you take a break, go down to the ER, and get that arm examined? You've been sitting here in pain for hours, and there is nothing more you can do for your fiancée."

"What if she wakes up?" Quinn's voice was hoarse with emotion, as if he feared she wouldn't.

"In that event, I'll send a nurse for you immediately." Trace always chose his words with care. The rule of thumb was never to promise *when* but never discourage with an *if*. He didn't want to upset a patient's loved ones, and he certainly wouldn't reveal that Hailey should've woken up by now. Not without more tests.

But Quinn was quick to pick up on the dodge. Cutting him a sharp look, he pounced. "*In that event?* You don't expect her to wake up?"

"That's not what I meant at all, Quinn." First names sometimes soothed people, and that's what Trace hoped would happen by addressing him informally. "Let's not jump to conclusions. Once I get the neuro results, I'll have more to go on. When I know anything, you'll know. Fair enough?"

Quinn rose, nodded once, and leaned in to drop a kiss on Hailey's cheek. As he shuffled toward the door, he paused and turned back. "There was a tiny dark-haired woman brought in about the same time as Hailey. She warned… she…" He cleared his throat. "She tried to help everyone get away before… Do you know what happened to her? Is she okay?"

Trace recalled hearing the story of how Annie Holt had thrown herself on top of Hailey in an effort to save her. Her heroic actions had cost her greatly, though he wasn't at liberty to say. "Ms. Holt sustained serious injuries, but she's holding her own." Trace checked Hailey's vitals as he spoke. "Annie was in distress over her missing dog. I'm fearful it didn't survive the crash."

"Actually, it did. I forgot about it until now."

"I've got a few of my staff making calls to find it. I wasn't hopeful, but perhaps we'll get lucky and find out what happened to it. God, I hope it isn't one of those yappy, frufru dogs with a name like Tink."

His groan earned a weary smile from Quinn.

"No, she's actually a sweet pup. She went a bit crazy during all the chaos, but she's fine. I had my brother pick her up and take her to a local vet for a thorough check." He looked uncomfortable for a second. "Um, can you tell me her room number? Annie, did you say her name was? I'd like to thank her for what she tried to do and let her know her dog's okay. Is she allowed visitors?"

Trace watched him, trying to determine if he should go against hospital privacy policies, then made an impulsive decision. The woman hadn't had any visitors in the hours since she was admitted, and the man *did* have her dog. She'd need someone to lift her spirits during the recovery process. Who better than a famous actor?

"Two-fifty-six. Here in the ICU, three doors down on the right. But she's sleeping, so get checked out first."

"Yes, sir." He had the feeling Quinn would have mockingly saluted if he wasn't so exhausted and wounded, to boot.

Trace narrowed his eyes. "I mean it. Arm first. Visit after."

CHAPTER 4

The second time Annie woke up, she was quicker to acclimate to her surroundings and took a mental inventory of her body. Not one area wasn't going to be covered in bruises, and although the mind-numbing pain medication helped, she still felt as if she'd taken on a semi-truck and lost.

One persistent thought permeated her brain fog. Tink had survived. Their connection was too strong for her to be wrong. But what had become of her fur baby was the question of the hour, and Annie's heart ached that, for now, she was lost to her. What if she'd been taken to the pound? All those heart-wrenching songs from ASPCA commercials flitted through her mind, and she pictured Tink in a cage, scared and feeling abandoned. The image was sobering and jolted Annie fully awake.

A low vibration hummed through her veins, making her aware of the other presence in the room. The pulse of this particular person was similar to a small electrical jolt. Moving her head was a supreme effort, but she managed to shift enough to see a dark silhouette in her visitor's chair.

"The hero of the hour finally wakes." Quinn Jensen's voice was like warm Mexican chocolate—*just plain yummy with the perfect hint of spice.* She could drink it in all day and night.

She blinked. Then blinked a second time and went for a third just to be on the safe side. Yep, he was really in her room. There was no blaming the drugs for a fantasy come to life.

Her hoarse "hi" was barely discernible to the human ear, but it was all she could manage while her ego mocked her about looking her absolute worst in front of her Hollywood crush. She wanted to yell at her inner voice to shut the hell up, but Quinn probably already thought she was a bit of a loon. Talking to herself around a witness would land her in a straightjacket.

Absently, she noted his sling and the few minor cuts on his face. It was doubtful they'd leave any lasting marks, but really, any small scaring would only add to the megastar's appeal. He was sex on a stick and likely knew it.

"How... how's your girlfriend?" she whispered, then winced, reaching for her sore throat.

"Alive, thanks to you. No internal injuries, but she hasn't woken up yet." Quinn rose from his seat, picked up a cup of ice from her tray table, and held it up as an offering. At her slight nod, he shifted the cup to his injured arm and spooned a few chips into her waiting mouth.

"First, let me start by saying your dog is at a local animal clinic to get checked out."

Tears burned behind her lids as she closed her eyes against the punch of relief.

"Thank you," she croaked. "I was so worried."

"You entrusted her to me. The least I could do was make sure she was taken care of."

Entrusted seemed tame. She'd practically broken his freaking ribs when she shoved the carrier into his hands at the airport.

As he spooned more ice chips into her mouth, he grimaced and shot her a guilty look. One she immediately recognized as feigned.

"You should also know I broke protocol and spoke with the nursing staff earlier. Seems you're pretty busted up. A nasty concussion, a fractured vertebrae, a broken hip and leg, a few cracked ribs, a collapsed lung, and a sprained wrist. You were in surgery for quite a long time." He spooned more ice into her waiting mouth. "They told me you were lucky. Apparently, the row of chairs next to you and Hailey took the brunt of the beam." His warm grin caused her heart to stutter. "If you're curious how Nurse Rachel knew, she heard it from the ER staff, who heard it from the first responders."

Annie nearly choked on a cube. She'd lay a-hundred-to-one odds the medical staff never thought twice about the standard privacy policy when Quinn flashed those pearly whites. Since she was flattered he'd cared enough to ask, she decided not to make an issue of it.

"It's called the triangle of life." She ran a tongue over her chapped lips. "I read about it once. If you're ever in a room with a collapsing wall or ceiling, you should try to stay next to the furniture. It provides a triangle of space and can come in handy for survival."

Cripes! Hating that she'd just word vomited all over him, she clamped her mouth shut and grimaced.

Eyes sparkling with humor, his engaging grin widened. Had she been any less sedated, her heart rate would've spiked, setting off alarms and bringing the hospital staff at a run.

"That's a handy fact to know."

"I'm full of random factoids." With an attempt at a smile, she accepted another ice chip and chose to ignore the humiliating image of herself with her mouth open, looking like a baby bird waiting for a worm. Thinking about Quinn's worm would get her in a *lot* of trouble.

"Why did you do it, Annie? You could have easily made it to safety. And how the hell did you know it was going to happen in the first place?"

Unable to meet his disturbingly hypnotic eyes, she gazed out the window. Night had fallen, and the glass reflected Quinn's image back to her. He seemed everywhere at once and all-too-powerful a presence. She sighed.

"I couldn't trust anyone else to react in time. No offense, but you were still trying to process what was happening with the security team and me. And as far as the premonition I had, I don't know exactly how to explain it."

"Try," he encouraged, feeding her another ice cube.

If he had been demanding or sounded skeptical, she would've told him to screw himself, but his curiosity was genuine, his caring real. Oddly, she felt she owed him an answer, but oh, how she hated describing her ability. "Again, I don't know how to explain in terms that won't make me sound batshit crazy, but—"

Two plainclothes officers walked in, cutting her off before she began. They were followed by a doctor who looked vaguely familiar.

A glance at his badge told her he was Dr. Trace Montgomery. For the life of her, she couldn't place him, but his mannerisms reminded her of someone she knew. Probably when she was less sedated and her brain was working at full function, she'd be able to recall exactly who.

The older of the two policemen stepped forward. His buzzed hairstyle did nothing to hide his balding head. Rotund, his gut hung low over his belt and jiggled with each step he took.

"Dude could stand to lay off the donuts."

Shocked gasps and a choked laugh echoed around her, and Annie could've cheerfully bitten off her damned tongue.

Heat infused her face.

"I'm sorry. I..."

What could she say? She wasn't mean by nature, and who didn't carry a few extra pounds around the middle? She certainly wasn't one to judge because she *loved* donuts and baby had back of her own. But the officer's edgy, cynical vibe had instantly gotten her back up. His irritated visage screamed he didn't want to be there and talking to her was beneath him. His pissy mood, combined with Annie's highly effective pain medication, had lowered her inhibitions and was likely to plunge her into hot water in short order. Again.

Expression a mask of pure pique, the senior of the two cops

glared. "Ms. Holt, I'm Officer Fields, and my partner is Officer Reynolds. We need to ask you a few questions."

Fucking great. She'd have no choice but to explain her freakish gift when all she wanted to do was crawl into a hole and hide until she was allowed to go home.

Dr. Montgomery was quick to tell her she only had to answer if she was feeling up to it.

"It's fine. I don't mind," she lied—badly. Annie took a few shallow breaths to stave off her building anxiety. Anything more, and she'd cry from the unpleasant pressure building in her chest. She hadn't noticed it before, but then again, Quinn Jensen was a superb distraction.

Reynolds looked at Fields, who shrugged as if he didn't give a shit that she couldn't breathe. Hell, they probably didn't know about her cracked ribs and hadn't cared enough to ask. They had a job to do, and her welfare didn't play into it.

The sharp rush of hurt threatened Annie's emotional well-being, and she closed her lids against the onslaught of tears. The mildly nagging pain throughout her body had turned excruciating and was making itself known. She shifted as much as her injuries allowed and tried to relax as Fields fired off questions. Most of her answers were an easy yes or no, but the tough part came all too soon.

"Ms. Holt, exactly how did you know the plane was heading for your terminal so long before it was visible? I mean, that *was* what your warning was about, right?"

CHAPTER 5

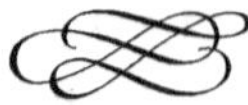

The silence was drawn out and awful as they waited for
Annie to answer.

Quickly summing up each person in the room, she attempted to
get a feel for how they'd react. Fields would be disbelieving. Dr.
Montgomery would be slightly less skeptical but still wont to doubt
her sanity. Reynolds might be more open to her ability, though.
Fresh faced and young, his golden-brown eyes held professional
curiosity. As for Quinn, well, he would be forced to believe,
wouldn't he? As a witness to the crash and ensuing madness, he
didn't have much choice.

"A premonition." A small kernel of gratification popped inside
her when she saw she'd been correct in her initial estimations.

"A premonition? That's what you are going with?" Fields sneered
with an exaggerated lip curled like a Vegas Elvis.

She flinched. Drugged as she was, she found it difficult to shrug
off his animosity.

"Yep. That's what I am going with," she retorted flippantly.

Rarely did she let it be known what she could do, but whatever
they'd dosed her with had effectively eliminated her natural reserve.
With the sure knowledge it would make them all uncomfortable—

herself included—she confessed, "I'm an empath with occasional psychic visions."

"An empath?" Reynolds questioned. Avid interest transformed his expression, and he leaned slightly forward as if to learn more. His curiosity earned him a scathing look from his partner.

"What the hel... ahem, what's an empath?" Fields snapped the question.

Annie paused a few heart-pounding beats. The intense regard of all four men was like a heavy weight around her shoulders, and the urge to squirm was strong. Their interview was about to take a turn for the ugly, and she didn't know how to stop it. Or even if she cared to at that moment.

She closed her eyes. Even groggy, the caress of the doctor's protective concern brushed along her nerve endings. When she lifted her lids, she gave him a half-hearted smile that eased his furrowed brow.

"I'm able to tap into other people's energy. I can literally *feel* their emotions and physical ailments."

Recipient of Fields's skepticism, she sighed. No one ever took her at face value. Why should they? Even to her, it sounded hokey, but a little demonstration was in order.

"Your right knee aches unbearably. Currently, you're experiencing a sharp pain just below the kneecap." Waiting just long enough for the stunned-stupid expression to cross his face, she continued. "Your left knee is sore, too, but in a different way." She squinted at him as she mentally reached for the source of his pain. "I'm guessing you've had knee-replacement surgery on the left and desperately need one on the right. But you're resistant."

Moving on from Fields, whose weathered countenance remained frozen in shock, she addressed Reynolds. "Painful urination. Get that one checked since it is accompanied by the itch." His cherry-red cheeks attested to her accuracy. "Oh, and there's a strong sense of shame and guilt. I'm going to venture to say one of you is in a relationship."

A choking sound emanated from Quinn, and Annie didn't dare

risk a glance his way, or she'd likely laugh, inappropriate as it was. After focusing on Dr. Montgomery, the urge to be bitchy died a painful death. Grief flowed through him, hammering at her psyche like forceful storm waves crashing against the shore, eroding the dunes and leaving them hollowed out. His unbearable sense of loss was palpable and destroyed her desire to be catty. She quietly stated she felt his sadness and left him alone.

Finally, she eased her head to the left to look at Quinn. "You want—"

"Enough! We get it." His tone was diamond hard, but Annie hadn't expected anything less. It wasn't difficult to understand why a widely famous person preferred to keep his secrets.

She nodded her understanding, but didn't look away.

She couldn't.

Quinn's uncompromising, impenetrable face was too fascinating. Too captivating. His expressive eyes too mesmerizing.

The weight of the group's awkward silence pressed down on her, and still, she couldn't break the spell he'd cast over her. Eventually, one of the men cleared his throat, and with great effort, Annie tore her gaze from Quinn. Suppressing a fiery blush proved more difficult. Once she realized the men were more embarrassed than she was, she smothered a grin. Causing her visitors to squirm was one of those things that tickled her funny bone. Her sister Sammy would be laughing her ass off right about now.

"Are you a witch?"

Fields's question would normally have set her off into peals of laughter. Perhaps if she could breathe with any regularity and without a significant amount of added discomfort, she'd have given in to her amusement. As it was, she compressed her lips and avoided eye contact with anyone, lest she lose it.

People justified her abilities in the most rudimentary ways. *Not* that she often shared what she could do. God, no! It wasn't fun to be the resident freak. But there were times, like these, when she had no choice. She hesitated to call her ability a gift. Hell, ninety percent of the time, she believed it was a curse.

"No, Officer Fields, I'm not a witch," she stated succinctly. "Please be sure to tell the townsfolk they can put away their pitchforks and torches." No one found her as hilarious as she found herself. Again, Sammy would've. Oh well, comedians couldn't win over every crowd, and Annie had never claimed to be a comic. "My ability showed up in early childhood, and I have been dealing with this crap ever since. I am as happy about it as you are."

Dr. Montgomery brought the conversation back to the original topic of discussion. "How does the premonition part work?" For a man who dealt with science, he would have a hard time swallowing her claim.

She glanced at the cup of ice in Quinn's hand, longing for more to soothe her parched throat.

Picking up what she was putting down, he offered a spoonful.

Annie gave him a grateful smile.

As she weighed the doctor's question, the ice melted inside her mouth, and nothing had ever tasted so sweet. All she wanted to do was have Quinn feed her ice chips forever, like a cabana boy with grapes. But the reality was he was only being kind.

"The premonitions," he reminded her, bringing her mind back from its side trip.

How the hell was she supposed to make them all understand? Half the time, *she* didn't.

"*Try.*"

From nowhere, the echo of Quinn's softly spoken encouragement flitted through Annie's mind, and she found the necessary words to explain.

"Energy is a living thing, mostly felt, but it also puts off subtle colors. Each shade is a clear indication of what is currently happening or about to happen in the near future. The auras of the passengers around me were all murky and dark. One or two, I could've shrugged off as illness, but wherever I looked, *everyone's* was charcoal gray."

For a split second, she was back at the airport, experiencing the mass terror and the sickening sensation of being snowed under. The complete claustrophobia of that moment was crushing, and she couldn't seem to catch her breath.

A warm, comforting hand on her forearm pulled her back to the present.

Annie gazed up into Quinn's concern-filled eyes.

God, she could get lost there.

The energy transference between them was heady. Seductive. Sweet and spicy, with fiery notes. Annie prayed he wasn't overwhelmed with sudden lust, because he'd likely never understand the burning desire came from her.

Ripping her arm away cost herself dearly. The sharp pain in her ribs and hips was unbearable when she jerked, and she gritted her teeth to hold back a cry. But better to let him think he repelled her than let on to the truth—she wanted to tear the buttons of his shirt off with her teeth. Sniff the delicious column of his muscled neck. Bite him.

Yeah, her and about twenty million other women.

Men that sexy were lethal to a woman's system. Mainly to her ovaries. Annie's had woke up and began spewing out eggs like a chicken factory the second they locked eyes across the airport. She was pretty sure she was ovulating, and it wasn't her scheduled time.

Fields cleared his throat, and his hostile stare had her wracking her brain to remember the conversation. Oh, right! The plane crash.

"Those with the darkest auras were closest to me, Gate 3, and the one adjacent. As soon as the image of the plane came to me, I reacted. I couldn't *not* warn people." While she didn't look directly at Quinn, she did shift her head slightly in his general direction. The compulsion to save *him* was what had prompted her to act. Saving anyone else had been an accidental bonus.

Annie described the futuristic flashes she sometimes received during an actual premonition. Full visions were rare, but when it involved her personal safety, she tended to receive images like a slideshow.

Skepticism hung heavily in the air. The information she'd provided was a lot to swallow even for the most open-minded person, and unfortunately, seasoned policemen could be notoriously closed-minded and disbelieving. They dealt in facts. Life was either black or white with little-to-no gray area in between, and Annie's ability fell under the category of palm readers, telephone psychics, and charlatans. For physicians, it was hit or miss when it came to a revelation like hers. They were a bit more willing to listen, but they defaulted to science and required proof.

Quinn was another matter altogether, and Annie knew he had no clue what to think. His emotions were running the gamut and affecting her like no one else's ever had. The urge to tell him to settle his thoughts was strong, but it would be like ordering the sun not to shine or the tides not to rise. He was going to need time to work through what she could do and apply it to what had actually happened.

A tidal wave of fatigue crashed over her, pulling her under—another side effect of tapping into other people—and she visualized standing in the center of a brick enclosure, blocking everyone out. It also served to divert her from the irresistible actor. However, it eventually brought her back around to her condition and the reason she was in this fucking bed, to begin with. Loneliness and the need to escape her life, if only for a weeklong vacation.

Emotional strain was another symptom of an energy overload, and a lone tear slid down her cheek.

She sought the calmest person in the room.

Dr. Montgomery.

Picking up on her distress, he ushered the officers out, with a head gesture for Quinn to follow.

Self-pity, that dangerous fucker, knocked on the door of her mind, and stupidly, she let it in. Cursing under her breath, she belatedly realized she should've asked the policemen to not leak what she'd told them. The airport accident was high profile, and people would view her as a crackpot if anyone found out what she could and did do.

It was too much to hope no one had filmed her crazy ass when she first reacted.

With a mental reminder to avoid the internet, Annie resigned herself to the fact she would need to make contact with Officers Frick and Frack again. Not that she had any faith they would honor her request, but she had to ask.

A strangely sympathetic vibe hit her, and she realized she wasn't as alone as she'd believed. There was no need to look to see who'd lingered. The sexual energy the man put off was a living thing.

"What do you want, Mr. Jensen?" Distance was essential, and using his formal name was the key—*or so she told herself.*

CHAPTER 6

Quinn had had one foot out the door when the sound of Annie's hiccuping sob reached him. Not wanting to bother her but incapable of leaving, he stayed. God, the whole situation disturbed him. Between her freak-out at the airport and the empathic mumbo jumbo, he didn't know how he should react. Still, he was unable to simply walk away, and he didn't know why.

As he approached her bedside, he mulled over her question.

Why was he drawn to her? What *did* he want?

Answers.

Only she could say why she'd saved Hailey specifically.

"Ah, yes. Hailey."

Her monotone statement nearly stopped his heart. How the hell did she do that? How did she pick up on his thoughts so effortlessly? At the airport, he would've sworn he'd heard her voice inside his head, telling him to kick Hailey to the curb. But he didn't know her well enough to ask if she'd implanted the thought there or even if she could. After Hailey had approached them, she'd started with the snide comments and superior looks, and Quinn had been thoroughly annoyed. Her catty behavior was a constant bone of contention between them.

He cleared his throat, uncertain what to say or do.

"Is her baby okay?" Annie asked in a low, subdued voice.

Baby? Mentally reeling, he stared at her in wonder. "How... how do you... know? Another premonition?"

She smiled wearily. "Her presence was... *more,* somehow."

"She never said." Christ! No wonder she'd been so tearful and emotional of late.

"Some women like to keep it to themselves until they know for sure," Annie replied, not unkindly.

A baby.

Quinn turned over the news in his mind and realized the idea of a child didn't terrify him in the least. In fact, it pleased him. He'd been toying with setting a wedding date and discussing a family over their holiday getaway. Hailey had been pushing him toward that end for a long while, and their Christmas vacation seemed like the perfect time to cement their plans.

Recently, burnout had hit him. *Hard.* Only last week he'd decided major changes needed to be made to his schedule. The unrelenting pace he'd set for his career could no longer be sustained. For the last eight years, he'd gone directly from one project to another without a break, and he was exhausted. It was well past time to re-evaluate his life. Maybe settle into a long-running sitcom or TV drama, with the occasional movie role to break the monotony. Theater might be a fun change, too.

"I have so many questions," he said softly.

"I'm happy to answer what if I can."

The petite, bruised-and-battered woman in the hospital bed looked nothing like the person he'd initially spoken to when Hailey went off to buy water and a fashion magazine. Quinn was a people watcher by nature, and when Annie slid into the abandoned seat— her dog carrier and computer weighing down her delicate frame— he couldn't look away. She'd appeared so lost, sitting there by herself, and he'd felt the need to approach her. To make her smile. The stoic, solitary expression was one he recognized. Even Hailey had never been able to ease his deep sense of isolation.

As he'd squatted in front of Annie's seat, he was impacted by her stunningly blue gaze. He couldn't recall ever seeing eyes that particular shade before. Or rather, none that weren't enhanced by contacts, anyway. But he could've easily gotten lost in those Caribbean-ocean eyes of hers. It was as if, with a single glance, she pulled him under the surface of her mystical sea and refused to let him go.

Where the hell had that drivel come from?

He mentally scoffed at the thought as soon as he'd had it.

"Are you going to ask your questions, Mr. Jensen?"

All this time, she'd kept her eyes closed, but when they flew open to meet his, he was transfixed by their soft, glowing light. He got the distinct impression she could communicate with him without a single word passing between them. When her lips twisted into a wry half smile, he was positive of it.

Disconcerted and more than a little spooked, he made a lame excuse and bolted.

———

As he sat by Hailey's bedside, Quinn cursed himself for being a coward. Annie was simply a kind woman who possessed a strange gift. Not someone he could ever truly befriend—the lack of privacy for his own thoughts would drive him batty—but still, she was honest and brave.

Pretty, too.

Pushing aside his disloyalty, he touched Hailey's stomach.

A simple blood test had confirmed Annie's prediction regarding the pregnancy.

Why hadn't Hailey told him? Maybe she'd been meaning to when they got to St. Martin. Maybe it was as Annie had said, and Hailey had wanted to keep the news to herself a little longer.

As he maintained a bedside vigil, he googled what to expect during a standard pregnancy, taking screenshots and typing notes when necessary.

When he'd questioned Dr. Montgomery regarding the imaging, Quinn was reassured by the doctor's response. "To put your mind at ease, the chance of any long-term birth defects or miscarriage from any of the tests we've conducted is minimal, according to the HP— which is a board on radiation safety. However, I *would* like to call in an OB to examine Hailey and do an ultrasound to check the baby's overall health."

A simple sonogram had shown Hailey was at the beginning of her second trimester. For at least three and a half months, she'd known and kept secret the fact she was carrying his child, and Quinn didn't know how to feel about it. Still, he couldn't believe he was going to be a dad. *A dad!* Wiping the pleased grin from his face was proving impossible.

As he daydreamed about holding his future child, a commotion in the hall caught his attention, and he rose to check it out. Nurses crowded around his twin brother, Ty, ooh-ing and ah-ing over whatever he held.

As Ty made room for Dr. Montgomery's approach, Quinn caught a glimpse of blond fur.

Annie's puppy.

Relief rushed through him, strong and swift as a river's current. They'd be reunited, and he could stop stressing about the little fuzzball. Annie had impulsively entrusted him with Tink's care, but Quinn hadn't spared the poor thing another thought until the doctor mentioned it.

As the group drew even with Quinn, the pup recognized him and lost her tiny mind. In her excitement, she struggled to reach him, twisting and turning until he feared she would break her damned back.

"Hey there, Tink." Quinn's soothing tone did to the canine what it had been doing to human females for most of his professional adult life. She whimpered and trembled with need.

"May I?" he asked Ty, holding out his good arm.

"With pleasure."

His brother readily handed over the squirming dog, and she

bombarded Quinn with aggressive kisses anywhere her tiny, wet tongue could connect, adding a nip to his nose in her enthusiasm.

"Okay, okay. Calm down there. Easy, baby."

As if she understood, she laid her head in the crook of his neck and let out a heartfelt sigh.

"Unbelievable. You certainly have a way with females—*of every kind*. First, my staff are practically tripping each other to get to you, and now this sad puppy." With a disgusted grunt, the doctor shooed everyone back to work and sauntered away, but not before saying, "I'd hate to see the betrayal in Annie's eyes when Tink refuses to leave you."

"Not funny, Doc," Quinn called after him.

"Not joking," Dr. Montgomery returned over his shoulder.

When Quinn looked down at Tink, she was gazing at him in adoration, with her tongue lolling to the side, about half the length of her body. Irritation welled up. If the doctor wasn't kidding, the female population was foolish as a whole. Quinn was just an average guy. Yes, he was relatively good-looking. Yes, he could act. But he wasn't anyone special. Each morning, after his essential caffeine consumption, he showered and dressed, then went to work like anybody else.

With a grunt, he shook his head. Tink's ears perked, and she gave him a half tilt of her head, questioning how serious he was about his disgruntlement.

Not very.

At least not with her. She must have been able to read him for the sap he was, because she rained more kisses on his chin. And damned if he didn't fall in love.

"She's *not* your dog, Quinn," Ty warned with a shake of his head. "Don't get attached."

"I'm not." Uncertain whom he was trying to convince, himself or his brother, Quinn strode off toward two-fifty-six. Pausing, he glanced back. "Will you stay with Hailey while I bring Tink to Annie?"

At Ty's nod, Quinn sought her out, only to find her fast asleep.

Intending to let her rest, he silently backed away. But Tink, hyper alert to her surroundings, spotted her mistress, and the puppy's struggle made the one with Ty look tame. The silly beast added high-pitched yelps to the mix.

"Tink?" Annie's trembling voice sounded as if she were waking from a dream and unsure whether to believe her eyes. "Ohmygod! *Tink!*" As she came more fully awake, she struggled to sit up, then hissed her pain, grabbing for her ribs in the process.

Sucking in a sympathetic breath, Quinn rushed to her side. "Jesus, Annie! I'm so sorry."

"Not... your... fault..." She spaced her words between pants. "Mine... forgot... moved... wrong..."

Miraculously, Tink stopped struggling and watched Annie, concern written on her fuzzy face. The almost inaudible whine damn near broke Quinn's heart.

With great care, he set Tink on the foot of the bed and couldn't help but smile as she daintily picked her way over the covers to offer a less aggressive greeting to her human mommy than the one she'd showered on him. Draping herself across Annie's shoulder like a mink stole, Tink instinctively avoided her owner's injuries. With her head tucked beneath Annie's chin, the pup let out a contented sigh and promptly closed her eyes.

"Poor baby. She must have been up all night, wondering what happened to me and why I didn't come back for her."

Silent, tragic tears rolled, one after the other, down Annie's face. "Thank you for finding her and bringing her to me," she said softly, accepting his proffered Kleenex.

"I'd like to take the credit, but my brother was the one who looked after her and took her to the vet. He was headed to your room when your gremlin recognized me." Quinn settled in the visitor's chair. "Being the needy little thing she is, she threw herself at me. I had no choice, really." Just enough truth and humor went into the statement to make Annie grin.

Slowly, her smile faded, and she became serious once more. "I must seem like an oddity to you. A woman who reads auras, energies, and whatnots. One who lives only for her dog."

After giving it some thought, he couldn't deny that she did, but not in a bad way. Just different. The moment had gone on far too long, and it appeared she didn't know what to say to fill the uncomfortable silence as she avoided looking at him.

Shifting forward, he said, "Look, I don't remember if I got around to saying thank you, but I owe you a debt I can never repay. I'd like to leave my assistant's number with you, and should you need anything, I'm happy to provide it."

"I won't."

"Nevertheless…"

She'd focused all her attention on the foot of her bed as if she was mentally distancing herself from their conversation and him in particular. Oddly, he despised the feeling of being dismissed by her.

"Annie?"

"I won't, Mr. Jensen. That's all you need to know. Thank you for bringing my dog back to me."

"Where do you intend to board her?"

The monitor spiked an instant before the machine sparked and went black.

"Jesus! Annie, are you all right?"

"Peachy," she muttered with a glare at the monitor.

Somewhere in the distance, an alarm could be heard. Quinn was still wrapping his mind around the faulty medical equipment when the door burst open and a harried nurse stopped in her tracks to gape at him.

"Ohmygod! Quinn Jensen!" she blurted, fluttering her hands in the area of her chest. In the time it took the woman to recover, she would've lost a critical patient.

"I'm over here. That's right, me, the one setting off the alarm," Annie snapped.

Rising on her haunches, Tink growled low in her throat. Lips curled back and fur standing on end, she was the animal equivalent of her owner. Two scrappy loners ready to take on the world.

The smartphone on the side table rang, breaking the tension. Too surprised to move, they all stared at the device for a few beats.

The first to recover, Annie glared. "Is someone going to get that? I would, but the broken body parts are preventing me from getting up and walking."

The nurse answered the call, listened for a moment, and held out the phone. "It's your sister."

CHAPTER 7

*A*nnie's ribs were throbbing, and normal breathing was impossible. For the sake of her personal welfare, she had to get a handle on the situation.

Tink—picking up her cue from Annie—cocked her head, let out a warning bark for her visitors, and found a spot to cuddle up again.

"Miss Holt, you can't keep that dog in the hospital. You need to make arrangements for someone to come get it, or you can call a local vet to see if they offer boarding."

The nurse didn't know how close she was to being strangled to death with the charging cord, but apparently Quinn did because he murmured some placating BS and urged the woman out the door. The nurse assured Annie she'd be back with a new machine to replace the broken one. With a last nod and a tight smile from Quinn, they left.

"Hey, sissy," Sammy said gently.

Self-pity clogged Annie's throat. Gah, she was a train wreck. When emotions ran high, she tended to close off from the rest of the world. Except for her sister. She was the only person Annie wanted to reach out to, but she was over five hundred miles away.

"It's good to hear your voice," she choked out.

"You scared us to death. Do you know how hard it was to find out where they'd brought you or to get the hospital to release any information? Christ. Margie had to be physically restrained from driving there, and I'm not convinced Jamie isn't already on his way." Sammy snorted. "He *said* he was running out for cigarettes, but we all know he doesn't smoke."

Sammy's running monolog made Annie's head ache. Sure, it was said to make her feel loved, but because of how practical they all were, her family would likely never make the trip unless she was literally at death's door. And Annie couldn't blame them. Her siblings were too involved with getting their own lives back on track after the trying year they'd had, and her parents were piecing their own lives back together.

Lately, they all found it harder to communicate because of those time constraints, and since Annie's divorce, she'd become a prickly bitch. It had taken a while, but she finally understood Margie's defeatist attitude and sense of failure after ending things with Scott.

"Yeah, well, you know me. Anything for a bit of the spotlight. Middle-child syndrome, right?" Annie quipped.

Sammy grew quiet on her end, but Annie could hear the muted background noises through the speaker. Her husband, Michael, continually fired off question after question about Annie's welfare. But she couldn't find it within herself to make light of the situation anymore. Her injuries hurt like hell, and she had no earthly idea how to care for Tink in her current state.

Seeming to sense Annie's mood swing, Sammy asked, "How bad is it, Annie? Does someone need to be on their way? The nurse wouldn't give me much by way of information."

There was irony in there somewhere. Quinn, a virtual stranger, had had no issue obtaining her medical condition, while her blood relative couldn't get the basic facts.

"Broken ribs, leg, hip, and fractured vertebrae. I also suffered a collapsed lung and a concussion. My whole body feels like it has been crushed by a building or something." Sammy's shocked gasp forced Annie to play it down. "Truthfully, I'm okay, sissy. It would be great if I could get you to make a few calls and cancel my vacation reservations, though. Also, find out what happened to my luggage. Do you think you have time for that?"

"Of course! Give me the name of the airline and the place you were supposed to stay."

"You can find everything you need in my inbox. If you have a pen, I'll give you the login info." After Annie provided the necessary information, they took an extra minute or two to catch up.

Extreme weariness was settling in, and Sammy quickly registered the change in Annie's voice. "You sound tired, sissy. Are you *sure* you are okay?"

How did she explain the overwhelming isolation and fear she was experiencing without triggering her family's guilt? She decided brutal honesty was best because Sammy wouldn't have pulled her punches.

"I *am* tired. A building fell on me. I ache everywhere, and I don't know what I am going to do with Tink while I'm recovering. She's just a puppy, and the thought of boarding her in a strange place for weeks on end kills me. But I won't be able to walk her anytime soon." Annie inhaled—or tried to. Anger at herself for her failed attempt to save Hailey burned in her gut. She had nothing to show for it but a broken body and a hospital bill she couldn't pay. "I'm going to lay odds this hits the national news, so a good half of the world will think I'm a crackpot soon. Cops have already been to my room, questioning my involvement in the accident. *Like I was part of some terrorist plot.* Jesus, Sammy. It was a commuter plane and pilot error. And I..."

She closed her eyes and sighed. Her mouth was a runaway train.

"It's not that bad, Annie. Come on. No one thinks you're a terrorist."

"It *is* that bad." In a hushed voice, she confessed, "I also short-circuited the heart monitor."

"Are you sure it was you and not faulty equipment?"

Although her sister was only trying to make her see reason, Annie's temper spiked. "It's all good. It doesn't matter. I get that you guys can't drop everything to be here. I really do. But I have to say it sucks to be incapacitated and to have no one to rely on but myself. Anyway, tell everyone there's no reason to worry. I've got this."

"Annie—"

"I need to go, Sammy. I have to call around and find someone to care for Tink. Maybe Charlie can, since his parents live close by. At least she knows him. I'm sure his new fiancée will have a fit because she hates anything that might get her fancy clothes dirty..." Suddenly, she was choking back sobs. She really was in a fix this time and bitterly hated to ask anything from anyone. "Don't worry," she croaked out a second time. "I gotta run. Talk to you soon."

"Annie, wait!"

Normally, she and Sammy were tight, but Annie was bone-tired, in constant pain, and completely stressed out. Too overwhelmed to give a flying fuck about anyone else's feelings, she disconnected the call. Sure, Sammy might freak out initially, but she'd eventually understand. As someone who'd been there, she'd come to realize Annie needed time to get her spiraling emotions under control.

The persistent ringing started again, but she ignored it, switching her phone to silent mode.

"It's you and me, baby." She kissed the black nose Tink used to nudge her chin. "We've got this, right?"

Tink's low, throaty growl coincided with a wash of ill intent. Chill bumps broke out on Annie's arms, and the hair on the back of her neck prickled. Easing her head sideways, she glanced at the door, but the shadowy figure she'd glimpsed quickly shifted out of sight.

"What the fuck?" she whispered.

Was a stranger with bad juju simply passing by, and Annie had picked up on their maliciousness? Or was it directed at her? But if so, why? What reason would anyone have to wish her harm?

THOUGHTS OF ANNIE AND ALL THAT HAD HAPPENED IN THE SHORT time since they'd met plagued Quinn the rest of the afternoon. He'd been so consumed with guilt he went back to apologize for being an insensitive jerk. For a brief second, he wondered if he should bother to involve himself, but just as quickly, dismissed his doubts. He owed her a debt for all she'd done, and he possessed the means to help her in multiple ways.

As he waited for the hospital maintenance man to exit with the dead monitor, he caught sight of his personal assistant.

"Paige, how did you… Did Ty send you?"

"It's my job to be there for you, Quinn."

The smugness in her smile irked him, but he put it down to fatigue on his part. Too many things were hitting him at once, and he'd had little sleep in the last twenty-four hours, not to mention his arm ached like a bitch.

Her expression shifted to conciliatory, as if she sensed his flare of annoyance, and she placed her hand on his upper arm, giving his bicep a light squeeze. "Let me help you, Quinn. It's what I'm here for."

Easing sideways, he broke the contact. It wasn't the first time she'd touched him without his express permission, but he understood some people were tactile in nature. *He* wasn't a touchy-feely person, at least not when it came to strangers or business, but he recognized others were freer with things like that.

"By now, you've guessed Hailey and I aren't going to St. Martin. Can you call the resort and cancel the reservation for the bungalow? The rental car, too. I'm okay with paying penalties if they insist on it." He rubbed the back of his neck and sighed. "I suppose I'll require a hotel room close to this hospital. Something with a private exit, so I can avoid any paparazzi. Please reserve it for at least a week."

"And your family?"

"I've already contacted Ty, and he's been by. But I don't want to worry my parents or my sister right now, so if you can work with him to keep my name out of the press, I'd appreciate it. By mutual agreement, my brother and I have decided to hold off telling

Hailey's family until we have to." He rubbed a hand through his hair and sighed. "I was hoping for news of her recovery before I called them."

"Of course. And I've already contacted the airline, regarding your luggage. They've assured me they'll call as soon as it's all sorted."

"Perfect." He glanced toward Annie's room. "I want a bouquet of flowers, as large as you can find, delivered to the woman in two-fifty-six. Something cheerful, with daisies or sunflowers. And another bouquet for Hailey's room, two-fifty-three."

Did Paige grimace when he mentioned Hailey? The motion was so slight, it was hard to tell.

"Her standard two dozen hot-pink roses with baby's breath?" she asked brightly. Almost too brightly.

"Yes."

"And what about a change of clothes? Yours are…" With a grimace, she gestured up-and-down.

For the first time in twenty-four hours, Quinn thought about his personal hygiene. "Ugh, yeah. I'll speak to Ty and ask him to get a change of clothes for me. I imagine I'll be staying here for the foreseeable future. But can you—"

"I'm happy to drive to your place and pick up—"

"No need," he clipped out. "My brother will take care of it."

"Of course."

She continued to stare at him, as if expecting something more. Too weary to figure it out, he lifted his brows and asked, "Anything else?"

"Oh! No. I was just curious about Hailey's condition. No one will release any information."

His irritation dissolved in the face of her caring, and he gave her a tired smile. "We don't know anything yet. She hasn't woken up, but I'm hopeful she will soon."

"Me, too." Her eyes darted toward Annie's room. "Why the flowers for two-fifty-five?"

"Two-fifty-*six*," he clarified, turning his head to follow her gaze.

The number was obvious on the wall plaque, but he didn't point it out. "She saved our lives. If you could follow up on those things I've asked you to do and spare me unnecessary questions, I'd be grateful." He gave her a tight smile, but really, he wasn't in the mood for idle chatter. Her perkiness wouldn't be well received in his state.

She shot him a sharp look and smiled. "Of course, Quinn. Right away."

In an effort to shake the oddness of her behavior and the disturbing feeling it left him with, Quinn rolled his shoulders and slowly shifted his head from side to side. More and more often of late, he was put off by her cloying personality. To anyone else, she appeared professional and efficient, but to him, she was almost *too* invested in his business.

The first chance he got, Quinn intended to discuss the issue with his brother. As a PR rep, Ty handled all media-related problems and publicity for him. He also managed their staff: landscapers, cleaning service, and other similar service providers. Paige happened to fall under Ty's employment umbrella.

With a weary sigh, Quinn entered Annie's room.

CHAPTER 8

*L*ost in thought, as if she carried the weight of the world, Annie hardly acknowledged him. A mere twitch of her facial muscles and a darting glance his way, but no eye contact. It only firmed Quinn's resolve to help her. There weren't too many people who actually needed him, but this lone, hurting woman did.

"Annie, I'd like to—"

"Forget it."

Being a fairly smart man, he should've realized it wasn't the time to approach her. He existed in an industry of temperamental artists, and he *had* dealt with pissed-off people in the past. A cooling-off period was essential. But Annie's dismissive tone set his teeth on edge.

"Excuse me?" He shifted closer.

"Don't tell me. Let me guess. You happened to be walking by and overheard my conversation. You, being the big movie star, with your gazillion dollars and endless resources, have decided you can come in here and make it all better. Why not just hire someone to care for my dog and use your personal assistant to manage my travel arrangements, right? After all, it's easy for you to throw money at a problem."

Quinn scratched behind his ear, uncomfortable with her accuracy. Well, yeah, that *had* been his plan. The solution was a fairly simple one. He opened his mouth to defend himself, but she wasn't finished flaying him alive.

"Let me save you some time. I *said*, 'forget it.' I don't want, nor do I need, your pity. So please turn around and walk your perfectly chiseled ass right back to where you came from and *leave me the hell alone.*"

Annie was in a snit. And if there was one thing women did well when they were in a snit, it was rant. However, hers was more of a rant with a pant. Tink chose that exact moment to stand and approach him, walking across the center of Annie's body to do it.

If it hadn't been for the agony on her face, Quinn would've left and never returned. But he couldn't abandon her this way. Ditching his sling, he retrieved her dog. "I've got her. And I've got you."

A harried voice answered the call button he'd just pressed, and he requested someone assist Annie. Before the RN arrived, Quinn said, "I'm taking Tink outside for a walk. Whether you want to accept my help or not, I'm not letting your dog suffer in silence."

He assured himself he wasn't a coward in the face of her palpable anger, and all during his twenty-minute walk, he'd almost convinced himself it was true. When he returned to Annie's room, he was pleased to note she'd calmed somewhat and that she was alone. There were things that needed to be said.

With a deep inhale for courage, he said, "Here's the deal. I'm going to take your dog back to the hotel with me until we can figure out an alternate arrangement." He cut her off as she started to speak. "Don't argue. I'm taking charge."

Quinn ignored her exaggerated eye roll, preferring to believe she'd be grateful in the end.

"I'll bring her back each day for a short visit. That way, both of you can see how the other is faring. I also intend to reimburse you for any money lost regarding your vacation."

Rejection was in every line of her face, and she opened her mouth, likely to decline his help. Acting impulsively, he placed his index finger over her objecting lips and waited until she quieted. The pillowy softness derailed his thought train, and he had to curb the reckless urge to stroke her pouty upper lip.

Good Christ, she had a great mouth! Cherry red and full, with no injections of any kind. There was something to be said for natural beauty.

Wide-eyed, she caught his wayward finger.

He was damned lucky she didn't go apeshit and break his other arm. A fiery heat crept up his throat and into his cheeks. As her stunned gaze sought his, all he could do was stare back in horror.

Holy shit!

He couldn't believe he'd given in to the desperate need to touch her. What the fuck was wrong with him?

"I'm so sorry, I…" He cleared his throat and hung his head.

How did he explain he'd gotten carried away through no conscious thought of his own? His action was wildly unacceptable. For fuck's sake, Hailey was in a coma a few doors down. Maybe he should check to see if the pain medication he'd been given listed impulse-control issues as a side effect.

Eventually, he remembered to pull back his offending hand. Unable to meet her eyes, he focused on the dog supported by his cast. The little beast gave him a knowing look, and he was hard-pressed not to clear his throat again.

Mentally grabbing his balls in hand, he finally met Annie's watchful stare. "When you're fully recovered and ready to rebook your trip, I want to treat you to your dream vacation. All expenses paid. Will you accept that gift in return for my life and that of the other passengers?"

Face a blank mask, she stared at him, and Quinn was left to wonder how she'd managed it. Until now, her expressive visage had given away her every thought. After an excruciatingly long moment that felt like hours, she nodded.

"Good." Quinn gave in to his relief and grinned.

Before Annie could comment, an orderly stepped into the room, bringing her afternoon meal. He placed the tray on the rolling table and gave her an absent smile before exiting.

Annie's disgusted face said it all—the meal was revolting.

First, she set aside the yeast roll, jello, and juice, then pushed the rest aside.

"You have to eat more than that," Quinn protested.

"I will if you will," she countered, her brows raised in challenge.

He squinted at the contents of the plastic plate, unable to make out what type of vegetable the limp green glob was supposed to be. "You win. I wouldn't touch any of it, either. What are you craving? I'll go on a food run."

"Mr. Jensen, you don't have to do that. I'll survive until breakfast."

"I imagine that is your first meal since you've been admitted. You need something more nutritious than jello and a dinner roll." With a dramatic fake sigh, he perched on the edge of her bed, cradling Tink against his chest. "You, my dear savior, are going to have to accept that I intend to spoil you while you're here. Plus, I'm hungry, too, and I absolutely hate to eat alone."

"I'm sure there are any number of people willing to dine with you," she said with an arched brow before biting into the roll.

The remainder of the bread crumbled onto the food tray, and he let the silence speak for itself as she struggled to chew. With his uninjured hand, he held the plastic juice bottle so she could rip off the aluminum tab.

"Together, we make one functioning adult," he quipped.

"I like Chinese," she choked out, struggling to swallow the bite.

Containing his laughter was hopeless, and he didn't bother to try. He picked up her cell and turned the camera toward her, triggering the facial recognition. Once the main screen appeared, he entered his information into her contacts. Why he'd impulsively given her his number when Paige's or Ty's would've been better, he didn't know. Maybe because he liked her and she didn't seem in awe of him. Well, not since their first interaction at the airport, anyway. He preferred Salty Annie.

With a severe warning look, he said, "This is my personal number, for when you need a meal delivered. Do *not* give it to anyone."

"I wouldn't dream of it. Put it under a fake name, in case my phone is stolen or hacked." Her blue eyes sparkled with a devilish light. "But it's probably already posted in the nurses' locker room. Aren't you Hailey's emergency contact? Trust me, your number has already made the rounds."

He paused in the act of punching buttons. "You're a bit of a ball-buster, aren't you? Besides, I have a secondary phone for stuff like that. It goes directly to my assistant, who knows to forward things to me immediately if there's a problem."

"Ah, so I'm *really* getting your assistant's number," Annie concluded, picking up her jello and holding it out for him to rip the lid off.

"Nope. I already said you're getting *mine*. I'll add it as Jen Quinn, so if you search for Quinn, you should find it easily enough." Once he was finished, he called his cell from her phone. "Now I have yours, too."

"No late-night dick pics. I'm not that kind of girl." Her eyes flew wide, and she paused with the spoon halfway to her mouth. "Oh, fuck! I... I..."

Her brilliant flush was too cute, and Quinn laughed. "Why Annie Holt! You've got hidden depths."

CHAPTER 9

*A*fter Quinn left, Annie allowed herself a smile. When he'd caressed her lip, her heart almost jumped out of her chest and twerked. If the second monitor gave up the ghost, the staff would know it was her screwy wiring and not a lemon electronic device. She was human enough to enjoy the attention of a hawt-as-fuck movie star.

She touched her still-tingling lip. Physically experiencing his desire to caress her had nearly melted her panties, or it might've had she been wearing any under the erection-killing hospital gown.

His impulsivity led to his flushed cheeks and the sudden avoidance of eye contact. It had been fine by her because had he bothered to glance up, he'd have seen her burning face, which had to have been hotter than the sun's surface at that moment.

Earlier, she'd almost scoffed at Quinn's little alpha routine regarding Tink's care. If Annie hadn't been desperate for a puppy sitter, she'd have protested his high-handedness on principle alone. For God knew what reason, the men in her life tended to view her as fragile, as someone who needed protection.

She wasn't and didn't.

But Annie was grateful for his insistence. She'd be up shit creek without the proverbial paddle.

Roughly twenty minutes passed, and she was beginning to drift off when her phone rang. Stupidly happy, she grinned when she saw *Jen Quinn* pop up on her screen.

"Hello?"

"Hi." His voice washed over her in a swift, sensual wave. That sexy hint-of-the-South drawl totally did it for her.

Her natural reserve had fled when he touched her mouth, and he'd accidentally awakened the devil inside her. One who liked to tease. "Who's this?"

"What do you mean, 'who's this?' It's Quinn."

She bit her lip and tried not to giggle at his put-out tone.

"Ohhhhh, *Quinn*. Right. Sorry, I thought you were a telemarketer or something."

His deep chuckle traveled through the connection, right down her ear canal, and straight to her penis flytrap. Closing her eyes, she shivered and savored the delicious sound.

"Nice try, Annie, but I'm on to your games now."

"I doubt that," she muttered.

He either didn't hear her or chose to ignore her comment.

"Anyway, Tink is safely in my brother's care, and I'm getting ready to call in our lunch. What can I get you?"

"One of everything. I'm starving."

"That can be arranged."

She smiled at his willingness to please. "I have the feeling you'd seriously buy me the entire menu, but I'll settle for egg fried rice and an order of crab rangoon, please."

"And for dessert?"

You.

"Dessert probably isn't a good idea." Because she'd pour chocolate over his entire body and eat him up like he was her last meal. "I'm stuck in a bed, immobile for the foreseeable future. The pounds are going to stick soon."

"Please don't tell me you're one of those people who count every calorie." His groan made her grin. "I was hoping for a chow buddy."

"A *chow buddy*, huh? If that's what I think it is, I'm in."

"Perfect. I hate eating alone."

"So you've said." Pleasure flooded through her. Questioning her desire to see him again was pointless. What person in their right mind would say no?

"Right. I'll be back in a half hour," he replied. "Do you like chocolate?"

"Am I human?"

He laughed and signed off.

Annie stared at the blank screen for an extra couple of seconds, then set the phone on her lap. Yeah, she already had it bad.

She must've dozed off because the ringing of her cell startled her and sent her heart racing. Not bothering to check the caller ID, she picked up.

"What did you forget?" she murmured sleepily.

"Annie?"

"James?"

"Hey, sprite." His warm, loving voice flowed through the line and gave her a hearty hug. Oh, how she missed him. Raw emotion clogged her throat, and she fought like hell to hold back sobs.

"Rumor has it that you were trying to stop planes with your scrawny body," James said.

She snorted. Leave it to her brother to ruin an emotional moment.

"Yeah, I have a Wonder Woman complex."

"You're not tall enough for the part."

"Rude!" She gave in and grinned.

Tone void of teasing, James asked, "So, you want to tell me how bad it is, or do I have to strong-arm a doctor?"

"Sammy didn't say?"

"She did, but I want to hear it from you. I need to know you're okay."

The urge to cry grew exponentially. "I'm pretty broken. Physically, at least."

"And emotionally?"

"Yeah, close, but I'm managing." Crowd noise filtered through their connection. "Where are you?"

"In the lobby of this fucking hospital, trying to find out what floor you're on."

"*What?* How? How did you get here so fast?"

"Your accident was yesterday morning. Did you think I couldn't assign work to my crew and drive here in a day?"

"Oh, Jamie." Love swelled in her heart. "You didn't have to."

"Yes, I did. Now, do you want to tell me what floor you're on, or do I need to bust some heads around here?"

Since her ribs wouldn't allow it, she curbed her desire to laugh. "I honestly don't know. Second floor, if I had to guess. My room's whiteboard reads two-fifty-six."

"See you in a few."

Just as Annie disconnected, Quinn sailed through the door, holding a bag high. "I got the goods. Let the feast begin!"

"You showered and changed. That doesn't seem fair."

"Had to. I couldn't stand my own stink, and it was pointed out that yesterday's clothes were disgusting."

"I'm jealous. What I wouldn't give to shower right now." She sighed her longing.

"I promise not to mention that you smell like hospital disinfectant," he vowed.

"Shut it, tool."

As she watched him spread their feast on the tray table, Annie's crush deepened. Yes, it was an exceedingly bad idea to lose her heart to Quinn; he was in a committed relationship with a pregnant woman, but who didn't adore a take-charge guy with a kind heart? The trick was going to be hiding her blossoming feelings.

"What's wrong?"

As if she could tell him!

She frowned as Quinn set an actual dinner plate in front of her.

"I was wondering what type of man has access to ceramic plates for impromptu lunch runs."

He laughed. "I may have purchased them along with the food. I despise disposable plates."

"Snob." She smiled to soften the word. "But you should've brought a third."

"Why's that?"

"Because my b—*Jamie!*"

James stopped just inside the door, a look of bewilderment on his tired, unshaven face. "What's this? Entertaining men behind everyone's back?"

Quinn looked nonplussed. Annie, on the other hand, experienced an immediate hot flash.

Thank you, embarrassing brother!

"*No!* No, Jamie. I'd never. It's not like that." She didn't want poor Quinn to think she had designs on his affections *or* that scrumptious body of his. Really, she *would* have designs if he was single, but as someone who was hurt when her husband strayed, she'd never put another person through that. Never poach another woman's man. Regardless of how much she might want him.

Jamie crossed to the bed and kissed her forehead. "Hush. I'm just teasing you, sprite. No need to sound like an outraged virgin." With a smirk, he picked up a triangle filled with creamy stuffing and prepared to dip it into the sweet sauce. "So, I believe introductions are in—*holy shit! Quinn Jensen!*"

Annie sighed. "He gets that a lot."

Quinn wasn't sure why Jamie's breezy entrance felt like a hot poker under his skin. Maybe it was the way the guy had walked in, as if he owned the place. Or perhaps it was something deeper. Something he didn't care to analyze. With certainty, it irritated the fuck out of him to see the dark-haired gym rat touch Annie in such a familiar way. Her flustered response caused his stomach to clench uncomfortably.

"I believe introductions are in order, Annie," Jamie said. He checked himself right before elbowing her, as if he'd only then realized she was hurt. Frowning, he tucked an errant lock of hair behind her ear.

Quinn fantasized about breaking Jamie's fingers, joint by goddamn joint. Where had he been yesterday when she was critically hurt? He couldn't be bothered to show up right away? His temper spiked.

Until Annie made a proper introduction.

"Jamie, obviously, you know who this is. Quinn, this is my overbearing brother, James."

Brother.

Offering a wide smile and a hearty handshake, Quinn was shocked when his pique dissolved as if it had never existed.

"I can wrangle up another plate if you're hungry, James," he said smoothly.

"Actually, I ate on the road about an hour ago. I *will* steal a spring roll, though." James glanced between them with a slight frown. "How do you know my sister?"

"Clearly, you don't watch the news."

"I was busy with work when our sister Sammy called. I headed up right away." Her brother shrugged like he didn't give a shit about the news, either way. "So?"

"She saved my life yesterday." Quinn smiled down at her. "And the lives of my fiancée and unborn baby."

James's blue eyes cooled, and the tension in his body couldn't be mistaken. The man had gone from slouched to upright and as dangerous as a Bengal tiger in a mere blink.

"Fiancée," James stated flatly. He squinted down at Annie and scowled darkly when she rolled her eyes.

"Jesus, Jamie. He's just here to bring me lunch as a thank you, not molest me. Chill."

"I didn't say anything."

"You didn't have to. I grew up with you, remember?" She eased forward and lifted her spoon, smiling tightly when Quinn rushed to offer his one-armed assistance. "Also, empath. You know more than most, Jamie. Our gifts never go away, and the overprotective-brother routine is unnecessary."

Based on the way she'd phrased her response, Quinn wondered if perhaps James had a special skill, too. If so, was it genetic? Did all her family have a freaky-as-fuck ability? He'd question her after her brother left. It was likely she'd be more forthcoming when James's domineering personality didn't suppress her desire to speak.

"Now that my selfless intentions are no longer in question, it's on to other important matters." Quinn whipped out his smartphone. "Do you practice any religion that would exclude your enjoyment of Christmas?"

Her bewildered expression told him she was delightfully confused.

He grinned. "No?"

She didn't strike him as someone easily surprised, and he felt a small thrill that he could achieve it.

"No," she said with a quick glance toward James.

"Perfect." When Quinn finished tapping out instructions to Paige, he dished up a plate, balanced it on his casted arm, and perched on the edge of the windowsill to eat.

During their meal, Annie and James traded sibling snark, but none of it was mean-spirited or meant to hurt. Whatever she dropped due to her awkward mobility, James was quick to retrieve or wipe up. The two of them had a bond similar to his siblings and him. They were there for each other, through thick and thin. As it should be.

The knock on the door was expected, and Quinn strode over to answer. When he saw the set-up crew, he checked behind him, meeting Annie's curious gaze across the distance and giving her a tentative smile. If she didn't like his present, he was going to feel like a prize idiot.

CHAPTER 10

"Okay, guys, bring it in." The astonishment on Annie's face was worth the effort it took Quinn, and satisfaction unfurled inside him at having shocked her into silence. "I didn't know if you had any sensitivities to pine, so I went with an artificial tree."

"No sensitivities," she murmured absently as her wide eyes took it all in.

James remained silent but looked none too thrilled by the interruption.

In fairness, Quinn had no idea her brother had intended to visit, or he wouldn't have scheduled the tree decorating. He'd assumed Annie would be alone for the holiday, and the knowledge didn't sit well with him. After Paige initially secured the necessary items, Quinn had recruited three men from the hospital's maintenance department. With quick precision, they fitted the limbs to the tree base and fluffed the branches to hang the ornaments. The entire process was done with minimal fuss. As they were about to top the tree with a delicate angel in a gold-and-white lace dress, Annie spoke.

"Wait."

Five heads turned in her direction.

She gnawed on her bottom lip, but her effort to contain her delighted grin was in vain. "I want Quinn to have the honors."

Though it would be awkward AF with only one useful arm, he was game if it meant making her happy. Stepping on the short ladder, he accepted a twelve-inch tree topper from the guy on his left and positioned it to face Annie.

"No. Since it's in the corner, it has to look out over the room," Annie directed.

"She should be watching over you."

"It's a decoration, not a real angel," she reminded him.

Forced to concede the point, he adjusted it according to her instructions. "How's that?"

"More to the left."

"Seriously?"

"Mm-hmm."

"Now?"

"A bit more. Nope! Too far. Back to the right a touch."

"Annie, has anyone ever told you that you can be a touch anal?"

She released an annoyed huff at the same time her brother's booming laugh rang out.

Quinn met James's amused gaze. "So they *have?*"

"Dude, you have *no* idea."

"I swear, Jamie, I'd punch you if I could," Annie groused, promised retribution in her glare. He blew a raspberry on her cheek as she grabbed her ribs with one hand and laughingly shoved at his face with the other. "I hate you."

"Nah. You don't."

Mesmerized by the animation on Annie's lovely visage, Quinn stopped what he was doing to watch her. One of the crew tapped the side of the ladder, breaking the spell.

"We need to get back to work if you're done, man."

"Right. Sorry." What the hell was wrong with him? Even at the airport yesterday, he'd been spellbound, unable to keep his eyes off her. It wasn't like she had extraordinary beauty. Hell, ninety percent of his time was spent in the land of drop-dead gorgeous people, for goodness's sake. Yet Annie held a strange draw for Quinn, a highly disturbing and unexplainable one.

Once more, he shifted the angel, fairly certain it was back in its original position.

"How about now, Annie?"

The low but firm "ahem" from James drew his notice, and Quinn turned in time to see Annie lift her gaze from his backside to the tree topper.

She'd kept him on the ladder to ogle his ass!

His "perfectly chiseled ass," according to her earlier comment.

Quinn narrowed his eyes.

No words were needed between them. The little she-devil knew she was busted, but the sparkle in her eyes was enchanting and emphasized by her pretty, pink flush. He couldn't be mad. She was too freaking adorable in her embarrassment. It wasn't as if she was the first woman to find his ass attractive.

Face averted to hide his grin, he climbed down and stepped aside so one of the crew could fold the ladder. He handed each of the three maintenance workers a thick envelope of cash. "Thanks, guys. I appreciate that you allowed me to take up your lunch break."

"Our pleasure, Mr. Jensen. Do you mind if we get a picture?"

Quinn dutifully posed, shook hands, and autographed whatever they had for him to write on. After they left, he faced the Holts, who were watching him with avid interest. The twin expressions made their resemblance more obvious.

James was burlier than most guys of Quinn's acquaintance. Even the majority of muscular men in Hollywood were lanky. Most actors of his acquaintance worked night and day on diet and exercise, so they didn't possess an extra ounce of fat. Yet Annie's brother was different. Although built like he could do damage in the boxing ring, James emitted a chill vibe—unless it came to his sister. The barely suppressed aggression lingering below the surface when they'd met was mostly gone, but the instinctive need to protect was there.

Annie, in direct contrast, was petite. Delicate. Perhaps it was the sight of her slight figure in the hospital bed, or maybe it was the fact Quinn knew she'd sustained unimaginably painful injuries to save others. But either way, her looks were deceiving. In the short time he'd known her, she'd displayed a core of pure steel, and he suspected her inner strength rivaled her brother's brawn.

"Thank you, Mr. Jensen. This was awfully kind of you to do." Her sweet voice wrapped around him, making him want to do more for her. To promise anything. Whatever magic she possessed, Quinn wanted a bit of it for his own.

But he couldn't have it.

Shouldn't even dream about it.

Any type of relationship with Annie was off-limits. Even an innocent friendship would be risky. The press would ruin her life with innuendos and slander her in the eyes of the world.

"It's Quinn." He shot her a tight smile. "It was the very least I could do. But now, I should leave you both alone to catch up."

A little of the light died from her eyes, but she gamely returned his smile.

His heart lurched in his chest. Her brilliant Caribbean-blue eyes should never shine with anything other than humor and happiness. He barely stopped himself short of shaking his head. What the hell was wrong with him? Perhaps he was the one who needed a CT scan of his brain.

"Actually, I have to get to a hotel and get settled in." James looked between them and rested his gaze on Annie. "I'd stay at your place, but I don't want that ninety-minute drive each way. Where's your pup? Are you boarding her?" When she shook her head, he said, "I can see if the hotel will make special arrangements."

Quinn knew he should remain quiet. Knew he should hand off the dog to James and be done with it. But he couldn't help himself. "I've offered to care for Tink until your sister's better. I'll be checking on Hailey every day anyway, so it's no bother to bring her by for a visit. If for any reason I can't, my brother can."

"Mr. Jens—uh, Quinn..." Annie stalled at his severe expression, but forged on. "There's no telling how long I'll be laid up. Jamie can take her home with him when he heads back to Florida, and I can fly down and get her when I'm mobile again."

She didn't sound as if she loved that plan. Her bond with her pet was too strong for her to go weeks, possibly months, without seeing her. Quinn hated it, too, though he refused to explore why.

"It's up to you, but really, it's no bother. Tink will be good company until Hailey wakes."

Until Hailey wakes.

Annie wanted to hurl up fried rice. For an hour or two, she'd forgotten Quinn was taken. Precisely how was up for debate. She'd seen with her own two eyes that he was with Hailey. Hell, they had basically mocked her at the airport. Or so his snooty fiancée had made it appear. Having met him, Annie found it hard to believe he'd take part in a mean-spirited conversation.

"I'm grateful to whoever wants to care for Tink in the interim." She hoped to leave the decision to James and Quinn. If she had to choose, she'd pick Quinn every time, if only to force him to drop back by. His presence made her forget how badly her body ached.

Annie toyed with what was left of her meal and heaved an internal sigh. Yeah, her brother was probably the smarter choice.

James kissed her temple. "Nothing has to be decided right now, and I need a shower. I'll pop back by later tonight with dinner, okay? Just text me what you're craving."

Quinn hung around after her brother left, making Annie wonder why. Guilt? Should she cut him loose and inform him he didn't need to cater to her every whim? Surely, he had better things to do with his time.

But she didn't want to.

Silently, he bent to plug in the tree, then switched off the main overhead light. The soft glow from the LEDs bathed him in its beauty, highlighting the sharp angles of his face and illuminating his handsomeness. Put simply, Quinn was a work of art.

When he turned to her and smiled, it occurred to her that she was already too late in sending him away. Something had ignited within her when he'd first approached her. Completely woke her up inside, and with every glance her way, every smile, she felt her inner self expand and shine in a way it never had before. She never wanted to be without that thrilling zing again.

The smile eased from his face, and an intensity sharpened his gaze. Annie felt the pull down to her pinky toes. How long they stared at one another, she couldn't say, but during that span of time, something significant altered between them.

A sharp knock on the open door brought them back to the present, and she shifted her head to see the newcomer.

"Paige?"

Before Sammy, Michael had been in a relationship with Paige. The woman had been a petty bitch, and the distaste on her pinched face indicated her personality hadn't undergone any life-altering changes.

"Annie." Paige's put-upon tone made her sound as if she'd rather be anywhere but there.

"You know each other?" Quinn's voice rose in surprise.

"Yes." Paige moved farther into the room as she spoke. In a possessive move, she clutched Quinn's arm and cast a sympathetic look at Annie. "I'm sorry to hear about Michael. How devastated you must be!"

Although the words *sounded* sincere, the pure malice behind them smacked Annie in the face. If the other woman hadn't been putting on an act, Annie might've mumbled a thank you and let it go. But as it was, her hidden bitch came out to play.

"The news of Michael's death was a gross misunderstanding. I'm happy to report he's alive and well."

Paige's thin lips turned pale as she pressed them together.

"Who's Michael?" Quinn's casual question seemed forced as he shrugged off the hand clinging to his forearm and strode to the bed to select another spring roll. All an act, of course, because they'd already gorged themselves and the food was cold after so long.

"My boyfriend." The challenging look Paige shot her, as if she had single-handedly destroyed their relationship, set Annie's teeth on edge.

"Technically, *ex*-boyfriend since he's been with Sammy since she graduated college." Annie couldn't resist a dig. She really despised the woman.

Gritting her teeth, Paige said, "Of course."

Quinn's head pivoted back and forth between them as if he was watching a tennis match. Their conversation had a soap-opera drama that would confuse an innocent bystander.

For a split second, Paige's perfectly made-up face twisted with dislike, and her thick, painted-on brows clashed together. Just as quickly, she smoothed her features into a serene mask, and a small, rueful smile shaped her mouth.

"Sorry, Quinn. I didn't mean to air dirty laundry. But I was devastated when Michael left me for Annie's sister Sammy. To be betrayed and left in the dust..."

The martyred expression was a bit much, but Annie stayed silent.

Quinn's narrow-eyed gaze landed on her, and she felt the need to defend the absent Michael.

"It wasn't like that at all, and you damn well know it." The fight not to glare at Paige was lost. Annie desperately wanted to say clinginess and blatant lies had sent him running. But she wouldn't. Partly because she felt awkward drudging up family history with someone she'd basically just met, but mainly, she didn't want to sound as if she were making excuses.

Although Quinn didn't give any indication in action or speech, his tension ratcheted up. If she touched him, she was sure to feel the bunched muscles beneath his clothing. The desire to remove some of his edginess was strong, and she fought the pull. He was in charge of his own emotions, and it wasn't up to her to soothe him.

"It was exactly like that, Annie, and you—"

"Paige, I think that's enough," Quinn stated quietly, effectively cutting off any venom she'd been about to spew. "It's personal information I don't need, and it's in the past, so let's leave it there." Dropping the uneaten egg roll, he wiped his fingers on a napkin. "I had you come by so I could introduce you to Annie. She may be calling for a few things she might need."

"Of course, Quinn," Paige purred with fluttering lashes and a butter-wouldn't-melt-in-her-mouth smile. A direct contrast to her bitchy vibe that screamed, *"No fucking way!"*

Annie was in agreement with Sammy's nemesis. It would be a cold day in hell before she accepted a damned thing from Paige. Quinn could keep the woman's number to himself.

"It's so good of you to care about a perfect stranger, the way you are." Ever the underhanded bitch, Paige paused for dramatic effect, and Annie knew the she-cat was about to take another vicious swipe. "But why isn't Charlie seeing to all your needs, Annie?"

And there it was!

Although she never blinked in her stare-off with Paige, Annie felt Quinn's questioning regard.

"Who's Charlie?" His tone was low, edgy, and it sent a small thrill through her. She wasn't silly enough to believe it was jealously, but his interest was there.

"My ex-husband," she replied with as much quiet dignity as she could muster. "My divorce was finalized last month. But even if it hadn't been, Charlie wouldn't go out of his way for anyone. Ever. I can honestly say that 'all my needs' wouldn't have been met."

Quinn gave her hand a light squeeze. "Jesus, Annie. I'm sorry."

"Don't be. These things happen." She shifted her arm away and gave him an impersonal smile. No way was she going to give Paige more ammunition for her long-running war against the Holts. "Would you both mind very much if we call it a day? I need pain meds and a nap, in that order."

The nagging discomfort from her injuries rivaled everyone's swirling emotions scratching at her. Including her own. Paige had succeeded in picking scabs off recently healed wounds and stirring up her special brand of shit.

"Thank you for the decorations, Quinn. It was a lovely gesture."

Silently, he studied her, and the seconds felt like hours. What was it he saw? Did he think she was as pathetic and sad as she currently felt? Probably.

"I'll see you tomorrow, Annie. If you need anything at all, call me or…"

He paused in jotting down Paige's number, likely because he'd grasped the situation.

No way in fucking hell was she ever going to call that bloodthirsty she-shark.

CHAPTER 11

Quinn left Paige outside Annie's room and returned to Hailey. He felt like he needed a palate cleanser. No love had been lost between the women, that was for damned sure. Even the most clueless individual could see they were vastly different. Paige had a brittle edge and tended to be overly familiar in her dealings with him. He'd always put it down to her desire to please in a world full of ass-kissers. Obviously, he hated the way she sucked up to him, but he couldn't find fault with her work. She was organized and productive, the best PA he'd ever had.

Annie, on the other hand, appeared kinder. More open and honest. Yet she'd become strangely reserved toward the end of his visit. He was coming to realize, if she didn't put up a wall between herself and the outside world, the emotional overload would leave her drained and broken.

The decision to have Ty replace Paige as his liaison to Annie was cemented. She didn't need the additional tension during her recovery.

As he sat beside Hailey's bed, he stared at her pale face. Even deathly still, she was stunning. Guilt began to eat at him. Not once today had he thought to decorate *her* room, but then again, she wasn't awake to enjoy it.

She might never be.

A shiver of awareness swept along his nerve endings, causing the fine hair on the back of his neck to lift and a tingle along his spine. Was that what Annie felt when she received a premonition? The physical dread? The *knowing* nothing would be normal after that exact moment? Was he being fanciful?

As Quinn held Hailey's hand and prayed to a God he wasn't positive he believed in, a nurse breezed in to check her vitals. Her name was Rachel, and she tried to engage him in small talk, batting her eyelashes and casting him flirty glances. With his attention purposefully focused on Hailey, he kept his responses short to discourage conversation. Yes or no, while avoiding looking directly at her. Finding minor things to fiddle with—the IV, the buttons on the monitor, a fluff of a pillow—she lingered and chatted inanely.

Quinn wanted to shout at her to get lost. To leave him the fuck alone. Rant that he needed quiet to gather his scattered thoughts. But he wouldn't be discourteous. His mother would tan his hide, full-grown adult or no.

Instead, he left to find coffee. Halfway to the cafeteria, he back-tracked to Annie's room. Although Quinn had expected to find her asleep, she was wide awake and staring contemplatively at the Christmas tree.

"Hey," he said softly. "I was about to head down for coffee. Can I get you a cup?"

"I rarely drink the stuff." She shot him a rueful grin. "It amps me up and makes me jittery."

"Tea, then?"

"Mr. Jens—"

"Quinn," he said firmly.

"Quinn. You don't have to cater to me. Really."

He narrowed his eyes and grinned when she ruefully laughed.

"Fine. I'd love a hot chocolate, if they have it. And thank you," she said primly.

"Anything else?"

When she shook her head, he left.

In a corridor a short distance from the main lobby, he discovered a gourmet coffee kiosk. After securing a drink for Annie, he ordered a double-shot espresso for himself. His ability to sleep tonight would be screwed, but he needed the extra boost to get him through the late afternoon.

As he waited, he noticed the thickening snow outside the sliders and sighed.

His plans to sit with Hailey and read emails were shot to hell. If he didn't leave soon, the weather would make it impossible to return to his hotel, and Tink shouldn't be left alone after all the upheaval she'd suffered.

He accepted the drink carrier with a nod and a large tip, then hustled to Annie's room. Her gratitude made the effort of stopping by worth it.

"Ghirardelli," she sighed after her first sip. "I'd recognize that flavor anywhere. I don't know where the hell you found it, but I'm thrilled down to my frosty tipy-toes."

"Your toes are cold?" He moved to the end of the bed, and without a second thought for permission to touch her feet, he lifted the blanket to wrap his toasty hand around first one foot, then the other. "Better?"

"Yes, but you shouldn't go around warming strangers' feet. I mean, it's a heroic thing to do and all, but the germs..."

Charmed by the sight of her high color, he laughed.

"So you're not only particular about decoration placement—yeah, don't think I can't tell that silver ball is bothering you—but you're also a germaphobe."

"I am not!" Her blush deepened. "But you should probably use the hand sanitizer by the door right away. I could have MRSA or something."

"This hospital stay is going to be torture for you, isn't it?" Seriously, it had to be a nightmare for someone who hated germs.

Other than to shoot him a mock glare, Annie didn't say

anything, choosing instead to sip her drink. After a short stretch of silence, she said, "Would you move the silver ball down and to the right, about two inches?"

He curbed his amusement and complied. "How's that?"

"Perfect."

A second check of the weather showed he still had a few minutes to spare. "Where were you headed for the holiday? Home, to see your family?"

"No. Actually, this is my first trip South in a long while—five years, to be exact—because my husband was an ass. We always did what *he* wanted. But my family is scattered this season." She had a far-off look as she toyed with a thread on her blanket. "I'd decided to head to the Florida Keys for a bit of R and R. Tink's never been to the beach. For some crazy reason, I thought it would be fun to watch her chase seagulls."

The idea of Tink antagonizing birds, tongue rolled out like a red carpet halfway down her chest, made him smile. He imagined if she were with them, she'd give a happy bark as if she, too, liked the idea of chasing those annoying sea pigeons.

"This is going to sound strange, but does Tink always agree with you?"

Annie grinned. "Mostly. But every once in a while, we have a difference of opinion."

The soft glow of love lit her eyes.

Lucky dog.

The person or pet fortunate enough to have Annie's unfailing devotion would hold an immeasurable gift. He shoved away the thought and tried to pull up Hailey's image. All he saw was the pale, still mask of an unconscious woman; he couldn't recall his fiancée looking at him with anything close to love, or even like, in recent months.

"Okay, I'll bite. How do you know when you're having a difference of opinion?" When she hesitated, Quinn perched on the edge of her bed. Crossing his ankles, he leaned back against the footboard. "I've got nothing but time on my hands. I can totally wait you out."

A small smirk played upon Annie's cherry-red lips. "It's her argumentative energy, of course."

"Ah, I should have figured as much," he replied with a chuckle. "And it couldn't be that she's right and *you're* the argumentative one?"

As she tried to suppress her answering laugh, a dimple appeared in her left cheek. Not both sides, just the one, and Quinn found her more attractive for the lack of perfection.

"What about you?" she asked. "What were your plans for Christmas? Surely, you had no intention of hanging around a hospital and putting up trees for bedbound patients?"

"Hailey and I were heading to St. Martin."

"Sounds ideal. Did I read somewhere that your brother is your twin?"

Uncomfortable discussing his private life, he gave a brief nod and didn't elaborate. But she wasn't done with her game of twenty questions, and it would have been churlish of him to refuse to answer.

"Why don't you spend the holiday with him? Are you not close? I thought twins were supposed to have a special connection or something."

"We are. Close, that is. If I'm in the country and not working, we spend holidays together. This year was different because of my recent engagement to Hailey. She didn't want a large family gathering, just a vacation for the two of us."

"Perhaps that's when she intended to tell you about the baby. I'm sorry you missed out."

With a forced smile, he said, "There's always time for a trip when she wakes up."

She caught her lip between her teeth, a sign of her sudden uncomfortableness with their conversation.

Dropping his feet to the floor, he sat straighter.

"What is it, Annie? Another premonition?"

"No. I..." The brackets on either side of her mouth deepened into a grimace, and her eyes were sorrowful. His stomach clenched at the sickening suspicion she was holding something back. "It's nothing, Quinn."

There was an *off* quality about her response.

What did she know?

Did she have a vision of Hailey and him separated? Was she not going to pull through? Was there going to be a complication to destroy all his future plans? A dozen more questions crowded his mind, and he curbed the impulsive need to ask. Yes, he'd locked on to Annie's obvious lie of omission, but other than the few brief visits they'd shared, he didn't know her well enough to call her out on it.

"Now that your plans are scrubbed, do you intend to stay close by for Christmas? I take it you live in the area?" she asked in a falsely chipper tone.

"I do. My brother actually lives in Sagefield, on this side of Stonebrooke, so I imagine I'll spend it with him or here."

"Really? I live on the far side of Stonebrooke, right on the border of Randolph."

"I know the area. Pretty lake."

"I was lucky enough to find a house overlooking the water. An older couple wanted to retire to Florida."

"Nice."

Plucking at the cover, she dropped her gaze. "The rest of your family is in Texas?"

"No." Disturbed by her invasive curiosity and her attempt to guess his family's location, he purposefully laughed it off. "What's with all the questions?"

"Oh, I'm sorry." She shot him a chagrined look. "I'm a genealogist by trade. I'm inclined to pry into personal facts. Accents, in particular, are a hobby of mine. Yours has a subtle underlying twang that screams Deep South."

The rambling explanation went a long way to ease his mind. "Genealogy, huh? What is the craziest thing you've stumbled across?"

"I don't know how crazy it is, but I've discovered more than one guy with multiple families over the years. Back before the digital age, a woman had no way of pinpointing her man's whereabouts. It was a lot easier to get away with subterfuge."

His brows shot up. Exactly why he was surprised by her discovery was beyond him. Deceit and games were the core of many people's everyday life. Honesty was the rarer commodity. One he valued.

"What else?"

"Hmm, let me think."

As Annie dredged up remembered discoveries, Quinn watched her closely. Of all the people he knew, she struck him as the most genuine and real when she probably had the most to hide.

"Perhaps familial closeness in marriage," she finally said.

"As in close kin?" His voice rose a notch with his surprise. The twinkle in her eye aroused his suspicion. "Are you screwing with me, Annie Holt?"

"Not at all. But I *do* love seeing the shock on your face."

He laughed.

Sweet Annie had a mischievous streak.

"You definitely shocked me. How close?"

She scrunched up her face.

"No! Brother and sister?" A nod confirmed his guess. "Tell me it went far, far back in history. That there were only five people in the entire town, and it was hundreds of miles from anywhere."

Her robust laughter was quickly cut off by a groan and a grab of her ribs.

"Shit! I'm sorry, Annie. Are you okay? Should I call the nurse?"

"No, I'm fine. I forgot about my injury for a minute. Damned broken ribs."

"I'm sorry, darlin'. I did, too."

Her expression shifted to wistful, almost sad.

Leaning closer, he touched her hand. "What is it?"

"My sister's husband calls her darlin'. Michael. The one Paige..." She cleared her throat and blinked rapidly. "When we thought he'd passed away, we were so devastated. I haven't seen him since it was discovered he's still alive." With a soft light in her eyes, she said, "I miss him."

"You sound half in love with him." Why her affection for another man bothered him, Quinn didn't know. Perhaps that's what had led to her divorce and the fact that no one but James had shown up after her accident. Maybe she was persona non grata in her family.

"Not in the way you suspect." She shot him a reproachful look. "He's just an all-around great guy. I've known him for the better part of ten years, and my entire family adores him."

"I hope you get to see him again soon," he replied stiffly, unreasonably irked by her closeness to a man he'd never met.

CHAPTER 12

*A*nnie didn't know what to think of Quinn's rioting emotions. Reservation, suspicion, acceptance, teasing, and finally sincerity. The man was thoroughly exhausting. Normally, she could drum up a defense against other people's emotion-packed energy, but with him, she found it damned near impossible.

When he suggested she was half in love with Michael, he'd sounded accusatory. *But why?* Quinn didn't know her from the next person. She could only assume he'd been burned in the past by a similar situation. There really was no other way to justify his gut reaction. Or it was possible that she'd misread him. Rarely did it happen, but her energy receptors were known to backfire, especially when she was ill or exhausted, like she currently was. Opioids didn't help, either.

To lighten the mood, she regaled him with stories of Sammy and Michael. Their relationship had all the makings of the perfect romance, with a host of hilarious situations thrown in the mix. Sammy, firecracker that she was, always kept Michael hopping.

The bonus for Annie? Quinn's laughter. Deep, rich, and toe-curling. She could bask in the sound of it all day long.

"You have a wonderful way with storytelling, Annie."

It was impossible not to preen under his praise. "Thanks. You should hear my brother retell a story, though. He's the master. I'd like to think maybe I learned a thing or two."

Quinn's engaging smile said she had.

"Other than your brother, who else is going to visit you for the holidays?"

The abruptness of his question left her breathless. How did she tell him no one was coming? True friends were rare for her, and the life of an empath was a lonely one. Those she'd been acquainted with were gained either through her business or her marriage to Charlie. But he took their mutual friends in the divorce.

"No one." Uncomfortable under his probing stare, Annie looked at the cheerful tree. "My friends will be spending time with their families, and like I said before, my family is scattered this year. Jamie assured me he'll be here through Christmas, though."

"Seems to me the others could return to check on you."

His anger was gratifying. More than once, Annie had thought the same.

"It's okay, Quinn. I promise, if my condition was serious, they'd all be here."

His mouth tightened, and he shot her a look of disbelief.

"This"—he gestured to her battered body on the bed—"isn't serious?"

"Yes, but not life-threatening." She shrugged as much as she was able and tried to explain. "They would've known to be here. Would have sensed it well in advance."

The next minutes were spent with him digesting and processing the information. He came to the proper conclusion. "They're all like you."

"To a degree," she acknowledged.

"Care to share?"

A little devil made her say, "I don't know if I should. We don't know each other that well. I mean, you could—"

"Point taken," he replied dryly. "How about we trade facts no one else knows about us?"

"Okay. What wouldn't anyone know about the great Quinn Jensen?"

He hesitated, as if searching for something not too personal.

To put him out of his misery, Annie said, "I'll go first. Sammy, my youngest sister, is psychic. Mom is, to a large degree, as well. Jamie can talk to spirits."

"Like a medium?"

"Yes. Exactly so. Would it freak you out to know he can see them, too?"

"Get out of here! You're making this up," he charged, edging closer.

"Nope. Scout's honor." She held up three fingers on her right hand.

"Did I hear you and James mention another sister? What hidden talent does she have?"

"Talent? That's a nice way to phrase it. To anyone else, we're witches, freaks, or liars." She hadn't meant to display bitterness, and his frown indicated his dislike of her confession, although she doubted his distaste was directed at her.

"My sister Margie can remember the past lives of those she's connected to. Her family, her children, a best friend, or even a lover."

His slack-jawed expression caused her to giggle.

"Tell me you're joking."

"Afraid not. It's the truth. Her fessing up to that particular gift is what started me down the genealogy path. I was looking for facts on one of her past lives."

"How so?"

"When she first started having dreams, she thought she was losing her mind. She wanted to verify what she believed were memories of previous lives. And because she didn't have the time, I decided to research whatever she could recall. After digging into the old records, I was completely floored by what I found."

"And I'm assuming you were able to verify all her 'previous lives'?"

She nodded.

"Unbelievable. I've never heard of anything like this."

Annie crooked her finger to gesture him closer. When he leaned in, she whispered as if imparting a secret, "She was on the Titanic with Sammy and Michael. Michael didn't make it off the ship."

"Seems poor Michael has a history of bad luck."

She hadn't thought about it before then. "I wonder if you're right and exactly how far back it goes." Annie met his warm, moss-green eyes and smiled.

With a suddenness that stole her breath, the air between them crackled. Carnal vibes shot through her like fireworks on the Fourth of July, and a desire to kiss him, to taste his minty fresh mouth, exploded like a Roman candle.

His thoughts or hers?

Hers. A mere glance at his sinful mouth was proof enough. But the question of the hour—*was it all one-sided?*

Incapable of freeing herself from his seductive draw, she stared into his confused eyes and wished she could stay linked with him forever. The buzz of his phone was the distraction Annie needed to control her wayward feelings.

What the hell had just happened?

Never in her life had she experienced anything of that magnitude before. An eleven on the Richter scale. And didn't Quinn appear affected? With a deep frown, he scooted until he once again rested against the footboard.

Annie mourned the distance.

"You were able to prove they were on the ship?" he asked after a quick peek at his cell. His voice was on the husky side of normal, and the telltale sound made Annie feel marginally better. She wasn't the only one experiencing the strange connection.

Pasting on a too-bright smile, she nodded. "Yes. Margie and Sammy were the Reddington sisters. Lucy and Rosalie. Michael was known as Andrew Hale, and he was Margie's—uh, Lucy's groom."

"*What?* Not Sammy's?"

Annie laughed in the face of his confused indignation.

"You weren't kidding when you said everyone loved him. Don't tell me you were married to him once upon a time, too." His playful scowl thrilled her in ways it shouldn't.

She relayed the facts as she knew them to be. "Lucy and Andrew were betrothed from an early age by their parents. Although Andrew always loved Rosalie, he wouldn't go against his father's wishes. There was a great deal at stake. So Lucy and Andrew entered into a marriage of convenience."

"This is like the plot of a dark and twisty movie." While he acted skeptical, his bright eyes shone with interest and delight. "What happened next? Other than the sinking of the ship, that is."

"Well, Lucy met the love of her life on board. His name was Sebastian, and unfortunately, he died the night of the iceberg, too." Annie reached for her water, and after a fortifying drink, she continued. "Apparently, Lucy and Sebastian believed Rosalie went below decks after a misunderstanding with her sister. But in reality, she'd sought out Andrew, presumably for comfort. Not knowing that, Lucy begged Sebastian's help to search for her. By the time they were deep into the search, the ship was in trouble."

"This is all verified?" he asked, incredulous.

"The people and deaths are, yes. The story of the Reddington sisters is what Margie remembers."

"Then how does she know it was her personal memory and not something she'd read or overheard?"

"Hand me my laptop."

Quinn did as requested, and Annie booted up the computer. After she found the file she was searching for, she pulled up an old photo of Lucy and a current one of Margie side by side on the screen. With a half smile, she turned the laptop toward him.

"*Jesus!*"

"Hold on." She replaced the photos with one of Rosalie and one of Sammy.

"It's uncanny. I really can't believe this. What about Andrew and Michael?"

As she set up two more pictures together, Quinn tucked his head next to hers and peered over her shoulder. His unintentionally seductive force began to wrap around her, stroking her and merging with her unprotected energy. With every inhale of his woodsy scent, she became increasingly lightheaded, falling further under his spell.

Cracker Jacks!

If he ever turned the full force of his charm on her, she'd be putty in his capable hands.

"This is Michael?" he asked.

"Huh? Oh. Uh. Yeah."

Quinn appeared not to notice the tremor in her voice. "Remarkable. And what about Sebastian?"

"I could only dig up one grainy photo. I *did* uncover that Sebastian Harwick actually existed and that he did indeed die when the Titanic sank. I've got the list of passenger names. Just a sec." With the fingers of her good hand, she hunted and pecked the keys to retrieve the information. More than once, she had to backspace since the mind-finger connection was interrupted by Quinn's nearness. "My sister Margie believes her fiancé, Gabriel, was Sebastian."

"I don't know what to say. This isn't some elaborate joke you play on unsuspecting strangers, is it?"

She giggled like a giddy teenage girl, then gave herself a mental slap.

"No joke," she said in an embarrassingly breathy voice.

"Wow. It's insane but incredible at the same time."

Annie tilted her head back to look at him.

Big mistake.

The exposed column of his throat and the hard line of his jaw tempted her in unimaginable ways. The desire to run her tongue over those corded muscles and nip his earlobe was a living, breathing thing, and she slowly inhaled to center herself. The action had the opposite effect, and his scent, clean and heady enough to scramble her brains, teased her. Taunted her with the forbidden.

In *way* over her head, she tried to act normal, but it required every ounce of acting ability she possessed. Admittedly, she had no skills in that area, at all.

"Annie, I..." Trace Montgomery paused inside the doorway and gave them an amused grin. "Why do the two of you look like you've been caught searching porn on the internet?"

She was so busted!

CHAPTER 13

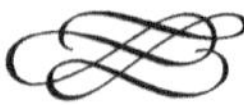

The interruption was a godsend. Well, that, and the fact Annie was essentially immobile from her injuries. Had the good doctor not appeared when he did, she might've latched onto Quinn like a blood-thirsty leech. Steamy sexual fantasies had hijacked her brain and stole her ability to speak. Under the doctor's hyper-vigilant gaze, her skin felt like molten lava. Probably looked it, too. Even her damned arms weren't exempt from her guilty flush.

And thank all that was holy Quinn never looked her way as he replied to Dr. Montgomery.

"Annie was showing me the most remarkable discovery she made in her research. Shit, I just overshared." He glanced down at her, chagrined. "Please tell me that's okay."

With an attempt at a casual wave, she mentally struggled for normal and dismissed his concern. "No worries. As long as it stays between the three of us, it's all good."

His delighted smile challenged her to not regurgitate every last bit of information she'd ever uncovered.

Silly Annie.

She jerked her gaze from his and pretended an avid interest in her computer screen.

"So what is this *remarkable discovery?*" Dr. Montgomery asked.

Did she detect sarcasm? She shot him a sharp glance. Yep. But his teasing was genuine and not malicious.

"Annie? You want to tell him, or shall I?" When Quinn turned his admiring attention on her, she lost her ability to think. Acutely aware of her shortcomings in the active brain cell department, she shifted the laptop closer to him with a flail of her hand.

Saints alive! She was in serious danger of embarrassing herself if he kept innocently praising her.

The consummate actor, his animated retelling of her story drew a listener in—even her—and she was the original teller of the tale! Quinn was superior in his talent.

Of course, Dr. Montgomery snorted his skepticism.

"She can prove it." Quinn placed a hand on her shoulder, and it was as if a white-hot poker impaled her sternum. She gasped, and he inhaled sharply, suggesting she wasn't the only one who felt the highly charged current.

"What the hell?" He'd yet to stop touching her, and she was subjected to his shocked reaction.

"Remove your hand," she cried. "Please!"

Jumping to comply, he appeared horrified by her plea.

The maelstrom inside her calmed after he broke their connection.

"I'm sorry. I didn't think." He shook his head, raising his hand as if to touch her again but thinking better of it. "Does that always happen?"

"No. Usually, I'm better prepared if I know it's coming." But it had *never* happened before. Sure, if she hadn't preemptively erected a wall, she might get a small charge whenever another person touched her, but nothing like what she'd just experienced with Quinn. Their situation was unique.

Electric.

And thoroughly terrifying.

Her entire life had been filled with bizarre and uncomfortable moments from her ability, but this was different-level shit. Otherworldly, cosmic shit.

Quinn Jensen was not hers—would never be—and establishing any form of bond with him, either emotional or metaphysical, was stupid to the extreme. Foolishly gratified by his concern, she sighed her relief and focused on the laptop. Worry was much preferable to pity or horror—two of the standard responses she'd received in the past.

"Annie—"

Turning the computer to her confused-as-hell doctor, she interrupted Quinn before he had a chance to delve deeper into what was happening between them. This was new and confusing to him, and being of curious mind, he'd want answers. Answers she wasn't prepared to give. Mainly because she didn't know.

"This is what Quinn was talking about. I present exhibit A." Her smile was forced, and she probably resembled a demented villain in superhero movies. She doubted she was fooling anyone, but she was damned well going to give it the old college try. When all else failed, bluff your way through the awkwardness.

Quinn's inquisitive stare weighed on her and was as real as if he'd brushed fingers across her skin, but she continued to ignore his unspoken questions. It wasn't the time or place to discuss what had happened when he touched her. She needed time to process it on her own first. Perhaps talk to her sisters and see if they had ever encountered anything of this nature. If all else failed, Annie could google the fuck out of the topic.

With the tap of a couple of keys, she said, "And exhibit B."

"Is this some type of joke?" Dr. Montgomery crowded in closer, forcing Quinn to shift sideways to give him access to the screen.

A relieved sigh escaped her.

She hadn't been aware of holding her breath until he'd moved away, and his bewilderment fed her guilt. He didn't deserve to be treated like a plague carrier, but she was immobile and doing her damnedest to cope. They had a stare off, and as hard as she tried, she was unable to dig up the strength to break it. What was it about this man that hypnotized her to such a degree? His inquisitive eyes were tractor beams, holding her captive, drawing her in.

Where the hell was her willpower?

"Annie?" Dr. Montgomery brought her back to herself, and she blinked slowly as if waking from a deep sleep.

"Sorry. Here's my final bit of evidence." She pulled up more pictures along with birth and death records for all involved. "Quinn, you haven't seen these yet."

"Is it safe for me to come closer?"

His snark caused her to grin. Call her warped, but his pique made her ridiculously happy. For whatever reason, he wasn't completely immune to her.

And didn't misery love company?

"Of course. I don't bite," she replied primly. "Not in polite company."

Both men chuckled.

As Quinn shifted closer, their gazes once again locked. The devil danced in his eyes, and Annie knew, without a doubt, he intended to touch her again to set her off-kilter. An experiment on his part.

She steeled herself.

As his hand brushed hers, heat rushed through her, but it wasn't as fierce as their initial contact, which meant his wouldn't be, either. She smirked at his confusion.

He narrowed his eyes. "You're going to tell me how you do that," he said in a low voice.

"Perhaps," she murmured.

If Trace happened to overhear, he was sure to think Quinn meant the documents. Only Annie knew what he'd really meant— that she'd successfully outmaneuvered him. When he winked, her jaw nearly fell off its hinges. His grin tickled her funny bone, and she smiled in return. In an instant, they became fast friends.

It was all they could ever be, and she'd take it.

"So, it looks like we're snowed in for the time being. Anyone interested in killing time with a game of cards?"

"What?!" Quinn dashed to the window and swore resoundingly when he witnessed the truth of the doctor's statement.

"Miss the weather alert?" Annie asked sympathetically. Winter weather below the Mason-Dixon line was unpredictable. Many southern states didn't have the resources to deal with blizzard-like conditions. Their rural area of North Carolina included.

"I noticed the snow was picking up earlier, but I lost track of time." His frustrated sigh spoke volumes. "And Tink is back at the hotel. How the hell am I supposed to feed and walk her if I'm trapped here?"

Worry rode Annie hard. "There can't be that many hotels close by. Maybe Jamie is staying at the same one?"

"It's worth a shot. If he is, I can call the manager and see if maintenance can let him into my room."

Annie shot off a text to her brother and practically held her breath, waiting for a response. It only took a minute for James to reply, but it was the longest of her life. The idea of Tink suffering in any way was a knife to the heart. As much as she wanted Quinn to stay and distract her, she needed him to take care of Tink more.

Dr. Montgomery pulled a deck of cards from his lab-coat pocket and began shuffling as Quinn spoke to the hotel's night manager and made arrangements for James to access his room.

"Spades?" her doctor suggested.

"God, yes!" Annie gushed. "I'm dying of boredom in this place."

"I'm thoroughly offended," Quinn said, phone tucked against his ear.

"No, you're not," she retorted with a grin.

By the end of the first game, Annie and Trace were all on a first-name basis. Before their fourth hand, Quinn had joined them, and Annie registered an odd, repetitive gesture of Trace's that seemed vaguely familiar.

"Do you have a brother, Doc?"

Quinn discarded. "Why? You need a date to the prom?"

"Sarcasm is *not* appropriate," she scolded, secretly delighting in the teasing. "And maybe. But I'm serious. He reminds me of someone."

Trace won the round, and amid groans, admitted he did.

"It wouldn't be *Stephen* Montgomery, would it?"

He looked up sharply from shuffling. "You know Stephen?"

"Yes."

Unable to cope with Michael's disappearance and presumed death, her sister Sammy was admitted to Brookhaven Hospital and treated by Stephen, then his colleague, for eight consecutive months.

Annie should've guessed that once she brought up the subject of Stephen, the good doctor wasn't going to let it go.

"How do you know my brother?"

Uncomfortable, she shrugged. "We met in passing."

"Did he treat you?" Card play came to a halt.

"No."

"Really? Because you're being cagey."

"I wouldn't lie about a psychiatric disorder, Doc." At his disbelieving look, she said, "Okay, I guess if I was unstable, I might. But I'm not—lying *or* unstable. Besides, he's in Florida."

"But he's not. He moved here last month," Trace replied smoothly.

"Here, here? As in Sagefield?"

"Mm-hmm."

Moisture beaded on her upper lip. The speculation in his chocolaty eyes had her sweating bullets. Why the hell was she nervous? She had nothing to hide.

Without comment, he whipped out his phone and dialed a number. Once the voice came through the speaker, Annie groaned and flipped him off.

"Way to put me on the spot," she muttered.

Quinn chuckled, and a ghost of a grin played on Trace's mouth.

"Stephen! So, I have Annie Holt here—"

"*Annie?* Is she okay?"

"She's fine, for the most part. After all, *I'm* her doctor."

She could imagine the hard eye roll on the other end of the line. It likely matched hers.

"Hardy-har-har." Stephen didn't sound entertained in the least. "Get to the point, Trace. What's going on with Annie?"

"As I was saying, I have Annie here, and I'm wondering how you two know each other."

She met Quinn's laughing gaze and grimaced. At least, *he* didn't think she was lying.

"As in, is she my patient?" Stephen asked carefully.

"Yes."

"No, she isn't."

"Told you, Doc," Annie retorted with attitude.

"Annie? Hey. Are you all right? What's going on, babe?" Stephen asked.

Quinn's brows shot up. "Babe?" he mouthed as Trace assured Stephen she was fine.

"I had a building collapse on me, Stephen. It was all great fun," she said.

"*What?*"

"You really need to watch the news more," Trace added with a scoff. "A small commuter plane crashed into our local terminal. Our Annie is a hero. She saved a lot of lives. *Including* a famous movie star."

Quinn shot him a black look.

"Premonition?" Stephen asked.

"How the hell did you know that?" Quinn demanded.

"Who else is there?"

"That would be the famous movie star, Quinn Jensen," Trace supplied with an evil grin directed at him. It was Quinn's turn to flip him off, and Annie huffed out a laugh.

"I'll be damned." Stephen let out a small chuckle. "I need to hear the full story."

"I'll fill you in later," Trace said. "Gotta run."

"That was mean," she scolded.

"But fun."

CHAPTER 14

annie's room phone rang, waking her from a sound sleep.
"Hello?"

Heaving breathing greeted her.

All sleepiness disappeared as she listened for signs of a bad connection.

"Hello?"

The purposeful silence was sinister in the darkened room. The closed door and snow-outlined windows created a deep sense of isolation, bringing to life every fucking horror film Annie had ever watched in her lifetime.

Infusing firmness in her voice, she repeated, "Hello?"

A chuckle was her caller's response, and it wasn't meant to be playful. The menace was hair-raising, and a chill settled into her bones.

"Speak, ass," she snapped. "Your mouth sure won't."

If terrified, the Holt sisters didn't cower. They grabbed their lady balls in hand and set about kicking ass. Of course, being bedbound didn't make it quite as easy to do, but Annie had plenty of gumption, if not smarts. What kind of brainless wonder antagonized a potential threat while they were wounded and incapable of movement?

"Bitch!" the computer-altered voice hissed. "You'll get yours. *Soon.*"

"Bring it." Okay, she really didn't want anyone to bring it. Ever. But she refused to be terrorized.

After disconnecting, she considered ringing the nurses station or reception, but a glance at her cell showed it was after midnight. There would be no one in the main lobby, and calls usually weren't routed through the nurses station, that she knew of.

To provide a small measure of illumination, Annie flicked on the TV and turned the volume to its lowest setting, comforted by the muffled sound in the stillness. Her thoughts turned to Quinn, as they seemed to do a lot since meeting him. Had he made it back to the hotel, or had he crashed in Hailey's room for the night? Trace had said he could use an on-call room rather than brave the roads during the freak blizzard. Annie hoped he had. Driving in winter meant white-knuckling it for a Florida girl, and she didn't want him to get hurt.

She only wished one of them, either Quinn or Trace, were there to keep her company at that precise moment. The inability to shake the terrorizing phone call was making her edgy as hell.

Contacting Jamie was out of the question. Uncaring if he got frostbite, he'd trudge the distance from the hotel to get to her. The big-brother protection gene was strong in him.

She toyed with the idea of texting Quinn to see if he was still at the hospital and possibly awake, but immediately rejected it. Relying on him was a recipe for disaster, and she would only set herself up for severe disappointment.

A light tap on the door startled her, and she choked back a scream. If she wasn't hooked up to a catheter, she'd have wet herself.

So much for being a badass.

Quinn eased the door open and peeked around its edge, and Annie exhaled a sigh of relief.

"Hey," he said softly. "I was coming back from the vending machine and saw the light under your door. Can't sleep?"

"Oh, no. I could, but late-night assholes like to wake me up."

His expression arrested, and she registered how her comment must've sounded.

"I don't mean *you*, Quinn. I meant some rando dickweed thought it would be great fun to call and threaten me."

"What?" His face was a thundercloud, and outrage rolled off him in monstrous waves.

She flicked her hand dismissively, dropping it the second she realized she was trembling.

"Yeah, it pissed me off, too." She shrugged and glanced at the snow-coated window. "And let's be honest, all horror stories start on a dark and stormy night. Or in this case, a dark and blustery one."

"Jesus, Annie. Are you okay?"

Comforted when he crossed the short distance to the bed and clasped her shaking hand, she smiled. "Initially, a little upset, but I'm fine now."

"No idea who it could've been?"

"None. And I suspect, with the late-night telephone rerouting, it would be hard to trace if I reported it."

"I'm sorry. Would you feel better if I sat with you for a bit?"

She nodded her relief, uncomfortable with how needy she felt.

"Want to split my chocolate?" Quinn held up a candy bar.

"You have to be starving if you were raiding the vending machines. I don't want to take your only one."

Like a magician, he produced a second and set it on her tray table. "I'm a squirrel. I stock up."

Laughing, she ripped it open and bit into the chocolaty goodness. As the sweetness of the caramel hit her tongue, she moaned.

"I think I adore you, Quinn Jensen," she mumbled around a second mouthful. "You're a god among men."

"So I'm told." His grin woke the slumbering butterflies in her belly.

"Thank you for caring," she said softly.

"You're an easy person to care about, Annie Holt."

Embarrassed by his warm regard, she searched her mushy brains for another topic. "Where did you bed down for the night?"

Great one, Annie. Now he knows you're thinking about him in bed.

But luckily, he was preoccupied with unwrapping his candy.

"Trace had a cot brought into Hailey's room, but sleep is impossible."

A grin curled her mouth. "Let me guess. Someone has been in once an hour to check Hailey's vitals and make sure you're comfortable?"

He grimaced and nodded. "Fame is hell."

"Hmm. I wouldn't know, but I'll take your word for it."

Cocking his head slightly, he gave her a bemused look. "Why don't you treat me like I'm a megastar?"

She frowned. "Do you want me to?"

"No. I actually like that you don't."

Annie understood his desire to be normal. His career was just that—a job and nothing more.

"Thank you," he said huskily.

"Hailey must treat you as a regular human being, right? You wouldn't be marrying her otherwise."

His one-shoulder shrug spoke volumes, and Annie wondered what he saw in the other woman. Hailey Newberry presented like a real piece of work. A mean girl from high school who strutted through the halls and ruled with an iron fist. For Quinn's sake, Annie prayed the adult version of the woman had a softer side.

"I don't want to talk about my fiancée." His tone was final, and Annie let it drop.

"No worries. I didn't mean to pry. You must get that a lot."

"Yeah, I do. I suppose I'm a little touchy about my personal life. Everything is fodder for the gossip rags."

What a sad existence! Unlike him, she wouldn't survive in a fishbowl.

Quinn glanced over his shoulder at the TV. "What are we watching?"

"I call it crappy-old-movie TV."

He snorted. "And why is that?"

"Have you *watched* what's on this station?" With an exaggerated eye roll, she gestured with her chin. "I've seen one of your earlier films on there, too."

"Wow! That was below the belt. I thought we were friends."

"We are. That's why I'm going to let you hide in here with me. The hospital staff rarely comes by, and if they do, they don't linger. They're all afraid of the village witch."

Giving her a wry look, he picked up the deck of cards Trace had left for her. "Rummy?"

"Sure, but we play for real money. A dollar for every point. I have to supplement my income somehow."

"You believe you're that good?"

"My sister is psychic and a card shark. I've had to be. I can even deal from the bottom of the deck, thanks to my dad."

Quinn dropped the cards on the tray. "I'm not playing you."

With a light laugh, she held up three fingers. "Scout's honor, I won't cheat."

"I find that highly improbable, but I'll take your word for it—for now."

The next two hours flew by, and Annie hated to end their party for two, but her pain was ratcheting up and she needed to call the nurse.

"You should go," she said regretfully. "I need meds, and you don't want to be caught hanging out in here."

"Yeah, I should limit my day visits, for the same reason."

His expression said he didn't want to, and Annie felt a burst of happiness mixed with sadness. For the longest time, she'd felt invisible to everyone. Charlie. Her family. No one thought to look deeper. But Quinn did, and she'd miss him when he stopped coming by.

"Same time tomorrow night?"

Her brows shot up at his suggestion. "Midnight visits? You don't think that will cause more talk if we're discovered?"

His amused grin was a thing of beauty. The flash of white teeth, the way his incredibly green eyes sparkled, his all-encompassing energy, it all seduced her in a mere instant.

"It isn't like we're getting it on, Annie. Half your body is in a cast."

"True," she acknowledged.

But she wanted to.

"Okay," she said. "Same time tomorrow, and I want a hot chocolate. I don't care who you have to kill to get it."

"Consider it done."

QUINN SMILED DOWN AT ANNIE, AND THE INEXPLICABLE RIGHTNESS of the moment hit him squarely between the eyes. He genuinely liked her and thoroughly enjoyed the time spent in her company. Admiration for her had taken seed inside him, and with each new trial she faced with her calm and wry humor, he felt it grow exponentially.

"Thanks for not putting me on a pedestal and treating me like a megastar, Annie." His voice was gruff, and he had the sudden desire to clear the building gratitude from his throat.

"I like real-life Quinn better than movie-star Quinn. He probably has stinky feet and farts in bed."

"I *don't* have stinky feet."

"I noticed you didn't deny farting in bed."

He laughed, and it occurred to him that he'd laughed more with her in the last few days than he had in the last year with Hailey.

"Only on Taco Tuesdays," he quipped.

"Same."

Besides his sister, Bec, no other woman on the planet would admit such a thing to him, jokingly or not. "Remind me *not* to get you tacos. You'll stink out the hospital."

"Rude. Now, get going. I need those pain meds."

Her plight was made real by her comment. He wanted to say, 'fuck the gossip,' and that he was staying with her to help if she needed it, but the dark circles under her eyes curbed his tongue.

Clasping her hand between his, he felt a jolt similar to the one he'd experienced when they were discussing her sister's past life. Annie's eyes flared wide, and she jerked her hand away, wincing and grabbing for her ribs.

"Sorry. I'll have to remember to not do that without warning."

"It's fine."

With great care and brows raised in question, he reached for her hand again. "Does this zing happen with everyone... for you?"

"No. Yes. I don't know. Maybe to a small degree." She stared down at their joined hands.

What did she feel? What was she thinking? Was it this bizarre familiarity he experienced whenever he was with her?

"Do you think we were friends in a past life, Annie?"

His question was whisper quiet, and he'd shocked himself when he asked it. But she gamely answered.

"Maybe." Locking gazes, she smiled softly, and although her face retained the bruises and cuts from the accident, she was beautiful. Luminescent. "It would explain the comfortableness I feel with you."

"It would."

"You feel it, too?"

He nodded. "I know some people are easy to be around, but with you, I don't know. It's like..." He shrugged. Trying to put it into words was damned near impossible. But he'd felt a bizarre sense of homecoming when he entered her room tonight.

"Yeah. I get it."

He supposed she did. She could delve into his deepest emotions if she chose to. And didn't that make him jittery? The idea that she could read him was off-putting. Not because he had anything to hide, but because, at his core, he was a private person.

"Get some rest." Before he could stop himself, he lifted her hand

and kissed her knuckles. "I'll be back tomorrow night with your hot chocolate."

"Don't forget the whipped cream."

"I'd bring you an entire can, but people would get the wrong idea."

"I might get the wrong idea, too. Best to only top the hot chocolate."

He chuckled. "Goodnight, Annie."

"Goodnight, Quinn."

With a quick check of the corridor, he slipped out and back to Hailey's room, only to find two hospital staffers lurking inside. Frustrated, he gave them a tight nod and pulled out his phone to text Annie.

2 showed up this time. At this rate, I'll never get any sleep.

Find an on-call room like Trace suggested. And lock the damned door!

Hmm. Not a bad idea.

It came from me. It's a great idea.

He almost laughed, but because his visitors were watching him like hawks would a field mouse, he maintained a neutral expression as he typed.

Anyone ever tell you that you're humble?

Annie's immediate reply was a row of laughing emojis.

CHAPTER 15

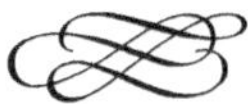

The next afternoon, Quinn popped in for another visit, bringing with him a mouthwatering lunch and her brother, James.

"Hey, lovely lady," Quinn said with a soft smile. "Roads were cleared early this morning, and I thought I'd bring you a present."

"The food or Jamie?" After a welcoming smile for them, she accepted the pasta bowl he held out with a happy sigh and watched as he opened another container with steak. "You're going to spoil me."

"That's what you're supposed to do for heroes." With a check of his watch, he said, "But your real present should be arriving any moment."

James moved away from the door, making room for the newcomers.

She gasped, and tears stung her eyes when she saw her youngest sister. Petite, dark, and full of sass, Sammy strolled in as if she owned the place, her husband on her heels with their newborn in tow.

"Sammy," Annie croaked. "How... The weather... I... I'm so glad you're here."

"Hey, sissy." Sammy approached the bed and pressed her cheek to Annie's. "Your actor chartered a private jet for us to come." In a whisper for Annie's hearing alone, she said, "He's a keeper."

"Not mine to keep," Annie murmured in return.

"Damned shame that." Sammy kissed her forehead and stepped back. "Michael, come bring our little pumpkin to meet her Aunt Annie."

Michael stepped forward, their daughter, Sophie, a tiny bundle in his arms.

"Hey, Annie." His voice was raspier than she remembered, and his face bore marks from his accident and subsequent surgeries, but he was still as handsome as ever.

"Michael." She felt herself getting choked up again. He'd meant the world to all of them for so many years, and they'd rejoiced when Sammy found him again. "I like the new look."

"Facial scars are all the rage these days."

"Hmm. Maybe that's what I should've strove for instead of broken body parts and a concussion."

"Yeah, I had those, too. I don't recommend." He grinned and followed Sammy's gesture, kissing her on the forehead. "But maybe you should stay out of trouble. Do we need to bubble wrap you?"

"It's a little late for that. Now, tuck my niece beside me so I can cuddle her."

Trace chose that moment to sail through the door.

"Annie. Quinn. I see you're breaking care-unit rules."

Quinn's brows lifted, but he didn't bother looking up from cutting Annie's food into bite-sized squares. "There are rules?"

"Apparently not for famous actors," Trace replied as he checked her vitals and pupil response. "How are the headaches, Annie?" he asked when she winced.

"Manageable."

"Want to tell me the truth?" Tucking his penlight into his lab coat, he entered whatever information he'd gathered into a tablet. "You're good at hiding it, but I'm an old hand at spotting someone who's suffering. And you, my dear Annie, are suffering."

"Fine. I've been getting migraines."

Quinn cast her a sharp look. "Why didn't you tell me? I'd have left you to rest."

"I've had plenty of rest, and your presence is actually soothing over the hospital buzz," she confessed.

"Nausea and sensitivity to light?" Trace asked.

She nodded as best she could.

"Okay. I'm going to order another head scan. It could be related to your neck injury, but I want to make sure we didn't miss anything the first time." With a cursory glance at everyone, he walked toward the door, stopping suddenly and pivoting back to stare at Sammy. "Annie's sister?"

"Yep. Sammy Anselin." She smiled. "Trace Montgomery, I presume." Sammy laughed and shook her head. "I'll be damned. You and Stephen look a lot alike. Same mannerisms."

"Well, we *are* brothers. Half, but brothers, nonetheless."

"He's told me a lot about you. All good, I swear." Giving him a wicked grin, she drew an X on the left side of her chest. "Cross my heart and hope to die."

"Uh-huh." Skepticism dripped from his voice, and he shook his head. "I understand everything now."

"I feel like I'm watching a soap opera," Quinn said as he set the plate on the bed tray and shifted it closer to Annie. "So many subplots I know nothing about."

"Mm. Stick around, and I'll break it down for you." She bit into her lunch and moaned when the taste of perfectly prepared steak touched her palate. "Dear Gawd! I think I love you."

He placed a napkin beside the tray. "You'd love anyone who brought you anything besides hospital food."

"It's true. I'm a food whore."

His deep laugh was more scrumptious than the five-star Alfredo pasta he'd brought her.

"Enjoy your family and your meal, Annie. I'll send Ty in later with Tink."

Knowing she had to ask, for the sake of politeness, she brushed her fingertips across his wrist to hold his attention. "How's Hailey? Any news?"

"Nothing yet." With a tight smile and an even tighter nod, he left.

"Annie," James's deep voice, filled with censure, drew her attention. "What the hell are you doing?"

It was too much to hope for that her brother had missed her longing whenever she looked at Quinn. He'd always told her she was an open book, but she decided to bluff her way through. "What do you mean?"

"I think you know. The movie star. You can't start something there. He has a girlfriend. A critically injured one, at that. Even if the other weren't a factor, you could never live in a fishbowl with your gift."

James hit on all the same things Annie had previously considered, and it was damned uncomfortable to be so transparent.

"Nothing is starting," she lied. Heat flooded her face, but she maintained eye contact.

His compressed lips and frown called her a freaking liar. And he was right.

"Don't be stupid, sprite."

"I resent that you think I am, Jamie." She went on the defensive. "That's the main problem with this family. Let's all protect Annie. She can't possibly handle the messy side of life all on her own."

"You're being ridiculous," he snapped.

"Am I?"

"You're too overprotective, Jamie." Sammy grabbed Annie's fork, took a bite of the pasta, and handed the utensil back to her. "But let's get back to the hot actor."

Annie flipped her sister off, then swirled pasta around the fork. "Let's not."

"Wouldn't it be fun to welcome a famous actor into the family?"

Both James and Annie sputtered.

Their sister had a knowing look in her eye to match her smirk. Yeah, she knew more than she intended to say, as evidenced by the way she pretended to zip her lip right before she straightened the covers over Annie's feet. All the Holt women had a tendency to rearrange things when they were in avoidance mode. Although the desire to plague her sister for answers was strong, Annie let it go. Sammy would talk in her own good time.

Her sister grinned and perched on the edge of the bed. "Spill your guts, sissy. How in the world do you have Mr. Movie Star at your beck and call? That man is sexy as fuck!"

Michael waved a hand in front of the two women. "Hello, husband right here."

"Shush! It's Quinn Jensen, for God's sake."

Sammy's best quality was her devilish humor during the most dire of situations.

"It helps when you save someone's life." Annie shoveled more pasta into her mouth, futilely hoping her sister would drop the line of questioning.

"Or draw him in with crazy amounts of sexual energy."

She choked. Eyes wide and tearing, she glared at Sammy. Although a mischievous expression was plastered on her face, there was an underlying worry to her sister's energy.

Was that what Annie was doing without being aware of her actions? How the hell had she been *emitting* sexual energy to begin with? It wasn't as if she possessed better-than-average looks, and currently, her body resembled a fucking mummy. It didn't scream sultry.

"He's engaged," Annie demurred, warm under the collar.

"Well, it isn't over until the fat lady sings."

"*Sammy!*"

"What? He's smokin', and you're single now that loser, Cheatin' Charlie, is out of your life."

"I thought you liked Charlie," James cut in.

Sammy waved him off with a flick of her wrist. "He was okay until he did Annie wrong. Then he became a total loser."

"Wait! He *cheated* on her?"

"Keep up, Jamie."

"He's a dead loser if I ever come across his sorry ass again," her brother muttered. Michael gave him a knuckle bump.

It was at times like these that Annie loved her family most. Their loyalty was second to none. They might all fight like mad, but no one else had better *think* about wronging one of theirs, or they'd be in a world of hurt.

The lunch service finally arrived, and Annie groaned at the indistinguishable blob on the tray. The congealed gravy triggered her gag reflex. "Please! Get it out of here."

"Jesus, what the hell is that?" James poked at what Annie assumed was Salisbury steak and sniffed the gravy on his finger. A shudder wracked his body. "Don't eat it, Annie. I think they're trying to poison you."

"A conspiracy!" Sammy cried. "This woman is a hero and deserves a decent meal!"

Michael laughed. "You're going to get us kicked out of here, Sammy Darlin'."

The rule-spouting nurse from Annie's first day strode into the room like a military commander. Privately, Annie had dubbed her Nurse Hatchet Face. The constant sour expression had frozen her features that way.

"Only two people can be in a care unit at once. And if you cannot behave, I'm going to have to ask you to leave." Her nasal, pinched tone was bad enough, but it was the snotty attitude that prodded Sammy over the line into battle territory.

Not one to back down from a fight, she threatened to call the Food and Drug Administration along with the CDC, certain there were guidelines as far as what could be served to the long-suffering patients of First Memorial Medical Center.

"Sammy, it's fine. I'm—"

"No, it's not fine. You are *not* eating this slop."

Annie closed her eyes and rubbed her temples in an attempt to ease the forming headache. Quinn had already provided a delicious meal, so Sammy's crusade was a moot point.

"Our dietitians work very hard to create nutritious meals to meet all our patients' needs," Nurse Hatchet Face self-righteously informed them with her hands on hips the size of a small destroyer.

"It doesn't help that she's a sanctimonious bitch, does it?" Jamie asked in an aside to Annie. "She's playing right into Sammy's hands."

"They always do."

CHAPTER 16

"Guys, can I have a moment alone with Sammy?"

Michael and Jamie shared a raised-brow look but exited the room and closed the door on the way out.

Sammy sat in the chair by her bed. Her pale-blue eyes were intent and penetrating. "What's going on, Annie?"

Searching for the words and rejecting everything she came up with, she finally settled on, "I want you to touch me and see if you get anything. I've a feeling something big is looming in the not-so-distant future, and I want to get a handle on it sooner rather than later."

"I can do that, but as you know, I can't promise I'll have a vision."

She nodded and opened herself up to Sammy.

Her sister picked up Annie's hand and closed her eyes. A frown tugged Sammy's dark brows downward, and she tilted her head, as if confused.

"Anything?"

"Yes and no. I—" Jerking, Sammy's lids popped open, but her ice-blue eyes were locked onto something Annie couldn't see. Goose bumps broke out along her arms, and she wanted to yank her hand out of her sister's grasp. This wasn't like asking if Marc Davis from her senior class would ask her to prom. Whatever images Sammy was receiving were sketchy at best, life-altering at worst.

After a massive energy swap, her sister dropped her hand and rubbed the back of her neck. Trying to ease her tension and get those pesky fine hairs at the base of her scalp to settle, Annie did the same.

"What is it, Sammy?"

"Nothing clear. More of a threatening vibe. It was like I was in her head and not yours."

"Her?"

"Yeah. Definitely female and definitely sporting a hard-on to hurt you." Her sister was more serious than Annie recalled seeing her in recent years. "You need to be careful, sissy. I don't like what I was feeling." After a watchful moment, she nodded slowly. "But you already know, don't you? You've picked up on the threat, or you wouldn't have asked me."

"Outside my room my first night, then again late last night. Someone called and said I was going to 'get mine.' I probably didn't do myself any favors when I told them to *bring it*."

"Annie!"

"I know. I know."

"Didn't you learn anything about antagonizing others by watching me?"

"Rabid Ronnie and Chester Molester Rob come to mind," Annie said with a wry smile.

"Exactly! And I wasn't a sitting duck."

"Way to scare me."

"You *should* be scared, sissy. The threat is real."

Weighing her words, Annie looked out over the snowy landscape beyond the window. "I might know who it is."

"Who?"

"Paige."

"Paig—wait, *what?* Paige as in Michael's psycho ex?"

"That would be her."

"Fuck, Annie! How? Why?"

"She's Quinn's assistant."

"You're screwing with me."

"Nope. No screwing here. He brought her in to offer her up as a personal liaison between us."

Sammy's icy gaze pinned Annie in place. "Did you tell them both to pound salt?"

"No. But I did tell him afterward about the connection and that it would be best if I didn't call her for anything." Trying to recall anyone else who might have an ax to grind, Annie shook her head. "It has to be her, right? I can't think of anyone else I've wronged."

"I don't know, but I'm damned well going to stick around until we find out."

"Sammy—"

"No. Jamie has a business to manage, and I'm not leaving you here without protection. If anyone can see what's coming, it's us."

"It's Christmas. You and Michael have found each other again, and you should be home, making Sophie's first Christmas special. Not hanging around a hospital."

"She's not going to remember this one, and besides, what if something happens to you, Annie? How do I explain to my kid that I let my favorite sister fend for herself with a psychotic hippot-watamus on the loose?"

An inappropriate laugh escaped. "Hippo*twa*tamus?"

"I've been saving that one for the perfect occasion."

Annie bit her lip, fighting back an explosion of giggles. "I love you, Sammy."

"I love you, too. Like I said, you're my favorite sibling."

All the years of feeling like the odd one out had her reacting strongly to Sammy's statement. She swallowed back the self-pity and resentment, allowing love to flow through. When tears broke free and trailed down her cheeks, her sister was quick to react with a gentle hug. As Sammy stroked Annie's hair away from her face, the sisters needed no words to communicate. All was felt through the warm, loving touch.

"I'm sorry. I don't know why I'm such a weepy mess lately."

"Are you kidding me? Annie, you were seriously hurt, you're in a place rife with pain and emotion, you've got one of the world's hottest movie stars paying attention to you, *and* you have a potential attacker on the loose. How can you *not* be a hot mess?"

"Thank you." Annie mopped up her face with the sorry excuse that served as tissues in that place and pasted on a bright smile. "I never asked, but how did you know Michael was the one when you first met?"

"From the second he touched me on the boardwalk in Flagler Beach, I was struck by a sense of rightness. And then again at the bonfire when he carried me away from the crowd." Sammy grimaced. "I thought I'd gotten it wrong when he rejected me and hooked up with Paige a few months later, but all's well that ends well, right?"

"And how did you know he was alive all that time? You were so insistent, even with the proof stacked against you."

A bittersweet smile graced her sister's face. "Honestly?" At Annie's nod, she continued. "I touched the coffin at the funeral, and I knew the body in there wasn't his. But I was such a hormonal, grief-stricken wreck that I didn't know how to relay it to anyone. I get that I must have looked insane, insisting I was right."

"I'm sorry we didn't believe you. I honestly don't know why we didn't."

"I do. Like you said, the proof was stacked against me. I mean, *someone's* body was returned to us. And it's all right that you didn't."

"I'm truly sorry," Annie whispered achingly. "I—more than anyone—should have listened and believed you."

"No, Annie. You couldn't have known. It's all right. I promise. I've found him, he's remembered our life together, and we're married with a baby. We have our whole lives ahead of us."

A micro expression flashed across Sammy's face, and Annie sensed her doubt. "What is it you aren't saying? What do you know, Sammy?"

"Can't hide a damned thing in this family, you know that?"

"Stop deflecting. Talk to me."

"I can't see our future, Annie. It worries me. Nothing past nine or ten months from now."

"Have you always been able to?"

"No. Actually, this seeing clearly into the future thing is fairly new."

"Then why are you worried?"

"Because of a second vision I had. I think Michael…" Her voice broke, and Annie clasped her hand.

"Don't! Don't you dare go there. You have both been through too much, and I refuse to believe you don't have a long future together with more beautiful babies for Mom to spoil." Annie sighed and released her sister. "Do you think perhaps it's residual fear?" When Sammy shook her head, Anne said, "Tell me about this vision."

"It wasn't completely clear. Michael and I were being held at gunpoint, and he stepped forward to protect me. The picture ends."

"Jesus!" Annie's stomach dropped to her butthole.

"I know."

"You said you feel it's not imminent?" *Please, God, let it not be imminent!*

"Right."

The smallest sense of relief flowed through her, and she squeezed Sammy's hand. "Then we have time to figure it out. Nothing is going to happen to him. I refuse to allow it."

With a soft smile, Sammy kissed Annie's cheek. "Your stubbornness alone would fend off an attack."

"So would yours, or did you forget I had to drag you into the shower to get the stink off you after Michael disappeared?"

"Shut it. I was allowed to grieve." Sammy stood and cocked her head. "Sounds like a commotion starting in the hall. That must be Jamie, and whenever he's causing trouble, the authorities aren't far behind. We all know the two never mesh."

"Pfft. Don't make me laugh. It hurts."

"Ah, yes. Those pesky ribs. Oh, and while we have a minute alone, you might want to work on that poker face when the hot actor is around."

"Don't go there."

"Just sayin'. You light up like that Christmas tree."

Annie's gaze was drawn to the angel topper, and a warm pulsing of peace infused her. "He had it brought in the other day."

Sammy's eyes flew wide, and for once, it seemed she was shocked into silence.

"How can I not fall for a guy who's so considerate?" Annie asked softly. "He's the polar opposite of Charlie."

"I'm sorry about Charlie. That fucker never deserved you."

"Your loyalty is duly noted." Annie had gone through her own grieving process when her marriage ended, but she wasn't upset the faithless bastard was now out of the picture. "Go keep Jamie from jail. And remember, I can't get out of bed to bail either of you out of the pokey."

Sammy, mischievous expression firmly stamped on her face, lowered her voice and said, "You could always get your hot actor to spring us." Laughter trailed her sister's petite form as she exited the room, leaving the door open in her wake.

Annie shook her head. The teasing was going to be relentless.

"Ah, speak of the dickweed!" Sammy cried out, a touch too cheerfully, catching her attention.

Charlie's once-handsome turning-to-jowly face was scarlet, and his thinning hair was standing on end from the abuse of his fingers.

He caught her eye beyond James's shoulder and tried to shove past him. It was a futile effort. Though Charlie outweighed her brother, Jamie was solid muscle.

"Annie! Annie, will you tell your gorilla of a brother to let me by? I just want to make sure you're okay, honey."

"Eat shit and die," she called back, turning the TV on and cranking up the volume. She didn't know why he was here, and she didn't particularly care. But she'd be damned if she'd deal with his fake fawning when she was unable to escape.

"You heard her, asswipe. Get lost," James ground out.

"You can't keep me from my wife, James!"

Annie had to strain to hear Sammy's retort.

"You lost that right the moment you tripped and your penis fell in your assistant's hidey-hole, Cheatin' Charlie. And we all know Annie signed the divorce papers. I suggest you get lost before we call hospital security."

Yay, Sammy!

Giving in to the urge, Annie turned her head in time to watch Charlie stomp away and her siblings high-five each other. Beyond them, a sickly thin, unkempt blonde stared at her, hatred in her eyes.

Charlie's girlfriend. Or rather fiancée. And dear ol' Daisy Jo must've overheard Charlie call Annie his wife. It had to sting. Well, so did finding out your husband was playing the slap and tickle with another woman.

Annie gave Daisy Jo a wave, then turned it into a one-finger salute.

Quinn rounded the corner in time to see her cattiness. "Nice. Who are you pissing off today?"

"Maybe someone is pissing *me* off. Ever think of that?" Annie snapped as she lowered the TV volume.

"Hmm. Fair." His grin took the edge off her irritation. "Did I just see your brother strong-arm a guy out of your room?"

"The ex. Apparently, he's concerned for my welfare. Insert eye roll here."

He placed a messenger bag on the counter under the television and faced her. "And the angry bleach blonde who resembles a two-bit crack whore?" he asked casually.

"The new love of his life." She frowned. "Although, calling her *new* after a two-year affair isn't quite right."

"Shit."

"Precisely."

"Want me to go flip her off, too? I will, if it makes you feel any better."

His offer cheered her immensely, even knowing he'd do no such thing. "Thanks for having my back."

"Sure. Not a problem." He dropped into the visitor's chair. "My brother, Ty, forgot to tell me he took Tink to the indoor dog park in

Stonebrooke. He'll be here in about an hour. Can your siblings run interference when he brings her here?"

Pure happiness filled Annie's heart to overflowing. "I'm sure they can, but you'd be the better distraction."

"Pfft."

Sammy poked her head through the door opening. "Hey, movie star."

"Hey, Sammy."

She grinned and directed her attention to Annie. "We're going to check into the hotel and get Sophie settled. Oh, and Jamie had some business requiring his attention. Will you be all right by yourself for a while?"

Quinn shot her a mock scowl. "What do I look like? Chopped liver?"

"Nope. You're premium-quality pâté, babe," Sammy replied with a laugh.

"I'll accept that."

With a snort and a shooing hand motion, Annie said, "Go. And give my niece a kiss for me."

All teasing dropped from Sammy's face. "We'll talk more tonight, okay?"

"I'll be fine, Sammy. Promise."

"What was that about?" Quinn asked after her sister shut the door.

"Nothing. She's worried." Hoping to change the subject, Annie shuffled the deck in front of her. "I thought you weren't coming around during the day. You know you don't have to hang out, right?"

"Yeah. Want to play?"

For the next forty minutes, they volleyed the win back and forth. She'd take one hand, and he'd take the next. But he grew progressively quieter, almost pensive, as the afternoon wore on.

"Quinn, you don't have to stay if you're bored."

He glanced up sharply from his hand. "I'm not. Just distracted.

And as for staying, I have some scripts to read over, but nothing urgent. Unless you want to be alone?"

"No!" Dear Lord, she sounded desperate! Annie smiled weakly. "I mean, I'd like the company, but I don't want you to feel you have to stay here if you have other things to… ah, do."

Smooth, Annie. Real smooth.

"I'm good," he replied. His smirk got on her last damned nerve, and she wanted to kick him. Probably would've too, if she didn't have pins in her leg.

After another ten minutes, Annie tossed the cards down. Apparently, distraction could be contagious, and she was finding it impossible to concentrate on the game. "How long has it been? Shouldn't your brother be here with Tink by now?"

With great patience, Quinn gathered and set aside the deck. He grabbed her hand in his and gave her a gentle shake—only enough to gain her undivided attention. "I'm sure Ty is on his way and everything is fine."

Since the accident, her worry for Tink had escalated. Her pup was in the company of strangers, and a new environment put a lot of stress on a dog. But Quinn's confidence in his brother made Annie feel marginally better. "Thank you."

He toyed with her fingers, as if reluctant to let her go, and she received a brief glimpse into his heart. Strangely, his strongest emotion was loneliness. How was it possible a man like him could be lonely?

"Why are you sad, Quinn?"

"I'm not." Without looking up, he released her and awkwardly shoved the cards into their case.

"Okay." With no real need to pry, she let it go. Picking up the newly loaded box, she tossed it to him. "You put them away too soon. New game. I want to learn poker."

"You've never played?"

"Only once, and I literally lost my shirt."

Her subject change lightened his mood. When he chuckled, her heart flipped in her chest and her stomach knotted. *Oh, to hear that sweet sound every day of her life!*

"You played strip poker? Well, sweetheart, it appears you have more hidden depths than I'd imagined," he drawled.

Just when she would've asked why he was imagining her depths at all, Trace entered her room.

"You living here now, Quinn?" he asked.

"It would seem so," Quinn answered dryly. "Pull up a chair. Things are just about to get serious."

"Yeah?"

"Yeah. Our Annie wants to learn how to play poker. I figured we can make a shark out of her in no time."

Trace glanced at his watch and shrugged. "I've got an hour to spare. Deal me in."

The warm smile Trace shot her didn't have nearly the same effect as Quinn's.

She was in deep shit.

CHAPTER 17

$\mathcal{A}$s Quinn dealt the cards and explained the basics of poker, it occurred to him that Annie was either a quick study or already knew the rules. He discarded, drew two, and as he tucked them into his existing hand, he happened to glance up in time to see a sparkle light her Caribbean-blue gaze. Frowning, he checked to see if Trace had noticed her devilish delight. The good doctor was too absorbed in his cards.

Quinn suppressed a laugh. It was a nice change. Since their meeting, Trace had been especially attentive to Annie. More than any doctor he'd ever seen.

"Doc, I think Annie's conning us."

Her outraged gasp cemented her guilt. "I would never!"

"Don't try to kid a kidder. Your acting ability is practically nonexistent."

"Not true. I can—" She closed her mouth, presumably because she'd realized his tactic. "Ha! Nice try. I'll take one."

After dealing her a single card, Quinn said, "Okay, place your bet."

"Twenty dollars."

"I thought we were betting clothes." A picture of her topless flashed through Quinn's mind, and he shook his head to clear it. Getting a chubby from imagining her naked was not the best idea in his current setting.

A blush tinted her cheeks.

Perversely pleased by her reaction, he grinned. She was adorable when she was flustered.

"I am not betting clothes, Quinn. I only have a hospital gown."

"I know," he replied silkily.

Trace snorted, but color surged up his neck. He cleared his throat and threw down his cards. "I'm out. Both are too rich for my blood."

"You're the damned Chief, Doc," Annie retorted. "You know you're rich."

Trace shrugged. "Not Quinn Jensen rich."

"What if we were playing strip poker? Would you stay in then?" she taunted.

The sudden flare of heat in Trace's eyes disturbed Quinn. What happened to that doctor-patient line? With a little more roughness than intended, he said, "Dr. Montgomery has too many articles of clothing. It puts you at a major disadvantage, Annie. Don't go there."

She bit her lip and looked down. If her dimple hadn't flashed, Quinn would have thought she'd taken the warning to heart.

"But I'll call you. What do you have?" he asked.

One by one, she laid down her cards.

Four aces.

He hadn't expected her to beat his full house.

He shook his head in disbelief. "Sonofabitch. You sneaky little—"

"Lose the shirt."

"What?" Surely he hadn't heard her correctly.

"I said, lose the shirt, Quinn. You lost."

"I am not taking my shirt off."

Trace laughed and stood to leave. "Looks like she schooled you, man. You two have fun. I've got charts to read."

Neither of them looked up when he exited the room. The

atmosphere had become charged as they hyper-focused on each other.

"Are you telling me you welsh on your bets?" Annie asked with faux innocence.

"Woman, you know damned well we were betting money."

"You were the one who brought up strip poker, my friend. I'm only calling in the marker."

"So if you lost, you'd be untying that gown right now?" Quinn challenged.

"Of course."

For a long moment, their gazes clashed, and hers was decidedly wicked. Finally, Quinn acquiesced to her ridiculous demand and pulled his shirt from his jeans. With a flash of learned caution, he grabbed her smartphone and moved it out of her reach.

"No pictures," he growled, then proceeded to undo the top button. He moved to the second, secretly delighting at her heightened color.

Her cell rang, bringing them both back to reality.

"Foiled again," she muttered as she held out her hand for the phone, looking entirely too disappointed. After a few minutes of conversation, she hung up and pulled a face. "You're off the hook for dinner tonight and, well, every night. My sister has decided to take charge of my care."

Quinn didn't want to examine his rush of dismay. Spending time with Annie allowed him to be himself in a world that only saw him as an actor, model, spokesperson, philanthropist, and/or sex symbol. With her, he was simply a man enjoying the company of a woman.

"You don't seem relieved," she said softly. "I'd have thought you'd be jumping with joy to have one less responsibility."

"Doing things for you isn't a chore, Annie," he replied gruffly. "You saved my life."

A flash of emotion crossed her face, and Quinn was ninety-nine percent positive it was hurt.

"Please stop," she whispered roughly. "Stop making me out to be a hero. I did what anyone would've done if they had my same ability."

"There you're wrong." He gathered the cards and shoved them into the cardboard case. "Many people would've saved their own ass first and not felt one goddamned moment's guilt about it." Leaning toward her, he tilted her chin and gave her a stern look. "Not you, though. Your first instinct was to warn others. That's heroic, lady, any way you look at it."

"Yeah, but look what I got for it. My body is broken, some parts I expect are beyond repair, a stranger is calling and threatening me for God only knows what reason, and Hailey is still in a coma."

She had a point, but it made her actions that much more courageous in Quinn's eyes. If he was being honest with himself, he'd have to admit Hailey wouldn't have done the same. She'd have been one of those who ran for safety and said, "fuck all" about anyone else. But he shouldn't be comparing the two women, because he'd have to admit to dissatisfaction with the one he'd selected to spend his life with.

Quinn stroked the petal-soft skin of her jaw with regret. "You sacrificed yourself. That's no small thing, Annie."

She opened her mouth as if to speak, but couldn't seem to find the words, so she pursed her lips in a grimace. He found it difficult to look away from that pouty, berry-red mouth. Thoughts of tasting her crowded his mind, and his heart rate kicked up. The desire to kiss her grew exponentially by the second. Never in his life had he been so tempted to disregard the promise he'd made. And what kind of fucking pervert did that make him, preying on an injured woman?

But then again, she was always welcoming whenever he stepped through her door, wasn't she? Always gazing at him with pleasure and happiness, and something more. Something he hesitated to define. No one ever truly looked at him that way. *No one.*

Closing his eyes, he sighed.

Perhaps her sister's phone call was divine intervention. Or maybe she'd already seen what the future held for Annie and him.

Star-crossed, never to be anything more than friends, despite the crazy chemistry building between them. And Annie felt it. He knew she did. No woman looked at a man like she did him if she didn't feel desire. One glance could singe.

When he lifted his lids, he caught sight of her longing gaze.

Yeah, she was in the same boat but without the towlines dragging her back to her old life, like him.

"It's no small thing," he repeated huskily, no longer talking about her sacrifice, instead referring to their attraction. She'd get it. She was an empath.

"You could still remove that shirt as one last reward," she whispered, licking her lips.

He groaned and shook his head. "Not a good idea, sweetheart. That road leads to trouble."

"All roads lead to trouble if you're not careful." Annie eased his hand away from her chin, and it shocked him to realize he'd not stopped touching her. "But we'll be forever friends," she stated in a firm, no-nonsense voice. "No more talk of repayment or thanking me, okay?"

Nodding, he swallowed hard. "But I'm going to point out that a hero would say the same thing, though."

Her light laughter was *his* reward.

Needing to break the seductive enchantment weaving around them, he checked his watch. Ty was overdue by about twenty minutes, and after the week he'd had, Quinn was beginning to get worried.

"I'm going to step outside and call my brother. See what his ETA is."

The door clicked open, indicating a visitor, and before he could turn, Annie focused her smile on the person behind him.

"I know he's your twin and all, but is he as smoking hot as you?" she asked in a thoughtful voice.

"No. Of the two of us, he's the troll."

Someone—probably Ty—smacked him on the back of his head.

"He's behind me, isn't he?"

Eyes dancing with laughter and a mock solemn expression, she nodded. "You've done it now."

Something small and wet swiped his ear. Either his brother had given him a wet willie, or Tink was making out with him. He shuddered and twisted to accept the pup.

"I don't allow that until the third date, Tink. You're being way too aggressive with your affections."

She slathered his chin with doggie kisses in response.

"Don't feel special, brother-mine. She swore her undying love to me not ten minutes ago when she saw where we were," Ty said dryly.

"Fickle bitch."

Annie laughed and grinned up at Ty. "Thank you. She's happier than I've seen her since this whole nightmare began."

"My pleasure. I'm Ty, by the way. Quinn likes to forget I exist." He held out a hand for her to shake.

"Annie. And my sisters and brother would probably like to forget I exist, too, if they could."

"I doubt someone as beautiful as you is forgettable in the least."

"So gallant," Quinn muttered, not caring at all for the flirty way Annie and Ty spoke to each other.

A slight frown drew Annie's brows together, and she gave him an inquiring glance. He shrugged away his annoyance and smiled. "Ty has all the moves. Watch out, or you'll fall head over heels. All the women do."

"Not true," Ty retorted with a snort. "Once they recognize you, I'm yesterday's news."

"Well, I don't know you personally, but I can tell you have a good heart." Annie lifted her chin and graced his brother with a blinding smile. Quinn's heart stuttered. "Any woman would be thrilled to date you."

With a roguish twinkle and a wolf-like grin, Ty brought the hand he had yet to release to his lips and kissed her knuckles. "What are you doing Friday night?"

"She'll still be here with me, I'm afraid," Trace said from behind them.

A quick glance showed the doctor resting a shoulder against the door and watching Ty with a hawk-like stare. Annie had more than one suitor vying for her affections, it seemed.

Quinn shoved away his instantaneous flare of jealousy. It wasn't his business. He couldn't let it be.

After carefully placing Tink next to Annie, he rose to his feet and stretched, gratified to see her eyes lock on his shirt where the fabric strained across the muscles of his chest. "Sorry, Trace. Friday night is poker night in the care unit. Annie's hosting the game, so you'll have me for company."

"Cockblocker," Ty murmured as he passed by to plop down in the visitor's chair.

Quinn smirked at a job well done.

"I don't remember saying I was hosting game night." Her arch look landed squarely on him.

"Really? Hmm." Scratching the back of his head, he pasted on a thoughtful expression. "I'm almost positive you did."

She was the first to end their stare-off with a laugh. "Fine. I said it. But I'm inviting Ty and Trace."

"Okay, but strip poker isn't going to be as fun."

"Speak for yourself. I fully intend to win."

Her happiness fled in an instant, and her eyes lost focus.

Tink whined.

"Annie?" Quinn dove for the bed when she didn't respond. Raising his voice, he called her name again and cradled her limp head.

"Back away, Quinn. Let me see what's going on." Trace had his penlight in hand and eyes on the spiking monitor.

Heart in his throat and dog cradled against his chest, Quinn backed away, giving Trace room to work. He shared a worried look with Ty.

"Does this happen often?" his brother asked.

"Not that I've seen, but I'm only here around mealtimes," he replied. "Christ! Is it a seizure or something? You mentioned the migraines, Trace. Could this be a result of something more serious?"

"This isn't that, and her pupils are responsive." The doctor eased her bed back, then listened for heart and lung sounds, checking the pulse at her wrist. Finally, he straightened and draped the stethoscope over his shoulders. Just as Trace reached for the call button, Annie blinked and gasped.

"Annie, can you hear me?" he asked.

Quinn was amazed by Trace's cool, collected tone. Personally, he was all kinds of freaked out.

Skin a sickly shade, she trembled and met his troubled gaze. "I'm okay. I'm… it was a… um, I had…" She placed her palm over her stomach and swallowed. "I'm okay."

"You're okay," Quinn agreed gently as he handed Tink to Ty and moved to clasp her hand. "You're okay." He said it again, as much to ease his own mind as hers.

"Annie, tell me what happened. What did you experience just now?" Trace asked, jamming his fists deep into the side pockets of his lab coat and watching her with rapt attention. "You gave us all a scare."

"Oh! Yeah… um, I'm sorry. That happens sometimes when I… when…" A blush crept up her neck, and she avoided eye contact.

Understanding dawned, and Quinn squeezed her fingers. "A vision."

Her gaze locked with his. "Yes."

"Want to talk about it?"

"No. Actually, I want to be alone, please." The distance in her tone was off-putting, and he released her. "Annie—"

"Please." The word held a hint of desperation.

"Okay." But leaving was the last thing he wanted to do, and his feet refused to move.

Ty stood and tucked a fretful Tink next to Annie. "Let's get some coffee, Quinn," he suggested, placing a hand on his shoulder.

Incapable of leaving her in her current state, he shrugged Ty off. "Annie—"

"I need to give her a more thorough exam anyway," Trace suggested. "Why don't you close the door on your way out and give Annie a few minutes to compose herself?"

"Yeah, okay." With a resigned sigh, Quinn followed his brother into the hall.

"Christ, that was fucking freaky." Ty shook his head. "I get the feeling you might know what the hell happened just now. Care to share?"

Curious faces were turned their way, and Quinn scowled at the invasiveness of it all. "Not here. Let's get coffee."

CHAPTER 18

"You had us all worried. Do you always check out like that when you have one of your... um, visions?" Trace didn't know what else to call them. Never in his life had he seen anything like what Annie professed she could do. But a long talk with his brother, Stephen, had assured him she was the real deal. Her sister Samantha was, too.

Stephen had told him all about Samantha's prediction and how she saved his colleague's life.

"This one was particularly bad," Annie confessed, burying her fingers in Tink's coat and giving her a rub. "And no, I don't always check out when I get a premonition."

"When you say particularly bad, what do you mean?" Trace leaned against the ledge of the windowsill and gripped the edges as he watched her. He didn't care for how ghostly pale she'd become.

"Like I told you the other day, I don't usually get visions at all. Mainly, I'm swamped with people's emotions. But this one..." She shook her head and, frowning, met his concerned gaze. "I think someone wants to kill me, Trace," she said in a strained voice.

His stomach lodged in his throat, and he stared at her in something akin to shock. "That seems, for lack of a better word, extreme."

She snorted, and some of the color returned to her deathly white cheeks. "You can say that again. I'm a hermit who traces family trees for a living. Why the fuc—er, why anyone would want to target me is a mystery."

"One we need to solve quickly." He frowned as he replayed what she'd said and considered security at his hospital. If he had a clearer idea of what she'd seen, he could pull in a few extra guards. "I'm assuming it will be soon. Is there a timeline we're working with here?"

"I'm not sure. I…" Her brows drew together, and she turned contemplative. "I don't think so. Or rather not one I can tell. The attack was in a parking lot."

"Attack?" Legs feeling decidedly rubbery, Trace moved to the visitor's chair and sat down. "You'd better tell me everything you remember. Maybe we can figure out what's going on and get the police involved."

"Pfft. Helping me would be the last thing Frick and Frack would do. They think I'm a lunatic."

"Frick and—oh! Fields and Reynolds. Good one." Placing his hand over hers, he gave it a light squeeze. "Stop stalling and tell me everything."

"It wasn't much. It was dark outside, and I was walking through a parking lot, or rather limping with a cane. There were footsteps behind me, quickening with every one I took." She shivered and brushed her hair back from her face. "I remember feeling unbearably cold, and I was desperate to find someone else close by, in case I needed to call out. But there was no one."

Again, Annie shivered, and her haunted eyes seemed huge in her heart-shaped face. Her lips appeared bigger and a deeper red next to the creamy whiteness of her skin, and Trace's heart stuttered in his chest. For the hundredth time since she'd first smiled at him, he reminded himself that she was his patient. "Professionalism in all things" was his motto.

And he still wasn't over losing his wife, Jessica. Although he'd promised her he'd do his damnedest not to mourn forever. But it had been a vow based on ignorance. He was so wrapped up in his sudden wave of misery, he almost missed her next words.

"An arm wrapped around my throat, and I felt a hard jab in the middle of my back. Like a hard punch, but the pain wouldn't ease. Then I heard a throaty engine sound as a vehicle sped away," she said, swallowing hard.

Rejecting the intense need to comfort her and that she'd just described being stabbed in the back, Trace focused on the facts. "Okay, let's set aside the horror of the attack and think about what else you might have seen or heard."

"Like what?"

"Start with the footsteps. Were they muffled like someone wearing runners, or a leather sole? Was there an echo of heels?"

"Muffled. And uneven," she said with a slow nod. "Almost shuffling."

"Good. That's a start. What can you tell me about the arm around your neck? Thick, thin, muscular, covered, or exposed skin?"

"Covered by a sleeve. Rough, though. Muscular underneath it, I think. Maybe a little fleshy and thick. The sleeve rode up, and I tried to grip his wrist but couldn't get my fingers all the way around it."

Nodding, satisfied she was recalling in-depth details, he probed further. "You said 'his,' so I'm assuming that's your first instinct?"

"Yes. The person was definitely taller than me. I felt the press of a protruding belly against my back."

"Okay, so not someone who spends their time in a gym, or not a lot of it anyway," Trace said with a tight smile.

"You're good at this." Her haunted look eased, but she still appeared troubled.

"Doctors are trained to consider all the facts before diagnosing a patient and determining a course of treatment." He shrugged. "It's not that much of a stretch to believe I'd be a decent detective if my current career choice didn't pan out."

Annie smiled as she scratched behind Tink's ear. "You're an excellent doctor and surgeon. I think your job is secure."

Because he liked her admiration too much, he looked away, making a show of removing a small notebook and pen from his pocket. Clicking the cam, he poised the tip over the paper. "Can you describe the parking lot? And what about the weather? You said you were cold. Was it snowing? Rainy?"

Frowning slightly, she closed her eyes, and Trace patiently waited for her to recall what she could.

"I can't see what I'm wearing, but the ground was damp. Like after a light rain or maybe early morning dew. The lot was almost empty, with maybe a handful of cars, but I could see the light from the safety lamp. Then, when I fell down, I noticed the glow from the building."

"Think hard, Annie. What did the front of the building look like?"

"Modern. Columns, with an overhang and sliding doors. I could see a lobby that was mostly gray with some pink accents. No one was at the reception desk, though."

Heart picking up speed, Trace shoved aside the sneaking suspicion he'd developed and asked for clarity. "How wide was the overhang? How many sliding doors? Just the one? Multiple?"

Opening her eyes, she locked gazes with him. "Wide. I can't say in feet, but there were two sliding doors, about the same width apart as one of the actual sliders." She gestured with her hands, then tilted her head. "You think you know where it is, don't you?"

"I do. Answer me this, were the columns round or square?"

"Square, with stone accents around the bottom and a bench under the overhang. Where was I?"

"Here, Annie. It's the front of this hospital."

"Ohmygod!" Her breathing became erratic, and she pressed a hand to her throat. "I think I'm going to throw up."

"Hang on." He jumped up, grabbed an emesis basin from the bedside table, and shoved it under her chin, just in case. "Breathe in for the count of four, then exhale for the same beats. If you vomit, your ribs will hate you."

A measure of color returned to her cheeks, and she gave him a dry look. "They already do. They haven't forgiven me for using my body as a human shield."

"Body parts can be obnoxiously unforgiving that way." She attempted to hand the basin back, but he waved her off. "Keep it in case the urge to vomit strikes again. Are you ready to call the police now?"

"And tell them what? I'm attacked in the parking lot at some future date by an unknown assailant?"

"When you say it like that, it does seem ridiculous," he agreed. The alarm on his watch beeped, reminding him of an upcoming staff meeting. "I've got to go. Are you going to be all right? Should I send Quinn back in to sit with you?"

"No. I'm good. And he doesn't need to be involved in my drama."

Her expression was wistful, as if she wanted him to want to be involved.

"You like him a lot, don't you?"

"He's nice. But—"

"Save the lie, lady. I know a fib forming when I hear one. But don't forget he's engaged, okay?" Trace issued the warning mainly because he didn't want to see her heartbroken. His own growing affection for her was a moot point. He wasn't ready for another relationship, and romantic involvement with a patient was taboo. His brother, Stephen, had fallen for Sammy, and Trace could now understand why. If she was even half as enchanting as her sister, remaining impartial would've been next to impossible. "I mean it, Annie. Be careful with your heart."

"Duly noted," she replied with a wry smile. "Don't worry about me, Trace. I know how to build walls."

He arched a brow. "But will you?"

"Tomorrow's Christmas."

About to bite into his burger, Quinn paused and stared at Ty. Carefully setting it down, he grimaced. "I forgot." At his brother's disbelieving look, he chuckled. "Yes, I know there are decorations everywhere, but my mind's been on other things."

"Like Annie, the super cute hero?"

If Quinn didn't know Ty, he'd have missed the underlying snideness in his tone. "You don't like her? You seemed friendly enough before."

"I don't know her, man. Not as well as you seem to."

"Out with it, Ty. What am I doing wrong here?"

"Your girlfriend—

"Fiancée."

"Fiancée," Ty corrected with a twitch of his jaw muscle. "Hailey is in a coma, yet you're spending all your time with Annie. What gives?"

"It's not *all* my time. I've spent countless hours every day by Hailey's side. And the longer I stay in that room, the more claustrophobic I become." Quinn sat back and sighed. "The fear sets in, and I'm terrified she won't wake up. What happens to our baby in that case? Can she carry it long term while in a coma? Is it good for a baby when the mother isn't moving? When I sit there, I can't breathe."

A sickly expression flashed across Ty's face, but he quickly recovered. "You can't worry about that right now, Kwee. She'll wake. She has to." His voice was raw, and his old nickname for Quinn spoke to much deeper emotion.

"Ty. What aren't you telling me? Have you heard something?"

"What? *No.* No, I… It's just hard seeing someone who was once so vital lie there without any life to her."

"So you get it."

"Maybe to a degree, but if she were mine, I wouldn't leave her side."

Guilt churned in Quinn's chest. His brother was correct. There he'd been, playing cards and enjoying himself with Annie, when he should never have left Hailey.

"You're right," he replied softly. "I've no excuse. It started with a thank you, but now, whenever I'm with Annie, some of the fear recedes. I'm in the moment and not swamped with self-doubts." He shrugged and stared down at the burger fat congealing on his plate. "And she treats me like *me*, Ty. Not a famous person."

"Does she? I'm pretty sure I saw stars in her eyes whenever she looked at you. Be careful you don't end up with another rabid fan who doesn't understand boundaries."

More than once, a follower of Quinn's had crossed the line. Their fantasy took over their real-world view, and he'd been the sole star in their universe. Police reports and restraining orders were nothing new to him.

"Annie isn't like that. There isn't a day that goes by when she doesn't ask about Hailey's welfare. Christ, she *saved* her. She's not the crazed fan you believe her to be, and she knows it's just an offer of friendship."

"If you say so."

"I do," he said flatly, wanting to end that particular discussion. "We should be together to FaceTime Mom and Dad tomorrow. It would mean a lot to her."

"Sure. Just let me know what works for your schedule."

They finished, and Quinn headed back to Annie, mainly to get Tink and return to the hotel for the night. *Or so he told himself.*

Raised voices from inside the room reached him, and he bolted toward the sound.

"What did I tell you the other day about that dog? She cannot be in here. This is a hospital," the night-shift nurse snapped.

Annie bristled, prepared for battle. "Really, Hatchet? Because I thought it was a—"

Quinn cut off her scathing comeback with a look and turned up the wattage of his charm to smooth things over. "What she really means to say is that her dog is a service dog. Legally, she's allowed to have her here."

The sour-faced biddy wasn't in the mood to be charmed. "I'll need to see the paperwork to confirm it."

"It was lost in the terminal crash," Annie lied with a straight face, impressing Quinn that she even could. Up to that moment, he'd have said every thought she ever had was reflected on her face.

"Until I receive documentation, the dog goes."

"There's enough of us. We can bury her out behind the hospital. No one would find the body," Sammy said drolly, and perhaps only *half* jokingly, from just behind Quinn. He jerked in surprise. In his rush to help, he never realized she'd entered the room accompanied by James.

But Sammy's comment did the trick, and the nurse beat a hasty retreat.

With a sad little sigh and a rub of her nose against Tink's, Annie looked at her siblings. "In all seriousness, I'll need either you or Jamie to take Tink and watch her until I'm released."

James stepped up to scratch behind Tink's ear. "I'd love to, but I'm behind on a number of projects, Annie. Once Christmas is over, I'll be working eighteen-hour days, and she's too tiny to take on a job site."

"Sammy?" The small break in her voice squeezed Quinn's chest.

"Sure. Tink will get along great with our Sassy."

"It won't be too much with Sophie and puppy training?" she asked.

Tears shimmered in Annie's eyes, and Quinn's heart spasmed. Who knew the sight of her tears could take him out at the knees?

"Does that mean I've lost dog-sitting privileges?" he asked teasingly. "I didn't think my care of her was so bad."

"I figured you were just being nice."

With a wry smile, he picked up Tink to snuggle her close. "No. I absolutely meant it. She's a sweetie and easy to love."

"You only want me for my dog," Annie said with a pout.

"It's settled, then. Since I live here and it would save you a trip to Florida to retrieve her, Tink stays with me."

"Quinn, I can't impose—"

"I want to. Really. She's good company when I get back to the hotel at night."

Something undefined passed between the three siblings, but finally, Annie nodded. "Don't fall in love with her," she warned. "I'm taking her back just as soon as I'm out of this place."

"I'm making no promises."

CHAPTER 19

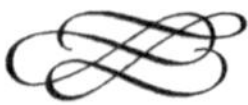

The next day brought Stephen Montgomery bearing gifts.

"Hey, beautiful. Merry Christmas."

"Hey, charmer," Annie countered with a wide smile. "Merry Christmas. Those for me?"

"For you." After placing the presents on the visitor's chair, Stephen leaned over her bed, dropped a light kiss on her cheek, and pulled back a few inches to stare deeply into her eyes. "How are you, Annie?"

Stephen had become like family to the Holts over the last few years, and Annie, like her parents and siblings, adored him.

The immediate sense of a third person's presence was accompanied by a tidal wave of outrage. The shock of the emotion caused her to jerk back and accidentally hit Stephen in the chest as an involuntary cry of discomfort was wrung out of her. She swore loud and long.

"What the hell did you do to her? For Christ's sake, can't you see she's not in any condition to be pawed at?" Quinn was at her side in an instant, smelling divine—all fresh-washed male mixed with baked goods. If she hadn't been so disoriented by his quicksilver temper, she'd have stuck her nose against his perfectly sculpted chest and inhaled deeply, broken ribs be damned.

The jaw-dropping surprise on Stephen's face would've been comical had Quinn's irritation not assailed her to the degree it did.

"Quinn, he wasn't pawing at me." She laid a soothing hand on his arm. "This is Trace's brother and my dear friend, Dr. Stephen Montgomery."

After introductions were made and Quinn's apology uttered, Annie eyed the to-go cup he carried, then the bakery bag he'd dropped on the bed when he initially charged across the room.

"Please tell me that's a croissant or some other wonderful confection and that it's just for me."

"Would a cronut work?"

"Bless you! I don't know where you found a bakery open on Christmas morning, but you're a god among men."

"So I've been told," he said with a droll expression. "By you."

"Whatever, just hand it over, and no one gets hurt. I'm starving." An appreciative sniff of the pastry nearly caused an orgasm. "Oh! I'm so glad I saved your life. Whatever this is will be worth every second of agony I suffered," she said a tad dramatically, with the back of her wrist to her forehead.

In reality, she was totally serious. Quinn could ply her with baked goods all day long, and she'd happily eat them while staring into his spellbinding eyes.

"Leave the acting for the professionals, kid." Stephen pulled the edge of the bag closer to him and peeked inside.

"Touch my cronut, and I'll gnaw your damned arm off," she growled, snatching her breakfast back.

Laughter burst from him. "I should've remembered that nothing comes between a Holt and their food."

"Looks like Annie just reminded you," Quinn said dryly. "I've only known her about a week, and I've already learned that lesson."

"Have either of you had the slop they serve here? No? Then zip it." Certain she looked rabid, she crammed a thick chunk of cronut into her mouth and blasted them with an evil eye for making fun of her.

"If she's anything like her sister, Sammy, then she'll demand hot chocolate and donuts twenty-four-seven."

She licked the blueberry goo from her fingers and sent him an arch look. "I'm sure no one asked you, Stephen."

Quinn fought back a grin.

Annie narrowed her eyes.

"For the record, Quinn, you're the only one on my good side this morning. Don't blow it."

With a long-suffering look, Stephen lifted a present and shook it. "Apparently, you've already forgotten my gifts."

"Okay, you're officially back on the good-side list, too."

"Whew."

She ignored Stephen as he pretended to wipe sweat off his brow and turned her attention to Quinn.

"How's my baby?"

"Hanging with my brother, Ty, at the hotel. He's promised to take her to the dog park at least twice today, despite the snow, and has sworn on his life to keep her safe. We swung by the pet store on the way home last night. Tink talked me into three different beds of varying thickness, two chewies, a rubber ball, and five packages of organic treats."

"That little beggar!" She bit her lip to stem off her laughter. "I should have warned you that she'll take you for all you're worth."

"Yes, well, you should bottle her charm. You'd be set for life."

Funny, she'd thought the same about him.

"Does it look like the pet store threw up in your hotel room?" Stephen asked.

"Abso-fucking-lutely."

Annie took a sip of her hot chocolate to hide her grin.

A bubbling energy alerted her to her sister's presence. Since there was no notice beforehand, she could do nothing to warn Stephen of Sammy's imminent arrival.

"Stephen? Ohmygod! Stephen!" Her sister flew across the room and nearly tackled him in her enthusiasm. The bittersweet ache he exuded was almost more than Annie could handle. With a deep sigh, she set her drink down and mentally constructed her barrier against all the raw emotions flying about.

"When did you get here?" Sammy asked as she pulled away.

"I've been in Sagefield for about a month. At your urging, if you remember." He glanced at Michael holding Sophie, and pain flashed in his eyes before he carefully banked it. "I've been meaning to get by to see Annie since Trace told me she was here. I didn't know you'd come up."

"Quinn flew us up to surprise Annie. But Michael and I were contemplating the drive before he called us." Sammy hugged Stephen again. "I'm so glad you're here, though. You can help keep Annie company. It'll perk her up."

"She's not perky enough for you, darlin'?" Michael asked with a laugh.

"Stephen knows what I mean."

Stephen's reluctant gaze found Michael's, and the tension was as thick as fog, created solely by the two men with an oblivious Sammy as the bone of contention between them.

"Asshole."

"Dickhead."

Their greeting sounded somewhat cordial.

"What am I missing?" Quinn asked in an aside, snagging a sip of Annie's hot chocolate.

"A three-way."

The liquid shot out of his mouth, and he began coughing like he had consumption.

"Christ, sissy! You almost killed the movie star! Who is going to bring you food and presents if he chokes to death?" Sammy rushed to pound on Quinn's back. "She *meant* a love triangle. But it's all resolved now. Michael and I are happily married, and Stephen will encounter the love of his life very soon."

"I will?" Stephen's look was highly amused, laced with affection.

"I'd forgotten that was supposed to happen after you basically ordered me to move here."

"Sarcasm isn't necessary, Stephen. Behave," Sammy scolded. "And I'm not wrong about anything but the timing."

With a wicked grin and a wink for Annie, Stephen said, "Maybe I've already encountered her."

"Keep it in your pants, lover boy." Michael crossed his arms and gave him a dark look. "She's not for you."

"You're all nuts," Quinn choked out, shocked disbelief on his face.

"That's why we have Stephen. He's the resident shrink." Annie gestured to Quinn. "Are you going to offer him the family discount, Stephen?"

She never heard his response as a wave of dizziness assailed her.

Trace's commanding voice called her back from the darkness as he waved a light in front of her pupils. The damned brightness blinded her with every pass and only added to the stabbing headache she was experiencing. With a loud groan, she pushed his hand away.

"When did you get here?"

"Annie, I need you to tell me what you were experiencing before you blacked out this time." His expression was grim.

Six concerned faces peered down at her, and she closed her eyes to shut everyone out.

God, her head hurt.

"What the hell does he mean *this time?*" Sammy stood over her with hands on hips, suspicion pinching her face.

Irritable, Annie waved her off. "Why am I facing the Spanish Inquisition? Can't a person fall asleep?"

"If you fell asleep, I'll eat the good doctor's stethoscope," Michael muttered from beside Sammy.

"So no one is going to believe it was a sugar coma?"

Brows near his hairline, Quinn shook his head.

Annie raised hopeful eyes to Trace.

He, too, shook his head, and she groaned.

"How long was I out?"

"Fifteen minutes," Stephen supplied helpfully.

It hadn't seemed like she was gone at all, but their worried faces were proof positive she'd fainted again.

"Right." Trace strode to the door and closed it with a definitive click. "Annie, this is the second time you've blacked out. I need to know what's causing that to happen along with those residual migraines you're experiencing after the fact. The CT scan didn't show anything yesterday, but I'd like to get an MRI with contrast."

Closing her eyes, she groaned.

"Don't try to tell me you don't have a headache. Your pain is as obvious as the nose on your face." He typed something on the tablet and, without looking up, asked, "Did you have another vision of the attack?"

"What attack?" Quinn demanded, indignation radiating from every pore on his body. "You were attacked? When? Why didn't you say anything?"

Annie glared at Trace, but he simply shrugged. "Obviously, you should tell them. But it's up to you."

"Yeah, I think you took that choice out of my hands, Doc. Thanks a lot."

Sammy perched on the bed and clasped her hand. "Start talking, sissy."

Quinn swore under his breath as Annie described the vision that came to her the previous night after she fainted. She'd been unusually pale and drawn when he returned for Tink, but she'd never said a word.

And it didn't sit well with him.

True, he had no claim other than friendship, but he thought they'd developed a special bond of sorts. He hated that she'd withheld what might be information vital to her safety. A testament to how poorly she must be feeling was the fact she hadn't tuned in to Quinn's unease.

Putting down the tablet, Trace met her irritated glare with a no-nonsense look. "I was going to move you from the care unit to a private room in the morning, but I'd like to run more tests first. "

"Do I have to? I'm sure it's nothing."

"I can almost guarantee no one here has witnessed an ability like yours, Annie. Myself included. I'm sure none of my colleagues would know what to do about your fainting spells if asked, other than order more scans and bloodwork, which is exactly what I intend." He sighed heavily. "Whether you've had them in the past or not—and here I'm going with not—I'm concerned about the blackouts and headaches. I think you should be, too, regardless of whether or not they're attached to your visions."

Annie frowned so deeply and darkly, her brows met in the middle of her forehead.

But Quinn understood the ramifications of what Trace was hinting at. The head trauma she'd received at the airport could be causing complications they had yet to discover.

His gut clenched.

Whatever mystical tricks she possessed might be putting her life in danger, and although it wasn't his place to say anything, he couldn't remain quiet if something serious was wrong.

"Annie."

She turned her head and met his concerned gaze.

"Please get the MRI."

"I don't have medical insurance, and it's another bill in a long line of many, Quinn. I'm sure it's pointless. It's probably just the pain medicine affecting me. My family can attest that I'm a lightweight."

"The airport's insurance should cover the damned tests, but whatever they don't pay for, I'll cover. Just get it done."

"I don't want you to," she said, her voice heavy with fatigue. "You're not my personal bank account. Enough with the savior-complex shit already. I can make my own healthcare decisions."

"Apparently, you can't," he snapped. Yes, his worry was clouding his judgment, but he had a very real fear that she'd caused herself unimaginable damage when she saved Hailey. And perhaps he was a little butthurt that she'd called him a bank account with a savior complex. "You refuse to do anything that might help yourself."

"Last I checked, you—"

Rising to her feet, Sammy held up her hands and laughed. "Okay, back to your corners. We're going to hold off on round two. I'm ringing the bell and tapping you out, Annie." To Trace, she said, "Schedule the MRI. She'll have it done even if I have to push her happy ass all the way to the machine."

"Sammy!"

"I mean it, Annie. Even for one of us, this isn't normal, and you know it."

Michael wrapped an arm across his wife's waist, and with a commiserating smile for Annie, he said, "You might as well give in. We both know your sister is relentless."

"Fine, but I don't know what anyone expects to find," Annie grumbled.

Stephen, who had been quiet the entire discussion, stepped forward and squeezed Annie's hand, placing a kiss on her forehead. Quinn had to fight the urge to rip his arm off, and Trace appeared to not like it all that much himself as he frowned at his brother.

"When you're ready, let's talk more about what you saw, okay?" Stephen suggested gently. "Perhaps we can discover clues you may have missed."

It occurred to Quinn that Stephen might not have been joking earlier when he said he'd already encountered the love of his life. And the thought tied his gut into a thousand knots.

"We already did." Trace elbowed Stephen out of the way to check Annie's vitals a second time. "We know it wasn't snowing and that it was late at night in our hospital parking lot. If she was walking on her own, it means it's still a few months away, when the casts come off her hips and leg."

"Great deduction, Sherlock," his brother murmured. Only Quinn was close enough to hear him say, "And no one is moving in on your patient. You can stop the pissing contest, Trace."

The doctor laughed and slapped Stephen's back in passing. "We're expected at Angelica's at noon."

"I've got to run, too. Ty and I are supposed to video chat with our parents soon," Quinn said to Annie. Part of him was still irritated she hadn't told him about her premonition, but he didn't want to get into an argument with so many people around. According to Trace, she was walking in the vision, which meant it was weeks from now. He felt comfortable leaving her alone.

She frowned slightly, as if she wanted to relay something to him but didn't know how. And when she touched his arm, an electrical current coursed between them. Breath nothing more than shallow gasps, her grip tightened, whitening her knuckles. The transference allowed him to catch a glimpse of what she must feel whenever she tapped into another. A throbbing headache, a dull ache around the ribs, and a sharper, more intense pain in his hips told him exactly where she was hurting.

As gently as he could, he peeled her fingers from his wrist and set her hand on the blanket, beside her.

"That was freaky. And I'm going to suggest Trace give you something more to ease your discomfort."

"Sorry." Bemused, she stared up at him with wary eyes. His weirded-out expression probably mirrored hers.

"It's okay. But maybe don't spontaneously grab my arm in the future," he said with a forced chuckle.

"Of course."

Her expression had dulled, and Quinn knew without a doubt he'd bruised her feelings.

"Annie—"

But she'd turned her head away and gestured to the packages Sammy had set by the door. "I'm tired, gang. Can I take a rain check on the company and Christmas gifts so I can take a nap?"

CHAPTER 20

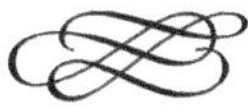

*D*eciding his family could wait a few extra minutes, Quinn hung back until everyone had cleared out before he addressed Annie again, knowing he had to make right whatever had gone wrong.

"Please don't." Her eyelids were at half-mast, and pain tightened her features. Whether it was emotional or physical, he couldn't say.

"Annie, let me explain."

"You don't have to. I get it, Quinn."

Frustrated with her assumptions, he crossed his arms and lifted an inquiring brow. "Really? Please, explain to me what it is you get."

"You don't care for strangers touching you. Me, either. It's all good."

"First, you're not a stranger. Or not completely, anyway." He dropped his arms to his side and sat on the edge of the mattress. "Second, I wasn't comfortable tapping into your personal—whatever you want to call it. It felt like an invasion of privacy, and as someone who constantly deals with boundaries, I didn't want to cross yours."

Her stubborn expression eased, and her eyes softened. An apologetic smile curled her lips. "Like I said, neither of us cares for strangers touching us. But I'm glad you were only freaking out because you thought you'd crossed a boundary with me and not the other way around. I'll never do that if I can help it."

"I know."

As he reached for her hand, the door opened, and the sour-faced nurse from the night before entered. Her eyes darted between them as Quinn rose and backed away to give her room to access the IV.

"Dr. Montgomery ordered another dose of morphine," she said. "And he's also ordered an MRI for this afternoon." With one last disapproving sniff for the two of them, she breezed out the door, her rubber shoes squeaking in her wake.

"I should let you sleep," he said.

"Will you stay? Just a little longer?"

The fretful quality of Annie's voice bothered him, and he shifted closer to brush the hair back from her forehead. "Want to talk about it?"

"I'm scared," she finally admitted. "Sammy was right. None of us have blacked out as a result of a vision or premonition."

"It's okay to let your guard down and admit to being afraid, Annie."

"Not for me."

"Yes, for you. It's scary business, but you've got this. You're one of the strongest women I've ever known." He laughed when she scrunched up her face. "No, I'm serious. With the exception of my mom and my sister, I've never met anyone with your resolve and ability to make the best of a situation. For what it's worth, I think you're going to be okay, whatever those tests show."

"I can't seem to get my footing back. Like all this"—she waved her hand around—"is spiraling out of control."

"I understand. It's the same for me, too." Casting a quick glance toward the door to make sure they weren't overheard, he said, "Hailey isn't waking up. There's a child I knew nothing about. And I've met the most amazing woman, who I can't seem to leave to her own devices."

"Hmm. Yeah, you have it much worse than me," she quipped.

He chuckled, as he was sure she'd intended. "I'm not making light of the fact you were hurt, Annie. Mainly, I'm just saying that I get it. This type of situation would be unusual and off-putting for anyone."

Her smile reached her eyes, lighting them, and Quinn was lost.

How the hell could he have a normal relationship with Hailey even if she woke up? This week with Annie had shown him what an easy relationship with someone should look like. Not the constant struggle to meet a partner's outrageous demands so they wouldn't throw a temper tantrum.

"I wish we'd have met under different circumstances," she said.

Understanding exactly what she meant, he nodded and drew back. "I have to go, but will you call me and let me know what the MRI results are?"

"I meant what I said. You don't have to cater to me, Quinn. It wasn't my goal to gain your gratitude when I saved Hailey."

Hailey. Until she woke and they talked, he was trapped. Guilt slammed into him, and he turned away. "Well, you have it anyway, and that's not all this is. I'm worried about you."

"Don't be. Like you said, I've got this."

His stomach flipped as he glanced back over his shoulder. Annie had her brave face on, but the tightness around her eyes and the slight downward droop of her smile told a different story.

"I'm never not going to worry about you, sweetheart. You're one of about five people I truly care about in the world."

With a slow blink, she smiled, and it encompassed her entire visage.

The drugs had kicked in.

"Okay. You can still bring me cronuts and hot chocolate."

He laughed and returned to stand over her. Unable to curb the impulse, he cupped her cheek. "Thank you. I don't know what I would do if you didn't let me feed you."

"You must be part Italian." With a gasp, she gripped his wrist, already forgetting their mutual agreement to keep touching to a minimum. *Though, he was one to talk.* "I have a great idea! Let me chart a family tree for you, Quinn. I'll discover all kinds of cool shit, and you'll love it."

Deciding the idea had merit, he nodded. "I'll put you in touch with my mother. She has all the relevant information for you to start."

"Is she into genealogy?" Annie released him with a jaw-cracking yawn. Lids drooping, she smiled sleepily. "That would be awesome if she is."

It amused him that she thought so. He found it difficult to recall if he'd ever met anyone as enthusiastic about their career as Annie was.

"Merry Christmas, Annie. Let me know if you want me to bring Tink by tonight."

But she'd already drifted off.

For a long minute, he watched her, terrified of the tenderness taking root inside him. A friendship for them meant keeping it a deep, dark secret. If the press caught scent of it, they would roast Annie alive. Thoroughly chew her up, and spit her out. As it was, Quinn had worked to keep any word of the terminal crash from reaching her. Already, the social media world had been unkind.

THE DREAMS, WHEN THEY CAME, SLITHERED THROUGH ANNIE'S MIND like a cobra: dangerous, dark, and twisty. Ready to strike at her sanity and poison her sense of self. In her dream state, she traversed empty hospital hallways with eerily flickering lights. The echoing slap of rubber-soled shoes gained volume behind her as she fought to flee. Just as she spotted the beckoning exit sign, the elevator doors dinged and someone called her name.

She turned toward the sound, but another caught her attention, jolting her awake.

A stocky man, dressed in navy-blue scrubs, was posed to inject medication into the line of her IV. Since his back was to her, she couldn't see his expression, but the pervading sense of his grim satisfaction sent her heart racing. As soundlessly as possible, she moved her hand and slowly eased the needle from her opposite arm, then drew the cover up to hide the fluid runoff.

He turned his head, and the second he was in profile, she snapped her eyes closed, trying to regulate her breathing. Desperate to remember the small glimpse of his hooked nose and acne-scarred cheeks, she mentally cataloged what she'd seen.

"Pleasant dreams, bitch," he snarled just above her face. His fetid breath was gag worthy, and Annie held onto her stomach's contents by a prayer. Violently retching while pretending to sleep would be a dead giveaway.

After an uneven, shuffling walk, she heard the thud of the spent needle hit the bottom of the sharps container, then the snap of his gloves as he removed them. She didn't peek until she heard the click of the door closing. The second it did, her eyes snapped open and she darted a quick glance around the room to make sure she was alone. Heart in her throat, she snatched up her phone and hit the last number dialed.

It happened to be Quinn's.

"Quinn?" she whispered frantically, eyes locked on the door, terrified to raise her voice, in case her would-be assassin was on the other side.

"Annie?

"Help me," she cried softly.

"Annie? What's going on, sweetheart?"

Her adrenaline surged, and the trembling kicked in. "P-please hurry. I think s-someone just t-tried to kill me."

"What?"

Through the connection, she could make out the sound of his running.

"Someone was j-just in my r-room, and h-he p-put something in m-my IV li-line."

Elevator doors dinged, and the running started again. "I'm on my way. What makes you think he was trying to kill you, Annie?"

"What the fuck?" James shouted in the background.

Quinn's muffled voice repeated what she'd said, as the pounding feet doubled.

"James and I are almost to your room. He's calling the police as we speak."

It said a lot about Quinn's fitness routine that he wasn't even the slightest bit winded, and Annie dismissed the random thought with a frown.

The door was shoved open, and an involuntary scream escaped her tight throat.

"Annie?" Quinn was there, reaching for her arm. "Annie, are you still with me, babe? Tell me you ripped the IV out before—"

"Christ, Annie!" James flew across the room.

"I'm o-okay."

"She ripped the IV out," Quinn told him, profound relief flashing across his face. "She ripped it out."

"Did you see who it was?" James gripped her arm as if to assure himself Quinn wasn't lying, then hit the call button. "Do you think you got that fucking needle out in time?"

She nodded, then burst into tears.

"God, Annie, don't cry!" If there was one thing that discomfited James more than anything else, it was a crying woman. Had Annie been less traumatized, she'd have laughed at the horror on his face.

In the distance, the repetitive whirl of sirens heralded the arrival of the police.

A security guard burst into the room with one hand on his holstered gun. He used the other to flip on the overhead lights. "Back away, fellas. Hands where I can see them."

"N-no," she cried through her sobs. "No. They're ok-kay."

"She's my sister," James told him at the same time.

The sight of Quinn, hands in the air, halted the guard in his tracks. "Quinn Jensen? Holy shit, man! I'd heard you were hanging around the care unit, but I—"

James growled. "Can you focus here? Somebody just tried to slip my sister a lethal dose of unknown shit."

The rabid aggression penetrated the guy's happy superstar-recognition haze, and the guard snapped to attention. "What happened?"

On the heels of his question, Fields and Reynolds charged through the door, followed by Trace and a floor nurse.

Trace rushed over, swiping up a tissue box and handing it to her. "What's going on?"

"We got a 911 call from a James Holt, saying someone just tried to kill his sister via her IV," Fields said, resting his thumbs in his utility belt as he cast Annie a suspicious look. "Anyone care to fill us in?"

His casual pose was a clear indication of his skepticism. Frick wouldn't be chasing potential perps down the hallways on her account anytime soon.

Annie cried harder, clutching her straining broken ribs.

"She's having an adrenaline dump," Trace said, pinching off her IV tube. "She'll be fine in a few minutes."

Quinn addressed Fields. "Annie had a premonition yesterday, and now, this is happening. Someone was just in here, trying to slip her a lethal dose of God-knows-what. I think you need to shove aside your doubts, for the time being, and take her statement."

"Of course." Frowning, Fields nodded at the security guard. "What is lockdown protocol? Do you have anything in place? If so, make it happen." Turning to Frack, he said, "Reynolds, call this in. We're going to need a team to take a sample from the IV line and dust the room. Call the chief and see if he has anyone to spare to question potential witnesses on this floor. I'm betting one or two of the staff saw something or someone out of place." Once his partner and the guard scurried off, Fields approached the bed and awkwardly patted Annie's shoulder. "Ms. Holt... uh, Annie, do you have reason to believe your assailant would target anyone else?"

"I d-don't even know why he t-targeted me," she replied, wiping her face with a tissue and trying to surreptitiously blow her nose. Snotting in public was another no-no on Annie's long don't-fuck-ing-embarrass-yourself list.

"Give me the basics, Annie," James demanded. "I need to know who I'm looking for."

His tone matched his hard expression, and Annie wouldn't want to be in the guy's shoes if her brother happened upon him.

"You're not looking for anyone. Let me do my job," Fields ordered. "These two, I know, but you, I don't. I'll need your ID and to know who you are in all of this."

"He's my brother," Annie said, covering James's balled fist with her hand. "And would it really hurt to have another pair of eyes looking?"

"Continue," Field said, pulling out a small spiral notebook and a pen.

After an aborted breath, she slowly exhaled, calmer than she'd been since the entire thing started. "The guy was tall. Built like you, Jamie, but thicker. Flabbier. And wearing navy scrubs." Closing her eyes, she recalled what she'd seen. "I only saw his profile, but his hair was greasy and a little on the long side. Maybe dark blond or medium brown. It was hard to tell in the dim light." Gratified to see Fields paying attention, she continued. "His nose was hooked, with a thick bump in the middle, like maybe it was broken once. And flat at the tip."

"A boxer's nose?"

"Yeah, maybe. There was a lot of acne scaring on the cheek I saw. His right one. That's pretty much it. I pretended to be asleep when he spoke."

"Spoke?" Quinn asked sharply. "He spoke to you?"

"More like *at* me." A shiver skated through her body at the remembered menace in his tone. "It's like he hated me. He said, 'pleasant dreams, bitch.' His breath was so rancid, I had a hard time not gagging." She met Field's thoughtful gaze. "You should look for someone with rotting or blackened teeth. That guy hasn't seen a dentist in his adult life."

"Got it. Anything else you remember?"

"No. I think that's it."

James bolted toward the door.

"Mr. Holt!"

But her brother was gone.

"Hothead!" With a frustrated sigh, Fields addressed Annie. "And again, you can't think of anyone you've upset recently? Anything that might've led to this? Break up or jealous ex?"

She shot a quick glance at Quinn and Trace, then faced Fields again. "Yes and no."

"Which is it, Ms. Holt? Yes or no?"

"My divorce was finalized last month, but my marriage was over long before. There's no one who would be jealous of me, or over me, for that matter. I've not dated anyone since before I was married."

Fields frowned and jotted a note. "What's the ex's name?"

"Charles Dutton. He goes by Charlie. But it wasn't him."

"Doesn't mean he didn't hire someone. Do you have a life insurance policy?" At her nod, he asked, "Who's the beneficiary?"

"It's divided equally between my parents and siblings. Charlie was removed from the policy the second I first discovered he'd cheated on me. That was about a year and a half ago."

"Smart. And for the record, the man's an ass."

She smiled at his gruff pronouncement. "Thank you, Officer Fields."

"In North Carolina, there is a year separation before divorce. To clarify, you didn't date anyone during that time frame who might be upset that you ended things?"

"No. No flirtation either." Heat was inching up her neck and into her face as she lay there under the watchful eyes of Quinn and Trace. "I'm pretty boring."

Quinn snorted. "Hardly."

She couldn't stop a responding smile. "Okay, well, not *this* week, but normally."

"Anything else you can tell me before I go?" Fields closed the notebook when she shook her head.

Quinn blocked the officer's path to the door. "What's the plan to protect her against this happening again?"

CHAPTER 21

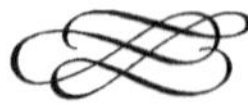

Quinn lost ten years when he received Annie's traumatic call for help, and his heart hadn't returned to normal since.

Fields was darting a questioning look between them as if he was waiting for either Annie or him to confess to a torrid affair. The man couldn't be further from the truth, but it still didn't mean Quinn intended to leave her to her own devices after what had just happened.

"It's doubtful he'll be back right away, with all the excitement and the other officers milling around, but I'll put someone at the door. No one will go in or out who doesn't belong." Fields faced Trace. "This is the care unit and should be limited to only a few visitors per room, right?"

"Yes. There are five rooms on each wall, with the nurses station in the center. Whoever came in here had to pass by the desk."

"Okay. I'll question whoever's on tonight and check security footage." He looked around. "Where did the nurse go? The one who entered with you?"

"To get a new IV set up. I told her to wait until you were finished here."

"Okay. And keep that tube pinched until Reynolds comes back."

Fields moved toward the door, then paused and returned to the bed to draw back the cover. "Smart thinking to remove the needle, Annie. If you hadn't been quick to react, I might be filing a very different report."

"I didn't know what else to do."

Annie frowned and darted a look at the red biohazard bin on the wall.

"What is it?" Quinn asked her. "Do you remember something else?"

"Yeah. He put a needle in the sharps container. I heard it thunk against the bottom, like maybe the bin has been emptied recently or there aren't that many in there." Nodding slowly, she looked at the officer. "He was wearing gloves. I remember the snap as he took them off, but I don't know if he tossed them into the garbage on the way out."

"I'll take a look. Maybe we'll get lucky with a fingerprint or two."

After the detective left, Quinn eased down on the mattress's edge, and because he had to touch Annie to assure himself she was unhurt, he reached for her. He felt the small tremble as they connected, and he gently squeezed. "Are you truly okay?"

"I'm getting there." Swallowing hard, she stared at their joined hands. "Thank you for rushing to my rescue." With a forced smile, she met his concerned gaze. "I guess that makes us even. You're a hero, too."

"I'm not sure what I'd have done had I encountered him. You made him sound like a fucking grizzly bear."

She laughed, and Quinn embraced his relief. Annie was unharmed, and that's what he needed to concentrate on, not the *what-if* of an unknown drug killing her.

"You had her brother as backup," Trace said with a quick glance at the monitor. "He wouldn't have let the guy ruin your pretty face."

Grinning, Quinn flipped him off. "I guess you've the easy job, standing there, holding a tube."

"Stick around. The difficult part comes with shifting an immobile patient to get the soaked sheets off the bed."

"Dude!" A dark scowl coincided with a wash of color in Annie's cheeks. "You make it sound like I peed myself and it's going to take a forklift to move me."

Laughing, Quinn released her hand and stood. "Recovering from that one is going to be tricky, Trace. Have fun with that."

"Where the hell are you going?" Trace called out as he strode away.

"To make a phone call. Annie's going to need private security."

"No! Quinn, I—"

He sighed heavily and faced her. "Does everything have to be an argument, Annie? Can you please just allow someone to help you for once?"

"Let him, Annie." Trace smiled down at her. "He has the resources."

"But—"

"Please." Quinn returned and brushed the hair back from her brow. Tenderness welled inside him as he stared down at her indecisive face. "You did an incredible thing for a great many people, Annie. Accept that someone wants to return the favor."

"But it's too much. You were supposed to spend today with Ty."

His grimace was automatic, and he straightened to turn away. "Yeah, that didn't go as planned. My brother is moody as fuck. It was better for all involved that I came back here to check on Hailey." He shrugged. "And I have a security detail for most events. I was about to book them regarding another project, anyway."

"Are you okay?" She tilted her head as she looked at him, and it was as if she could see clear through to his soul. He squirmed inside, certain she believed him to be a great guy. He wasn't. The opposite was true. Quinn could be a demanding prick on his best day. Only with Annie did he feel different. Like maybe he was a decent person.

Making a face, he turned the tables. "I should be asking you that. And yeah, I'm good."

"What our friend isn't telling you, Annie, is that the crowd of fans and reporters outside the hospital has become unreal." Trace's amused expression bordered exasperation, and his voice was heavy with the constant frustration Quinn felt on a daily basis. "His security team is meant to strong-arm a way through the throng to get inside."

"Oh." Her voice was small and her eyes worried. "I guess it doesn't help that you're probably fielding questions about the plane and the terminal collapse."

"Do you not read the news?" Traces's disbelief was stamped on his slack-jawed face.

Color flared in her pale cheeks, and she became charmingly flustered when Quinn laughed.

"She doesn't!" he crowed. "How refreshing!"

"I've been a little busy here, guys." Even her growled response was cute. "You know, recovering and kicking your asses at poker."

"Maybe Trace hired someone to off you so he doesn't go broke."

"Hardy-har-har. You're funny, movie star." But Trace chuckled. "Go check on Hailey and make your calls. I'll stay here until the police arrive."

As if he'd conjured them, Reynolds and two other uniformed officers entered the room.

<hr>

By the time everyone left and a new IV was inserted into her arm, Annie was exhausted. Her brother had returned to nap in the visitor's chair, and an armed policeman had taken up residence outside her door. The entire situation felt surreal, as if she'd stepped onto the set of a movie and been shoved into the middle of a scene she hadn't received a script for.

Sleep was elusive. Every time she closed her eyes, the terror returned. Knowing she was safe did little to ease the clawing fear.

A man out there hated her enough to kill her.

A bone-chilling cold seized her and refused to let go. Her teeth began to chatter. Loud enough to wake James.

"You're going to be fine, sprite. Promise. I don't care if I have to sub out every single job on my book and sleep on the floor in your room. I'm not going to let anything happen to you."

Tears pricked her lids and escaped to run down her temples. "If I knew why, I think I could handle this better," she choked out. "But I can't understand how anyone could hate me so much. What did I do?"

"Maybe it's a case of mistaken identity. But even if it's not, we'll find him." James perched on her bed and placed a hand on either side of her. Leaning in, he rested his forehead against hers. "Sleep. I'm on watch. And I don't care how big the grizzly bear is; I'll take him down."

"I see you've been talking to Quinn." She laughed and kissed his cheek. "I love you, Jamie. You're the best big brother a girl could have."

"Damn straight. It's about time I was appreciated around here." He straightened to his full height and tugged her fresh, dry blanket up to her neck. "I'm serious, Annie. I'll kill him before he gets to you a second time. I'm not letting anything happen to another one of my sisters. Our family has been through enough."

Her reply was locked behind a lump in her throat, so she nodded her understanding. She felt the same. If she had to lay down her life for any of her siblings, she would without hesitation. Both Sammy and Margie were happy now, but the road to get there had been long and had extracted a mighty toll.

"And I love you, too," he said gruffly. "Get some rest, then we'll talk about your blackouts."

"Ugh! You sure know how to ruin a perfectly good sentimental moment."

His grin encompassed half his face. "That's what big brothers are for."

"Tool."

"Snot."

Their insults were loaded with affection, and their warmth chased away the relentless chill Annie's would-be assassin had left behind. To appease James, she closed her eyes, but her thoughts drifted to Quinn, as they did a lot these last days.

He was such a good person. Yet he tended to play it off, refusing to believe it himself. It was strange that anyone that intelligent, attractive, and wildly successful could have self-esteem issues. But he did. She'd sensed it more than once, especially when it came to his brother, Ty. Their dynamic was off for identical twins. They should be closer than they were, but during their visit the other day, she'd felt Ty's animosity. Not toward her, but for Quinn, if she wasn't mistaken. Although Quinn was the actor, Ty was the one playing a part.

Should she involve herself? Neither man would appreciate it if she stuck her nose in where it wasn't wanted. The part of her developing feelings for Quinn wouldn't allow her to remain quiet in the face of whatever strife awaited him on the horizon.

"I can practically hear you thinking, Annie," James said from the comfort of the recliner. "Christ, can't you turn that big brain of yours off?"

"You're such a dick," she retorted with a laugh. "And I can't sleep. My hips hurt, and I'm sure as shit sick of lying in one position. This is hell for a stomach sleeper, I'll have you know."

"Wait. Let me dig out my tiny violin to play a heart-wrenching tune."

She snorted and shook her head. "James Holt, if you don't be nice, I'm telling Mom!"

The door swung open as she said it, and Sammy entered. "Is he being a dick again?"

"Ha!" Annie laughed. "See? She gets it."

James gave her a dirty look. "Is Michael with you, lil bit? I need to get away from this harridan and find a cup of coffee."

"Oh! Harridan! Big word for such a small IQ," Annie teased.

"See? She's relentless."

Sammy laughed and took his place in the visitor's chair. "Sorry, bro. Michael's not allowed in. They are holding to the strict policy of only two family members in the care unit. But you can find him in the cafeteria and send him up if you're worried." Leaning against the headrest, she smiled. "If it makes you feel any better, there have been no visions. I think it's safe for you to go stretch your legs."

After he left, Sammy rolled her head sideways to look at Annie. "Now, tell me everything that happened and exactly how that gorgeous movie star saved the day."

"You're incorrigible."

"I know. But don't act like you're not half in love with him. I'll call you a damned liar." An arrested expression crossed her sister's face.

"Sammy?"

"It's nothing."

"You're lying," Annie said flatly. "What did you see?"

"Really, sissy. Compared to what happened earlier, it's nothing. I'll tell you when I understand it better."

"Fuck."

It was never good when Sammy had to decipher her own visions.

CHAPTER 22

$\mathcal{L}$ater that evening, Quinn showed up with takeout containing a variety of Chinese dishes. As he spread the cartons on the tray table, Annie gushed her gratitude. Her stomach had been growling since her mystery-meat lunch was taken away untouched.

"I've been living on rolls, jello, and whatever you happen to bring. I know I said you don't have to do these things, but thank you for being so amazing."

"It's my pleasure. And because I knew you liked it, I ordered orange chicken again, but I can go back for something else if you prefer."

His concern was so sweet, Annie's teeth ached. Every time he arrived with a meal for her, he took up more space in her heart. Whoever said the way to a man's heart was through his stomach didn't know the Holt women.

"It's perfect, Quinn. I never tire of it."

"Good. What do you want to start with?"

"The crab rangoon, followed by the orange chicken and steamed rice." She sighed with delight as he placed a heaping plate in front of her. "You'd think I couldn't eat all that, but I'm going to give it the old college try."

He laughed and fixed a plate for himself, careful to leave the bulk of the remaining rangoon triangles next to her.

"Is that molten-lava cake I see for our dessert?"

"As I was leaving earlier, I ran into your sister. She happened to mention it was one of your favorites."

"God bless her meddlesome heart," she muttered as she shoveled another bite.

"You have quite the interesting family."

"Don't I know it."

"Do you want to talk about what happened this morning?" he asked quietly, watchful for any change in her demeanor.

"What's to talk about? Some rando wants to off me. Seems my family attracts trouble from those types." At his questioning look, she told him about the events of Sammy's stay at Brookhaven and about Margie's four-month-long captivity. "The unsavory sorts love to target us."

"If anyone makes your life into a movie, I want a role." He grinned around a bite of chicken, and Annie paused to admire his beauty. How odd that she'd always been drawn to the man through his films, to his particular magic reflecting back at her from the big screen, and how in real life, that magic had woven a spell, bewitching her and capturing her heart. Possibly forever.

"What? Do I have broccoli in my teeth?"

She laughed and shook her head. "No. I was just thinking how kind you are for an actor."

"Know many actors? I can promise they aren't all arrogant pricks. Just average Joes trying to make a living doing the work they love."

"I know. I guess I assumed arrogance went hand in hand with the career choice. But you've disabused me of the notion."

"Awesome. My job here is done," he quipped.

"I know you were supposed to be on vacation over the holiday, but when do you have to return to work? What are you going to do about Hailey?"

He paused in scooping up rice, then set his fork down with a distasteful twist of his lips. "I'm hoping she'll wake soon. Trace said they still can't figure out what the hell is wrong with her."

"I can ask Sammy to visit her room. See if she can get a read… but only if you want," she added hurriedly, seeing his wariness.

"Do you really think that's a good idea? What can she really tell me that the doctors can't?"

Plenty. But Annie kept the thought to herself. "The offer's open if you want to go that route."

With a brisk nod, he returned to eating.

"So, Stephen Montgomery. You two developing a romance, or what? You know it's going to piss off Trace if you are."

She choked on her chicken.

As tears streamed down her cheeks and her lungs caught fire, she glared at Quinn. For the love of everything holy! What had made him ask a question like that?

With a laugh that sounded distinctly hollow, he handed her a napkin and a cup of water. "Sorry."

"You're not." She leaned back to ease the pressure on her ribs. "And it was a cruel thing to ask me, knowing the reaction you'd get."

"I didn't know!"

"Right," she muttered darkly. "Stephen and I are only friends. He boinked Sammy, so I'm not going there."

It was Quinn's turn to choke.

"I thought your sister said not to kill the movie star," he said when he had himself and his incredulous reaction under control.

Annie giggled and threw a fried triangle at his head.

His energy shifted from light and fun to moody and contemplative. "What about Trace? He likes you, ya know."

"He's my doctor, and he's being kind."

"You're not that naive, Annie. Especially as an empath. You have to be able to read the signs."

"I keep my mental barriers up. I rarely know what someone else is experiencing unless I lower the shield and search their energy." She shoved the rice around her plate and shrugged one shoulder. "It's safer that way."

"How so?"

"I don't have to be hurt by negative emotions or disappointed because someone views me in a different light than I view them."

Nodding slowly, he watched her closely. "So you don't know how someone feels about you until they tell you?"

"Mostly, yes."

"I suppose that's good. Keeps the mystery alive."

She laughed.

Unable to simply let the matter of Hailey rest, she probed again. "Quinn, what if Hailey doesn't wake up? Are you prepared for that?"

"No. And she's going to. Wake, that is."

Expression hardening, he shut down, and she decided it was better to let it go.

"Tell me about your oldest sister. Margie, did you say her name was?" Quinn asked, trying desperately to switch the subject. Until the accident, he'd had life goals and had set about making them happen. One of those had been to marry Hailey and start a family when the timing was right. The crash never figured into his plans, and he didn't have an alternative in mind.

As Annie painted a picture of the idyllic relationship between her sister and the sister's boyfriend, Gabriel, Quinn watched her animated face. To her, Gabriel was the end-all, be-all.

Quinn could understand why she thought the guy was hot. She'd described a six-four man who was chock-full of muscle, with dark, wavy hair and piercing silver eyes that would make him one helluva on-screen sex symbol if he'd decided to choose that profession, according to her. Having seen his picture, Quinn couldn't argue. However, hearing she found another man "smoking hot" made him uncomfortable and perhaps a little irritable.

"And he's a stand-up person. Sticking despite my sister's best efforts to screw up her relationship with doubts and fear," she concluded. "Makes him one in a million."

His brows shot up at her skeptical tone. "In your opinion, men don't stick?"

"Based on my experience, they don't. But I'm the common denominator." She laughed, raised her brows, and took another forkful of food.

"Don't sell yourself short, Annie. Any man would be lucky to call you his own."

"Women aren't chattel in this day and age, Quinn," she teased.

"I'm serious."

Grimacing, she put her fork down. "You don't live with me or this gift on a daily basis. It's difficult for *me* to handle, and I've grown up dealing with it." She took a sip of water and an extra minute to form the rest of what she intended to say. "As for a relationship, it isn't fair to subject a partner to the invasive element of it all. The constant need to guard against having their thoughts and feelings read twenty-four-seven. Men think they know what they are signing up for when I tell them, but the reality is far worse."

Hadn't he thought the same thing upon meeting her? Now, living like that didn't seem too terrible if one went in with their eyes open. "If there's nothing to hide, how is it a problem?"

"I believe you've hit the proverbial nail on the head."

"*Your* husband cheated," he stated flatly. The idea of anyone hurting her in such a manner was sickening. "That's not all men, Annie."

"He did. *For two entire years.* As did the boyfriend I had before him and the one before him." She dropped her gaze to her plate, then pushed it aside. "Honestly, I think they wanted to see if they could get away with it. See if my *Spidey* senses would pick up on the infidelity."

Curious in spite of himself, he asked, "Did it?"

"Yes. With the first two, there was no question. With my husband, Charlie, well, let's just say he made me doubt my sanity.

Gaslighting at its finest. And I'm not one to throw that term around loosely."

"Jesus, Annie. I'm sorry." And he was. Picking at old wounds wasn't a thing Quinn did. Mostly, he was a live-and-let-live kind of person. But with her, he was quick to pry, and his conscience gave him a stern lecture.

"Don't be. I'm better off without any of them. Unfortunately, the whole marriage experience has left a sour taste in my mouth."

"Understandable. But you'll find love again." And he had to say it, though he didn't want to. "Trace is a decent guy."

"But we have that doctor-patient taboo happening. And I'm not certain the chemistry is there."

"Really?" *Why was he prying?* "The man's impossibly good-looking, has a respectable career as chief of surgery, *and* he's single. What's not to be attracted to?"

"You're obsessed." Annie laughed. "Sounds like you should date him."

"Maybe I should."

Biting her lip, she picked up another crab rangoon and, distractedly, broke the crispy edges off.

"I think he's mourning. His lingering grief makes me think he lost someone close to him." Annie met his inquiring gaze, and her eyes were filled with misery. Not for herself. In the short time he'd known her, Quinn learned she felt the world's problems keenly and had an unfailing desire to fix them. "His pain is so fresh."

"So not Trace, then," he responded softly.

"Not Trace," she agreed. "Anyway, enough of my tragic tale. Are you excited you're going to be a father?"

"I am." Quinn couldn't contain the shit-eating grin. He'd been dreaming about children for a long while, well before hooking up with Hailey. There were times that he believed what he really wanted from her were the kids she could give him, and not the conditional affection she was so stingy with. "Can't you tell?"

"Yes, and you'll be a great dad."

"You say it with such conviction. I'm terrified I'll screw up the little guy."

"Little girl," she corrected absently around a forkful of food. "And you won't."

Girl?

"Wait! Annie, are you saying I'm going to have a daughter?"

"Crap!" One hand flew to her mouth. "I'm sorry. That's probably something you wanted to find out with Hailey."

Reeling from the information, he shook his head in wonder. The image of a cherub-cheeked baby filled his mind. One with thick dark hair and enchanting blue eyes. The daydream was so real, he jerked, nearly knocking the food off the rolling tray. Quinn shied away from the fact his imaginary infant resembled Annie and not Hailey.

"I'm so sorry," she repeated.

"No, it's fine. Really. But how do you know?"

"Trade secret," she laughed. "But I promise, I'm not wrong."

"A girl." Yes, having a daughter felt right. He shook his head, awed by the news. *"A girl!"*

"Do you plan to cut back on the moviemaking? Maybe shoot for a series or some other project to keep you closer to home?"

"It's funny you should ask. Before the crash, I'd been thinking along those same lines. Hailey expressed her desire to start a family. She's been pushing me for the last six or seven months. It isn't as if I don't want children, and I figured I wasn't getting any younger. I also thought that if her biological clock was ticking, I should probably shit or get off the pot, you know?"

"I do. Charlie always found a reason to put off having kids. Ultimately, I think he was afraid any child of ours would be cursed, like me."

"You're not cursed," he said, angry on her behalf. Fucking Charlie needed his clock cleaned.

Pursing her lips, she blew out a breath. "Not to anyone who hasn't lived with unexplained emotions not their own and premonitions out of the blue. There are days I would give all I own to be normal."

The sadness in her voice didn't sound like self-pity. Merely a woman who had seen more than her fair share of shit. Quinn didn't dare draw her attention to what the press was digging up about her —or who they'd quoted.

"I'm sorry, Annie. For what it's worth, I think you'd make an amazing mother to some lucky child."

"Let me see if I can keep Tink alive first. I might forget I have a child when I hit the mother load of all records during my research. Once I worked through the night. Twelve solid hours with no break."

He chuckled and held the trash bin as she swept the remains of their food into the garbage. "You didn't open all your Christmas presents. Want to do that now?"

"I thought I had." Her confused frown was delightful.

"Looks like you've been a good girl this year. Santa dropped off more." With a nod toward the bag he'd left by the door, he grinned.

"I don't want to know who you paid off to get gifts on Christmas Day." But she held out her arms and made a give-me gesture by wiggling her fingers.

"Actually, I got a few over the last couple of days."

"Quinn! I didn't get you anything."

"You gave me the gift of three lives. My child, Hailey, and mine. The greatest gifts of all."

"And I'd do it again." Squinting and wrinkling her nose, she amended her statement. "But preferably without the self-injury part."

Setting the gift bag on the bed, he stood sentinel next to her, prepared to lift or shift whatever he needed to so she wouldn't experience discomfort.

"Ohmygod! This is my first Coach bag."

"Truly?"

"No, but I thought it would make you feel special if I said it was."

She winked and pulled the stuffing from inside, taking her time to check every pocket as if she'd never seen a purse in her life.

"The color was bright, and I thought the flowers were cheerful. Like you."

"You really need to bottle that charm, Quinn. I swear to God, you'd rake in more than what you do for those movies of yours."

Laughing, he moved the purse to the chair and gestured to the next present.

Like a small child's, her excitement was contagious, and he found himself enjoying the exchange more than he'd believed possible. In his world, gifts were much more extravagant than what he'd given her. Cars, houses, boats... and it never seemed to be enough for some people.

After she was finished, she gestured him closer, and closer still, until he leaned over her bed. Bracing herself on the rails, she stretched forward and kissed his cheek.

"Thank you," she said softly. "I can't remember a Christmas as lovely as this one."

Turning his head, he met her sparkling eyes. "Ever?"

"Ever."

"I find that hard to believe," he said huskily. From nowhere, the desire to kiss her cherry-red lips struck, and though he was tempted to throw caution to the wind, he held onto his control with an iron fist. Helping her get settled, he adjusted her pillows, then backed away. "You know what would've made this holiday better? You not in a body cast from the waist down."

"True dat!" She flared her eyes wide and nodded. "There's always next year."

"True dat."

Their gazes locked, and her expression shifted to one of wistfulness. He supposed if he examined his own feelings, he might be experiencing the same emotions. Like her, this was the best Christmas he'd experienced in a very long time. Minus the attempted murder from that morning. But they wouldn't be spending the holiday together next year. She'd be back to her regular life, and he'd be with Hailey and his daughter.

Heart kicking up its pace, he continued to stare, unable to break the bizarre link they seemed to have created.

"I have to get going," he finally said.

"If you have to."

"Are you afraid to be alone? You don't have to be, you know." With a head tilt toward the door, he clasped her hand. "Fields has an officer outside at all times."

"What if he has to go to the bathroom? Or get a drink?"

"The guy I hired will report for duty at seven tomorrow morning, and there's another officer between now and then." He squeezed her hand gently. "The hospital staff all know to look out for you, too. No one is going to hurt you again, Annie."

She offered up a tight smile.

And all he could think was, *"Famous last words."*

PART II

CHAPTER 23

$\mathcal{E}$ndless days, then weeks, flew past with no change to
Hailey's condition. Trace brought in specialist after
specialist at her family's urging, and they all repeated the same trite
phrases. Really, they were as stumped as Trace. There was no clear
medical reason for Hailey to remain comatose. Her brain activity
was normal, and there were no underlying conditions anyone could
uncover.

Quinn was stuck in a holding pattern of wait and worry, then
wait some more. Hailey's family rotated in and out with decreasing
frequency, with the exception of her mother, who took up primary
residence in the room. Sitting and listening to Gloria Newberry's
sobbing remorse and lectures was no better than torture, and Quinn
sought refuge elsewhere when he was at his wit's end.

Annie helped break up the monotony with her playful smiles,
card games, and ancestry discoveries. But she was looking paler by
the day. More wan and jumpy should anyone show up unexpectedly, as Quinn did from time to time. The MRI results showed
nothing out of the ordinary, and she had been moved from the
intensive-care unit to a long-term-care room.

That morning, as Quinn waited in line to order Annie's favorite hot chocolate, he was jostled. Hard.

Tired from broken sleep the night before and thoroughly irritated by the lack of courtesy on the jostler's part, he turned to speak his peace, but the burly stranger was hustling off. About thirty feet away, the man turned, and Quinn sucked in his breath.

Hooked nose and acne-scared cheek!

With no conscious thought for what he'd do if he caught the guy, Quinn dashed after him.

Hooked Nose's survival instincts were sharp, and as he caught sight of Quinn giving chase, he bolted. The man was out the door and lost in a sea of paparazzi before Quinn could catch him.

Frustrated beyond belief, he shoved a particularly aggressive cameraman's equipment out of his face. "What the fuck are you hoping to get at this point?" he snapped. "Seriously, it's just me walking in or out of the door to this hospital like I do every goddamned day."

"You're news, Quinn," one sympathetic photographer said. "Pictures of you go for top dollar, man."

"What's your name?"

"Jason."

"Okay, Jason. Did you see the guy who just flew out of here?"

Jason nodded, curiosity furrowing his brow.

"If you or your cronies ever see him come through here again, snap a picture of him, his vehicle, and a license plate if you can get it. I'll pay you a reward."

"And if we can get a name or physical address for him?" another photographer asked with a crafty grin.

"I'll pay for that information, too. How does five thousand for each of those things sound?" Quinn suggested.

"So to be clear, you're offering 25K for his face, car, plate, name, and address?" Jason asked.

"Yes. And it has to be an easily identifiable image of him or no deal."

"Done."

Quinn shook hands with him. "You know where to find me, gang."

"Hanging out with the psychic chick?" The question came from a sickly thin, balding man with coke-bottle glasses and sweaty armpits.

The snideness of the comment got under Quinn's skin, but he shrugged it off. "Fishing for information won't work with me. Have a nice day."

"Not fishing. We already have the information. Seems you spend more time with her than your own fiancée. Care to comment for The National Star?"

"No, I don't. Go fuck yourself."

"Can I quote you?"

Quinn snorted. "You will, anyway. Had I said nothing, I'm sure you'd make something up."

A few people laughed, but the look in The National Star reporter's eyes turned ugly.

Quinn had just made an enemy of the press. Something he tried to never do.

Fuck.

Whipping out his phone, he strode back inside and joined the line for the coffee kiosk. He typed out a message to Ty.

> I need you to take care of a potential problem.

What?

> I pissed off a reporter at the National Star.
> Can you squash a story?

Details?

Quinn typed the explanation and description of the guy, then forwarded the information for his brother to handle. As a PR rep, Ty had mad skills and could charm the pants off magazine and newspaper editors alike. It also helped that he'd sneak them exclusive details regarding Quinn's upcoming projects without ever breaking any contracted privacy clauses.

Ten minutes later, Quinn was parked in Annie's room, listening to her ramble on about whatever records she'd found that day.

"You okay?"

He glanced away from the wilting bouquet he'd been blindly staring at. "Yeah, sorry. Just have something on my mind."

"If you have other things to do, you don't have to entertain me."

She wasn't being coy or needy, merely courteous, but the comment triggered his last nerve.

"No, I don't. And I'm not here for entertainment value. Not for you or anyone," he snapped.

Had he spoken like that to anyone else, they'd have reacted badly. Annie, however, smiled softly as she tilted her head and studied him.

"What?" His voice still held on to his residual irritation, but he was curious about her lack of reaction.

"Someone needs a nap," she said with a laugh. "I'd offer this bed, but I'm still in it."

And suddenly, the idea of snuggling next to her was prominent in his mind. Of holding her and whispering naughty sexual innu-endos as she giggled. Of touching her and burying his face against her sweet-smelling neck.

Her teasing expression dissolved, and a small bloom of color tinged her cheeks. Either she'd picked up on his amorous energy, or he wasn't as great at hiding his thoughts as he believed.

"I've got to go," he muttered, surging to his feet.

"Quinn."

Turning back, he met her concerned gaze.

"Tell me what's wrong?"

"Nothing," he muttered.

"Something is."

"Leave it alone, Annie. I don't like my privacy invaded."

She jerked as if he'd slapped her. "Got it. Thanks for the hot chocolate, and I hope your day gets better."

The need to apologize, to fix whatever he'd just thoughtlessly altered between them, was strong. But caution held him back. That prick reporter was right about one thing. Quinn was spending more time with her than Hailey, and people were noticing.

"I have things to do tonight, so I won't be back, but I'll have dinner sent over."

"No need. Sammy and Michael are back in town. They can grab something for me."

With an abrupt nod, he left.

ANNIE SIGHED HEAVILY AND LOOKED DOWN AT HER LAPTOP SCREEN. From the moment he'd stepped through the door with her hot chocolate, Quinn's energy was off. But she hadn't wanted to plague him with questions, preferring instead to let him mull through the problem and speak if he intended.

Yet when he became more reserved and distracted, she'd felt the need to inquire. What a mistake *that* had been! It was difficult to shake off the sense that he was putting her in her place with the privacy comment. Especially after their previous conversation about how the men in her life hated what she could do. It was as if Quinn had exploited her main insecurity on purpose.

Still, he wasn't wrong. He deserved to keep his thoughts private. After all, she was holding hers close to her chest. The suffocating secret she was hanging on to could never be spoken aloud.

She loved Quinn.

The once-in-a-lifetime, forever kind of love that didn't let a woman move on to another relationship after she'd experienced it. But it wasn't as if she wanted to. Men were more trouble than they were worth. Or so she tried to convince herself.

Her mind was so consumed with him, she failed to hear him return.

"Annie?"

Across the room, he stood, as if unsure of his welcome, and she didn't know if she *should* welcome him back. Wouldn't it be better if he left her alone for good? Would it allow her to finally dispel any lingering fantasies of the two of them together?

The silence stretched to painful.

Whatever Quinn wanted to say to her was locked inside him as he waited for her to speak first. She didn't.

"Look, I owe you an apology," he finally muttered.

"You don't."

"Yes, Annie, I do." Closing his eyes, he hung his head. "I'd like to explain why I was such a dick."

"So explain."

"You aren't going to deny I was a dick?" His droll tone made her laugh.

She shot him a cheeky grin. "Nope."

"Pfft."

For the next ten minutes, he detailed the incident by the coffee kiosk, his conversation with the paparazzi, and his subsequent request for Ty to fix his faux pas with the skeezy reporter.

"You were frustrated you lost the guy and pissed off by the jackass reporter's comment. I get it, Quinn."

"Yes. I'm not making excuses, simply giving you the reason for my foul mood." Lifting her hand in his, he perched on the edge of the mattress. "I'm sorry I took it out on you."

"I sensed your underlying anger, but I thought maybe you were sick of me droning on about my work."

Toying with her fingers, he shrugged. "No. I quite like hearing your excitement. But this time, I was in my head about the other stuff and didn't hear a word you were saying."

"I know." She smiled when he lifted his head and met her eyes. "I know because the information I found was for *your* tree."

"What?"

His confusion made her laugh. "Yesterday, I finished the project for my client, and with nothing but time on my hands, I gathered the facts your mom sent me to start your family tree."

"Oh, Annie. I'm doubly sorry for being a grump."

His sincerity flowed through their connected hands, and she hugged it to her. Her gift hadn't been the issue this time. It wasn't to say it wouldn't be in the future, but for now, Annie was content to know *she* wasn't the problem and Quinn still wanted to remain her friend. She was truly pathetic in settling for scraps.

Another thought occurred to her, and her stomach sank. "I suppose we need to call the police to let Frick and Frack know my would-be murderer is back."

CHAPTER 24

"When did you first know Hailey was the one?"

Annie's question gave Quinn pause. It had been two weeks since he saw her attacker in the hospital lobby, and with each passing day, he'd grown closer to her. His vision of a future with Hailey had dimmed during that time, too. But he'd struggled with doubts long before Annie ever asked, and if he bothered to delve deeper, his true feelings—or lack thereof—for Hailey were what had made him reticent to start a family with her last year.

"I'm not sure I ever *did* know," Quinn found himself admitting. "I care about her, and our careers make our lives compatible. We both knew what we were getting into. The constant press, a relationship under a microscope, living in the public eye, and the constant separation from out-of-town trips to film on location."

Annie squinted her disbelief. "You… Are you saying you don't love her?"

"No, I do. Of course, I do." Her shocked response made him squirm.

"You don't sound sure, Quinn. That's not a good thing to be."

The fortune cookie in his hand suddenly required all his attention. If he looked up, he was sure to see censure in her eyes to match her tone. How could he explain that before the accident, there had been no question? Yet, after spending weeks in Annie's company, doubts were plaguing him.

"I'm not comfortable discussing this with you, Annie," he mumbled.

"Oh. Yeah, okay."

Shit.

Her movements were aggressive and jerky as she gathered the remains of the dinner on her tray table. A clear indication of her distress. He'd only wanted to end the interrogation, not upset her.

"Annie, I didn't mean to hurt your feelings. I just don't want to discuss my relationship with Hailey, in general."

"You said, 'with you, Annie.'"

"I should have said *with anyone.*"

"I understand." But her small voice said she didn't.

"Do you? Because you don't sound like it."

Her head came up, and she glared. "Quinn, I get it. No matter what we've been through and how many times you've visited me, we're strangers. You deserve to keep your thoughts and feelings to yourself. I imagine privacy is hard enough to come by without every Tom, Dick, and Sally asking about your love life."

He grabbed her busy hands, halting her manic cleaning. "We aren't strangers, Annie. Not anymore."

"Okay, maybe not strangers, but we aren't besties or confidants. So yeah, you have the right to your secrets."

"There are ears and eyes everywhere, and I shouldn't have said what I did," he replied in a low voice. "I'm not going to discuss my relationship where anyone can overhear and print it." With a squeeze of her fisted hands, he released her. "But we're not strangers, okay?"

"I'm sorry. I'm testy."

"Lack of sleep?"

"Did the dark circles under my eyes give it away?"

"Actually, yes. That and Logan, your night guard."

She frowned.

"Apparently, you've cried out in your sleep a few times. He said he also hears you typing at all hours of the night. Nightmares keeping you up?"

"On occasion," she admitted.

"Same one, or different?"

"Still the parking-lot dream. I don't know what to make of it, but I don't want to rehash it."

Breaking open a cookie, he handed her the fortune, then changed the subject. "There aren't anymore surgeries needed for your back, right?" Annie nodded distractedly as she read the slip of paper. "So you're still scheduled to be discharged in a few days?"

"Yep, then months of physical therapy, according to Trace. I want to rent a place closer to the hospital so I don't have so far to go for PT."

"I'd miss you desperately if you did, but why not go back home?"

"Trace told me about the new equipment they purchased last month. The latest and greatest for cases like mine. Also, he'd like to keep an eye on my recovery, and he suggested I shouldn't drive under the influence of the pain meds, since they make me loopy."

"Sounds like Trace is trying to keep you close," Quinn teased.

Her blush was accompanied by an eye roll. "Knock it off, Matchmaker Mike. Still a doctor-patient taboo. And he's still grieving."

"But your blush tells me you don't want it to be."

"Whatever."

Not exactly comfortable with his own goading, Quinn stood up and collected the trash Annie had neatly piled from their meal. His own jealousy over a possible relationship between Trace and her was ridiculous and inappropriate. The only explanation he allowed himself to believe was that he'd be losing his friend. Until Hailey recovered or the baby was born, he'd be in a holding pattern of endless boring hours at the hospital. He'd have no one to talk to when Annie returned to her research and added a lover to her mix.

In his head, he saw Trace and Annie embracing and preparing to kiss. The picture stabbed him right in the fucking heart, and the pain was so great it stole his breath.

"Quinn? What's wrong?"

Her expression bordered on panicked, with her gaze locked on his shirt. Glancing down, he dropped his arms, embarrassed to find them clutching his chest.

"Nothing." He cleared his throat. "Nothing's wrong. Heartburn, maybe," he added when her frown deepened.

Even as she carefully studied his face, a wave of heat crept up Quinn's neck. In less than two seconds, she'd know him for a fucking liar. But she didn't call him out on his bullshit. With a small smile that didn't reach her worried eyes, she shifted and grabbed her water from the tray table then took a hearty sip.

Had she become overly warm when he had? A random thought distracted him from his embarrassment. What would it be like to make love to an empath like Annie? Would it heighten the experience to be connected on a cosmic level? Would he experience the shocking surge of energy like he had that first time he touched her before she'd put up and maintained her guard?

"I can feel you thinking." Giving him a sharp look, she lifted her chin. "Or rather smell the smoke."

He laughed, but a small part of him suspected she'd tapped into his sexual thoughts, and he wasn't at all bothered by it.

Annie didn't know how to respond to Quinn's earnestness from earlier. Was he saying they were good friends? Were they developing something more? Was he admitting he was no longer sure about his relationship with Hailey? Thinking about any and all of it made Annie's head hurt and her heart wistful.

When Quinn had changed the subject to a lighter topic, she was relieved. Her only problem was his sweet, playful mood. Whenever he teased her, he created havoc with her system. Without trying, he could weave a dreamworld around her, giving her a glimpse of what everyday life with him would be like if she were the lucky one he loved.

But the image was false. Here, they were in a cocoon, with the outside world kept at bay. In her room, he wasn't a famous person hounded by the press and she wasn't an oddity. They were a man and a woman on mutual footing, enjoying time together. The sensation was heady.

"How's our patient?" Trace's voice drifted to them from the hallway.

"She has company. I intended to check back," replied a woman who sounded suspiciously like Nurse Hatchet Face.

Annie and Quinn shared a panicked glance. What had been overheard? She'd been too wrapped up in his seductive energy and had never sensed the other woman's presence. That was another serious problem for her. When Quinn was near, she could only focus on him.

"Why am I not surprised to find you here again?" Trace laughingly said upon entering.

"I practically live at this hospital now." Quinn grinned and shrugged, but Annie could see his underlying unease. "Your rounds are late today. You just missed lunch."

"I had another patient who required my attention."

The tone of Trace's voice was off. Quinn was quicker with his response than her.

"Have you come from Hailey? Anything I should know?"

"All her vitals remain good, but there's no change to report. I'm sorry, Quinn."

"The baby's okay?"

"Yes, so far."

Annie didn't need to delve deep to see Quinn was hurting.

"Quinn, do you mind if I have a private word with Annie?" Trace nodded in her direction.

"Certainly." He stood and bussed her cheek. "I'll check in later for your dinner preference, if you'd like."

"Sure, but only if you're going to be back out this way. Don't make a special trip."

After he left, she faced Trace. "What's going on, Doc?"

"Today's scans show the initial swelling is down. The fracture has healed well. I think you can be released in the next couple of days, after your cast comes off and if there are no further complications."

"That's good news!"

He smiled. "It is. I imagine you want to get the hell out of here and started on your PT."

"I guess I need to start searching for apartments."

"There's a new complex about six blocks from here. Gated, with a doorman and a private parking garage. You should talk to Quinn. I think he's signed a short-term lease there."

It probably wasn't a good idea for her to move anywhere close to Quinn. If she rented a place in his building, he would think she was fishing for more.

"What's with the frown? Do you have questions about your back?" Trace rested against the windowsill and crossed his arms over his chest.

"No. I'm taking it all in." She crinkled her nose and made a face. "I suppose I wasn't expecting a positive report when you walked in."

His indulgent smile vanished. "Real truth?"

"Real truth."

"You're never going to be as good as you were, Annie. Your leg and pelvis were shattered and had to be rebuilt. The hip joint was damaged, and the replacement surgery will only last you for ten or twenty years, depending on your activity level. The pins will never be removed." He shook his head. "With physical therapy, we might get you back to ninety percent. The inflammation took a long time to go down, and you may be facing arthritis earlier than you would've. You also mentioned a cane in your vision."

"I'm a little nervous, Trace."

"Me, too."

She sputtered a laugh, surprised she could after the weight of his revelation. "You're not supposed to admit that. You're *supposed* to tell me there's nothing to be nervous about."

"Damn. I always get those two things confused." He smiled and placed a hand on her shoulder. "You're going to be fine, Annie. *Better* than fine. The best surgeons on the East Coast have rebuilt you."

His words had a ring of truth, and she believed him.

"Like the bionic woman."

"Like that," he agreed with a light laugh.

"Thank you. And just for that, I'm going to have Quinn get me something truly awesome for dinner and you can share with me."

"It has to be better than what our cafeteria has."

"Ah, so you admit the food here is crap," she teased.

"I admit *nothing!*" His chocolaty eyes were twinkling, and their warmth made her happy. Over the last two months, his grief had taken a backseat.

"It's good to see you bouncing back. Stephen's doing?" she asked.

"No comment. And I have rounds." With a backhanded wave, he sailed out the door, whistling off key.

Annie didn't wait to call Sammy. "Hey. Looks like I'll be released sooner than I thought."

"Mmm. Less time for you to win the movie star's heart."

"Give it a rest, Sammy. He's engaged."

"To a vegetable."

Putting a hand to her mouth, Annie choked back a laugh. Really, she shouldn't, but her sister's outrageousness was always in fine form. "You're horrible," she groaned out when the fear of hysterical laughter had passed.

"Oh, for fuck's sake. You know you love him, and I know you love him. Hell, the hospital staff probably all know you love him. He's the only idiot who doesn't know."

"He's not an idiot. And I'm very reserved around him."

Robust laughter carried through the line. "Right!"

Annie hung up.

CHAPTER 25

That night brought both her sisters to her door and tears to Annie's eyes. She'd expected Sammy, but Margie's arrival was a wonderful surprise.

"Hey, sissy," Margie said.

It was all either of them needed for the waterworks to start.

"Don't do that!" Margie embraced Annie, and together, they had a good cry.

When they finally composed themselves, Sammy rolled her eyes. "Well, now that we got that out of the way, tell me the latest on the movie star."

"Oh, good grief, Sammy."

Margie's laugh was music to Annie's ears. There was a time, after her sister's abduction, when Annie believed she might never laugh again.

They caught up on family gossip as Sammy opened the cooler she'd brought with her. Removing plastic margarita glasses with one hand, she raised a bottle of booze with the other. "It's been too long since we had a girls' night. Let's get this party started."

Annie shook her head. Although a party sounded fun in theory, she wasn't sure she should consume any alcohol with what she was currently taking.

"We won't let you do anything embarrassing." Sammy handed her a brimming glass. "Promise. Now can we get our drunk on?"

"I'm going to say you are breaking all sorts of rules with this impromptu party." Annie felt compelled to point out.

"Pfft! Since when did you become the Nelly Naysayer? That's Margie's job."

"Hey! I resent that!" Margie scowled, flipping Sammy off.

"Yes, but it's going to make that rebellious side of you let loose and have a drink. Am I right?"

Suddenly, their oldest sister laughed. "I love you, Sammy."

"Ditto." She poured a second drink and handed it to Margie. "Here. First one's on me." After Sammy's own margarita was poured, they all tapped glasses together for a toast. "To the Holt sisters. Forever fierce," she said.

"Forever fierce!" Annie and Margie echoed.

THE THREE SISTERS WERE LAUGHING HYSTERICALLY WHEN QUINN entered Annie's hospital room. Without any of them the wiser, he leaned one shoulder against the wall and watched them interact. They were a sight to behold, each stunning in her own way. But his attention was constantly drawn to Annie, who was animated and giggling with abandon. The happy flush looked good on her.

As if she sensed his presence, she attempted to zero in on his location. Her bleary-eyed expression had him chuckling.

"Quinn!" she exclaimed excitedly. "Come join us!"

He put a finger to his lips and shut the door. "People are sleeping at this hour, ladies. You might want to keep it down if you don't want Nurse Hatchet Face to throw the lot of you out of here."

"She's off duty. Monica is on this floor tonight, and she doesn't care." She sighed happily and held out her hand. Damned if he wasn't forced to respond by reaching for it. As she gazed up at him with those incredibly bright blue eyes, he had the disturbing desire to kiss her senseless. Mentally shaking off the compulsion, he released her, unnerved by his response to a simple innocent touch.

Once his polite mask was in place, he shook her elder sister's hand. "It's a pleasure to finally meet you."

"Isn't he dreamy?" Annie gushed.

Everyone froze.

Sammy's delighted laughter rang out. With wicked intent, she put Annie on the spot. "Who? Quinn?"

"Huh?" Annie was charmingly confused.

"You said, 'Isn't he dreamy?' And I'm asking 'who?'"

"No, I didn't!" Annie denied hotly, glaring at her margarita in betrayal.

"Uh, yeah, ya did," Margie snorted.

"I hate you all. For that, I'm not introducing you to my friend."

Quinn couldn't help but laugh. Drunk Annie was hilarious and so fucking cute, and apparently, unable to hold her liquor. When she finally declared *he* was the friend, his unease at being called dreamy vanished. He preferred she didn't have any romantic feelings toward him. The complication didn't bear thinking about.

Margie waited for her to take another sip. Sharing a secretive smile with Sammy and shooting Quinn a wink, she asked, "Annie? Who is your friend?"

Annie, once again bubbling with happiness, said, "Quinn! You have to meet my sister, Margie!"

A fourth plastic glass was produced. What was left of the bottle of premade margaritas was poured for Quinn, but he did his best to escape.

"I didn't intend to interrupt your party."

"Think nothing of it. I brought a spare glass just in case." Sammy waved away his objections. "The more, the merrier."

He perched on his usual spot on the side of Annie's bed, and as he sipped his drink, he got lost in the play of emotions that crossed her face.

She watched him in return, albeit a little less focused.

"What cologne do you use?"

He nearly sucked the booze into his lungs. "Excuse me?" he asked on a cough.

"You smell incredible, and I'm so sick of hospital disinfectant. Come here and let me sniff you."

Trying not to laugh, he leaned in so his throat was close enough that she didn't have to stretch forward. The deep inhale and the sound of her subsequent sigh hit him low in the gut. He wasn't one to get turned on by a simple exhalation, but he was quickly discovering nothing was normal around Annie.

As he pulled back, his lips accidentally brushed her jaw, causing them both to jerk in response. Had he ever felt anything as soft as her skin?

Get it together, Quinn.

"I think you've had enough," he said, snagging her glass before she dumped it on herself.

"No, I get to drink tonight. I'm celebrating going home!" She hiccuped the last word.

He stilled. Had he heard her correctly?

"Annie? You're being released tomorrow?"

"Am I? I don't think so."

He sighed in relief.

"Maybe," she said with a frown. "No. Coupla daysh."

"Why didn't you tell me?"

Her head bobbed drunkenly in answer. "I got a brain tu-mah." Even blitzed, her Arnold Schwarzenegger impression was spot on. Or at least she thought it was as she sat back giggling, spurred on by her sisters.

Suddenly, Quinn wasn't in a celebratory mood. He set his drink on the bedside stand and did the same with hers. "Annie, can you be serious for a minute?"

Her owllike expression attested to her attempt to comply. However, she couldn't maintain it for long and broke into giggles.

"Annie!" he barked, latching onto her arm.

She jerked as if he'd slapped her. A current raced through his arm and shot straight through his entire body. The sensation made him light-headed.

Sammy surged forward to break their contact. "Holy shit! You can't grab her without some prior warning!"

"What the hell was that?" he demanded hoarsely. "That's the third time I've felt something similar to electrocution when I've touched her. How can that be?"

"*That* was my sister in an unguarded moment. On a normal day, she would have tempered the energy exchange. But when she's vulnerable, touching her is the equivalent of a small power surge."

Annie's head lulled back on the pillows. Her eyes were closed and her mouth slightly open.

His gut clenched even as he struggled to get his heart under control. "Did I hurt her?"

Sammy's sudden laughter didn't pack the punch of Annie's. "No. She's a lightweight and passed out from one too many."

Relieved, he compressed his lips to hold back a chuckle. "I see."

"Drink up. We are celebrating sisterhood." A frown tugged at Sammy's brow, but she waved a hand in dismissal and shoved his discarded glass at him. "I mean, you're not a sister, but you can still hang with us. We'll wake Annie in a few minutes."

"Maybe she should go easy on the booze," he cautioned, downing the rest of his margarita and rising to his feet.

"Don't worry about Margie; she can hold her own."

"I was talking about Annie. She's still taking pain medication."

"Oh, yeah, she can never handle more than one or two, at the most," Sammy confirmed absently, digging into her cooler for another bottle. "Has something to do with her mojo."

As he got a glimpse of the cooler's contents, he shook his head in wonder. There were two more containers of alcohol. Sammy was serious about her partying.

"What was Annie saying about a brain tumor?" he asked.

"You're like a damned dog with a bone, aren't you?" Margie complained, refilling her drink.

"And the two of you like to avoid answering questions," he countered.

"Touché, actor man! Touché!" Sammy laughed and pointed at Annie. "She was joking. There's no tumor. Ah, she rallies!"

"Time for a toast," Margie chirped.

Quinn decided to go along with their party attitude—*for now*—but when he had Annie alone, he'd discuss her future plans and perhaps help her get settled.

Sammy whipped out her smartphone, cued a song, and encouraged Annie to sing. Oddly enough, as soon as the music began, all signs of drunkenness disappeared. Annie's voice was pure and haunting, and Quinn sat back against the foot of the bed, enjoying her impromptu performance.

As she sang a song of lost love, their gazes locked and his heart swelled with an aching tenderness. An emotion he couldn't remember ever feeling for anyone before. It was as if no one else existed in the world right then, and he was in awe of the emotion. Of the sudden desire to steal her away and keep her forever.

"We need something a bit more upbeat," Margie complained.

Sammy nodded her head. "I'm on it."

While the two sisters bickered back and forth over which song they wanted to play, Annie sat across from him, smiling serenely. Quinn sucked in a breath. Had he ever experienced a more perfect moment? Regardless of the fact she was injured and he was otherwise committed, he wanted to freeze this instant in his mind.

His heart lurched in his chest. Once again, he reminded himself she wasn't his and he had other commitments. He belonged to Hailey and his baby. Yet when he was with Annie, he forgot all that. The struggle to remember what the soon-to-be mother of his child looked like was real, and at times, he even forgot she was in the same hospital.

This bizarre attraction he'd developed would fizzle out as soon as Hailey woke and life returned to normal. It had to. The entire situation made him moody and somewhat surly, and when Annie's smile turned bittersweet, he silently questioned if she was picking up on his mood.

But the longer he remained with this trio of women, the more he wanted to stay. As he listened to them tease and joke with one another, his respect for them grew. These three, despite their recent trials, found a reason to celebrate. They sang. They danced. They made merry. All because they had the spirits of warriors and a zest for life.

If only he could capture some of their magic for himself!

CHAPTER 26

*A*nnie woke with a headache to end all headaches.

Ugh! What had she done?

Peeling back an eyelid, she glanced around to see who was in the room with her. She suspected she knew, but she needed to confirm that suspicion. Quinn was dozing in the recliner with Tink cuddled in his lap.

Her heart pinged at the sight.

Love swelled within her. To find a kind, considerate guy willing to go out of his way without ever being asked was a rarity. Without fail, Quinn showed up again and again, making sure she had everything she could ever want or need. How could she not fall for him?

The door cracked open, and she put her finger to her lips to shush her visitor. A zing of awareness chased down her spine, and she experienced momentary confusion.

Only Quinn had that effect on her!

As the visitor drew back the curtain, her mouth dropped open. Whipping her head to the right, she realized her mistake. Ty was in the recliner. With his longer hair and scruff, she should've immediately realized it wasn't her Quinn.

Her Quinn?

Flaming fucks! She was in deep shit.

"Mornin'. I see Ty brought Tink for an early morning visit."

Keeping her voice low, she said, "He was sleeping when I woke up."

"Ah. Well, I told him to bring her up while I took a detour and gathered breakfast for us."

Her stomach churned at the idea of food, and she would've bet good money that her complexion had turned green.

With an evil chuckle, he shook the paper bag. "Only two things cure a hangover. Greasy food or a hair of the dog. I assumed you didn't care for more booze."

She couldn't prevent the grimace. "Are you trying to make me yak? Is this revenge for making you sing last night?"

"Maybe a little." He whistled the tune to *Call Me Maybe* as he spread the food on her tray table.

"You're evil."

"He really is," piped up a scratchy voice from beside her. "One time when we were kids—"

"Don't you dare tell that story, Ty!" Quinn warned. "I won't give you the waffles Cookie made."

"If they were anyone else's waffles, I swear I'd spill my guts. But no one makes them as good as my beloved Cookie."

Annie found herself grinning. Their lighthearted teasing lifted her mood considerably. "Who's Cookie?"

Ty answered. "She initially started working as a cook for our mother when we were kids. Quinn, heartless bastard he is, stole her away from Mom when he moved out on his own. I can only assume he tempted her with fame and fortune but now keeps her chained to his kitchen island."

"Yes, well, great waffle cooks *are* hard to come by," Annie replied.

"See? She understands." Quinn placed the food before her and smiled. "For you, I grant the first waffle."

"This isn't greasy food."

"True. I just wanted to see if I could make you suffer a bit." He removed a thermos and put it on the side table.

"For that, I'm going to have Ty tell me that story you're trying so hard to cover up."

"He's sworn to secrecy. If he tells, he has to shave not only his head but also his balls, then run around the outside of the house naked—*twice*."

She laughed and shook her head. "As much as I'd love to try these, I can't. I don't think I can hold it down." The explosive scent of warmed maple and fresh cinnamon caused her stomach to rumble. "Okay, maybe I can try."

The brothers laughed as Annie took another appreciative sniff.

"Dear God! I don't know how much you're paying that woman, but from the smell alone, it isn't enough. And I'm here to tell you, if she knows how to make a decadent hot chocolate, I intend to steal her for myself. I don't care if I have to work three jobs."

Quinn chuckled as he picked up the thermos to pour her a steaming cup of rich cocoa. "Careful, it's hot," he warned as he handed it off.

Reaching into his never-ending bag of goodies, he removed a can of whipped cream.

Desire struck Annie hot and hard. Seeing her freaking dream man holding that can had sexual fantasies by the dozen crowding her mind. All entirely inappropriate for the current time and place, considering she was bedbound and, after this week, going to have limited mobility, he was in a committed relationship, *and* his twin was sitting right beside her.

She blinked.

The added fantasy of twins knocked on the door to her brain box, and she tried her damnedest not to answer.

And of course Quinn made a flawless swirl with the cream on top of the drinks. Annie sighed at the perfection of it all.

"Bacon?" Ty asked, as if his plate weren't already threatening to overflow. Ever hopeful, Tink shoved her head under his arm, and her nose went to work overtime as she investigated his breakfast.

"It's the thing Cookie does best."

He offered Annie four perfectly crisp slices from another

covered dish he'd produced.

"Okay, Ty can keep your secrets."

"You're so easy," Quinn teased.

"Totally." She sighed heavily, enjoying the taste of the bacon.

Ty roared with laughter, but it was Quinn's seductive chuckle that skittered along her nerve endings and caused goose bumps to break out on her entire body.

The three of them sat together, with Annie and Ty inhaling their breakfast feast as Quinn snuck bites to Tink. She couldn't fault the brothers in their care of her dog, but she missed her pup so much. And if she were being honest with herself, she was feeling unloved and jealous that her dog currently preferred Quinn to her.

"Ty, what do you do?" Annie asked. "I'm sure Quinn probably told me, but I have Swiss cheese for brains ever since the concussion."

"I own a PR firm. I rep for Quinn and a few other well-known celebs."

"Do you like it?" The question came on the heels of the sensation of discontent emanating from him.

"For the most part."

She frowned but kept her suspicion to herself.

The rest of the meal was finished in silence, mostly because the food was scrumptious and it would have been rude to talk with their mouths full.

Ty excused himself and left as soon as he was done eating, commenting he needed to make a few phone calls. Left alone with Quinn, Annie didn't know whether she should bring up her impressions of his brother or not.

"You should just come out with it, Annie."

She whipped her head around and met Quinn's sardonic gaze.

"What makes you—"

"Are we really going to play that game?" he asked, irritation heavy in his tone. "I didn't take you for the game-playing sort."

"I'm not! I..." She paused and shook her head, frustrated at her inability to put her finger on what was off about his brother.

Heaving a sigh, she said, "It's really nothing. I've been trying to figure out what I was reading from Ty's energy."

"He's been conflicted for a long time. I wouldn't worry too much."

Taking the conversation at face value, she picked up her drink and sipped it. "This is the best cocoa I've ever tasted."

"Really?" He took it from her and guzzled some down. "Tastes like regular hot cocoa to me."

"There's no hope you'll ever become a chocolate connoisseur. Your ability to distinguish good chocolate from bad is questionable."

"Damn. There goes *that* career choice. I guess I'm stuck being a crappy old actor."

"There is nothing crappy about your acting."

"Ah, so you think I'm good?" he asked, a teasing grin in place.

"I think you're fishing for compliments."

"How's the hangover?" His sudden change of subject had her head spinning.

"Mostly gone."

"Good. There's something I wish to discuss with you."

The seriousness of his statement had her nerves jumping. "Oh-kay."

"When are you scheduled to go home?"

She closed her eyes, rested her head against the pillows, and sighed. If she spoke to him about her living arrangements, he'd tell her he didn't have an issue with her renting in the same complex. Hell, he'd probably give her one of his guest rooms. But she wasn't positive her heart could stand living in the same town, much less the same building, as he was. Every day, she was falling more in love. Soon, it would be impossible to keep her feelings to herself.

"Annie?"

There was no point stalling or putting him off. He was a damned dog with a bone.

"Trace said likely this week. They need to remove the cast tomorrow to reevaluate and check mobility, but if everything looks good, a few more days at most."

"But that's great news." Understanding dawned on his face. "You haven't found a place to rent yet, have you?"

"No. Trace suggested I try the new complex on Louden Way because it has decent security, but he also mentioned you live there."

"And that's a problem?"

"I don't want you to think I'm trying to wrangle my way into your life or invade your space," she confessed. In her nervousness, she fiddled with the covers, folding the edge and smoothing the line of the fold.

"I don't think that. I never could." He rubbed a hand back and forth along her shin soothingly. Unfortunately, it had the opposite effect and brought her nerve endings to life. "Annie, this is a small town, and we both know the rentals are limited. I agree with Trace, for what it's worth. I like the idea of security and, more importantly, the fact you would be close in case you need anything. I could walk Tink in the mornings."

"It's too much," she cried in her exasperation. "Quinn, you're doing way too much. Seriously. I can hire a dog walker."

"I know, but I've come to love that sweet-faced gremlin."

When he seemed satisfied she didn't intend to argue anymore, he busied himself stowing the extra food into their original containers. "Also, I may have reserved an apartment for you already."

"Quinn!"

His interest in her welfare was as flattering as it was disturbing.

"If you don't love the place, I'll get the deposit back. But if you do, it's yours."

"I don't know if I want to thank you or tell your meddlesome ass off."

"My vote is thank you," he replied cheekily.

"Well, at least you didn't suggest I take one of your guest rooms," she complained.

"I thought about it, but I knew you'd reject it out of hand."

Laughing, she lay back against the pillows. "I don't know if I should tell you this, but I think with your looks, charm, and refusal to accept no for an answer, you could rule the world."

"That's my next course of action."

He checked his watch, the third time since he came to visit her, and frowned.

"You don't have to hang out, Quinn. I'm sure you have things to do." Although she wanted nothing more than for him to keep her from boredom, having him around was selfish and added to her unrequited feelings.

"Nope. I have the whole day free. I need to visit Hailey and get the latest update from Trace, but if there's still no change, I'm all yours."

And wasn't that the problem? Annie didn't want there to be any change. If Hailey stayed in her coma, he would continue to hang out with *her*. But once his fiancée awoke, all the fun would stop and their friendship would end. Hailey would cut off her own arm before she allowed the bond between Quinn and Annie to continue growing.

"We could watch a movie," he suggested.

"Don't think you can force me to watch your crappy acting," she teased.

"Looks like you've figured me out."

"I like Disney movies."

He paused in picking Tink up, something akin to a sickly pallor creeping up into his face. "Say it isn't so," he demanded.

"Sorry, not sorry."

"Okay, but after the movie, you help me pick scripts."

"Pick scripts?" She didn't know what that entailed, but maybe it was more interesting than watching something she'd seen a dozen times.

"Yes. That's nonnegotiable."

"What do I have to do?"

"Read through a stack and tell me which ones sound promising. It'll help me select my next project."

"Sounds simple enough," she agreed. "Let's do that instead."

She should have known by Quinn's wicked chuckle that she'd signed herself up for a nightmare of work.

CHAPTER 27

More and more over the last two months, Quinn found himself simply watching Annie. When she let her guard down and became animated, she was striking. With her empathic ability, she was forced to maintain a shield between herself and the rest of the world, but to see her unguarded with her family, and oftentimes with him, filled him with a sense of wonder that bordered on happiness.

And as they read in companionable silence, jotting notes on pads of paper, their gazes would connect, and every admiring look from her was like a caress to his dick. More than once, his jeans had become uncomfortably tight. And fuck if he could concentrate on work around her. He needed his damned head examined. What was sexy about a woman in a nondescript gown, trapped in a hospital bed?

Absolutely nothing—unless it was Annie, with her sparkling eyes and welcoming smile.

Ty was right. There were stars in her eyes, and it was all his fault. He'd made himself available at every turn, catering to her every whim.

And once again, she was quick to pick up on his rapidly deteriorating mood.

"What's wrong?"

"You need to ask? Can't *you* tell *me*?" He came across as a sarcastic ass, but it had finally hit home that he was in grave danger of becoming too involved with her.

Leave it to her to immediately delve into the root of the matter.

"Quinn, you don't have to stick around. Not for me."

Because he needed the buffer of his shitty relationship, he said, "I'm not staying for you, Annie. I'm here for Hailey."

Her sharp indrawn breath made him cringe inside. Still, the truth was paramount and should be stated. To have either of them believe anything was happening between them other than friendship was to allow them to live in a fantasy world.

"Then you should be on your way to see her. I need some downtime from visitors, anyway."

He could detect very little emotion in her voice. She'd managed to hide her feelings well—*if* one didn't happen to be looking at her eyes. Those large blue orbs spoke volumes about her hurt and disappointment in him.

"I can stay," he found himself blurting.

Shifting her head, she gazed out the window, effectively blocking him from her thoughts. With a sad half smile and a voice almost too soft to hear, she said, "No. I'd like to be alone now."

Unable not to, he approached her and stroked her petal-soft cheek. "Annie..."

But what was there to say? She had to be getting confused as fuck with his hot-and-cold routine. Hell, *he* was confused. This helpless female had him tangled in knots, and he didn't know which way was up. He should probably stop visiting her, but damned if he could make himself. "I'll stop by later."

"That's not necessary." She eased her face away, breaking their contact. "You've done your duty for the day with Tink's visit."

Why did she suddenly sound defeated? And why was his heart

hammering in his chest? *Fuck.* This was all too much. "If that's what you want."

"It is." She cleared her throat. "The scripts I've read are on the tray table. Here are my notes." After handing him the pad of paper, she snuggled back onto her pillows.

Knowing he'd messed up and that he couldn't leave on a sour note, he set the notepad on her tray table. "Annie—"

"And I think it's better if you don't come back anymore, Quinn."

"What?" His stomach dropped, and he wanted to fucking vomit. But hadn't he been thinking something similar a moment before?

"I'm... You... Our lives are too different to sustain this on the outside. And if Hailey wakes—"

"*When.* When Hailey wakes," he corrected, unsure why he was still pushing the point.

"When Hailey wakes," she dutifully replied. "She's not going to like that we've spent so much time together."

With dawning dread, he asked, "You've seen The National Star article, haven't you?"

"Among others." She gazed out the window, sighed, and met his panicked eyes. "Researcher, remember?"

"Annie, I'm sorry."

"It's a good time to end this... friendship."

"No. Maybe the visits, but I'll always be available if you need me. You know that, right?" Because it was important she knew he wouldn't abandon her like others had.

She simply smiled, and it tore his guts up.

"What should I do with Tink?"

"If you or Ty can watch her for another day or two, I'll collect her when I'm released."

"I don't mind walking her. I said I would."

God, why couldn't he allow her to cut the ties?

"It's better if I hire a dog walker and we end this now, Quinn."

Was it? He wasn't as sure as he'd been minutes before. The draw he felt had its challenges. Every day, he told himself he would only pop in for a short time to check on her. And every day, he found himself spending hours in her company instead. During those occasions, he convinced himself he was only keeping her from boredom. She deserved as much for saving his life. However, the reality went much deeper—he couldn't stay away.

But he needed to start. Annie was right to send him away. Hailey would wake soon. She had to. And when she did, she deserved all his focus. Deserved a man who was one hundred percent present and committed. Hell, if he were honest with himself, she deserved it now. But he found it difficult to sit by her bedside, waiting in vain for her to wake. When he wasn't holding one-sided conversations with his baby, he wondered what Annie was up to. Wondered what new mysteries she'd uncovered in her genealogy research. Wondered if Trace was keeping her company. The thought of her killing time with the handsome doctor—regardless if it was in a friendly fashion—made Quinn salty as hell.

"I'll see you tomorrow." Irritated, with no one to take out his aggression on, Quinn stalked from the room.

He needed air.

As he cleared the front doors, a small group of photographers jumped to their feet and ran toward him. He almost backtracked, but Jason caught his eye and tipped his chin. Quinn met him halfway.

"What do you have for me?"

Jason produced a flash drive. "Everything you asked for."

"Excellent. You intend to stick around another couple of days? I may have another job for you." At the affirmative nod, Quinn smiled. "I'll have a check for you in the morning."

"Quinn?"

He turned back, and Jason edged closer. "There are a few other images on that drive for you to pay special attention to."

Frowning his confusion, Quinn nodded. "About the grizzly bear?"

"Grizzly bear?" Jason grinned.

"That's how I've been referring to the guy with the hooked beak. He's huge."

"Yeah, and not someone you want to tangle with."

Pulling him off to one side, Quinn glanced around to make sure they wouldn't be overheard. "Obviously, you know more. What can you tell me?"

"He's got a record. Been arrested on numerous assault-and-battery charges. Never serves much by way of jail time because none of the witnesses last long enough to testify."

Quinn's butthole tightened.

That fucker had Annie in his sights.

"What else?"

"Not much, other than he's been meeting with a woman who seems to stir him up."

"Stir him up how?"

"His temper. But he treats her with respect, like a sister or girl-friend. Though I'd be surprised if she was the latter. I haven't seen any sign of that type of affection." A contemplative look flashed across Jason's face. "Unlike you and Annie Holt."

"What the fuck are you talking about?"

"There's footage of the accident that's leaked recently. You might want to take a look at it." He nodded to the drive. "And those additional pictures? I'm going to give you the chance to buy them first."

Nausea rolled in Quinn's stomach. He'd been a fool to believe no one could see into the second-story windows of her room. No wonder the sleazeball reporter from The National Star had insinu-ated more.

"How much?" he asked coldly.

"Don't even want to negotiate?"

"No, Jason, I don't. But whatever I pay you comes with a contract and a gag order. Got it?"

"Yep." Jason handed him a business card. "My number, for when you're ready to talk numbers."

"I'll want the originals."

"You'll have them."

Livid and filled with an irrational fear that Annie's and his lives were about to take a turn for the worse, Quinn snatched the prof-fered card and stalked into the hospital.

Belatedly, he heard another reporter—the one from The National Star, if he wasn't mistaken—question Jason. "Hey, man, what was that intense-as-fuck conversation about?"

"Fuck off, Dooley. As if I'd tell you." Jason's triumphant laugh sickened Quinn. Trustworthy people were few and far between in his world.

Since Hailey's room likely had her mother or sister, Jeri, reviewing the file would only raise their curiosity and invite questions Quinn didn't want to answer. An out-of-the-way bathroom was his best bet for privacy. He almost laughed at the absurdity of using a restroom as an office.

After perusing the images and brief on David Rice, he swore softly. Jason was telling the truth; the guy was bad news. Seven suspected murders. Zero proof. That meant David was clever and always one step ahead of the police.

Quinn withdrew his phone and scanned all the documents, then scrolled through his contacts until he landed on the number for a PI he'd worked with before. It was well past time to call in rein-forcements.

"Mac?"

"Hey, Quinn! What's going on?" After hearing a rundown of the events to date, Mac whistled. "That's some shit. Send me what you have, and I'll see what I can find. My wife will send you an invoice for a retainer. Same as last time."

"Be careful, Mac. I don't need to tell you this guy is dangerous, do I?"

"No. I've dealt with his type before. I know the score."

"Call me when you have something."

Although he hated to do it, Quinn had to inform Annie about David. She had a right to know how perilous her situation was. When he reached her room, the curtain was drawn and she was conversing with Trace.

He almost made his presence known, but Trace's next words

held him still. He didn't want to interrupt an exam if he could help it, and what he needed to reveal about David Rice should be for Annie's ears alone. Afterwards, she could decide who to tell.

"I don't want you to worry about your recovery, Annie," Trace was saying. "You'll be up and about today, now that your cast is off."

"I'm not worried. I have a lot on my mind."

"Anything you want to talk about?" She must've shook her head, because Trace continued speaking. "Where's your champion?"

"Which one?"

"I think you know."

From his vantage point, Quinn could see Trace making notes using his trusty tablet, and he glanced up when Annie said, "He had shit to do."

"I'm surprised he couldn't do it from the visitor's chair," Trace joked, but it fell flat.

"Are you fishing, Doc?" She sounded salty as hell, and Quinn grinned. He couldn't help it; he adored Salty Annie. "You could just ask."

"I thought I did."

"I'd tell you where to go, but I have to be nice to you since you're in charge of my recovery."

"Why can't you just admit it, Annie?" Trace asked. "You are in love with him. That's why you are so anxious to check out."

"All I know is I can't take another day trapped in this damned bed. I'm going insane, and I have to get out of here."

"I see it every time you look at him."

Unease settled around the edges of Quinn's brain.

"You don't know what you are talking about," she retorted.

"Oh, I don't, huh? Trust me, I know what love is. I know because I've lived it. But believe me when I tell you, unrequited love doesn't end well. You need to at least admit it to yourself, if not to him," Trace argued.

"I'm not doing this right now. Besides, what's it to you? What difference could it possibly make if I do?" Annie demanded.

Quinn saw Trace's expression alter. It *did* matter to him. Trace

Montgomery cared about her and, if Quinn was any judge, in more than a doctor-patient way.

The muscles of his gut clenched.

Annie must've had her barriers in place and been sleeping to miss Trace's reaction because the visually impaired could see it made a whole shitload of difference to the good doctor. He shifted and glanced toward the door, probably in a piss-poor attempt to hide his feelings.

They locked wary gazes.

"You want me to say I love him, Doc? Fine! *I love him.* But it doesn't matter how I feel because he'll never see me. Not in that way. Why? Because he's engaged to another woman." Annie was clearly mad enough to be oblivious to it all, and she huffed out a breath.

Quinn was about to quietly leave, but stopped as the next half of her rant registered.

"His cheating-ho fiancée isn't going to wake up. Not because she can't, but because she doesn't *want* to! Probably doesn't want to deal with the parental shitstorm about to happen."

Roaring started in his ears, and black dots altered his vision.

She must have finally sensed Quinn's presence or noticed Trace's arrested expression.

"Oh God!" she whispered.

Quinn couldn't be silent any longer. *"What the fuck did you say?"*

CHAPTER 28

Quinn had never been so enraged. The sheer ridiculousness of her statement had fury pounding through every part of his body.

How dare she!

Of course Hailey was going to wake up.

Shame and uncertainty contorted her features. But she didn't cower. Resolve straightened her spine, and her chin lifted.

"That wasn't meant for you to overhear."

"But I did, and I want you to clarify what you said," he replied silkily. For the moment, he chose to ignore Annie's confession of love. One crisis at a time.

"I can't."

"Bullshit! *Tell me.*"

She remained mute. When she looked at Trace for support, he stared back in stoney silence, offering none.

"Goddamnit, Annie! Tell me what you meant and what you think you know."

Trace strode for the exit. "This is between you two, and I have patients to check on. My advice is to keep it down if you don't want to see it online."

The door shut with a decisive click.

"Please, Annie. I've never asked you for anything, but I'm asking now. What do you think you know about Hailey?"

"She's not going to wake up," Annie said achingly.

"A vision?" he croaked.

"Yes."

For the longest minute, he simply stared at her, unable to comprehend what was happening. What it would mean if Hailey died.

"No." He shook his head, denying whatever she thought she knew. "No. She will, and Serena's going to be okay. She's going to have a mother and a father, and..." Heart hammering, he bent at the waist, put his hands on his hips, and tried to suck in air. He felt like he'd just run ten miles at top speed and couldn't get enough oxygen.

He couldn't lose his baby girl. His one governing thought was to get to her, and he ran.

"Quinn!"

Annie's voice broke, and the plea was evident in the way she called his name. That heartbreaking catch halted his exit, but he couldn't look at her.

All this time, he'd believed Annie was his friend, and she'd been silently hoping Hailey would die. Rarely had he ever wanted to hurt someone like he wanted to hurt Annie right now. The feeling scared him into silence. Whatever he said in the moment, there would be no coming back from.

Scathing words struggled to break free, and Quinn mustered self-control from a place he didn't know existed. Stepping farther into the room, he slapped the manila envelope on the tray, wearing a mask of disdain.

"This is David Rice. The man who injected..." It occurred to him that perhaps none of it was real. According to Logan, there had been no other attempts on Annie's life. No one even close to suspicious lurking around the halls. Maybe David's presence had been a setup to draw Quinn in further.

"Quinn, please. I'm so sorry." Her tears caused the thready quality in her voice.

He acknowledged her apology with a single nod and turned away. In the process of his escape, he recalled the rest of what she'd said. He paused mid-stride, swung back, and ate up the distance between them.

"What do you mean by *parental shitstorm?*"

But the dread on Annie's face, the solemn knowledge in her eyes, couldn't be denied.

"You called her a cheating-ho," he said almost to himself as he tried to piece together the jigsaw puzzle of her combined comments. "Hailey *cheated* on me?"

Her eyes flared wide.

"How long have you known?" Quinn rasped out, his stare cold.

She remained mute.

Although his stomach felt like lead and his chest ached at seeing the compassionate expression on her face, he was furious. Charging forward, he only stopped when he was towering over her.

"How. Fucking. *Long?*"

"Leave her alone, movie star," Sammy warned from behind him. "She—"

"What?" he snapped, spinning to confront her. "She hasn't been lying to me? Colluding with you to make me question my relationship?" Sammy pushed past him to clasp Annie's trembling hand, and Quinn sneered at the sweet sight of their unity. "She wasn't fucking asking after Hailey's health at every turn, like she truly gave a shit!"

Fury clouded his vision, but not so much that he didn't see Annie recoil from his verbal attack.

"Quinn..." Her tone was as broken as her spirit, and her ever-bright eyes were dull. "Quinn, I swear I didn't—"

"You're crazy if you think I'll take your word for anything," he ground out. "Why can't you just admit you played me, Annie? That you supposedly love me—your words—and you fucking played me to get what you wanted?"

She paled under his furious regard. Her lips compressed, and tears streamed from her tightly closed lids. "Honestly, I've never expected anything from you, nothing more than what you've already given me—the friendship you've offered. I swear."

"You're a liar."

Sammy wedged her way between him and the bed, giving him a shove. "You need to leave. Right now, or I'll kick your sorry ass."

"I'm going." He looked at Annie with all the hurt and disgust he felt for being a chump. "Whatever debt I owed you is done, Annie."

"I never expected repayment," she retorted, her eyes snapping open and blazing with fury. Her rage caused her voice to quaver. "I repeatedly told you not to bother. You think you got played? *Fuck you!* You played *yourself* for a fool, Quinn."

Grim satisfaction curled Sammy's lips as she stared at him, daring him to say one more goddamned thing to Annie.

But Quinn was done with the lot of them.

"So much for friendship," he muttered, turning on his heel and stalking toward the door.

"You wouldn't know friendship if it bit you in the ass, movie star," Sammy retorted.

Unease settled around the edges of Quinn's brain. Like he'd done or said the wrong thing. But he hadn't misheard. They were the ones making up lies and taking a wrecking ball to his well-ordered life.

He was almost to the door when it occurred to him there might be a way to verify the truth. Returning to the bed, Quinn never took his eyes off Annie. She sat paralyzed under his glare.

"Who's Serena's father?"

"No. I'm not doing this. You can't claim bullshit, call me a liar, then demand facts, Quinn. You can go to hell."

"Annie, I am not going to ask again. Start talking. *Now!*"

"Oh for God's sake. Just tell him, sissy!" Sammy said. "It's not like he'll believe you, anyway."

"It isn't my place to say," Annie said, stubborn to the last.

His hand sliced the air separating them. "Give me a damned break already. You detonated your truth bomb, *sweetheart.*" He couldn't help the viciousness he was feeling. If Hailey had cheated, he wanted to know whose ass to kick. "Shrapnel is everywhere. Fires burning. What's one more nugget of information?"

Cupping her palms over her eyes, she took a deep breath, then another. When she lowered her arms, she looked defeated, but Quinn was too upset to care.

"No."

He was sure he hadn't heard correctly. *"Pardon?"* he asked, incredulous.

"I said, no. Look, I was mad. I shouldn't have spoken about something I couldn't..." She paused and grimaced. "I don't know if what I suspect is one-hundred-percent accurate, and I am not going to say anything else."

Quinn stalked to within an inch of her face. He loomed above her, furious beyond reason. He knew the stance would be intimidating to a tiny woman, but he didn't care. The importance of her discovery was too great. He needed to know the truth. Regardless of all her hemming and hawing, he would force her to reveal what she knew.

"Speak!" he growled.

ANNIE HAD NEVER FELT SO THREATENED. YET, BECAUSE OF WHO HE was, she knew he wouldn't physically hurt her. Or at least, she hoped he wouldn't. She continued her silence.

"Annie, *I'm not fucking around,*" he bit out. "I want an answer, and I want it now."

Heat rushed throughout her body. Desire coursed through her, making her want to grab him and pull him close, to bury her hands in his hair and crush her mouth to his. Jesus, what was it about this man that caused her sexual juices to flow when he was so oblivious to her? *How inappropriate could one person be?*

Anger was always the key to unlocking her lips. This time was no different. She was pissed at both herself *and* him. Herself for being unable to control this never-ending lust for a man who couldn't currently care less if she was run over by a bus. And at Quinn for being so insistent about her slip. Why couldn't he let it go? Why make her the one to tear his heart out?

She shot a look at Sammy, questioning what she knew. Her sister nodded.

"I suspect she was having an affair with Ty. The baby's his."

Had she whipped out a bat and hit him with it, Quinn couldn't have appeared more stunned. Whatever he had been expecting, she was certain it wasn't that.

"You're delusional," he spat. Fury vibrated across every syllable of his declaration, and if he could've slammed the door in his hurry to leave, he would have.

Sammy rushed out on his heels, probably to deliver a few choice words.

Had Quinn bothered to look back, he would have seen the agony his words had caused. He would have observed her grief well up and race down her cheeks in the form of hot tears. Witnessed her self-doubt and pain as those same tears dripped off her face to soak her hospital gown.

Coincidentally, she'd heard those words once before—*the day her husband told her about his affair with Daisy Jo and informed her he was leaving.* Charlie had told her she was delusional on that horrible night a year and a half ago. He'd pointed out her lack of friends due to her "gift." Relished rubbing it in that she scared everyone around her and no one wanted to be anywhere near her. Certainly not *him* when he couldn't find a private moment with his own thoughts or feelings.

They'd been friends as well as lovers. But slowly, over the years, Charlie had pulled away. He'd become less concerned with her feelings, and when he vented, he didn't bother to speak with anything resembling tact. What he thought flew out of his mouth, and the words *"you're delusional,"* with their coating of disgust, had been the worst.

And now, it had happened again. At thirty-three, Annie told

herself she should have known better. Even her own mother thought she had her head in the clouds most days. It might have been mentioned a time or two that she was too far *out there* for normal people. The deterioration of every relationship she'd had was because of her ability.

Yet somehow, Quinn's words hurt so much worse than Charlie's ever had.

But perhaps both men were correct.

She *was* delusional. She saw things as she wished them to be, not as they were. Tried to take people at face value, but always ended up with egg on her face for believing in them.

As of today, it was all going to change. From this day forward, she would no longer be the person who tried to heal everyone else's emotional pain. She would no longer subject herself to the hurt and rejection. The time was at hand to live life for herself.

Fuck everyone else.

Determined to find a Zen state of existence by the time the morning dawned, Annie inserted her earbuds and allowed her playlist to take her away. Her new plan would be to walk, work out a schedule for her PT, and get the hell out of this fucking hospital.

When she saw Trace again, she'd tell him she wanted a new room. One that was private and where no one could find her. Not murderers. Not Quinn. Especially not Quinn, because right now, David Rice would be doing her a fucking favor if he gave her a lethal injection.

Though, why bother to move? It wasn't as if Quinn would be dropping back by for a visit. She wouldn't see him again. Not after she'd made it plain she thought his fiancée was a ho. Along with the therapy exercises, perhaps she could learn exercises in zipping her damned mouth. She had to stop telling people what they didn't want to hear.

It was a long afternoon of berating herself before she finally succumbed to exhaustion.

She jolted awake, disoriented by the inky night sky outside her window. The activity outside her door wasn't its normal daily shuffle, but it wasn't as quiet as the midnight hour was. Not so late then.

With a quick glance at the tray table, she registered that the manila envelope was missing.

Someone, probably Sammy, taken the file on David for reasons of her own.

Her mind began a rousing round-robin game of what-ifs.

What if she'd slept through Dastardly Dave's murder attempt? Would she have taken her secrets to the grave? Would Quinn be happily awaiting the child he thought was his? What if she'd just held her tongue when Trace was prodding her? Would Quinn be with her, whiling away the long, lonely hours?

Refusing to feel sorry for herself, Annie opened a reading app. Yet after scrolling through her recent online book purchases and seeing Happy Annie's optimistic booklist, Surly, Down-in-the-Dumps Annie scowled. A romance novel would make her vomit and self-help books were a joke.

What she wanted most was to confide in a friend, but it was obvious the walls of this hospital had ears. Annie and Quinn had found that out the hard way. Keeping her own council was best at present. As the ideas for a way to pass the time shifted in her mind like a kaleidoscope, the main one that stuck was writing or journaling.

Perhaps she'd take a page from her sister's book and begin a career as an author. She could tackle a different genre than Sammy and create intricate murder mysteries where everyone died in the end. It would be a great way to satisfy her bloodlust. There were plenty of people in her life to base the main characters on. The longer she sat there, the more the idea gained merit.

Whipping open her laptop, Annie started to type. The story seemed to take a life of its own. She scarcely noticed the hospital staff as they checked her vitals or the food tray when it was delivered. She continued to write throughout the night, pouring her frustration into the murder of the main male character. That he bore a striking resemblance to Quinn was not a coincidence.

Asshat!

It was doubtful her plot was CSI-proof, but so what?

People had to die.

Painful, tragic deaths.

She wrote until she was exhausted and emotionally purged.

Finally, she dosed off.

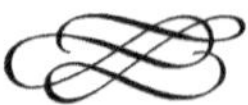

CHAPTER 29

*W*hen James arrived at the hotel early the next morning, Quinn was waiting in the far corner of the lobby. He'd heard what had gone down, and although he felt sympathy for the shitstorm about to hit the actor, he wasn't in any way happy with how Quinn had treated Annie. Had Sammy not already called him to tell him Quinn had discovered information on Annie's attacker, James would've been a helluva lot more surprised to see him.

However, he'd hoped Quinn would take the hint and move on, because he knew what his sister didn't—the actor would break her fucking heart, if he hadn't already. Annie wasn't capable of living in Quinn's world even should he decide to cast aside his bitch of a fiancée, which Jamie very much doubted he'd do.

"What the fuck do you want?" James asked, crossing his arms to show he wasn't happy with the visit.

"To talk, if you can take your head out of your ass for a minute," Quinn replied. His expression was forbidding, but James didn't give two fucks about the man's temper.

"Don't you have a girlfriend to visit or something?" Sure, he was taunting him, but he was a Holt, and dickhead comments were built into his DNA.

"Don't you have a house to go build or something?" Quinn snapped back.

"Not today. Today, I intend to comfort my sister. Apparently, some fuckwad ruined her life." He paused for the count of five. "That means you, in case you're too stupid to understand."

In response, Quinn linked his hands behind his head and yawned like he had nowhere to be in a hurry.

James nearly laughed. It was such a Holt move.

"Wow, you boys should just take out your dicks and measure them. Biggest one wins," Sammy said as she joined them.

Humor won out, and James hugged his youngest sister. "Nice. I'm telling mom you said *dicks*. She'll want your mouth washed out with soap."

"Pfft. As if." She strolled over and eyed Quinn with distaste, as if he smelled like three-day-old athlete's socks. "To what do we owe this unsolicited visit?"

James opened his mouth to answer, but was cut off by Quinn. "It seems your family has an inability to mind their own fucking business, so I thought I'd repay the favor."

Sammy's twinkling gaze turned toward James. "Is that so?"

He narrowed his eyes in warning. She was up to something, and he could feel it in his bones.

"I seem to recall you never wanted to talk to any of us again less than an hour ago," she said to Quinn, tapping her chin as if trying to remember.

James cast a contemplative look between Sammy and a scowling Quinn. What was her endgame here? God, he hoped it wasn't to push the guy at Annie. It would be the worst thing possible for her with her gift.

"I still don't. But if the threat against your sister is real, don't you think the information I have is useful to you?" Quinn taunted.

"It is real. Annie's not a liar like the women you're used to."

Sammy's ice-blue eyes would've frozen a polar bear. "Jamie, why don't you go find coffee for us."

"And why would I do that when I've got a fresh cup and you're carrying two?" he asked dryly.

"So you and the movie star don't argue like wild dogs over a fresh kill?" she retorted with no little humor.

Her good-natured rebuke was enough to shame James. He'd been acting like an ass in his attempt to protect Annie, and his sisters were perceptive enough to figure it out. Fuck all if he didn't hate being called out. He glared but finally conceded defeat. Sammy's triumphant expression irritated the ever-loving piss out of him.

"Fine. I'll behave."

"Actually, I want to address what I've uncovered, if you'd care to stick around." To Sammy, Quinn said, "The envelope you stole from Annie's tray table, if I'm not mistaken." He gestured to the curled manila folder sticking out of Sammy's bag.

She shrugged off her guilt, took a coffee cup from the carrier she was holding, and handed the other to Quinn. "I knew you'd be here," she told him when he raised a questioning brow. "Continue."

"I had the idea to turn a few of the lingering reporters into investigators. They came up with the name of Annie's hooked-nose assailant."

James's heart kicked up its pace in his eagerness to settle the score. "Sammy mentioned you'd given them information when she called me. Who is it, and what are we dealing with?"

"David Rice. A local."

"And the address?" he ground out.

"Won't do you any good, James," Quinn said as Sammy passed the information to him. "His trailer has been abandoned, and he's a ghost. I hired a professional investigator today to see if he can find him."

"Annie would have your ass for that," James informed him with a snort.

With a wry smile on her face, Sammy nodded her agreement. "She'd say it's too much, Quinn. And really, this isn't your problem."

"I'm not going to leave her as a sitting target, especially when she can't help herself." His reply lacked warmth, and James could hear the underlying surliness.

Yep, Sammy's suspicion, the one she'd shared with James during their phone conversation, was most likely correct. The actor was as invested in Annie as she was in him. A fucking recipe for disaster, if anyone bothered to ask James. But they hadn't and wouldn't. When the time came for Annie to heal her broken heart, he'd be there for her if she needed to talk.

James bent the tabs and opened the envelope, carefully memorizing all the relevant details. His gaze locked with Quinn's, and he refused to speak out loud what he'd just learned. Good ol' David was a serial offender but a smart one the local police had never been able to nail. Charges never stuck, because witnesses tended to disappear before trial.

"Annie tells me you communicate with the dead," Quinn said softly. "Perhaps, if you actually can, you'll find the evidence you need to put this guy away."

Carefully, James pushed the papers and photos back into the envelope, trying like hell to temper his rage and terror for Annie's sake. Handing the folder to Quinn, he nodded his thanks. "Keep me in the loop with the investigator, please. And let us know his fee. I'll cover it."

With a tight smile, James hugged Sammy and strode out the door. Maybe he'd renovate Annie's bathroom as he thought about his next move. He sure as shit needed to smash something, and that green seventies tile might be the thing since David Rice's head wasn't available.

OVER THE NEXT TWO DAYS, TRACE CHECKED ON HER IN THE EARLY morning, during his rounds, and once during her scheduled cast-removal appointment. He remained professional, and his cold disapproval hurt.

There were no more card games to pass the down times of his shift. Quinn had made himself scarce. No midnight margarita parties, hot chocolate, script readings, or movie marathons. Her siblings had become scarce as well, and Annie was lonelier than she had ever been in her life.

She wanted her dog.

At least, Tink would've been able to help ease the aching sadness. The pictures and text updates she received from Sammy and Michael showed Tink was doing well at her lake house, but the images hurt her heart even more. It seemed no one needed or wanted her.

When she wasn't making use of her rebuilt lower body, Annie tried to keep herself busy with genealogy work, but the excitement she usually experienced when she made a new discovery was gone. Quinn's tree was abandoned. Someday, when she could look at his name again without feeling as if her heart was being used for target practice, she'd finish the project and send it to his mother. For now, that gift idea seemed stupid.

Pausing after the third circuit around her room, Annie wiped the sweat from her brow with the back of her wrist. One more, and she'd take a break. Then maybe she'd be too tired to replay the events in her mind, and she'd get some blessed sleep.

"That's enough for today," Trace told Annie from the doorway. With his arms crossed, he rested one shoulder against the frame.

She almost smiled, but bit it back. Just because Trace appeared more laid back, didn't mean he was or that he currently viewed her in a charitable frame of mind. For all she knew, he could be nursing a grudge.

"You're like a fucking ninja. I never heard you come in." Giving in to the wisdom of his command, she inched her walker around and painfully scooted toward the bed, grateful when he joined her and hovered until her agonizingly slow progress got her to her destination. "I'm glad you called a halt. I didn't want to embarrass myself, but I'd have cried if I got stuck on the other side of the room and had to call for help."

"You maneuvered the space well." With a tap to her walker, he said, "Just remember to hold onto the handles when you lower yourself onto the bed or into a chair."

Seeing her grimace, he smiled.

The sight of his compassion brought an ache to Annie's chest. She missed their friendly banter. "I will," she promised.

"It won't be forever. You'll be zipping around before you know it."

"Thanks, Doc."

After he left, Annie went right back to stressing about her scheduled release the next day. Yes, Quinn had mentioned a deposit on the apartment in his complex, but she no longer knew if that was an option, and when she'd inquired, she was told no other units were available.

Rehab was going to be hell. Oh, she knew her eventual recovery would turn out well. Sammy had assured her of that. What had her worried was the pain, healing, and physical therapy she'd endure. There was a lot to consider for when she was finally released. Who was going to help her initially? Groceries and meals she could have delivered, but she needed someone to clean her house by her standards in addition to a dog walker.

She lined up the items on her tray, largest to smallest, then decided she'd like them better with the tallest item in the center. Annie was on her third tray rearrangement when Quinn knocked on her door.

"It felt odd not stopping by and bringing your meals," he told her by way of greeting.

"I thought we agreed you were going to be a less frequent visitor." She sounded bitchy, but she couldn't stop the words from pouring out of her.

His mouth pinched, and his hard stare made her squirm inside. She'd be damned if she backed down, though.

"Do you want me to go?" he asked.

Did she detect a softening in his attitude?

With a muffled sigh, she shrugged. "Not really. And the hospital food isn't so bad. Sometimes Sammy brings me lunch."

When he didn't reply, she started her fourth tray arrangement, sneaking glances at him as his eyes followed her every move.

"I can only imagine your place must be spotless."

Drumming up the courage, she asked, "What are you doing here, Quinn?"

"I wanted to drop these by." He waved a set of keys and placed them on the nightstand. "I signed a lease for your apartment. It's three months with the option to extend it if needed."

"You shouldn't have done that. Your debt to me is over, remember?"

"I know what I said." He didn't choose his normal spot at the end of her bed, instead sitting in the visitor's chair, with his back to the window. "But the apartment was before…"

"Yeah, okay. Thanks." Christ, this was awkward. She hated how stilted their conversation was. Hated how stranger-like he'd become. It was nothing more than she deserved. "I'll write you a check. For that and for all the food—"

"I don't give a shit about the money, Annie," he snapped. Closing his eyes, he shook his head. "Sorry."

"No worries."

"Can I ask you a question and get an honest answer?"

She wanted to say she'd always been truthful, but there was such a thing as lies of omission.

"Sure."

Interlocking his hands in front of him, he stared down at the giant fist he'd made. "You said Ty and Hailey slept together. Were you saying it to hurt me, or do you believe it?"

Her heart ached for him, but she wasn't into self-torture, and she steeled herself for the conversation about to take place.

"It's from a recent vision." After toppling her stacked items in the center of the tray, she rested against the pillows and met his chilly gaze. Yeah, she'd only imagined the softening earlier. Angry Quinn was only there for answers. The apartment keys were an information payoff.

"I'm not infallible," she said softly. "I make mistakes quite frequently. Misinterpret things."

"How long have you known?"

"Not long enough for it to matter. It came to me while I slept, and I was trying to process it. To decide if it was real or just a vivid dream."

"But you don't have those often, do you? Vivid dreams? Not without them signifying something else."

Phrased as such, his questions were more statements of fact. His mood hadn't softened, and his energy grew more aggressive the longer she took to respond, though he hid it well behind a polite mask. He knew her enough to know she couldn't deny it. Knew she believed what she'd seen.

"Either way, you'll have to discuss this with him. Anything else is supposition on my part."

"Tell me everything."

"You're awfully demanding."

His brows shot up, and a hint of dark amusement came and went. "*I* am?"

Scowling, she sat straighter and reached for her tray, but he moved it away and shifted to the edge of her bed. Her heart thudded, and it felt like a manual transmission in an old junker, shifting and clunking hard at frequent intervals, stalling out at stops.

"The vision, Annie," he said in a low, lethal tone. "I want to know everything."

As she relayed the details, Quinn fiddled with his phone, as if taking notes. It sickened her to think he was collecting evidence of any sort to use against his brother. Since Hailey wasn't going to wake up anytime soon, if at all, there was no one else for him to focus his vengeful energy on.

"That's it."

"To be clear, it was Ty, and not me, in bed with her?" His mossy eyes sharpened as he watched her. "Not some twisted fantasy in your mind."

Heat surged up her chest, and she wanted to spew the lime jello from lunch. "If you think seeing you with another woman is a fantasy, you're cracked."

His gaze narrowed. "Wanted it to be you, huh?"

"Fuck off," she snapped, thoroughly disconcerted by his sudden seductive tone, but angry as hell at his goading.

One side of his mouth curled, and for the first time since she'd met him, he looked cruel.

"There was a football-shaped birthmark on the man's right ass cheek," she stated coolly. "From what I remember of your naked ass on screen, you don't possess one."

He paled, and his lips tightened into a straight line. "I've heard enough."

"Really? Don't want me to detail the dick penetrating her p—"

"Enough, Annie!" He was breathing heavily, as if unable to drag in air. The high color in his face wasn't from embarrassment.

It was murderous rage.

CHAPTER 30

The next day, Quinn was running late for a conference call to discuss an upcoming film he'd contracted, prior to the hiatus. After all these weeks with no change in Hailey's condition, he'd decided he could no longer put his life on hold. Hailey's sister, Jeri, had promised to visit Hailey regularly and give him updates whenever Quinn was out of town on set.

In no way was his decision based on the fact he couldn't bear to be at the hospital anymore. Not at all because his friendship with Annie was a flaming pile of shit and his only feeling for Hailey was pure loathing.

He was about to pull out of the hospital parking lot when his cell rang.

Ty.

Quinn hadn't been able to confront his brother yet. After he pieced together the remaining facts, he would, but for the moment, he had to draw on his talent and pretend everything was fine. Failing to fully contain his resentment, his tone was cold when he answered.

"What do you want, Ty?"

"You okay?"

"Fine. Busy. What's up?"

"Have you seen the media blitz today?" Ty asked.

With little prompting, the muscles in the back of Quinn's neck tightened. "No, why?"

"I think you should."

"What now?" His stomach plunged through the SUV seat.

"You aren't going to like it, man."

"Jesus, spit it out already, Ty."

"It's an article about Annie. And *you*."

The air left his lungs.

"There are some intimate conversations quoted by an unnamed source."

Sick with dread, Quinn switched to speakerphone and typed a list of the so-called entertainment sites carrying the article into his notes app. "Thanks."

"I can spin this however you'd like, but you need to find out what she's told them."

"She?"

"Annie. She's the only one who could've given this type of info to the press."

Denial was Quinn's first instinct, but he tamped down the protest. He needed to read the story first. "I'll call you back."

Blowing off his meeting, he sat and scrolled through the local paper, Sagefield Chronicle, along with other bigger-named papers. Even The National Star had a sleazy version of the tale.

The story alluded to an affair between Annie and him, suggesting their meeting at the airport had sparked love at first sight. The report quoted anonymous hospital staff members stating he'd had a tree brought in for Annie while ignoring his own fiancée's barren room. It went on to detail conversations he'd had with Annie in private. A picture of the two of them reading scripts and another of him smiling down into her glowing face was captioned with some stupid, syrupy comment. The reporter even went so far as to interview Hailey's parents.

There was nothing complimentary about Quinn in their opinion.

Sonofabitch!

Ty was correct. Either Annie or one of her family had caused the media maelstrom.

Betrayal cut deep. Quinn's appetite abandoned him, and he left his vehicle long enough to dump his breakfast in the trash. Heart heavy, he drove to his penthouse. Once inside, he paced off his steam.

The night before, Sammy had dumped Tink on him with the excuse that Sophie and Michael were down with a bug and she couldn't take care of one more thing.

How was Quinn supposed to reject a helpless dog?

Now, Tink watched him from where she sat, head on her paws, on his sofa.

"Your owner did this," he told her, trying to keep the accusation from his voice. "How could she? We were friends."

Her only response was a sad, heartfelt whine.

"That's what I get for trusting a stranger."

Annoyed at his own gullibility, he called Ty. "I need you to squash this. I also need you to contact Annie and get one of her family members to take her dog back."

"I can handle the dog problem a lot easier than the other, but I'm on it."

"Thanks. I guess I trusted the wrong person, once again."

"Kwee…"

His brother cut off whatever he'd intended to say, and Quinn got the impression it would've kicked his world off its axis. But he needed to ask all the same. If Ty confessed, they might have a chance to repair the damage.

"What is it, Ty?" he asked tiredly.

"I only wanted to say I'm sorry this is happening to you. You don't deserve it."

Not what he was going to say originally, but Quinn was weirdly glad for the reprieve. "Thanks. See if you can head this off. If you can't, maybe we can minimize the damage. In the meantime, I need to call the Newberrys."

Two hours later, Quinn stalked through the corridor of the hospital. The judgmental stares infuriated him. It wasn't as if he wasn't used to his share of attention, but this type of negative scrutiny, where everyone was waiting for him to take one step out of bounds, shredded his last nerve.

He didn't bother to stop by Annie's room, instead heading straight for Hailey's. He sat amid the massive flower arrangements Paige had ordered, and stewed. These bouquets were over the top and made him look foolish. Sickened by the overpowering scent of roses, he wanted to throw them in the garbage.

Soul-weary, he pressed his forehead into his palms.

"I thought I'd find you here."

Quinn lifted his head to find Michael right outside the doorway. "What do you want?"

"May I?"

"I thought you were sick. And since when have any of you bothered with my feelings?"

Perhaps he was being harsh, but he was hurt by Annie's part in all of this.

"I can go."

Quinn studied the blond man. He was quieter than most. Much more quiet than the family he'd married into. Michael was a watcher. Quinn recognized the type. Actors needed to make a continuous study of those around them, perfecting mannerisms and emotions.

With a jerk of his head, he indicated his assent.

Michael entered and shut the door behind him. Nodding toward the four massive floral arrangements, he said, "Isn't this overkill?"

"Not my call. My assistant was trying to overcompensate for the article."

"I figured as much. You don't seem the type to do foolish gestures."

"What do you want, Michael?" Quinn asked wearily.

"I was in to see Annie this morning. She looks pale and sad."

"Does she?" His words were cold, but he didn't have it in him to be nice. Especially after she dragged his name through the mud.

"You should talk to her," Michael suggested softly. "She's hurt by this, too."

"Maybe she should've thought about that before offering up everything to the press," Quinn snapped, standing to confront him.

"She didn't. You *know* she didn't."

"I don't know anything."

"I think you do, Quinn. In your heart, I think you do." Michael sighed heavily. "I've known this family for going on thirteen years. Not one of them would betray a trust. Especially not Annie."

"Pardon me if I don't take your word for it," he sneered. But Quinn had to give the guy credit; Michael remained calm in the face of his wrath.

"You don't have to. I only ask you to search your heart. A woman who risks her life to save others? Yeah, she's not the type to be spiteful or attention seeking."

Quinn stilled as the words sank in. Although he desperately wanted Michael to be right, no one else had been privy to their private conversations.

"They reported things I've only ever said to her. How do you explain that?" he asked hoarsely.

"I can't. But maybe you should ask Annie, and not condemn her without proof." Michael shifted to gaze down at Hailey's still form. Nothing in his expression revealed his thoughts. Finally, he faced Quinn again. "You should keep in mind that you're in a public building. There's no way to know how much can be overheard at any given moment."

"Either way, it's better if I don't see her again."

"Maybe. But the very least you can do is give her a proper apology and say goodbye."

Quinn shook his head. "If I see her again, it will add fuel to the fire."

"Fair enough."

As Michael turned to leave, Quinn called his name. "The dog? Will one of you be able to care for Tink?"

"Of course." Michael smiled, but it never reached his eyes. The scar on his cheek made his expression harder than it probably would've been without it. "Something tells me you'll never be convinced of her innocence. It's a damned shame. Remember, Annie's family has a lot of things they don't want public." He shook his head and gave Quinn one last nugget to chew on. "Do you honestly believe, with their abilities, they wouldn't be subject to a shit-ton of bad press if anyone found out? You might want to think about *that* before you accuse her of callously setting you up to spill your secrets."

He'd given Quinn a lot to mull over. And for the next few hours, he did just that. He didn't like the conclusions. While Michael had valid points, there was still no way for anyone other than Annie to know what they'd discussed.

CHAPTER 31

"Is this your revenge?"

A device clanked on the hospital tray, jolting Annie awake.

Quinn.

And his sour mood hadn't sweetened since his previous visit. His entire vibe screamed accusatory.

"Go away." She flipped him off and shut her eyes to block him out.

A day had passed since the article was published, which was exactly four days after he'd initially accused her of conspiring with Sammy to ruin his love life and two since he'd left in an aneurysm-inspiring rage.

Five days too many of brutal self-reflection. Annie hated herself and practically everyone else on the planet who drew air.

"I asked you a question," Quinn said, exasperation heavy in his tone.

"Fuck off."

Michael had detailed his conversation, unknowingly wounding her in the process. To think Quinn believed she would offer up the intimate details of his visits pureed her heart, leaving only sludge for an organ.

She'd half suspected their confrontation would've taken place sooner, but she was happy for the reprieve. It had given her time to lecture herself on lost causes. Harden up. Gird her loins.

Sure, the coward in Annie had wanted to keep her head low and sleep her life away, but the fighter in her wanted to flay him alive at the injustice of it all. He was convinced she'd wronged him. And there was no coming back from that.

"Annie."

As his voice washed over her, his emotions were a churning tide. But his standard warmth was lacking, and she knew whatever barriers she'd erected weren't high or thick enough. They never would be. A sense of raw pain burned the back of her throat, and all the words she wanted to scream were held there by the thinnest of threads. Unable to look at him without losing control, she picked up a pen.

"I need to speak with you."

"No, you really don't." She clicked the pen off and set it parallel to the notebook she'd been using to write out her PT exercises.

"Did you…" He cleared his throat. "Did you speak to the press? Be honest with me, please."

Rage fired up every single one of her cells. The blaze engulfed her, burning her to the point she couldn't reply even if she wanted to. She aligned her laptop with the rest of the items on the tray.

"Annie."

Her eyes scanned the hard surface to avoid his probing stare.

Something was off with her arrangement.

She picked up her water bottle and wiped the condensation with the sheet's edge before she set it back down. Next, she removed the spiral notebook and pen. When Quinn called her name a third time, she moved the laptop to the center of the tabletop.

He gripped her wrists to stop her fussing.

"Why did you do it?" he demanded.

She jerked free and shoved at his offending hands. "Go. *Away!*"

"I trusted you," he spat out, his temper finally letting loose. "I trusted you, and you…"

His accusations stung. Damn if they didn't. Her gaze flew to his. "Get out of my room, and don't come back."

"I want an explanation," he ground out.

"And I want to stab you in the neck with this pen for believing I would talk to anyone about what you've told me," she retorted, throwing it at his stupid head.

His eyes grew marginally warmer, and he gently wiped at the tears she hadn't realized she cried.

She slapped at him like a pesky fly. "Don't touch me."

Irritation and something more elemental flared to life in his eyes.

She caught her breath, waiting for him to act on whatever urge he was experiencing. Wanting him to. *Needing* him to. Her entire body tightened with that need. Never in her life had she challenged another person to defy her demand and lay claim to her. Not as she mentally did with Quinn. Apparently, some long-dormant and hereto-unknown desire wanted him to go all Captain Caveman, tug her hair back, and ravish her.

But that fucking desire could pack right the hell up and go back to where it came from. She had about a hundred problems, and Quinn was at least ninety of them.

His disturbingly hot gaze dropped to her mouth, and her tongue flew out to wet her suddenly dry lips. He visibly shook himself, breaking free of the spell he'd created over them both.

"I'm sorry."

Her jaw became unhinged. "For what?"

"For touching you without your permission."

Yeah, okay, there was that. Disappointment doused the flames of her rage, leaving only sadness in its place. She'd wanted him to apologize for *doubting* her. For believing she would purposely set out to hurt him. Not for losing his cool and giving in to his instincts. Once again, tears blurred her vision.

Bugger her blind.

If he didn't leave soon, she'd be a sobbing mess.

"No worries," she said, wincing when her voice cracked. "Now, if you don't mind, I have work to do."

"You didn't speak to the press, did you, Annie?" he said softly. Knowingly.

Not quite over her snit, she snorted. "Give the man a gold star."

"Jesus, I'm an idiot," he muttered as he plopped down on the edge of her bed and scrubbed his hands over his face.

She traced the apple on her computer, neither confirming nor denying his comment. But if pressed, she'd *definitely* confirm it.

"But if *you* didn't, how the hell did that reporter get such detailed information? I can't wrap my head around it."

She let the silence fill the room.

"I'm sorry, Annie."

His sincerity begged her forgiveness. But she couldn't even look at him. Her feelings were too raw to converse. Although she knew she loved him, she hadn't realized the extent of it until the moment he'd said her name today. Friendship was pointless, and it was far better if he left, never to return. Better if he believed the worst of her so he'd never contact her again. So one day, she might think back on this with a laugh at all the silly misunderstandings between a stupidly handsome movie star and a hermit who lived in the past.

But she didn't really want that, either.

"Can you give me an idea how long you're going to stay mad at me?" he asked as he grasped her wrist to hold her palm against his cheek. "I miss my friend."

Ah, hell!

The man must've spent half his life in charm school to possess those mad skills.

"We're not friends," she muttered sourly, proud she could muster some surliness and strength of will.

He straightened and gently rested her hand on the blanket. Features arranged in a polite mask, he said, "My mistake."

Her hurt burst from her. "If you viewed me as a friend, you would've asked me straight away about those goddamned articles.

You wouldn't have believed the worst of me, Quinn. You blew in and used me to occupy your time while you waited for Hailey to wake up. Our supposed friendship was only to ease your fucking boredom."

"That is so far from the truth it's ridiculous. I'm here because…"

"Because why?" She lifted a brow in challenge.

His frown deepened.

"Yeah, I thought as much," she scoffed.

Quinn shoved aside the tray table she'd begun rearranging and leaned over her, trapping her against the mattress. "I'm here because I like you, Annie. Because despite the circumstantial evidence to the contrary, I *do* believe you." His minty breath caressed her hot face, and his eyes—those soulful, glorious green eyes—bore into hers. "I'm sorry. Tell me how many times I have to say it before you believe me." Shifting, he gathered her close. "Please forgive me," he whispered into her hair.

Being held in his arms for the first time felt like heaven, and she never wanted him to let go.

Incapable of resisting, she returned his embrace, pressing her hands into the muscles of his back and squeezing. Regardless of the reason, she'd savor the feeling. It was likely the only hug they'd share.

Fuck all! She was such a sucker.

A light knock sounded at the door, breaking them apart. Quinn took an extra few seconds to grab a tissue and dry the last of her tears before he dropped a light, lingering kiss on her cheek.

"Did you lock it?" she asked incredulously.

He shrugged, and she watched in amazement as color crept up his neck. "I didn't want our conversation to be interrupted."

"Dude! Now you've done it. Someone is going to report we were bumping nasties."

His laughter flooded the room, and everything was bizarrely right between them. Or mostly right. He didn't love her, but he liked her, and she had to believe she could live with that.

PART III

CHAPTER 32

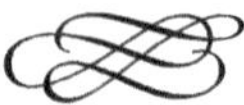

*I*n his kitchen, Quinn fixed a hot chocolate in addition to his standard morning coffee before he realized what he was doing. Over the last week and a half, it had become natural to sneak down to Annie's for breakfast. To simply sit with her, talking about anything and laughing at everything. To walk Tink at regular intervals whenever Annie had a difficult time after a particularly rough therapy session or sometimes in the early mornings after she first woke up.

He headed out the door with both drinks in hand. On the off chance she needed him today, he intended to help her.

Recalling her dry jokes always brought a smile to his lips. He was honest enough to admit to himself that he missed her when he couldn't see her every day. The truth was, he enjoyed her openness and warped sense of humor. And she'd forgiven him his ridiculous accusations.

She was kind, his Annie.

Coffee cup frozen halfway to his mouth, he swore.

His Annie?

Where the hell had *that* drivel come from?

Quinn looked from paper to-go cup, filled with hot chocolate, to the trash bin by the elevator door and debated tossing it. Developing deeper feelings for Annie was a continual complication he didn't need.

He'd heard her admit to Trace that she loved him. Did she sit around all day, weaving romantic fantasies about the two of them? Did he want to feed into her feelings by continuing their friendship, or should he let it die a natural death as he got on with his life? If he no longer visited her, would she eventually cease her silly crush and return to reality?

His good mood went south.

It absolutely had nothing to do with how good she'd felt in his arms the day he questioned her involvement in the article's release. Or the fact that in holding her, he'd experienced a wholeness for the very first time in his life. Or that she was the one other person who understood his grievance with his brother, who he'd *still* avoided confronting and who he talked to as infrequently as possible for fear he'd lose his goddamned mind and say regrettable things.

Fuck it.

He'd check on her once more. But that was it. After that, he needed to finalize the travel arrangements for his next project and get going. She'd have to hire a dog walker. In fact, he'd do a search later.

And wasn't that the same thing he told himself every day since she'd moved into his complex? But he was repeatedly stalling the film studio to the point they threatened to fire him and hire another actor. Quinn was in breach of his contract, but he couldn't work up the enthusiasm to give a shit.

When he knocked on her door, there was no answer. Frowning because it was unusual for her not to be awake at this time of the morning, Quinn keyed in the code and eased the door open.

"Annie?" he called softly.

Tink padded over and greeted him with a down-dog stretch and a poof of gas.

"Nice," he muttered. "I used to get kisses from you."

Rounding the corner from the foyer, he found Annie asleep on the couch with her computer precariously close to falling from where it rested on her abdomen.

He figured she'd gotten lost in her research again, as she was wont to do.

Setting the drinks down on the coffee table, he picked up her laptop. The least he could do was charge it for her. No one liked waking up to a dead battery. As he was closing the top, the words on the screen captured his attention.

After getting comfortable in an armchair, he propped his feet up, sipped his coffee, and began reading. He was lost in the final chapter when she gasped, indicating she was awake and more than a little outraged to find him reading her work.

Sheepishly, he met her stormy blue gaze.

Her expressive eyes seemed to say everything they couldn't vocalize. Yes, she was irritated that he'd invaded her privacy by reading what she'd written, but her pique ran deeper. He couldn't recall if she'd been grumpy upon waking, in the past.

"So you decided to kill me off, huh?" he finally asked, gesturing to the screen.

"Who said it was you?"

The struggle not to laugh was real, and he let his raised brows do the talking.

Her nose crinkled, and she shrugged, knowing she was busted. "I was expanding on what I wrote over the week you refused to speak to me."

"Death by honey and fire ants? You don't think that's a little brutal?" He smothered his laughter by rubbing his hand back and forth across his mouth.

"Nope." Her chin was in the air and her challenging attitude firmly in place.

"Well, *I* do. I never pegged you for a cruel woman, Annie. And my punishment was much more severe than Nurse Hatchet Face's. It's unjust," he teased.

"I had to create a murder that wouldn't lead back to me... uh, I mean to the protagonist. These CSI units have all those high-tech tools to crack a case. I figured fire ants would eat all the evidence," she reasoned with a shrug.

He nodded his understanding, then proceeded to point out the obvious. "What about the gallon of honey she purchased? There would be a transaction history."

"Dammit! You're right." Annie grabbed for the laptop he held toward her and typed out a note in the margin of her current work in progress. "Addie's going to have to dress in disguise, drive to a small-town beekeeper, and pay cash."

Quinn pursed his lips in an effort not to laugh. She was taking this murder plot of hers very seriously. It was no coincidence that the main character was named Addie any more than the victim, modeled after him, was named Quill.

"Better," he said with a nod. "I mean, not very solid, if it came to it, but doable. You'll need an alibi and a way to bypass street cams."

Wicked amusement danced in her eyes, and a smirk curled her berry-colored lips. It wasn't long before they were grinning like idiots. Laughter followed immediately after. When their hilarity abated, he shifted seats, settling next to her.

Leaning into her, he placed his lips next to the delicate shell of her ear. "You know, there are far more pleasurable things to do with honey."

She stilled, and the ratcheting tension in his body matched hers.

Where the hell had that come from?

Hadn't he lectured himself about leading her on?

What the fuck was wrong with him lately?

Reaching down, he clasped her hand and threaded his fingers with hers. He needed to convince her he was sincere about his upcoming apology, and she'd know it was true if she could feel it through their connection. What he hadn't expected was for her to withdraw her hand. He looked up sharply.

She turned away.

"I'm sorry, Annie. Truly."

His somber, husky voice created a riot of emotions in her, and she had the overwhelming urge to cry. She sucked in her lower lip, fighting to stave off the pesky tears. Why the hell was she always a basket case around him? She hadn't cried nearly as much when Charlie left her. Or at all, really. By the time her ex was history, her only feeling was relief. Good riddance to that douche canoe.

"Yeah, no worries, Quinn. But if you don't mind, I'm kind of tired from the all-nighter."

Please, God, any excuse to get him to leave! If she appeared vulnerable in front of him again, he'd think she needed a therapist.

Concentrating on the to-go cups in front of her, she turned the design so they aligned in front.

Annie sensed his unspoken, *"What the fuck?"* but she could no longer deal with the constant turmoil. She was too raw from it all. Too in love with him. Maybe she should've gone back to her house in the country, after all.

Having Quinn treat her like his buddy was sheer torture. But pity or teasing her about her unrequited love? That she couldn't—*wouldn't*—tolerate.

"Annie, look at me," he demanded softly. "I'm not going anywhere until you do."

Furious, she glared at him. "There. I've looked at you. Now please leave."

Frowning, he glared back. "What the hell's the matter with you? I am trying to apologize for an inappropriate comment. The least you can do is listen."

"Jesus Christ!"

"Don't take the Lord's name in vain," he said absently, as if parroting something he'd heard all his life. "And I'm *sorry*, okay."

"Well, I don't accept your stupid apology," she snapped.

"Are you kidding me? What the fuck has you so cranky today? It's not like you."

"Maybe you don't know me as well as you think you do. Did you ever consider that?"

"Today, as a matter of fact."

His retort surprised her. Enough to jolt her out of her anger. "Really?"

"This is ridiculous, Annie. I honestly don't know why we're fighting." He lifted Tink, who'd begun to whine, and held her, cheek pressed to cheek, with both of their beloved faces toward Annie. "And we shouldn't fight in front of our child."

She laughed. "You're an idiot."

"That goes without saying." He handed Tink to Annie and threw an arm around her shoulders, laying his cheek on the crown of her head. "What's really bothering you?"

"The headlines are getting more extreme."

"Ah. So that's the real reason you don't want to be my friend? You're afraid of a little gossip?" After a quick, platonic kiss on her temple, he released her and climbed to his feet. He reached out a hand to help her up. "If they report anything about you, I'll sue them for slander."

"They already did, or have you forgotten? Do you know today's story made me out to be some wild gypsy fortune teller you're shacking up with as payment so you can talk to your fiancée on the other side?"

He grinned.

"It's not funny!" Annie forgot herself and shouted.

"It kind of is." Quinn laughed and caught her hand as she shoved his chest.

"You're an asshole," she grumbled. "It's not going to be so funny when they entangle us in a love triangle or write about us keeping Hailey in a coma to use as an incubator for our love child." Seeing his humor disappear, she nodded her head in triumph.

"I think you're getting carried away here. How did we stray so far from the main topic?"

"Because everything's a joke to you," she retorted.

"Oh, for fuck's sake." He threw up his hands. "I'm sorry, okay?"

"That's a lousy fucking apology. Shove it up your ass," she spat.

"You're being ugly and unreasonable," he growled.

"And you're being an arrogant fucking prick. Of the two of us, I like my viewpoint better."

"Someone should've washed your mouth out with soap when you were a child. Maybe you wouldn't have such a filthy vocabulary now," he said as he gathered his cup to leave.

"You know what? I'm going to revive Quill just so I can devise another torturous death. How about *that*?"

He turned to look at her in horrified disbelief. "You're insane! You know that?"

"Then why do you keep visiting me?" she taunted.

Quinn stormed away without replying.

"Don't think I'm not going to murder you again!" she hollered after his retreating back.

With nothing left to do, she sipped her hot chocolate and clicked on the television. Of course, the first channel she tuned in to was playing her favorite of all Quinn's movies, *No Limits*. Inasmuch as she loved that one, she switched the station.

Cold turkey from here on out. No more Quinn, no more love, no more pathetic relationships.

Ten of the thirteen channels had his movies running.

"What the fuck?"

Of all the days for her to watch the boob tube, she had to stumble across a marathon? Convinced cosmic powers were conspiring against her, Annie pressed the off button and glanced down at Tink.

"I suppose I should take you out to do your business, huh?"

She eyed the leash on the counter and sighed. Mornings were the hardest part of the day for her. Without exercising through a full range of motion, her back and hips tended to seize. But maybe a long walk was what she needed.

After employing her cane and limping to the kitchen counter, she rested her head on the cool surface and gritted her teeth. "Just one more minute, baby. Then, we'll go."

Annie had just picked up the leash when she heard Quinn growl, "Don't even think about it."

In the doorway, he stood, six-foot-plus of virile, irritated male.

She wanted to yell. To tell him to get bent and that she didn't need him. But in truth, she was as helpless as a newborn kitten, and her pride was in tatters.

"I can do it," she lied.

Not bothering to hide his pissy attitude, he strode over, snatched the lead from her hand, and scooped up Tink.

"Drink your hot chocolate and relax, crazy lady. I'll be back in twenty."

"Screw you."

"Wouldn't you like to?" he retorted.

Behind his back, she nodded. Maybe her surly mood had more to do with not getting laid and less to do with actual annoyance at Quinn. She should look into ordering a new BOB.

He snorted a laugh, and she met his dancing eyes in the foyer mirror.

Mortified, she flipped him off and limped toward the living room to drown her sorrows in her hot chocolate.

In the next chapter, Addie was totally killing Quill in the most horrendous way possible.

CHAPTER 33

Quinn was chopping vegetables as she entered her kitchen. When he glanced up, his moss-green eyes swept her body from her freshly combed damp hair to the tips of her bare toes. "Feel better?"

"Yes," she lied straight-faced as she bypassed the dining room for the balcony and dropped onto a patio chair.

The truth was that today's therapy had been grueling. Not only the physical aspect, but the emotional one. Everyone's judgmental eyes had been on her, and she could feel their disdain. Feel their curiosity. How could someone like her garner all Quinn Jensen's attention? What magic did she possess to lure him away from Hailey Newberry, with her supermodel looks and waif-like body?

After following her outside, he squatted in front of her. "You're a terrible liar, you know that?"

"So you've said."

"I've missed you." The honesty shone from his bright gaze. "I didn't expect to. Or at least, not as much as I have."

Three days prior, he'd flown to LA to meet with his agent and a studio rep to iron out his contract. The studio had drawn the line in the sand, and he either met with them in person or they intended to sue him. He'd had no choice but to go.

For once, Annie gave herself the freedom to trace the hard lines of his face. She nodded her understanding.

"I've missed you, too," she admitted. "More than I should've or had the right to."

"We're in a bit of a pickle, aren't we?"

"I know I am."

He laughed and shifted to kneel between her thighs. Lips barely an inch away, he said, "I'm going to kiss you. If this isn't what you want, say no right now."

Morally, it was wrong, and yet she refused to deny herself. Her curiosity propelled her forward, but the unexpected explosion of pleasure kept her anchored in the kiss. One of his large hands cradled her head as the other snuck around her waist and hauled her to the edge of the chair. His tongue swept her mouth, teasing and tantalizing in its seductive dance. He tasted of peppermint and coffee, a heady combination, and an addictive one, at that.

Needing to feel the contact of his chest with hers, she inched forward. Before she could blink, she was straddling his lap as his fingers dug into her ass, having hauled her close. She ignored the nagging discomfort in her back and hip. This was *Quinn*, and she'd waited a lifetime to feel this way.

The fingers and thumb of his hand wove into her hair, and he manipulated her head to gain access to the side of her throat. Head thrown back, she moaned in response.

"You're so fucking hot, sweetheart," he rasped in her ear.

And damned if his words didn't fire her passion all the more. Annie tilted her hips to better connect.

He hissed out a breath.

Reaching between them, she tugged up the edge of his t-shirt and ran her fingertips across the rock-hard ridges of his abdomen.

"*Good fucking duck in muck!*" Awed that anyone's body had so little fat and that muscles could be that solid, she drew back and glanced down, trying to witness the proof with her eyes.

He laughed, and the rumble traveled down to her pleasure center, making her instantly wet.

"I can't have sex with you," she blurted.

"You can't?" His voice was growly and low, as if torn between humor and frustration.

"No. You've got the body of an Olympic god. I'm… well, I'm…" At a loss for words, apparently.

"Annie, you're perfect."

Slap her twice and hand her to Mama; he meant it!

She could feel his sincerity.

His lips zeroed in on the erogenous zone beneath her ear. Soft, lingering love bites made her question her sanity. What kind of nutter turned down the opportunity to sleep with Quinn Jensen?

A banging echoed through the apartment, and they froze as they heard footsteps in the foyer.

Her horror at getting caught was mirrored on his face.

"Annie?"

She sagged against him when her sister's voice rang out.

"Oh! *Hel*-lo!" Sammy giggled as only she could. "Isn't this awkward?"

Quinn had yet to release her, and Annie was finding it difficult to let go of him, too. His gaze dipped to her lips one last time before he shifted, rising to his feet with her crushed against him. Oh, the strength it took to do that! An appreciative sigh escaped her.

"Can you stand?" The spark of humor in his tone irked her. She hated that she was the only one affected by their kiss.

Sammy snorted, and Annie shot her a glare.

"Do you mind?"

"Not at all." Her sister crossed her arms and didn't budge.

The boom of Quinn's laughter could be felt against her belly. Her grip on his neck tightened before she forced herself to release him.

"You probably want to straighten your clothes. Maintenance is on their way up about the dripping faucet," Sammy supplied helpfully.

"You're a pain in my ass," Annie growled.

"Does that mean you don't want me stopping by unannounced anymore? Perhaps you can hang a ribbon on the doorknob when you're, well, playing with Quinn's knob?"

Her sister was taking great delight in teasing her, and had anyone else been the recipient, Annie would've laughed herself sick.

"I should go," Quinn said as he smoothed down her mussed hair. Was there tenderness in his tone? She certainly imagined she saw it in his expression. "I have to fly back to LA in two days, and there's a million things to do."

His casual smile scored her heart, and she felt dismissed. How could he claim to miss her, kiss her until her panties went up in smoke, then abandon her mere days later? And how could she be so fucking clingy after a soul-branding kiss?

Because it had been a soul-branding kiss, Annie!

She understood Hailey's possessive scene at the airport much better now.

He frowned. "Are you okay?"

"Uh-huh. Yeah. Yes." Waving her hand in a flighty fashion, she backed away from him. But her damned knees were too weak to hold her, and her ass barely managed to hit the chair as they gave out.

Quinn followed her down, squaring her hips and balancing on the balls of his feet between her splayed thighs. Dropping another light kiss on her throbbing mouth, he said, "I need to check on Hailey and see how the pregnancy is progressing. Can I call you?"

She shared a look with Sammy. Did she dare bring up the subject of him not being the father again?

"Sure." As he stepped away, she tugged on his index finger, needy to the last. "Does this mean the offer for lunch is off the table?"

His look was regretful as he withdrew. "I have to go, sweetheart."

Crushed but refusing to show it, she gave him a sunny smile.

Stepping forward, Sammy curled her hand over Annie's shoulder. "Actually, Michael and I have something planned for you."

"Oh, Sammy, you shouldn't have gone to the trouble."

"It's your birthday. How could we not?"

"Birthday?" Quinn did a double take. "Annie! Why didn't you tell me?"

"It's not a big deal." She shrugged her embarrassment. The truth was she hated birthdays. Hers, anyway. So what if she was born thirty-odd years ago? Who really cared but overzealous sisters who loved to celebrate every silly milestone in life?

"Fuck. Okay, new plan. We need to celebrate. Will you be home tonight?"

"Quinn—"

Placing his index finger on her kiss-ravaged mouth, he shook his head. "No objections. I'll swing back by unless you plan to go out."

Feeling decidedly guilty for all he'd already done and all she knew he planned to do, Annie gripped his wrist and drew it down.

"She's got no plans, movie star. None she can't reschedule."

"Shut it, Sammy," she growled, promising retribution for another interruption. To Quinn, she said, "If you truly want to celebrate, we can do it when you return from LA. Run your errands."

"I can find the time."

"Not convincing, Quinn," she said, infusing humor she didn't feel into her tone.

He frowned and wrapped a finger around a lock of her hair. "I'll call you later this afternoon."

After he left, her sister's upbeat mood disappeared, and Sammy gazed at her with something akin to pity. "Annie, what are you doing? He's not free to start anything."

"Don't lecture me. Not right now. Let me enjoy this as my birthday present."

But the next ten minutes were filled with a tedious discourse about unavailable men and Annie's poor tastes in males in general.

"Enough, Sammy!" Annie limped to the kitchen and pulled out containers to put away the vegetables Quinn had cut up. "I don't need you to tell me how to live my life. He isn't a forever thing. I get it, okay? Let it go."

"You're going to get hurt when he walks away."

"Is that what you've seen?"

"Yes."

That single three-letter word was a punch to the solar plexus, and it sucked the fire right out of Annie's fight. Presenting her back, she shoved the containers into the fridge in a willy-nilly pattern that made Sammy gasp and rush to reorganize.

"What the hell is wrong with you?"

Annie's laugh bordered a sob, but she managed to check the emotion at the refrigerator door. "I'm too tired to care if the labels are lined up."

"Where is my sister, and what have you done with her?" Sammy demanded, outraged on behalf of clean freaks everywhere.

Ignoring her, Annie eased herself onto a stool at the counter.

"I sensed you were lying to Quinn. You and Michael don't have anything planned, do you?"

"Does pizza count?"

"No." Annie stared out at the scenery. Finally, when she could no longer contain her resentment, she asked, "Why the hell did you make such a big deal? You couldn't just let me enjoy myself for one damned minute of one damned day?"

"Would you have me watch a train wreck and say nothing?"

"Are you so sure it would be terrible? I love him, and I think he feels something for me, too."

"He no doubt does, Annie, but that doesn't mean he's able to act on it. Do you really want to sneak around for the next year?"

"What about Hailey? You know as well as I do that she cheated on him. He hasn't even confronted Ty. Should we let him continue to live in denial, believing she's a freaking saint?" And the true question finally emerged. "Why can't I have something *real* for a change?"

It was a long moment before Sammy answered. "No, for sure, Hailey was a lying skank. I saw it the day I snuck in her room to touch her, but you're going to be the one who comes across as the bad guy in all of this, Annie." She leaned her elbows on the counter. "She's not waking up. We both know it. Give him time to come to terms with it on his own. If you push now, you won't like the choice he makes."

"I'm not the one pushing, Sammy. He keeps coming back to *me*. Trust me, it isn't as if I can chase him," she said in disgust and pounded a fist on her leg.

"Okay, fair enough. But ask yourself this: do you think you can handle living his high-profile life? Handle the constant scrutiny and ridicule that comes with being the love interest of a famous person?" Sammy slapped the granite top in her frustration. "What happens if the press gets wind of your budding affair for real this time? You only had a taste of the ugly these last weeks. Do you know how badly they will tear you apart?"

"You've made your point." Annie wasn't ready to listen to another long list of reasons why she and Quinn shouldn't be together. "I'm hungry. Tell me you already ordered the pizza, at least."

As soon as the words left her mouth, the doorman rang to inform them of the delivery.

"You must be psychic," Sammy quipped.

They shared a laugh, but their usual goodwill was absent.

Sitting in Hailey's room brought with it all kinds of self-recriminations for kissing Annie.

What had he done?

Quinn had been overcome with loneliness. Even surrounded by the studio's cronies and his fawning agent, all he thought about was getting back to her, to ensure she was eating healthy meals and to assist her with Tink, but mainly to experience the soul-soothing peace she brought him. He'd spared Hailey the occasional thought, but most of his concern was directed toward the baby. This, if nothing else, made it clear marriage to Hailey wasn't what he wanted.

From nowhere, the heaviness of the room suffocated him. The

desire to flee was pressing down and causing anxiety. Before he'd even cleared the elevator, his phone was in his hand with his mother's number on the screen.

"Hey, Mom."

"Quinn! What's wrong?"

In the quiet of his vehicle, with no chance of being overheard, he laid the problem out to her.

Maybe he'd expected compassion or the advice that he should follow his heart, but instead, he received a stern dressing down. He was told to step up and do his duty for the baby. A decent man married his child's mother. A decent man didn't waste time with another woman when his fiancée lay in a coma. A *decent* man didn't lead another woman on when the relationship could go nowhere.

Quinn wasn't a decent man.

He couldn't be, because all he wanted was Annie. The physical need kept him up nights. In more ways than one. A decent man wouldn't question if the child was his, but would treat it as if it were his own, regardless.

A decent man wouldn't want to murder his brother for ruining his life.

CHAPTER 34

The next week flew by, and Annie was grateful to be in her own apartment, away from the illness and negative energy that floated around the hospital. Thankful that each day she became a little stronger. It was doubtful she'd ever walk without the cane—the damage to her leg, hip, and back had been substantial—but she was learning a new normal. She'd been told that, with alternate therapies and continual massages, her sex life could return to normal.

She'd almost laughed in Trace's all-to-serious face. Her sex life hadn't been normal in years.

Of Quinn, she saw little and heard even less. He'd blown off a birthday celebration, and other than sending a dog walker to help Annie with Tink, he never contacted her to reschedule. In fact, over the last four days, he'd taken to avoiding her, going so far as to wait for the next elevator if they happened to arrive or depart the building at the same time.

She didn't need to ask why. He was in an impossible situation and probably held residual distrust over the Hailey-is-a-ho revelation.

"I'm not the candy man, and I'm not going to sugarcoat shit," she muttered to herself as she entered the elevator.

From the beginning, she'd known there was a shelf life to their friendship. Their kiss had been over the line, and after he'd had time to think about it, he bolted.

She couldn't blame him.

And if Annie cried into her pillow on those rare nights of self-pity, no one was the wiser but Tink.

The doors to the lobby swished open, and she allowed Tink to exit first.

Quinn and their doorman, Harold, stood side by side, sending her into a barking frenzy. The leash jerked from Annie's hand, and her little traitor launched herself at the men. Pure joy radiated from her trembling body.

Pleasure lit Quinn's face as he scooped her up, and Annie was envious of her dog.

"Sorry. Some days she's a handful to walk." One more thing she couldn't control in her life.

"Which is why I hired the dog walker." Quinn gave her an exasperated look. "Why the hell did you turn him away?"

"It's a waste of money. I can walk her."

"Right, because she didn't just escape you—"

"I've got a few minutes, if you need a hand," Harold suggested, giving her a warm smile.

Annie shook her head, tired of being a charity case. "No, that's okay, Harry, I—"

"Let him help you, Annie," Quinn snapped.

"I don't need him to." Why she was being stubborn was anyone's guess. She could use the assist, but accepting it meant she wasn't as self-sufficient as she wanted to be.

"Nonsense," he argued.

Harold reached for the leash. "Seriously, Annie, it's all good—"

The vision came with no warning. In it, he was lying in an ambulance as paramedics performed CPR to revive him. Annie and Harold both staggered back as if choreographed. Pale as death, he stared at her in horror, and she felt sorry for him. It was always a jolt to be on the receiving end of her gift.

"What the hell was that?" Harold whispered. His fear was a brick to the chest.

"I'm sorry." Her stomach cramped, and sweat beaded along her temples as she fought the urge to vomit. The revelation of what she'd seen—Harold facing certain death—was as shocking as it was tragic. "Th-these things come without any ad-advanced notice."

She swiped the back of her wrist over her clammy forehead.

"Annie, what did you see?" Quinn asked. His visage was the picture of concern, and the urge to punch him in his perfect fucking face was strong. After abandoning her, he suddenly cared again? Fuck him!

Her outrage firmed her spine and cleared her mind.

"That's between me and Harry, Quinn." She reached for Tink, taking great care to not touch him. There was no telling what she would relay or receive, and she couldn't take the chance.

He shot her an incredulous look. "If you saw something happen, I want to know."

Addressing Harold, she said, "Please go get checked out, Harry. Today, okay?"

"Annie!" Quinn called to her retreating back, but she ignored him and kept limping.

She should've been prepared for Quinn's touch. Had she given it a moment's thought, she could've predicted he would demand answers. But she was too busy trying to shut away that part of her failed love life.

The shock buckled her knees, and she dropped. He caught her against him, arms cradling her close and his clenched-jaw face mere inches from hers. Immediately feverish, her hands found their way up his chest to wrap around his neck, and her fingers dug deep in his luxurious mane of hair. Giving him no warning, she dragged his mouth to hers.

She met no resistance.

Their current kiss put the previous one to shame. There was no

Sammy to stop their passions from running away with them. No hospital staff or pesky brothers. No thought but to taste. To feel. To relish the experience. To cling to him so tightly.

As their kiss dragged on, she didn't know where her body ended and his began.

The hard length of his erection nestled against her belly, and all she could imagine was stripping bare, impaling herself on his dick, and riding it until they both succumbed to the mind-melting pleasure.

A sharp bark shattered the sensual spell, and they pulled apart. Harsh breaths, his and hers, mingled in the humid early-morning air. When Quinn groaned and closed his eyes, she wiggled to free herself from his grasp.

Idiot woman!

She'd thrown herself at him, infecting him with her oversexed energy.

"Stop moving, for fuck's sake," he hissed. When Quinn's hips pressed forward, Annie got the feeling it was instinctual, not intentional. And she fought her body's response to rub against him like a damned feline in heat, yowling until she was satisfied he'd done the job right.

But she reached behind her to grip his wrists and tug his hands away from her ass.

"I dropped Tink's leash." A lame excuse, but she needed to get away, and that one did the trick.

"Stay put. I'll get her."

Helplessly, she complied. If it hadn't been for her fur baby, Annie would have escaped as fast as her wobbly jello legs would allow.

In seconds, he'd jogged the few feet to where Tink was resting in the grass and captured her lead. His ease of movement made Annie irrationally irritable, but she was careful to keep her focus on Tink's happy grin, so he wouldn't catch a glimpse of her feelings.

"Thanks," she muttered. "I'll take this escape artist back inside now."

"We need to talk."

"We really don't."

"Annie, this thing between us..."

He didn't finish, and she didn't care to comment. She held out her hand for the leash, which he disregarded. Contrary man!

"Come on, I'll walk you up."

Quinn squatted to pick up her cane, and Annie's humiliation was complete. Red-faced, she accepted it and headed for the side entrance of their building. Wordlessly, they rode to her floor.

After keying in the entry code, she continued into the foyer, not bothering to check if he followed. His pervasive energy told her he did.

"Thanks for your help. You can go now."

As if she hadn't spoken, he unhooked the clasp of Tink's harness and watched as the beastie raced around, rubbing her face along the carpet.

"How about offering me a cup of coffee?"

"I don't have any. Besides, I have PT in thirty minutes."

"Fine. I'll take you to the hospital."

"I don't want you to take me to the hospital," she snapped. "I don't want anything to do with you. I want..." She broke off and stared into his impassive face.

Him.

In spite of everything, she wanted him.

"What? What do you want, Annie?"

Resting her head in her palms, she shook it back and forth. "Can't you just leave me alone, Quinn? Whatever your reasons for this recent hot-and-cold routine, I just don't have the energy for it. I'm tired."

"I'm not sleeping." His confession caused her to glance up. "Not for more than a few hours per night. Since our first kiss, you're all I think about. Dream about."

"Bullshit," she spat. Righteous anger brewed inside. *"Bull. Shit."*

"It's the truth, sweetheart. I miss you all the time." At her outraged snort, he said, "I do."

"You ghosted me!"

"I distanced myself. There's a difference."

"Not from my perspective."

He swore savagely. As he paced the foyer, the words she longed to hear tumbled out of him. "I care about you. You make me feel alive. Alive in ways I've never experienced before. It's as if I truly matter. Me. Myself. Not Quinn Jensen the actor. Not the famous twin."

But she had to put a stop to it for all the reasons she hadn't contacted him over the last week. The main one being he had to clean up his house first and settle things concerning Hailey.

"You know what you feel, babe? An illusion." She put a hand on his chest and pulsed all her sparking energy in his direction. The current shocked them both, but she was prepared.

He wasn't.

Smiling grimly at his yelp, she said, "Nothing but a fucking illusion. You think you're attracted to a normal woman, but you're not. I'm a freak of nature. You're drawn to the unusual and unknown. That's it." Resigned, she dropped her hands to her sides. "Quinn, I can promise you, if you had to deal with this every day of your life, you'd run and never look back—just like the rest."

Annie painstakingly made her way to the door and yanked it open. "Please leave."

"No." He stormed to her and slammed the door.

Stubborn fucker with his beautiful, belligerent face! And damned if she didn't want to rip his clothes off and do him right there on the tiled entry floor. What was it about this willful bastard that had her ready to jump him at every turn? The more demanding he became, the stronger the pull.

Genetic defect. It had to be.

"I don't run, Annie. I won't. Not now, not ever."

"You will," she promised. "Nothing about me inspires men to stick around."

"Can we go back? To the beginning, before all the strife?"

The heartfelt plea was a sledgehammer to her anger *and* to her resistance.

"I don't think it's that easy." She sighed and opened the door again. "I really do have to go, Quinn."

"I'll drive you. I'm not taking no for an answer," he said, quietly closing the door a second time.

"You're setting us both up for a heartache."

"How so?"

"The press. They hang around that damned hospital like buzzards on carrion."

He smiled and trailed his fingers down her cheek. "You have me there, but you know what? I don't give a shit."

You will, she thought but didn't say it aloud. Quinn would continue to insist it didn't matter, only to regret it later.

"I'll be ready in five. I need to grab something to eat," she finally said.

"We can get cronuts, for old time's sake."

"It's not fair that you know my weakness," she complained, halting the hand tracing her lower lip and weakening her already faulty knees. If he didn't stop touching her, she'd be a goner. Also, he'd be picking her molten body up from the floor.

"And I'm not ashamed to exploit them," he murmured.

Crowding her against the closed door, he bent his head to nuzzle the sensitive spot below her ear. Her eyes rolled back in pleasure, and her hands found their way under his t-shirt. The ridges of his abdomen were a magnet for her fingers, and her desire to see those ridiculously hard abs was becoming an obsession. The big screen was great and all, but up close and personal, he was positively divine. If only he'd follow through with taking off his clothes when he eventually lost, she'd suggest another game of strip poker.

She knew how to cheat.

"This is an exceedingly bad idea, Quinn," she warned when reason allowed, following it with a moan as his hand found its way under the edge of her bra to toy with her breast.

"I don't care." He lifted his head. "Do you?"

"Do I what?" She guided his lips back to her neck. Even the puff of expelled air against her throat, indicating his laughter, was a turn-on.

"You're so easy," he murmured.

"I thought we'd established that."

An alarm on her phone went off and broke up their make-out session.

"I have to go." *Was her tone as whiny as she felt?* "Trace will have my ass if I skip my appointment."

"Do you need to cancel your other ride?"

"No. You distracted me. I forgot to set one up in the first place."

He chuckled and pulled back to straighten her shirt. "Are you going dressed like this?"

She glanced down at her gray yoga pants and bright-orange t-shirt.

"This is my workout outfit," she said, sounding defensive to her own ears.

"I'm not picking on your clothing, sweetheart. I'm used to women who feel it's necessary to pair their workout clothes with their biggest and brightest diamonds and a designer handbag." He dropped a quick kiss on her pouting lips. "It's refreshing to find a woman comfortable with her appearance."

Except she wasn't. Especially after he told her *that* stupid bit of information.

"I might forgo the diamonds, but I'm not opposed to nice workout clothes and a coach bag," she finally admitted.

"Remind me to show you what I wear to the gym."

"Please tell me it's nothing."

His eyes flew wide before crinkling with laughter.

She choked on her own spit. "Fuck me! That slipped out, didn't it?"

"Come on, let's get you to your appointment. Then we'll explore this"—he gestured between them, his hand lingering over her heart—"when we get back home."

CHAPTER 35

$\mathcal{A}$fter Quinn dropped her off outside the door of the therapy center, he found Trace for his daily update on Hailey's condition. The next forty-five minutes were spent speaking to their baby and scrolling through his phone to kill time until Annie was finished. He hadn't realized he'd dozed off until a soft hand touched his cheek. He jumped as if shot.

"*Jesus, Annie!* You about gave me a heart attack! What time is it?"

"I finished fifteen minutes ago. Your car was still in the lot, and I decided to come find you. I figured you'd be in here."

"I'm sorry. I guess I dozed off."

She patted his shoulder and moved to the side of the bed.

Deciphering what she was thinking was impossible as she stared at the ever-growing mound of Hailey's belly. The slightest smile played about her mouth, and she reached out a hand. Before she connected, she glanced his way. He understood she was asking permission, and he nodded, curious what she was about.

When she touched Hailey's abdomen, her expression turned tragically sad.

"You don't know what you're missing," she said as she leaned in.

"If you don't wake up, you're going to lose out on the very best thing in your life."

His heart shifted into his throat, pulsing double-time, when he realized she was speaking to Hailey. He wanted to shove Annie away from the unnaturally still form, to stop her from encouraging a return to the living. But hadn't he been doing much the same thing whenever he visited Hailey? However today had changed everything, and if she woke up, Annie would disappear from his life. As it was now, he wasn't sure he could face not seeing her every day. Not touching her. Kissing her.

Annie's solemn gaze drifted over the figure on the bed, and she lifted her hand from Hailey's abdomen.

"What did you see?" he asked hoarsely.

"Quinn…" She sounded tortured, and his gut clenched.

"Tell me, Annie. I know you did. *Please.*"

Eyes shut as if in great pain, she again touched the baby bump. As if making a sudden decision, her eyes snapped open and focused intently on him. There was a world of trepidation in her eyes, and he was seconds too late to tell her to keep her damned secrets as the words he never wanted to hear tumbled from her lips.

"I'm confident Ty was the one Hailey had the affair with. The baby… Serena… I'm almost sure she's his."

"No!" Denial, hot and fierce, swept from him. Something ugly unfurled inside him. *"No!"*

"This isn't news, Quinn. You asked me before, and I'm confirming what I saw. It's Ty's baby."

All his daydreams of his daughter were going up in smoke, and he fought to extinguish the fucking fire.

"You're mistaken," he said flatly.

"I'm not." She sounded too sure of herself.

From the first, she'd seemed sure, but Quinn hadn't confronted his brother, preferring to think she was wrong. He'd told himself it wasn't her fault, that sometimes the universe sent mixed messages or showed people what they wanted to see. His anger had simmered below the surface, and he'd avoided Ty in case he saw for himself the truth of Annie's words. His denial was going strong because if he believed her, his bond with his brother would be severed for good.

"Then you're a goddamned liar! Ty would *never* do that."

She flinched, but her expression turned stubborn, and her jaw lifted in challenge. "You shouldn't ask what you don't want to know."

Her refusal to back down was proof positive.

"No. He wouldn't…" Quinn couldn't breathe. Couldn't drag in enough air as darkness gathered on the outskirts of his vision. "He… wouldn't. My brother… he wouldn't."

Without being aware she'd moved closer, he felt her delicate hand curl over his shoulder as the fingers of her other brushed his cheek.

"Breathe, babe, please," she urged from next to his crouched form.

He knocked her hand away. *"Don't touch me."*

"Quinn." Her voice was achingly sweet, and he longed to be deaf. To not hear the pity and pain she experienced on his behalf.

"Go. Away."

"I'm sorry," she whispered. "You have to believe I'm so sorry."

The catch in her words slayed him. She honestly believed what she was saying, and as such, he had no choice but to believe her, too.

"Get the fuck away from me, Annie, or you won't like what I'm going to say," he rasped out.

Before he could blink twice, he was alone. Footsteps passed by the door, and he felt the curious eyes of the hospital as he sat on the floor, staring at the opposite wall. Voices came and went, and staff tried to catch his attention.

"Quinn?"

His lids came down over his burning eyes.

Ty.

The voice of betrayal.

Black fury possessed him. He wasn't aware of rising from the floor. Not aware of gripping his brother by the throat or hammering him with balled-up fists. He never felt the return blows as Ty fought like hell to stay alive under Quinn's murderous rage.

He was scarcely aware of being dragged away or of Ty slumping to the ground.

The monster who'd possessed him stared with cold detachment. He watched as blood flowed from Ty's nose and the broken skin on his face darkened to an angry red, only wishing he'd have done more extensive damage.

"You're no brother of mine," he snarled.

With eyes halfway to swollen shut, Ty glanced up. The knowledge he'd been found out was plain to see. Something like regret mixed with anguish twisted his features as he reached out a hand, but Quinn turned away.

Shock and horror filled the faces surrounding him.

Less than ten feet away, Annie leaned against the wall, her hands over her mouth as if shocked by his brutality.

"*You* caused this," his inner monster snarled at her. "You couldn't leave well enough alone, could you?"

For the first time since they'd met, he didn't care that she was distraught. Didn't care if his fury overloaded her. Didn't care what happened to her once he left this goddamned place for good. He outright despised her for her fucking interference and the havoc her cursed abilities had caused.

After her initial shock at his savagery, rapid recognition of his boiling emotions registered on her pale face. What little light was left in her eyes died out, and with tears flowing freely down her face, she staggered away.

This time, he had no desire to chase after her. He wanted nothing more to do with her or the chaos always traveling in her wake. Silently, he cursed that godforsaken day at the airport. He'd have been better off if the fucking plane *had* taken his life. Anything to spare him this horrific pain of betrayal and complete loss.

Ty was rushed away to be treated, and Quinn's monster yawned and patted himself on the back for a job well done. After he slithered away, Quinn remained, staring at the spot where he'd last seen Annie.

People skirted the statue he'd become.

He only glanced up when Trace skidded to a halt in front of him, two armed policemen steps behind him.

"Let's get you cleaned up."

Like a traumatized child with no will of his own, Quinn followed him to an empty room, barely listening as Trace ordered the officers to wait outside.

"Talk to me, man. What the fuck happened out there?" he asked in a low voice.

Quinn couldn't be bothered to answer.

Nurse Hatchet Face poked her head in, and with a disapproving look in Quinn's direction, she informed Trace that Ty had been taken for a CT scan.

"Thanks. You can go. And please close the door on your way out," Trace said. After she had left, he cleaned the blood from Quinn's swollen knuckles and tested the movement of each finger.

"If you don't start talking, you're going to face charges."

Quinn shrugged.

Unsuccessfully trying to reach beyond the frozen wall he'd erected, Trace continued to question him as he applied ointment to the broken skin and wrapped his hand. With nothing left to do, he stood aside as the police hauled Quinn away for assault.

"You're free to go."

The cell door swung open, and an elderly corrections officer offered him a hand up. Quinn's body felt like hell, so he accepted the assistance with a grateful nod.

"Why?"

"The guy you attacked refused to press charges. Usually, our D.A. won't pursue a conviction without the victim stepping up."

"Victim." Quinn snorted his anger. "Yeah, he's the victim, all right."

"You aren't going to pursue your vendetta, are you?"

He met the man's concerned brown eyes. "No. No point. I had a moment of insanity. It won't happen again."

The officer slapped him heartily on the back and ignored Quinn's wince. "Glad to hear it. You got a ride?"

"How would I have anything lined up? I didn't even know I was being released."

The older man chuckled as if Quinn had said something funny. "Do you have that car-app thing? What's it called?"

"Uber. And yes."

As they cleared the cell area and walked toward Admitting, the corrections officer gushed ad nauseam about his favorite Quinn Jensen movies. "Do you think I could get a selfie with you? It would mean the world to my daughter."

"Of course. Can I have a minute to clean up?" he gestured to the restroom across from them.

"Oh, sure, kid. Take your time. I'll pull your personal items from lockup."

"Thanks."

Quinn stared at the haggard face in the mirror. Doubtless, there would be a backlash from yesterday's fiasco. What had possessed him to attack his own brother? His ugly-ass mugshot, appearing like one of those strung-out-looking actors, would show up in the tabloids before noon, if it hadn't already. It was no more than he deserved.

He could already hear the lecture from his mother.

All night, every time he'd closed his eyes, he was haunted by Annie's pale, devastated face. One would think his give-a-damn was forever busted, but he was sick with the knowledge that, once again, he'd treated her poorly. He'd been reactive to the truth. A truth she hadn't created, just spoken aloud.

Quinn didn't deserve her forgiveness this time, and he didn't intend to ask for it. She'd probably pardon his behavior. Rule it as temporary madness. But he'd never be able to look at her again without remembering the pain of his brother's betrayal.

Savagely, he rubbed his forehead, hoping to erase the memories. How did he get past this? A splash of icy water added a bit of color to his cheeks. Giving his image one more disgusted glance, he put on his movie-star persona and went to take a selfie with a fan. Likely the only one he'd have left after today.

In the back of a blacked-out SUV, he scrolled through the online news. Video after video of his attack on Ty popped up in his social feed, but he only watched it once and didn't bother reading the thousands of vitriolic comments.

The entire situation made him ill.

Next, he checked his voicemails and text messages. Unsurprisingly, the majority were from his parents. Only one was from Ty.

"I'm sorry."

Two words. As if two words could erase the fact his twin had fucked *his* girlfriend. Yet those two words reached in, pulled out, and shredded what was left of his heart.

Nothing from Annie.

No call, no text, no go to hell.

Nothing.

Had he really expected her to contact him?

No.

He rode the lift to her floor but didn't have the courage to leave the security of the elevator. The doors closed, and he couldn't bear the distance. He pressed the open button and held it. If she stepped into the hall, he'd have no choice but to speak with her.

Five more times he pressed the fucking button.

And five more times she didn't appear.

Another resident made his way down the corridor and cautiously eyed Quinn on the threshold of the elevator.

Yeah, he was lurking like a Chester Molester. So the fuck what?

With one last glance at Annie's place, he stepped back and pressed the button to close the doors. A dickhead move when the tenant was only a few feet away, but he didn't care.

He punched in his key code for the penthouse suites, and a handful of floors later, he wearily traversed the hall toward his apartment.

A sealed letter was taped to the door.

His heartbeat tapped out an unsteady rhythm as he tore open the envelope and scanned the contents.

Quinn,

I've thought long and hard about what to say. Nothing profound came to mind. But I couldn't let ugliness linger between us. I'm sorry for my part in all of this. It went against my instincts, but I told you, anyway. The truth should've come from Ty, not me. Either way, I should have stayed out of the whole mess. I'm sure, had the situation been reversed, you would've encouraged me to speak with my sibling first.

None of that matters now. The bottom line is that I'm sorry. Deeply. Of course, I don't expect this to change anything. But I do hope maybe one day you can look back with affection on the early part of our friendship. Maybe you can drum up a smile now and again for memories of the good moments we shared.

It goes without saying, the next few months are going to be an ordeal for you. Please, try to understand where Ty is coming from. If there was one thing I understood from the vision, he truly cared for Hailey.

Thank you for your many kindnesses during my hospital stay. I wish you nothing but the best.

Annie.

Her poignant, heartfelt apology poured salt into his already exposed wounds and made him feel lower than slug slime. With a vicious curse, he balled the paper and threw it to the ground, stepping over it to enter his apartment. As he was about to shut the door, a shiver of awareness halted him.

The elevator dinged, and he turned, but no one appeared to be there as the doors swept together. Drawn to the crumpled yellow note at his feet, he bent to retrieve it, smoothing it against the wall.

The letter was her goodbye, and his heart ached at the fucking unfairness of it all. Perhaps in another time and place, if there had been no Hailey, no cheating brother, no demanding career in the public spotlight…

The fleeting thought hit that maybe, like Margie and Gabe or Sammy and Michael, he and Annie had known each other in a past life. If so, maybe they'd get it right in the next lifetime.

nnie ducked into the elevator, breathing hard, as if she'd run five blocks instead of limping five steps. As a thank you for the premonition that inspired his life-saving checkup, Harold had given her access to leave the note, and she'd stayed longer than intended, nearly getting herself caught.

When she heard the elevator ding, her internal voice had warned her of Quinn's arrival. She didn't want him to discover her in the humiliating action of taping the envelope to his door, so she'd hurried to the far side of the hall to avoid detection. Luck was with her for a change, and he failed to check behind him, instead going straight for his apartment. It allowed her to slip inside the elevator unnoticed.

The absolute fatigue on his disillusioned visage was heart-wrenching, and she wanted to go to him. To hold him and promise him it would all be okay. But it wouldn't. If he didn't see the inside of a courtroom from aggravated battery, he certainly would for a custody hearing.

The latter was the vision Sammy had had.

Annie lingered long enough to watch him read and crumple the letter. On the ground, discarded like yesterday's trash, was her answer. In all honesty, she couldn't say she'd been looking for him to have a miraculous change of heart. But she had hoped for forgiveness for foolishly blurting out the information about the affair.

As he crossed the threshold to his apartment, she let the doors close and her tears flow. Although she didn't regret a minute spent in Quinn's company, she had to acknowledge her brother and sister had called this one right from the start.

Annie had indeed gotten her heart broken.

How the hell had things gone so terribly wrong in less than two hours? One moment, Quinn's lips were scorching her neck and he was telling her he intended to stick. The next, his blazing hatred was consuming her from the inside out.

When the doors opened on her floor, she wasn't in the least surprised to see Sammy and Michael sitting cross-legged on the ground, waiting for her to arrive.

"Oh, Annie." Sammy jumped up and rushed to her. Loving arms embraced her, no permission asked or needed. Annie craved the contact, and her sister understood. Together, they collapsed as the wretched sobs shook her frame.

"Michael," Sammy said.

He lifted Annie and carried her the short distance to her door.

"What's the code again?" he asked.

"Twelve-nineteen."

"The day of the crash," Sammy added with a laugh. "Anyone ever tell you that you're warped?"

"Only you," Annie replied with a watery chuckle.

"Where would you like me to place you, m'lady?" Michael asked, effecting an old-world English accent. Or at least an attempt at one.

"Has anyone ever told you that you do a terrible Englishman?" Sammy crowed. "I tell him all the time. Does it stop him? No."

"Shut it," he growled, but the twinkle in his eye belied his words.

"At the counter is fine," Annie said.

He set her down on the stool and kissed her forehead. "I'll go get a box of Kleenex. Then I'll leave you and Sammy to talk. Tink and I need exercise."

"I love you, Michael," she said.

"I love you, too, Annie." His sweet smile made her feel marginally better, as if good people still existed in the world.

After he left, Sammy placed a box of donuts in front of her. Annie hadn't realized she was hungry until she bit into the powdered lemon pastry. "Holy shit! Where did you find these?"

"A place called Divine by Design. It's a bakery in Stonebrooke. I think it's my new favorite place."

"Mm-hmm," she agreed around another bite. "So why wait in the hall? You had the code."

Shrugging a shoulder, Sammy dug out napkins and handed one to Annie. "I knew you'd be home soon, and I was trying to be supportive without being invasive."

"That's a switch."

"I know, right? Pretty impressive, if I say so myself." Watching her for a moment longer, her sister picked out a donut to casually examine. "Want to tell me what that fuck-face movie star did?"

"Don't call him that."

"He treated you like shit, and he broke your heart. Why the hell would you defend him?"

"I've broken my own heart, Sammy. I foolishly let him in."

"He didn't give you a choice, did he? He showed up every single day, showering you with presents, pouring on the charm. You were pretty much a captive audience, don't ya think?"

Understanding the simmering rage was on her behalf still didn't make it easier for Annie to handle.

"Don't."

"Don't what?" Sammy snapped.

"Don't attack him. We both witnessed what went down with his brother and Hailey." She held up her hand when her sister would've argued. "It had to be awful for him. He hadn't finished processing what I told him before Ty showed up. The video made him look like a psycho."

Sammy rolled her eyes.

"Don't try to deny that you saw it, sissy. It has to be everywhere by now."

"Yeah, I watched it. What I saw was a monster beating the hell out of his brother, then looking at you like you were the dirt beneath his feet. To say nothing of his blaming you for his wretched situation," Sammy stated in a huff. "For that alone, I should kick his ass."

"He'd just received the shock of his life. Everything came crashing down."

"You aren't going to let me be angry about his atrocious behavior, are you?"

Annie flashed a tired half smile. "No. If anyone gets to be angry, it's me, and I'm not there yet. First and foremost, I want to lick my wounds and the inside of a few of these lemon donuts."

"They *are* great donuts," Sammy said, biting into the one she'd picked for herself.

They sat in companionable silence, devouring pastries right along with their feelings.

It was the Holt way.

Sammy brewed hot chocolates and passed one of the mugs across to Annie. "What's your plan now?"

"Other than drowning my sorrows with donuts for days?"

"Yeah."

Annie shrugged. "I have another month and a half of Trace's sadistic PT. Then I'll move back to the lake house and transfer to a doctor's care there. My lease is set to expire in two months anyway. I could extend it, but I want to go home." She licked out more filling. "After that? I don't know. If my business hasn't taken a major beating with all this negative press, I'll dive back into research full time."

"He's a fuck face." Sammy's brows shot up as if daring Annie to reprimand her.

"Cut him a break. We need to be understanding right now."

"You understand too damned much, you know that?" her sister

retorted. "I wish you'd get good and angry once in a while. Maybe break someone's nose."

"Pfft. Think Stephen has a room in his ward for me? Maybe there will be a Rabid Ronni for me to take on."

The sisters laughed over the memory of huddling in the medical center of Brookhaven while an unstable and highly enraged woman bent on murder, roamed its halls.

"I thought I'd die a thousand deaths when I saw the vision of you getting stabbed. How about we never repeat anything like that?" Annie said as she used the side of her hand to swipe the powdered sugar into a tidy pile. But she still couldn't shake her own fear of being stabbed. They still hadn't caught David, and Annie refused to make late-afternoon or evening therapy appointments for that reason.

"I'm afraid you're—"

Sammy's words were cut off when Michael trotted a worn-out Tink into the kitchen on a quest for water.

"That dog is a beast! She thinks she owns the neighborhood."

Annie grinned. "Yeah, she's a badass. Was it the pit bull from the fifth floor?"

"How did you know?" He shook his head. "You'd think she'd tangle with something her own size. A Yorkie or Maltese."

"Y'all staying here tonight?" she asked with a yawn. "There are fresh sheets in the guest room."

After being assured they would, Annie went in for a nap, hoping, when she woke, she'd be in a better frame of mind. Yeah, her love life was bleaker than ever, but at least she could take comfort in knowing she had a kick-ass family who had her back.

<hr>

ANNIE WOKE TO RAPID-FIRE WHISPERS AND DEBATED INVESTIGATING the reason for Sammy and Michael's hushed conversation. If she had to venture a guess, she was being vilified in the press again—

just as she'd been over the last six days, since the incident at the hospital—and they were trying to hide the evidence.

Last night, she'd made the mistake of checking social media.

The vitriol ranged from calling her a gold digger to a home-wrecking ho, and everything in between. She supposed if the public was attacking her, they were most likely leaving Quinn alone.

Moving to the far side of the world was looking better by the day.

With a muffled groan, she sat up and petted Tink as her pup thumped her tail in support.

"I need a new body, baby. Know where I can get one?"

A soft whine was her answer.

"I didn't think so. Who knew thirty-four was going to suck so bad?"

"Thirty-four? *Aw, fuck!*"

Annie laughed. "I'm going to assume my sister is standing behind me, in the doorway. Otherwise, you sound remarkably like Sammy, Tink."

"Funny," Sammy said as she entered the room. "We forgot to reschedule your birthday celebration!"

"We had pizza. I wasn't going to hold you to anything more than that." Annie smiled her understanding.

"But we missed cake. You have therapy today, right?"

"At two, but I'm thinking about calling off sick."

"You can't. It's not like you work there, you nerd."

Annie released a heavy sigh. "Yeah, well. I'm still tired of the whole thing. I could do the same exercises in the gym downstairs."

"Your problem is impatience."

"Says the woman who refused to let the doctors of Brookhaven help her." Annie rolled her eyes as she limped toward the bathroom.

"I wasn't sick! If you recall, I *knew* Michael was alive."

"Yeah, yeah, yeah. Potato, po-tah-to."

"What flavor cake do you want, you ungrateful bitch?"

"I don't want any cake," Annie said around a mouthful of toothpaste.

"That's sacrilege," Sammy scolded, lingering in the doorway. "Who are you, and what have you done with my sister? She never turns down cake."

"Your sister is getting old and chubby. All those sympathy donuts over the last week didn't do her any favors." Annie spit into the sink and rinsed her mouth. "She's definitely turning down cake."

"Oh, shut it. You're curvy. Men love curvy. And stop talking about yourself in third person."

She pointed the toothbrush at Sammy. "No cake. I mean it."

"Pfft. I'll do what I want. You're not the boss of me."

"Thank God," Annie muttered.

"I heard that."

"When are you and Michael heading back to Florida? Today?"

"Stop trying to change the subject, Annie. We're having a belated birthday party for you, and you're going to love it."

"Well, right now, I'd settle for breakfast."

"What about heading to Divine by Design for biscuits and gravy? What do you think?" Sammy gave her a tempting smile and a waggle of her eyebrows.

"Sign me up."

Within fifteen minutes, the three of them were heading to the public elevator—because Annie avoided the private one at all costs. The doors opened, and Annie's heart plummeted to somewhere around her ankles. There, leaning his shoulder against the wall, arms crossed against his chest, was Quinn.

"What the fuck?" echoed inside her suddenly pounding head. Why couldn't she catch a break?

Sammy, ever the faithful champion, wrapped a supportive arm around her shoulders. "We'll take the next one."

Quinn's cool green gaze clashed with Annie's across the short distance as the doors swept together. She breathed a sigh of relief until, after another second, the signal dinged, and the doors swished open again.

"Seems you're stuck with me. The other one is undergoing

maintenance," Quinn said smoothly, hand on the button, preventing the lift from going up or down.

Inhaling a deep breath for strength, Annie stepped into hell. Maybe she'd get lucky and the elevator would plunge her to her death.

CHAPTER 37

They entered, and Annie was quick to take the corner farthest from Quinn. But fate had decided to conspire against her, and the damned car stopped at every floor. He maneuvered closer to her with every new occupant. Before long, their shoulders were brushing.

She shrank away and tried to make herself smaller.

"You never said what flavor cake you want, Annie."

"Give it a rest, Sammy," she growled.

"Cake?" Quinn asked in a hushed tone.

Panic was taking hold of her, and a tingling began along her raw nerve endings, making her antsy. "Is this stinking elevator broken or what? Shouldn't we have reached the lobby by now?"

A few of the other occupants looked to the panel with concern. A snort, sounding suspiciously like a laugh, came from Quinn's direction. She shot him a glare. Lowering her voice for his ears only, she said, "I'd think you, above everyone else, would be eager to get out of here."

"I've nowhere special to be," he told her.

"Contrary bastard," she hissed.

A finger lightly traced her arm.

She knew that touch!

Annie sucked in a breath. Or what should've been a breath. Instead, her spit filled the pipe that should've been reserved for breathing. Her coughing fit had the other five apartment residents inching away, as Quinn placed a hand on her back.

"Breathe, sweetheart," he urged with concern in his voice.

The endearment smacked her right in the fucking face, and she froze. Of course, she sucked in more spit, coughing harder. An unopened bottle of water was produced by a sympathetic neighbor. Quinn uncapped it and held it up to her lips.

"Slowly," he encouraged. "Good, girl. Better?"

A glance at the mirrored panel showed her red-faced with raccoon eyes.

Fucking great!

With the heels of her hands, she swiped at the offending mascara.

Quinn's arm never left its place around her waist.

Annie tried to inch away, but his fingers tightened. Certain everyone could hear her heart pounding, she was twenty seconds from passing out. Only the sound of her heavy breathing echoed inside her ear cavities. She wanted nothing more than to knock his arm away, but she didn't dare create a scene.

Finally, the doors opened, and everyone piled out. When she would've followed Sammy and Michael, Quinn held her back.

"Let me go," Annie hissed.

"I can't seem to do that."

Her panicked gaze flew to Sammy's surprised face. With a considering look, her sister watched Quinn, only relaxing when he gave her a nod, silently communicating whatever it was she was searching for. With a small smirk and wink, Sammy promised to bring Annie back something good from the bakery.

"Traitor!" she hollered.

Sammy's laughter was the last thing she heard before the doors whooshed shut.

Quinn hit the number for her floor, and they whisked upward without stopping.

What the hell?

A conspiracy was afloat. She was sure of it. The Universe hated her.

They didn't speak until the door of her apartment closed behind him.

"My brother had me served." Anger laced Quinn's words, and Annie took a step back. Even knowing the emotion was directed at Ty, she half expected him to rail at her.

"Served?"

He crossed to the arm of the sofa where Tink was perched, begging for his attention.

Annie was surrounded by turncoats.

Gently, in direct contrast to his volatile mood, he stroked the pup's chest. "Seems he wants to be in charge of Hailey's care because of the baby."

Annie remained silent. What the hell was she supposed to contribute in the face of this situation, anyway?

He pinned her with a hard stare. "Nothing to say?"

"Nope. Nada. Zip. Zilch," she squeaked.

The brackets around his mouth deepened. "You've always been outspoken about everything else. I somehow expected you'd have two cents to add."

"Why are you even here, telling me this?" she asked, unable to contain her morbid curiosity.

"Because you're my friend. Aren't you, Annie?" There was a silky menace in his words. A challenge of sorts.

"No, Quinn. Not anymore. I'm nothing to you." No one would ever accuse her of being intelligent after she waded in when she should've retreated.

His banked fury took on a new edge, and the crackling energy could practically be felt in the air. He abandoned Tink to stalk her, and with no idea of his intent, Annie backed around the couch, trying to keep the furniture between them. When she ran out of tables and chairs, she cursed her minimalist lifestyle. Back pressed against the wall, she also silently berated herself for being a coward.

He closed the gap and hooked an arm around her waist. His free hand cradled the base of her skull, and he tangled his fingers in her hair to tug her head back, forcing her to look at him. Her limbs had a mind of their own and crept around his mouthwateringly wide shoulders. She assured herself it was only for support.

"You're wrong," he growled right before savaging her mouth.

His taste, his smell, the familiarity of him—it was as if she'd come home the second he touched her. It didn't help that she'd missed him unbearably.

She hadn't been aware she was crying until he pulled back and rested his forehead against hers.

"Did I hurt you?" he asked raggedly.

"Huh?" It wasn't an exaggeration to say her mind had melted into a puddle of mush.

With his index finger, he tenderly swiped at the moisture on her cheek. "You're crying. Did I hurt you?"

"N-no. Not the w-way you think."

His exhale of relief expelled mint-scented breath across her dampened lips. She turned her mouth to his, needing to taste him again. Their second kiss was much more gentle and, blessedly, a whole lot longer. It drugged her mind and eliminated any modicum of resistance she'd imagined she possessed.

"Are we done denying this, Annie?" His passion-filled voice was gruff and sexy as hell.

What choice did she really have? She nodded, in no doubt of his intent or what "this" was.

"I believe we are," she murmured her agreement.

He nodded.

As he lifted her, she jumped and wound her legs around his hips. They fell against the wall as his mouth covered hers again. The forceful impact made her wince, and a whimper escaped.

"*Shit!* I forgot about your back." He immediately eased her away from the wall. "Are you okay, sweetheart?"

"Yeah. Awesome. And I kinda forgot, too." She met his concerned gaze. "But maybe, if your intent is to pound the hell out of my vajay-jay, we shouldn't do it against the wall."

His bark of laughter triggered hers.

Hands clamped against her ass, he turned in a slow circle, then lifted a brow. "The couch?"

"Would it be too ordinary to request a firm mattress?"

His grin told her it wasn't.

His mouth descended again, and when he finally lifted his head, he murmured, "The bed it is."

AFTER SETTING ANNIE CAREFULLY ON THE MATTRESS IN DEFERENCE TO her previous injury, Quinn caught a glimpse of her desire-laden face and sucked in a breath. Her cheekbones were flushed a becoming pink, and her parted mouth was swollen from his kisses, silently begging for more. When her tongue dipped out to moisten her lips, he groaned.

Was there anything sexier than a woman in the throes of passion? Anyone more beautiful and real than this woman resting on her elbows and staring up at him? He didn't believe so.

With great deliberation, he tugged his shirt up, and right as he exposed his abs, her hand lifted, pausing midair as if she wanted to touch, but didn't dare. Quinn bit back a satisfied smirk. Sure, he needed to maintain a ripped physique for his career, but even if he didn't, he would count the hours spent at the gym as worthwhile. The wanton desire darkening Annie's hungry eyes was worth any price.

She sat up and placed her hand over his as he reached for the button on his jeans.

"We can't do this," she croaked.

At first, the words didn't penetrate his passion-induced fog. But when they did, his disappointment rose to the surface. "Why the hell not?"

No meant no, and he would honor her wishes. However, wrapping his brain around *this* particular no was next to impossible because he was finally realizing he'd wanted her from the moment he saw her.

"Look at you," she said on a wistful sigh, tentatively trailing her fingers over his eight-pack. She took an extra few seconds to toy with the hairs on his happy trail. "You're a freaking god."

Her words were breathy, causing him physical discomfort at not being able to touch her.

"Mere mortals shouldn't hope to reach for the heavens, Quinn. It's playing with fire, and I don't want to get burned." She slowly shook her head, never lifting her eyes from his bared torso.

As quickly as it had developed, his irritation evaporated. "I'm only a man, Annie. As human as any other. I have fears and desires. And I want *you*."

She closed her eyes and inhaled sharply. "I want you, too. More than I've wanted anything in my entire life. But my body is scarred and ugl—"

He placed a fingertip over her lips. Kneeling on the floor between her legs, he leaned forward and cupped her face.

"You're beautiful, sweetheart. Both inside and out."

Her eyes opened, and one crystal tear shimmered on her lower lashes.

"Truly," he confirmed her unasked question.

Annie transformed before him. All doubt disappeared, and in its place was wicked delight with a plate of mischief on the side. The mercurial change left him momentarily paralyzed and speechless. *She* was the one descended from heaven to tempt mortals, not him.

"Then what are you waiting for? Let's get naked."

"Oh, thank God," he muttered.

Her laugh had him shucking his jeans faster than he'd thought possible.

"Impressive," she murmured.

"I'm glad you approve." He lightly tugged on the V of her neckline. "You're wearing too many clothes, Annie."

She hesitated for a second, and he took over, not allowing her doubts to cripple her again.

Quinn lifted her shirt over her breasts, then eased the material over her head. Next, he unclipped her bra, throwing it God knew where, as he took a brief moment to appreciate the fullness of her perfect Cs.

"The women I know pay good money for tits as beautiful as yours," he said, cupping them and running his thumbs over the hardened tips.

"You say the nicest things."

Meeting her humor-filled gaze, he laughed. "It wasn't a comparison. I'm simply grateful I'm benefiting from what the Good Lord blessed you with."

"Benefit away."

With a grin, he bent and closed his mouth over her dusty-rose nipple. Her low moan reached all the way to his dick, causing it to twitch as his blood pulsed through it. He drew back to lightly blow on the wet tip of her breast and smiled as it pebbled.

"Wow. I think I'm the one benefiting the most," she said in a husky voice.

"Oh, no. It's definitely me," he assured her.

Annie laughed and tugged his head back to her chest. But he abandoned it to trail his lips down along her smooth abdomen, pausing when he reached the scars. Tears unexpectedly stung his eyes as Quinn thought about her heroism. The remaining resentment he'd been holding onto dissolved, allowing his awe and gratitude for her sacrifice.

With great care and taking his time, he worshipped every inch of her body that he exposed as he stripped her bare. She remained silent as if she understood his need to touch and give back to her what had been taken.

If only he could.

But Quinn had the ability to pleasure her. To bring her to the heights of passion, take her over the threshold, and catch a brief glimpse of heaven. After working her to a fever pitch, that's precisely what he did. With his mouth, his fingers, his body. As he eased into her welcoming warmth, their eyes locked.

Was she experiencing the same wonder as him?

She cradled his hips with her knees and, keeping her heels on the mattress, lifted her pelvis to accept him fully. Her eyes closed, and a blissful smile curled her mouth. "Mmm."

"Annie." The desire to have her look at him, to really see him, consumed his mind.

And thank God for her ability to read and recognize what he wanted because she lifted her lids and met his gaze.

"Quinn." Her fingertips caressed his face, and butterfly soft, she traced each individual feature. From the arch of his brows, to his cheekbones, to his jaw, lingering on his lips. Her eyes filled with adoration, and he knew it was for him, not for some character he'd portrayed.

Relief surged through him, and the words he longed to say became lodged behind an emotional blockage in his throat. He could show her how he felt, though.

His second thrust was as slow and smooth as the first, and his eyes almost rolled back into his head as her heat enveloped him.

"So fucking good," he murmured.

She grinned her agreement and gripped his ass. "I had no doubt."

"Hmm, you didn't worry I'd be a one-pump chump?"

"Nah. Two at the very least."

He laughed, realizing it was the first time he ever had during sex. The act had previously been to provide an orgasm for his partner before getting off. Where had the teasing and wonder been?

"Where did you go just now?" she asked curiously. It said a lot for her that she didn't get offended he'd taken a side trip.

"I'm worried if I tell you, it might upset you."

"Then don't tell me," she said simply. "Not unless you want to."

Resting on his elbows, he stared at her, studying her relaxed visage. He withdrew to plunge into her again, his stroke smooth and steady.

He grinned at her happy meep.

"I was thinking about the sex I've had in the past," he confessed.

She blinked once but didn't comment.

"And how this is better than any I've had before. The laughter, the teasing, the fucking perfection of our joining."

A blinding smile transformed her face from pretty to heart-wrenchingly beautiful, making Quinn breathless.

"I can't see how any of that would upset me," she said. "And I was thinking much the same thing. But how about we stop thinking so much and get busy?"

With a chuckle, he kissed her. The sweet, simple peck turned exhilarating as she opened under him, and she swiped her tongue across the crease of his mouth. Her teeth grazed his bottom lip right before she gave him a love bite.

Groaning, he sank into her and began to pump in earnest as she drew his soul from his body with her passion-drugging kisses. Quinn reached between them and parted her folds to brush her clit. With his thumb, he circled the nub with tantalizing slowness. As if it had a life of its own and sought his touch, her body arched up, pressing into him and his hand.

She broke their kiss with a low moan, and the welcoming walls holding him tightened with a swift graduation of force until the pressure was almost painful. But the flip side of the coin was pleasure, and he pushed forward, seeking more.

"God, yes," she groaned.

Her entire body shuddered as her orgasm swept through her, as if she was electrified. Gratified his sexual musings were right, that their lovemaking would be epic due to her gift, Quinn felt her orgasm like it was his own. His body responded in kind, with urgency and increasingly harder thrusts. With every stroke, she cried out, gripping his ass and drawing him tighter to her.

"Yes, yes, yes," pounded through his mind and out his mouth as the intensity built and his balls tightened. His orgasm exploded through him, and Annie's legs locked around his waist for his wildly bucking finale.

She arched her back, exposing her throat, and all he wanted to do was bite her like some wild animal marking his mate. So he did.

Crying out, she tightened around him, her body milking his, and he benefited from her second orgasm. As she clung to him, he experienced a feeling of rightness. As if every event of his life had culminated in that moment. Yeah, he was being fanciful, but so fucking what?

"Jesus!" she panted. "Who knew a bite could be so damned hot?"

He laughed, eased his weight from her, and drew her against him. "It's good to know you liked it. I couldn't have stopped the compulsion if I tried."

"Please, never stop your compulsions. If you have one, act on it."

Chuckling, he kissed her, and she melted into him, weightless.

"I'm starving," she mumbled sleepily a few minutes later.

"For more sex or food?"

She lifted her head. "Is more sex an option?"

"Oh, fuck yeah."

"Would I be a glutton if I wanted to mix the two?"

Compelled by the wicked gleam in her eyes, he rolled atop her. "Tell me what you want, and I'll ensure you get it."

CHAPTER 38

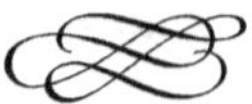

"You're glowing."

"Mm-hmm." Annie snuggled into the blanket, tracing patterns on the ridges of his stomach. "Multiple orgasms will do that to a woman."

He chuckled and stroked the damp hair back from her forehead.

"I can feel you thinking," she said softly.

His thumb traced the arch of her brow. "Hmm, can you? Somehow, I don't doubt it."

With an upward sweep of her lashes, she shot him a mischievous look, provoking him to roll on top of her.

"I'm thinking I never want to see you lose that glorious glow. How many more orgasms do you suppose it will take?"

"Not sure. Probably countless." Annie wove her fingers into his hair and tightened her hold. "Let's find out," she whispered against his lips.

Thirty minutes later, Annie wanted to purr and stretch like a cat, but she was too worn out and felt more like a gooey pile of marshmallow fluff. Her bladder was screaming at her to at least make an effort to move, but her bones were pure liquid, and her muscles refused to obey any of her commands. Also, she was too fucking happy and didn't want to disturb their little love nest.

Positive she couldn't wipe the obnoxiously satisfied smile from her face, she rolled toward Quinn. "Six seems to be the magic number. And now, I can die happy."

His deep chuckle caused her abdomen to contract. How did a simple sound do that? How did the mere timbre of his voice cause such a physical reaction?

Love.

It had to be. Because she desperately wanted to declare herself, she faced away from him. Some small bit of self-preservation held her back. Admitting she loved him hadn't worked out so well the last time. Yes, he probably knew. It wasn't like she'd told him any differently, but she hoped he'd never bring it up until he was ready to return her feelings. If he was ever ready.

Soon enough, he'd remember he was committed to a woman in a coma, and he'd freak the fuck out over what had transpired here. He would try to distance himself from Annie once again. If she confessed her feelings, she'd make it happen that much sooner. She sighed and buried her head half under the pillow. A silly attempt to hide because she felt too exposed.

When his fingertips brushed the scar on her back, she jumped.

"Does it still cause you pain?" he asked.

"Sometimes, but not right now. You startled me more than anything."

A tender kiss replaced his fingers. "I'm sorry you were hurt on everyone's behalf."

Eyes and nose burning from the sudden onslaught of tears, Annie stayed hidden and forced a light laugh. "It adds character."

"You have plenty of that, sweetheart," he replied.

Quinn placed one last lingering kiss on her scar and shifted to rest his back on the headboard.

Annie already missed the contact.

With a contented sigh, she faced his direction and opened her eyes. Quinn's wary gaze greeted her, and her smile slipped.

Aw fuck!

"Annie, I have to go."

The heaviness stole all her joy from moments ago with a swiftness that took her breath. Her "glow" died a quick, painful death. How did she save face when all she wanted to do was mourn the loss of him in her bed? Why did it feel like he was one more guy who couldn't wait to beat dust to the door?

She infused a chipper note into her voice as she said, "Mmm, okay. Do me a favor and lock the door on your way out, won't you?"

There, that sounded sophisticated and casual enough, didn't it?

His hand trailed along her lower back, and she shivered.

"I'm sorry." His voice held more regret than his expression had seconds ago.

The desire to weep was stronger still. "No worries, babe. I'm not expecting a ring and shit. It was just sex."

The hand caressing her halted.

She twisted to sit up and wished the fall of her thick hair was enough to cover her. With a tug of the comforter from beneath Tink, the dirty bed stealer, she cloaked her body with the heavy bedding. Sure, she'd left Quinn in nothing but his birthday suit, but his physique was perfect. Not an ounce of cellulite to hide.

Regret poured off him and into her. The weight of both their emotions was suffocating.

Here it comes.

Now that the orgasmic bliss had ebbed, his doubts were crowding his mind and, as a direct result, hers. She'd failed to replace her psychic barrier, and the barrage messed her up, big time.

"Don't ruin what just transpired. Please." She shifted to face him and pulled the blanket tighter around her. "I don't expect anything. Today was fun, but I know nothing's changed for you. You don't need to spoil it with unnecessary words."

"Annie..." He cleared his throat. "Annie, I—"

She wanted to scream. Wanted to say, *"Jesus, Quinn! You're killing my postcoital buzz. Can't you let me enjoy a few minutes of afterglow before hammering me with regrets and recriminations?"*

But she didn't. Every person was in charge of their own emotions and their own reactions to another's inner turmoil when it came to light. Annie would remain calm. Focused. Casual. If not, she'd fall to her knees and beg him to stay with her forever, and Holts weren't clingy. Her DNA was woven with steel.

His solemn stare was nearly her undoing. She couldn't seem to shut up.

"I realize for you this was probably mediocre, run-of-the-mill, but for me, it was the first great sex I've had in years." She eased to her feet. "I mean, I wouldn't mind having more of it. More glow, but it's cool if you don't want to."

Shut the fuck up, Annie!

Where was a gag when you needed one?

He frowned as he climbed from the bed.

Fate was on her side, and as he opened his mouth to speak—likely to tell her she was as nutty as a walnut tree—his phone rang, distracting him. It was all the time she needed to flee for the bathroom.

"Annie—" he called out, preparing to give chase.

Putting on the biggest performance of her life, she cast him an impersonal smile over her shoulder. "Potty break. Take your phone call."

His frown eased slightly, and she was free to escape.

Snippets of his conversation could be heard through the door, and it didn't sound positive. His forceful knock startled her.

"Annie? I have to go. Hailey..." His voice sounded choked, and she whipped open the door.

His devastated expression told her more than any words.

"Quinn! Let me get dressed. I'll go with—"

"No." His fierceness shocked her into silence. Though the intensity of his rioting emotions never lessened, he delivered his next comment in a calmer voice. "It's not a good idea. I've got to go."

She'd suspected the recriminations were coming, but she hadn't expected them so hard or quickly. There was time for her heartache later. For right now, she needed to relieve his suffering.

"This"—she gestured between them—"isn't on you, Quinn. Not solely. Please, don't feel bad. You go do what you need to. We can discuss this later if you want."

She raised her hand to cup his jaw, but he flinched away, as if her touch was toxic. Once again, she'd miscalculated, and she couldn't shake the sensation of being used and discarded. Her stomach flipped, and the small snack they'd shared between sexual calisthenics threatened to come back up the way it went down.

"You should go." Pressing her palm to her belly, she nodded and forced another smile.

He dressed without speaking, and when he reached the hallway, he partially turned to address her over his shoulder.

"I'll call you," he said, not making eye contact. But he wasted no time beating a path to the exit.

When Annie sensed she was alone, she sank to the edge of the tub. He might be back, but if he returned, things would be drastically different. Every time he ran away, he crushed another piece of her heart.

Perhaps he wasn't the man she believed him to be. Maybe she shouldn't have trusted someone with his acting talent, because looking back, his seduction felt like a calculated act. A woman in her circumstances, one who loved him beyond reason, was an easy mark.

Of course, she'd seen in him what she wanted to see. His attention came at a time when her ego was battered by Charlie. How could someone live to be as old as she was and still be so naive? Her emotions fired off, one after the other. Anger, betrayal, regret, heartache.

"Silly, Annie," she whispered as she stared at her distraught reflection. "When will you ever learn?"

Two days later, as she was checking out of her therapy session, Annie overheard two employees gossiping.

"Did you hear about Hailey Newberry?"

"No. Tell me."

"She went into cardiac arrest two days ago. She didn't make it."

One of the female therapists had the nerve to laugh. "I can't say I'm brokenhearted. It means Quinn Jensen is on the market again, and I'm happy to ease his suffering."

Their callousness was a hot poker under her ribs, firing up Annie's anger.

"How dare you!" She wasn't aware she'd rushed to confront them until she was up close and personal. "If it's true what you say, the man lost someone he cared about. What the fuck is the matter with you?"

Their expressions ran the gauntlet from shock to indignation to disdain to recognition.

"Wait! I know you. You're the psychic from television," one woman said.

Psychic from television?

"Holy crap! It *is* her!" the other exclaimed. Completely clueless to Annie's rage, the woman had the nerve to ask, "Can you predict the future? Do you do readings?"

Annie's fury reached its highest peak, and when that happened, she couldn't feel anyone else's energy. Being angry took all her own.

"Go to hell," she snapped. "And have some fucking respect for the dead."

As soon as she exited the facility, she limped toward the main hospital. Halfway to her destination, overexertion forced her to sit.

"Annie?"

Lost in her tumultuous thoughts, she hadn't heard Quinn's brother approach.

"Hey." With a half-hearted smile, Ty gestured to the spot next to her on the bench. "Mind if I join you?"

She did, but she wouldn't be awful enough to say it. Scooting to her left, she gave a single nod at the seat.

"I suppose you heard about Hailey."

He studied her face while she returned his regard. What was he hoping to discover by talking to her? She couldn't detect a hidden agenda.

"For the first time, just now," she admitted.

"Quinn didn't tell you?"

"There really wasn't any reason for him to call."

"I disagree. You risked your life to save her."

He had a point.

"Is there going to be a service for Hailey and the baby?"

"Wow, you really are out of the loop. Serena—that's what Quinn named the baby—survived." His lips twisted into a semblance of a smile, but it never reached his eyes. "She's in for the fight of her little life, but she's alive."

"I don't understand," Annie admitted.

"Hailey went into labor, and because she was far enough along, it was decided to take the baby by C-section. But Hailey's heart stopped on the table. An embolism."

Annie could scarcely breathe at the impact of what had happened. Quinn had been in bed with *her* while Hailey was rushed to surgery and had died on the table. No wonder his behavior was so abysmal. Looking back, she could say with one-hundred-percent certainty she'd have behaved the same way had the roles been reversed.

"Poor Quinn!"

Jaw clenched, Ty glanced out over the parking lot. His anger prickled her skin, and she rubbed her arms.

Question after question ran through her mind. Did he know she'd been with his brother during Hailey's final moments? Did he hate her for it? Or was the residual anger about her ratting them out? Through the myriad of sensations, a small bubble floated toward her. And in the center of the bubble was the truth.

Ty wasn't as angry as he was grief-stricken.

"I'm sorry. I know you cared about her." Annie geared herself up for the contact, then touched his forearm. "Can you forgive me for meddling where I shouldn't have?"

"It's water under the bridge, Annie."

"Somehow I doubt that, but thank you."

When he smiled at her, the smallest hint of humor shone in his eyes, and he resembled his brother to the degree that her heart pinged and her stomach clenched.

"You love him, don't you?" he asked softly.

She wrinkled her nose and stared at her scuffed sneakers.

"I can tell by your silence that you do. We're a pair. I'm in love with a dead woman. One who never loved me, and you're in love with a man who…" He trailed off, perhaps to spare her additional pain.

He didn't need to vocalize that Quinn didn't love her back. She already knew.

"We should go get drunk," he suggested.

"A brilliant idea on your part. One I can completely get behind." She pulled her damp t-shirt away from her body. "I need a shower first. My therapist is a sadist."

"Need a lift?"

Once again, she'd forgotten to arrange for a ride. "I do. I'm afraid I was too in my head earlier to make arrangements."

Ty escorted her to his black SUV and opened the door right as a sizzle of awareness hit her. "Your brother is close by."

"Damn, woman. Sometimes you creep me right the fuck out."

She laughed. Ty had an easygoing charm she found appealing. "I get that a lot."

"Don't look, but he's bearing down on us. Ten o'clock. And he doesn't look happy," he said.

"Do we make a run for it?" she asked, one foot in the vehicle, one foot out.

"Nah. I say we torture him a bit."

"Doubtful he'll be tortured by anything I do, but I'm game."

"You'd be surprised," he whispered with a wink. "If he thinks I want one of his toys, he's likely to lose his shit."

Quinn stopped just shy of touching her and ignored his brother completely. "What are you doing here?"

"I have physical therapy three times a week," she answered, calm and concise, feeling anything but.

"I know *that*. Let me clarify. What are you doing with my brother?" he ground out the question.

His jealousy was gratifying, if only to a small degree. "He offered to give me a ride."

His attention focused sharply on a point over her shoulder, and his face lost all expression, reflecting nothing but polite indifference. "We're being spied on, Ty. I'd appreciate if you'd see her home."

"That was my intent," his brother answered as blandly as Quinn.

"Try not to sleep with her, huh?" Quinn delivered the dig before casually sauntering off as if he didn't have a care in the world.

The shock of his comment stole her breath, and Annie gasped.

"Bastard," Ty muttered.

"I can call for a lift," Annie said, embarrassed by the whole scene. "I don't want to cause problems between you."

"Sweetheart, that ship has sailed. You're a troublemaker all the way." He placed a hand on her butt and gave her a small shove into the SUV. She chirped her surprise, and he chuckled.

Right before he closed the door, Ty leaned in and murmured, "Nice ass."

A quick glance toward the hospital showed Quinn staring in their direction. No doubt he'd witnessed his brother *helping* her—as Ty had intended. There would be hell to pay when they saw him again.

CHAPTER 39

Ty was kind enough to walk Tink while he waited for Annie to shower and dress. He ended up taking her to a quaint place called McAdams Pub in downtown Stonebrooke. The bar had been established in the early 1800s and boasted a large eat-in area for the restaurant, along with a private dining room off to the side. Along the far wall, the L-shaped bar ran from one end to the other. Between the main area and the bar was a sectioned-off space for dancing.

"This place is huge," Annie said in wonder.

"Yes, it's easy to get lost in here on a Friday night."

"Sounds like a familiar haunt for you."

When Ty smiled, it never reached his haunted eyes.

"Thank you for suggesting this place. I love it." Annie discovered the pub was still family owned by the server who delivered their food. The knowledge made her genealogist's heart sing. She could see herself spending time here in the future, perhaps enjoying a meal on occasion.

"Quinn and I used to come here a lot," Ty told her as he inspected his burger and salted his fries.

"You miss him," she concluded.

"And you don't miss anything," he replied. Lifting his beer in a mock salute, he nodded and took a long swig.

"It's true. Even when I want to, I find it hard to shut out other people's energy."

"Are you truly psychic?" There was no judgment in the question, merely curiosity.

Annie narrowed her eyes. "You're the second person to mention the term 'psychic' today. Why?"

"Where have you been living?"

"Apparently, under a rock. Spill your guts."

"You're famous in your own right now."

Annie could feel the color leach from her face. "What do you mean?"

"I'm sure you know the news got ahold of your name as the person who saved all those people at the airport. There was a follow-up story about you locating a little girl who was abducted about four years ago. The media reported it not long after."

"I was foolish to ever believe that would stay hidden."

"Why would you want it to?"

"To keep away psychic seekers and anyone desperate to find missing loved ones."

He grimaced and sipped his beer. "Makes sense. But you're screwed now. Tangling up with Quinn exposes you to the media sharks. And to put it mildly, you've caused a feeding frenzy."

"I didn't know about the earlier articles," she said, choosing to ignore the mention of Quinn. "One of the therapists in PT asked me if I could read her fortune. I thought she was mocking me."

"Doubtful. More like she was serious."

Annie swore and chewed the inside of her cheek.

"I can see why Quinn is attracted to you." He smiled softly when she looked up sharply. "You're not what I was expecting."

"I'm not what anyone expects," she muttered and pondered what being 'famous in her own right' meant. "You're in PR. How long does it take for this stuff to die down?"

Ty shrugged, took a bite of his burger, and contemplated the question. After a long minute, he said, "It won't. Not until you distance yourself from Quinn. Even then, this story will be dredged up periodically when tabloids or entertainment outlets need a filler article for my brother. I have a feeling you don't know half of what's been reported about you both."

"Do I want to?" Annie dropped her burger on her plate and sagged back.

"Probably not."

"I'm not psychic. Not in the way people think," she said. Avoiding his knowing gaze, she made a show of dunking her fries in ketchup. "My sister is."

"Seriously?"

"Yep. She can touch a person or object and see events unfold. Sometimes, she gets a vision of the past. But there have been times she's received nothing."

"I saw her coming out of Hailey's room a while back. I wondered why she visited that day. It was to confirm your suspicions, wasn't it?"

"Yes."

"Regarding her ability, it's not consistent?"

"Not really. Those in our family with the gift of sight can usually see things for blood relatives, but as far as seeing the future for an outsider, it can be hit or miss."

"Interesting. Quinn told me you were an empath. Something about reading auras and energy?" At her nod, he asked, "How does that work? Is it hit or miss, too?"

"No. My ability is on twenty-four-seven. I don't have much choice." His curious frown encouraged her to continue. "Think of it this way. Every living thing puts off energy. Some stronger than others. That energy reaches out to mine and mingles unless I create a barrier or I'm alone."

"A barrier?"

"I visualize a bubble or wall to put between me and others."

He nodded as if processing her explanation.

"Quinn mentioned you actually had a premonition the day of the accident." Ty had abandoned his food and crossed his arms on the table in front of him. She smiled at how engrossed he'd become in the conversation.

"I did," she confirmed. "I like to think it's an early warning system from my ancestors. If I get a chill and it's not winter, I better take heed."

He chuckled along with her. "I won't pry anymore," he assured her. "I get the feeling it's uncomfortable for you."

Reflecting inward, she compared Quinn and Ty. They were physically similar in so many ways, but the truth was, Quinn was in a league of his own. Untouchable.

"You know, when you think of my brother, you turn sad." Ty waved a fry in her face. "Eat something, and let's try not to be the pathetic losers we are."

"Want to talk about Hailey?" she asked, not letting him change the subject.

"Nothing to tell. Boy meets girl. Girl falls for boy's brother. Boy suffers in silence until one day she throws herself at said boy. Boy loses all brain cells and sleeps with his brother's scheming girlfriend."

"Boy gets girl pregnant," Annie concluded with sympathy.

His head came up, and his sharp focus made her uncomfortable.

"You think Serena is mine." There was no question, and the statement made her squirm.

"I do."

"We gave DNA samples for a specialized test yesterday. We're waiting on the results."

Full of compassion for his plight, Annie entwined her fingers with his. A vision smacked her at the moment of connection.

Two visions in one day was unheard of for her.

"Ty?"

"Hmm?" He'd gone back to eating his now lukewarm burger.

"Don't take this the wrong way, but you need to contest the results. There's going to be a mistake, I think."

"You weren't kidding when you said you thought she was mine."

"I wasn't kidding," she said. "But it was more than a thought or feeling. This image I received showed me a mix-up in the samples. If you want Serena, demand a second test."

"Quinn will hate you for this. He's already in love with that baby. Has been since he discovered Hailey was pregnant."

He wasn't telling her anything she didn't know, yet it hurt to hear it. Especially from him, who knew Quinn better than anyone. "She deserves to be with her real father."

Ty cleared his throat and took a chug of beer to compose himself. When he was able, he thanked her.

"You're worried you can't repair the break between you and Quinn, aren't you?" she asked with sympathy.

"No offense, but can you get out of my head for a bit? Put your wall up or something? Because this is getting really uncomfortable."

"Pfft. I don't need to be an empath to know you're hurting. Your hangdog expression tells me you miss your brother." Annie offered him a smile right before sipping her drink.

He grimaced. "That obvious, huh?"

"That obvious."

"I'm scared," he finally admitted. "Scared I'll lose Serena. Scared I'll lose my brother. Scared the rest of my family will hate me either way. If I take the baby away, Quinn has nothing left."

Annie winced. Ty hadn't meant the direct hit, but nevertheless, his words struck at the core of her feelings for Quinn. Thankfully, he missed her reaction.

"What if I'm a shitty dad? I don't know anything about raising a kid," he said broodingly, concentrating all his attention on the beer label.

He was earnest in seeking reassurance, and Annie desperately wanted to give it to him. "This conversation proves you're going to be an exceptional father, Ty. You're considering everyone else's feelings first. Quinn's..." Did she choke on his name? "Your family's, Serena's. I promise you'll be all she needs you to be. Kids only require a loving parent, willing to listen without judgment."

The suddenness of his sunny smile jolted her. Had she not been in love with Quinn, she'd have been floored by the stunning beauty of it. The Jensen genetics were a thing to behold. DNA gold. Of course, he was as close to the mirror image of the man she loved as one could get, so maybe that had something to do with his impact.

"I'm glad I ran into you today," he confessed. "I didn't realize I needed the therapy session, but you've worked wonders. Quinn's all kinds of an asshole for—"

Annie waved a hand back and forth. "Please don't go there. He's in an impossible situation."

"Why are you defending him?"

"I'm not. But I can see it from an outsider's perspective. You have to know what you did was wrong, Ty. Yet I believe she played you. Played on your feelings for her. Quinn is the one ultimately paying the price. He's lost his fiancée, his child, and his brother."

"And just like that, our therapy session has made me feel like total shit again."

He scrubbed his palms over his face as she'd seen Quinn do multiple times. The similar gestures tore at her soul. Had Hailey not been a true monster? Had she desired Quinn to a degree of desperation? To a level of seeking solace with his brother when he wouldn't give her what she needed? As hard as she tried, Annie couldn't find sympathy for the woman. She'd destroyed two brothers with her games.

"I didn't mean to, Ty. You asked, I answered."

He lifted his beer to toast her. "Fair enough."

Annie shoved her half-eaten food away and sipped her wine. The alcohol was the mind-numbing medicine she needed.

QUINN WAS IN HELL. FOR THE LAST FOUR NIGHTS, HE'D BEEN UNABLE to sleep. Seeing Annie with Ty had left his thoughts tangled and his emotions scraped raw. She wasn't the type to play games. He had to keep reminding himself of that. She'd claimed Ty was giving her a lift home, and she was telling the truth. She didn't know how to be anything but honest. He wasn't jaded enough to not recognize honesty when he saw it.

He knew he'd been an ass when he left and never called. Making love with Annie had been earth-shattering. He imagined he could still smell her on his skin, and he wanted her even now. It was doubtful he'd ever tire of her. However, coming to terms with the fact he'd been in her bed while Hailey lay dying was difficult, and he couldn't shake the guilt. He'd royally fucked up, and what did that make him? Granted, Hailey had cheated on him first, but she'd *died* while he was sleeping with another woman. And the worst part? His baby could've been lost to him forever and he wouldn't have known until it was too late.

He reached one hand through the hole in the incubator to touch Serena's tiny toes. The contact eased the crushing weight in his chest. Hailey's funeral was in two days' time, and he had yet to shed a single tear. Had he ever truly loved her? His continued detachment bothered him.

The only thing he knew for certain was that he intended to be the best father possible. Serena deserved a hands-on parent who put her first. And Annie? He needed to let her go. Whatever this connection between the two of them was, it could go nowhere. She wasn't built to be the girlfriend of a Hollywood actor, and Quinn needed to use all his emotional resources to give Serena a normal upbringing. He didn't have extra energy for a woman like Annie. Even if he did, he doubted he could ever look upon her and not be swamped by guilt for what he'd done.

His phone buzzed. Knowing he couldn't ignore the rest of the world any longer, he lightly squeezed Serena's foot, which was no bigger than his thumb, and left to take care of business. He was halfway to the elevators when Trace caught him.

"We need to talk."

Quinn frowned at the doctor's dire tone. What remained to be said? Serena wasn't his patient, and Hailey was dead. "What's going on?"

Trace did a visual survey of the area around him. "It might be better for me to address this in private."

"This? What's this? Say what you have to say, Trace."

"Annie called early this morning. She claimed there was a mix up with the DNA samples." He winced when Quinn swore. "Ty called about an hour later. He wants a second test because he's convinced she's right."

Black rage blinded Quinn.

"Annie? *Annie* said that?" His heart was pounding as hard as his head from the insta-tension.

How dare she betray him like this!

"Yes."

"You told me the other day this type of test was conclusive," he charged.

"I did. Technically, it is, but I hadn't accounted for lab error." Trace placed a hand on Quinn's shoulder. "Annie told me she had a vision of the samples being mislabeled."

"No!" Quinn barely controlled the urge to put his fist through the wall. "No. This has to be some kind of game the two of them have concocted." Never mind that he'd just ruminated about her honesty, there was no way this newest development wasn't a con or payback for some imagined slight.

"His attorney faxed over a letter of intent to contest the results, first thing this morning." The sympathy on Trace's face was too much.

"*Goddammit!*"

"Shhh. Unless you want this as tomorrow's news feed, you need to keep your voice down."

Trace's warning didn't go unheeded.

"Fine. They want their fucking second test, they'll get it. Serena is mine. How do we do this thing?"

"Come with me. We can head to the lab right now."

As they walked side by side down the corridor, Quinn was struck by another thought. "How do we make sure the same *mistake* doesn't happen again?"

"I intend to assign two lab techs to the testing. Preferably ones who aren't flustered by your fame. There will be a double verification of the DNA draw and testing process."

Quinn nodded, satisfied. "I want this to be over so I can take my daughter home when she's ready."

"Quinn."

The warning in Trace's voice caused Quinn's neck muscles to bunch. Following the direction of his gaze, he witnessed his brother chatting Annie up.

He saw red.

In the blink of an eye, Quinn stood in front of them, ready to do battle.

"Isn't this cozy?" He'd infused the perfect amount of contempt and coldness into the words. They couldn't mistake his anger.

Warily, she met his furious gaze.

Good.

Let her feel the full impact of the anger that had propelled him to confront them.

"I'm only going to say this one time, Annie. Stay the *fuck* out of my life. Don't meddle where you're not wanted."

"Quinn!" Ty's tone was harsh with warning.

"It's okay, Ty." She patted his brother's arm and shifted to go. "We're done here, anyway. Good luck."

"Annie—" His brother tried to halt her progress, and Quinn checked the urge to do the same. Together, they watched her limp down the hall, leaning heavily on her cane.

Forcefully knocking into Quinn's shoulder as he moved by him, Ty said, "You're a fucking ass."

Yes, he was. But his feelings weren't unjustified. With one hand, Quinn stopped his brother. "Are you going to deny she encouraged you to pursue another DNA test?"

"Yes. I am. She told me what she saw when she touched my hand. The decision to fight was mine."

"No, it wasn't." Quinn ran a shaking hand through his hair. He was coming down from his anger, but not fully. "If you believe she didn't manipulate you, you've been conned by another woman. She went behind your back and called Trace today to tell him the results were fucked. About an hour before you, if I'm not mistaken. What do you think of her innocence now? Huh?"

"I think it's firmly intact. Annie is blameless." Ty leaned close, careful to keep his voice low when he said, "Having seen your ugliness, I'm confident in my decision to raise my own child. It will be a cold day in hell before you get her."

CHAPTER 40

The apartment door opened and closed, signaling the arrival of her sister.

"Hey. Someone need a ride?" Sammy's affectionate smile was a sight for sore eyes.

Annie had been toying with saying to hell with it and avoiding Hailey's funeral service, but Ty had encouraged her to go. Even so, she wasn't sure she could handle another confrontation with Quinn, and after the new test results, there was bound to be.

Where had it all gone wrong? Where had her sweet friend disappeared to? Had his kindness all been a lie? And what about their lovemaking? Surely, that hadn't been a mistake. Nothing so beautiful could be. And yet, he clearly hadn't felt the same. He'd never tied affection to the act. If he had, he'd be with her now.

Coming to a decision, she told her sister, "I'm staying home."

"Pfft. Not happening."

"*Why?* Why do I have to go? I didn't know the woman. No one cares if I attend or not," she argued.

"Ty wants you there for support. You're being a friend. Probably the only one he has right now. And also because you're a Holt, and Holts are made of sterner stuff."

"All those people will be grieving. The impact of it, Sammy. I don't think I'm strong enough."

Sammy smoothed back a strand of Annie's already slicked-back bun and gave her a brief hug. "You are. When I say it's important for you to be there, then it's important. No arguing."

"Sammy, please." Annie's voice was raw and aching. "I can't take his hatred. It's like a hot poker under my skin." There was no need to vocalize who she was referring to. They both knew damn well she was talking about Quinn.

Annie swallowed hard.

"The press will be there, recording everything," she said, shaken by their constant presence in her life. "It'll be a feeding frenzy. You know my poker face sucks."

"We aren't letting any of those shits stop us from doing what's right. You hear me?"

"Is this payback for me making you go to Michael's service?"

Sammy smiled sadly. "No, sissy. I needed to go that day. If I hadn't, I would never have known the truth. As horrible as it all was and what happened after, it led me back to him."

Annie had deeply regretted forcing her sister to go to the memorial in Michael's honor back when they thought he'd died. The resulting chaos continued to feed her guilt.

"Annie?"

She glanced up to see Sammy's soft smile. "I promise it's all going to work out the way it should. Maybe not right away, but eventually."

"Have you seen something else?" Hope flourished in her chest.

"A glimpse. Nothing definitive yet, but today is part of the overall picture. Now let's shake a leg," Sammy urged. "We're going to be late."

"I'm going to regret this, aren't I?"

"It builds character."

Annie almost wept when she remembered Quinn's sweet words from two weeks before.

"You have plenty of that, sweetheart."

Yes, if pain built character, she certainly had plenty.

THE CEMETERY WAS PACKED.

Annie texted Ty for an escort through the tight security line. Although Hailey's funeral hadn't been publicized, her family lived in North Carolina, and loads of her celebrity friends had flown in to attend. No one without an actual invitation to the service was allowed. Of course, that didn't stop the media from hanging about the fringes with their long-range cameras. Annie imagined she heard the continuous clicking of lenses as she painstakingly made her way to the front of the line.

When Ty showed up and hugged her, she felt better about attending. He'd been through a lot and needed the support of his new friends since the old ones had abandoned him.

"Ty, this is my sister Samantha. Sammy, this is Ty Jensen."

"We've met. Briefly. You really are identical," Sammy said by way of greeting.

"No, they're not," Annie blurted. Two sets of brows lifted. Her face flamed. "I just mean, Ty is more boy next door. Quinn is more GQ."

She waved her hand helplessly, and Ty's lips twitched. Okay, so her explanation was feeble and oh-so pathetic, but whatever. He understood.

He chuckled and gave her a one-armed hug. "I'll take that as a compliment. Thank you."

As they all strolled up the hill toward Hailey's family and friends, Annie caught sight of Quinn. He hadn't noticed them yet, and she expected he wouldn't be pleased to see *her* in particular.

Why had she come here?

She was a fool.

Halting her forward movement, she was about to voice her concern when Quinn spotted her. The wave of cold outrage rolled across the expanse of space between them and hit her squarely between the eyes.

"Reinforce that wall, sissy," Sammy warned. "Mr. Movie Star is on the warpath."

Leave it to her sister to state the obvious.

"Fuck him. He doesn't own the planet," Ty retorted.

Both sisters gaped at Ty.

"I thought I told you to stay away from me?" Quinn's aggression pounded against Annie's well-constructed wall, doing serious damage and exposing her to his emotions.

Paige rushed over, and Annie distracted herself from him by focusing on the impossibly high heels the woman sported. Who the hell wore five-inch stilettos and tried to wobble her way across a grassy cemetery? It was a great way to break an ankle.

"Quinn, come back to the graveside," the annoying blonde bitch purred as if asking him to come back to bed. "They are waiting for you to start the service."

Annie hated Paige so fucking much at that moment. The cloying perfume and clinginess pissed her off to hell and back. Belatedly, she recognized the feeling as jealousy, something she'd never truly experienced in her life. Not even Daisy Jo boinking her husband had set her off as much as Paige sidling up to Quinn.

"Hello, Paige." Sammy's cold disdain jerked the skank's head in her direction.

Horror registered on Paige's overly made-up face as recognition struck. Hatred flashed in her eyes before she could bank it. She added her glare to Quinn's and wrapped her hand around his elbow as if she possessed the right to touch him.

Annie wanted to snatch the bitch bald.

Shrugging off Paige's hand, Quinn stepped to within a foot of Annie. "*Go. Away.* You're not wanted here. This is for family and friends only."

"She has every right to be here. She saved Hailey's life," Ty ground out.

"Did she? Because if she did, my fiancée wouldn't be in that casket right now."

Annie reeled from the ugly onslaught. Quinn couldn't be any plainer, and he cemented the undeniable truth once and for all. *She wasn't wanted.*

"I'll go," she said, surprising herself that she sounded cool and collected when she was anything but.

"Good," Quinn snapped.

Because she found it impossible to look directly at him, she shifted her gaze to the oh-so-smug Paige, who now rested the offending hand on Quinn's back. The urge to claw her gloating eyes out was stronger than the instinctive urge to flee. But Annie wouldn't. There really was no point in trying to defend what wasn't hers.

Quinn waved over a security officer.

"See that she's escorted from the premises," he ordered over Ty's objection.

From nowhere and everywhere, flashes blinded the group, shoving them from all sides. Discombobulated, Annie lost her balance.

Quinn was the first to reach her as she collapsed. Lightning fast, he gripped her upper arms and held her steady. Their rioting emotions merged, and black dots peppered her vision.

Shit, she was going to faint.

Or puke.

Or both.

"Take your hands off my sister, you fucking tool," Sammy snarled and launched herself at him.

For the paparazzi, it was Christmas all over again. The gift of Sammy attacking Quinn would hit the internet before her sister unfurled her balled hands. More photographers surged forward, and it became a free-for-all. Quinn somehow dodged Sammy's flying fist, adjusted his grip on Annie to lift her, and charged for the parking lot.

"I'm helping her, you crazy-ass woman!" He held Annie tight to his chest as his long legs ate up the distance. "Where's your car?"

"Please, put me down, Quinn. I can walk."

Why did her voice have to sound so damned breathy?

"Where's your car?" he repeated, tone pure steel.

"Blue one on the left."

He deposited her by the door. "Can you stand?"

When she nodded, he stalked away without a second glance.

As the press continued to snap shots of her and Sammy, Annie averted her burning face and climbed into the vehicle. All the paparazzi vied for her attention at once as they banged on her window. The shouted questions came fast and furious.

"Annie, why did Quinn kick you out of the service?"

"Annie, are you really psychic? What other predictions do you have for us?"

"Annie, what can you tell me about the kiss on your balcony?"

"Annie…"

"Annie…"

Stone-faced, she raised her handbag to block the sight line from the passenger window as Sammy inched the car through the throng of reporters.

"I'm sorry, Annie."

"Maybe someday you'll tell me why you put me through that fucking torture." The chill encasing her was reflected in her tone. "I can't believe you didn't know this was going to happen."

"I'm sorry," her sister said again.

Once they'd returned to her house, Annie made a beeline for her liquor cabinet. Today's fiasco called for something strong to forget.

"Annie? Please, tell me you're okay."

For once, Sammy sounded tentative and concerned. What did she expect? Annie would come through the door, skipping and whistling as if the whole world was one big happy playground? Her life was a shit show. It always had been. It always would be. She'd been cursed at birth with this damned empathic ability. All she wanted was a normal life.

"Annie?"

"Go away, Sammy," she screamed. "Just go the fuck away!"

Her sister's sharp inhale spoke of her shock.

Annie was the kind one. The sibling who never hurt anyone else's feelings. Well, *fuck that!* She was tired of being nice. Where had nice gotten her?

"Annie, we should talk."

"What does *'go away'* mean to you? I understood it when Quinn said it. I think it's pretty self explanatory, don't you? It means *leave me the fuck alone.* Get lost. Stop pestering me."

"Annie, please."

"I want to be alone. I can't process this shit. And, to be honest, I blame *you.* You forced me to attend that fucking funeral when I clearly stated *I didn't want to go,*" she yelled. For the first time in her life, she gave into a temper tantrum and flung her glass across the room, shattering it against the closest wall. "Do you know what you did? You made him hate me even *more,*" she cried. A sob welled within her chest. "The press is going to have a field day and paste my pathetic attempt to... to..." She threw her hands up, knowing she wasn't making sense. Shaking her head, she glared at her sister. "I'll be all over the internet, Sammy! *Again!* I can almost guarantee I'm going to come across as a deranged stalker. Or at the very least, some lovelorn spinster."

"You can't be a spinster. You've been married," Sammy retorted.

The desire to do her bodily harm must've been reflected in Annie's face, because her sister immediately changed tactics.

"It's going to be okay," she assured her softly. "I swear."

Annie's temper vanished, leaving her deflated and hollow.

"I don't want your promises right now, Sammy. I just want to be left alone," she said, weary to her very bone marrow.

"I'm sorry."

"Not half as sorry as I am."

"Do you want me to go back to your house for the night?"

She glanced up, surprised by the offer. "No. I'm going to sit out on the balcony and let Tink bark at the neighbors, because fuck the world. The first person who bitches gets my size six right up their ass." She ignored Sammy's chuckle. "You don't need to leave the apartment unless you want to head back and see Michael and Sophie. I only want alone time to regroup. I'll talk to you in the morning.

"I can make dinner."

"If you want."

"You *must* be traumatized." Sammy bent to pick up the glass shards.

Annie eased into a squat to help. "Why?"

"You don't let anyone in your kitchen. You're as anal as they come."

All her life people told her that, and it never became less annoying. Sure, she was a bit OCD about her surroundings, but not completely over the top.

"I'm turning over a new leaf. I'm calling it my *I don't give a shit about anything* leaf." After she tossed the glass into the garbage, she scrubbed her hands for a solid minute.

Sammy wisely held her tongue.

Pulling another tumbler from the cabinet, she poured herself a two-finger shot of tequila, downed it with a gag, a gasp, and a grimace, then poured a second.

"Be careful, lightweight. I'd hate to have to pick you up off the floor or try to cart your ass to bed."

"Are you still here?" Annie asked. "Hmm. I could have sworn I said I wanted to be alone. More than once."

"Fine. But for the record, you also said you were going outside. I'll hide in the guest room until you decide to vacate the kitchen."

She toasted Sammy with the second shot and poured herself a third to nurse.

"Stop at three unless you want to pay the price of sleeping on the floor. I can't lift you," Sammy warned.

"Call reinforcements. I'm not stopping until I'm good and wasted. I may become a full-fledged lounge lizard who wears leopard print and sex-kitten heels."

"Yeah, sure you will."

CHAPTER 41

Quinn observed the casket being lowered into the ground with a heavy heart. He shouldn't have ordered Annie to leave. He wasn't even sure why he did. All he *did* know was seeing her walk toward him with her hand on Ty's arm had sent him over the edge of reason. This was the third time he'd lost his cool over an innocent interaction with his brother. What the hell was wrong with him?

He mentally cringed when he recalled his own behavior. At the very least, he should apologize the old-fashioned way. Later, he'd personally send her flowers and a note. If he asked his assistant, there was no telling what pushback he'd get from her.

He frowned.

Speaking of Paige, he still needed to have that discussion about her familiarity. As an employee, she was positioning herself to take more and more liberties. Currently, she created a spectacle as she pressed into his side. He shifted to break the contact. Lately, he'd been too distracted and, frankly, uncaring to follow through on replacing her. Breaking in a new assistant required time and energy, and Quinn had lacked both. Tomorrow, however, he intended to correct his mistake.

Across the grave opening, Ty stared at the casket. The frown on *his* face was deeper and darker than Quinn's own. Why had he deceived him? Ty had been his closest confidant and best friend the entirety of their lives. The betrayal went deeper than the Mariana Trench. *So fucking deep.* Quinn didn't know if he could ever heal the gaping hole left behind.

The *why* of it all bothered him. Why had Ty slept with Hailey? Was it out of spite for some unknown reason? Jealousy because of his fame? Ty could've had it if he'd chosen. Their mother had put them both in the spotlight early on, but his brother swore he hated it and refused to go to auditions. Ty had claimed it was Quinn's gig, not his.

Perhaps he should try to rein in his resentment and judgment long enough to have a conversation. Maybe if he approached Ty, brother to brother, like a reasonable adult, and left the recriminations on the table, they could have an honest talk.

Quinn noted the softening of Ty's features. The sorrowful look in his eyes as he gazed upon the casket was the answer Quinn sought. They didn't need that conversation, after all. He understood what Annie had been trying to tell him.

But what were they to do now? How did they move forward and bridge the gulf?

A good start would be for Quinn to not contest the DNA results when they finally returned Ty as the father. And they would. Try as he might, he couldn't see Annie lying about the baby. She knew how much he'd been anticipating being a dad. Knew by taking fatherhood away, she'd tear him apart. Could she be that spiteful? It didn't fit with what he knew of her. Yet he hadn't thought it was possible for his own brother to be disloyal, either.

And then there were the mysterious pictures of the kiss on the balcony outside her dining room.

Someone had to have set those up. No one should've been in the courtyard to see them. They couldn't have known he'd be there when he was or that he'd even kiss her when he did. But she'd walked directly there from her shower and he'd followed her magnetic pull. Had she known he would?

Logic told him she was responsible for the pictures, along with their private conversations at the hospital.

His heart denied it.

The game of round-robin in his brain was maddening, and he wanted to scream. Instead, he looked to the sky and sent up a silent prayer that Serena was his and Hailey would find the peace in the afterlife that she never found on earth.

The mourners began dispersing to head to the Newberrys' reception, and Quinn realized he hadn't heard a single word of the service. It was just as well. If anyone tried to paint Hailey as a saint, he'd probably lose what was left of his mind.

A heavy hand gripped his shoulder, startling him from his tormented thoughts.

"Son, you and I need to talk after the ceremony."

His father was normally the jovial type. The earnestness behind John Jensen's words caused butterflies in the pit of Quinn's stomach. His worry ran from financial troubles to illness to death.

"On a scale of one to ten, how important is this, Dad? I don't know if I have the energy to tackle another problem today."

"It has to be today. Your mother and I fly home tomorrow afternoon. I want this mess resolved by then."

Ah, so not illness or death. Bonus.

"This mess? Why do I get the feeling this involves Ty and me?"

"Because you're smart and I'm not going to put up with foolishness."

Quinn gazed at his mirror image across the grave opening. Ty hadn't moved or stopped staring at the hole in the ground. The pull was strong to offer him comfort, and to combat the urge, he buried his hands deep in his suit pockets.

"We can talk, Dad, but I'm not ready to forgive quite yet."

"But forgiveness will come?" his mother, Pauline, asked from beside his father.

"I need time, Mom." He leaned forward to kiss her buttery-soft cheek. "Why don't you go see how he's doing?"

She patted his chest and picked her way carefully to where Ty was talking quietly with Bec. Mom enfolded him in a tight, loving embrace, comforting him as only a mother could. The afternoon light glistened off the teardrop trailing down Ty's cheek.

That goddamned tear was a fist to Quinn's stomach. When Ty hurt, he did, too.

"You two are killing your mother over your feud, son. She's not made to handle this type of conflict," John scolded.

Quinn would've laughed had he been able. Their mother was a force of nature.

"We can talk about it back at the house, Dad. This isn't the time or place." To prove his point, he nodded in the direction of the reporters speaking to some of the departing mourners. "My life is always on fucking display."

"Watch your tongue, boy."

"Yes, sir." The response was instinctual, as was his father's correction of his language. Some things were ingrained.

On the ride back to the Newberrys', his cellphone rang.

Annie.

He scowled at the screen.

By the fourth ring, they all grew irritated.

"Aren't you going to answer it?" John asked.

"No." Quinn sent the call to voicemail.

Thirty seconds later, the ringing started again.

"For God's sake, Quinn, answer the damned phone," Ty snapped from beside him.

"I have to be trapped in this fucking limo with you, Ty. But I *don't* have to like it, and I sure as hell don't have to take orders from you."

"Do you honestly think Annie would call you if it wasn't important? Especially after the way you treated her?"

His neck grew hot, and worry plagued him.

Ty was right.

In the past, she'd only messaged Quinn whenever he messaged her first. The exception was her concerned text when he failed to call her the night of her birthday. Never in a million years would she actually call unless she was having an emergency.

Like the attempted murder in her hospital room.

They still hadn't caught her attacker. Images of bloody apartments, car wrecks, and other equally horrendous disasters flooded his mind.

Quinn answered her third call on the first ring.

"Hello?"

"You're an ashh-hole," she hollered.

Relief swept away his anxiety, and he bit his lip to stem an inappropriate bark of laughter. Tilting his head far back, he stared out the moonroof.

"Yeah, I can be," he agreed.

"No, you *are!*" she retorted. "I shro… shro… show up to shrow my respect, an' you—"

She was cut off on her side by Sammy.

"Jesus, Annie! Are you drunk-dialing? Give me the freaking phone."

He pinched the bridge of his nose. Great. His earlier tirade had goaded Annie into tying one on.

"Hello? Who is this?" Sammy demanded.

"Quinn."

"Oh. Yeah, well, sorry but my sister's wasted."

"I got that impression," he said dryly. "Is she all right?"

"As if you care," she snapped. "Fuck all the way off."

He silently stewed. Of course he cared. Did he need to cut out a kidney and hand it over to prove himself?

"She's fine," Sammy grudgingly said before disconnecting.

His family ranged from indignant to amused. Ty being the latter. Quinn cut him a warning glare to keep silent. If Ty laughed now, Quinn wouldn't be responsible for his actions.

"Was that the troublemaker from the funeral?" Pauline demanded. "She seemed so nice in her emails. You never know who's going to scam you."

"Mom, let it go," Ty encouraged.

"How did she get your number?" John asked.

"I gave it to her," Quinn said simply. "We're friends."

"Were friends."

He glared at Ty. "What?"

"You *were* friends. I doubt she considers you one after today. Hell, probably not since you slept with her and didn't call again."

"She told you about that?" Outraged and beyond shocked, Quinn gaped at him. He couldn't believe Annie had told Ty about their intimate moments.

"You had sex with that crazy woman?" his mother screeched. They all winced. "What would cause you to do that? You'll never get rid of her now."

Quinn and Ty ignored her tirade.

"No," Ty said with an air of smugness. "*You* just told me. You're a piece of work, you know that?"

"Me? *Me?*"

"You boys need to stop this nonsense right now," John snapped, shoving a booted foot between them. Quinn had the fleeting thought that you could take the man out of Texas, but you couldn't take the Texas out of the man.

Again, the two of them ignored their parent.

"*I'm* the piece of work? You sleep with Hailey behind my back, and *I'm* the piece of work? Classic." Seething, Quinn tucked his hands under his thighs so he didn't clock his brother in the mouth.

"Hailey was in a *coma* while you were making time with that poor biotch." Ty snorted and gestured to the phone. "And royally screwing her up, I might add."

"Don't ever call her a bitch again." Quinn's warning tone was pure venom. "And *fuck you.*"

Ty's lip curled.

"I said biotch, not bitch. Your irrational behavior is telling, though, isn't it?" he said before turning to stare out the window.

Minutes ticked by under the weight of his family's harsh disapproval, but Quinn didn't care. He pressed the call button for the driver. "I need to make a detour."

CHAPTER 42

Quinn climbed from the vehicle and leaned in to inform his family he'd find a way to the Newberrys' home for the reception. His parents' and sister's expressions held twin looks of confusion. Ty, on the other hand, shot him a smirk, and satisfaction lit his knowing eyes.

He gave Quinn a mocking salute. "Tell Annie I said hi."

Other than a narrowed-eye glare, Quinn didn't react to his brother's jibe. He jogged up the stairs in lieu of the elevator, eager to see Annie and assure himself she was okay. Her door opened as he lifted his hand to knock.

"What the hell are *you* doing here?" Sammy asked, zero welcome in her tone.

"I came to check on Annie."

"Dude, seriously?" She attempted to shut the door in his face, but he blocked the action with his foot. "Look, buddy, I don't know who the hell you think you are or what you get away with when it comes to other women, but your crap won't fly here."

"If Annie wants to kick me out, that's her option. Until then, move aside."

"No, movie star, I don't think I will." She stuck her middle finger straight up, within an inch of his nostril. "Get lost."

Rubbing the space between his brows, he counted to ten. If he strangled Sammy, Annie might never forgive him.

"I don't want to manhandle you, but if you don't move out of the way, you'll give me no choice."

"Try it. You'll be picking up your teeth. Think anyone is going to want a toothless action hero?" she sneered. "I don't."

He'd never used his height to intimidate a woman, but he did now. "Dammit, Sammy. I'm not messing around. I need to see her."

"Why? You haven't done enough? You humiliated her in front of the world today. Get bent, you fucktwat."

Once again, she attempted to slam the door in his face. The weight of the heavy wood on his foot a second time smarted.

"I'm not leaving until I see her," he growled.

She stopped fighting him. "Why?"

"Does there have to be a reason? Why can't I just check on her?" Irritated and bewildered as to what she could possibly want him to admit, he threw up his hands.

"Because if you haven't figured it out, you shouldn't be here. You shouldn't be anywhere near her. Stop confusing her with the on-again, off-again routine." She paused in closing the door, and her expression transformed into a look of wonder. The sudden change in demeanor disconcerted him. "You poor bastard. You don't even know, do you?"

"Know what?" He'd stepped into a real-life version of Alice in Wonderland. Up was down, and down was up. No one and nothing was as it should be, and he was confused as hell.

She sighed, shook her head, and opened the door to its full extent. With a wave of her arm, she allowed him entrance. He tentatively stepped forward, worried her pleasantness was a ruse.

"Where is she?"

"Balcony. And if you make her cry, I'll cut you."

"Anyone ever tell you that you have violent tendencies?"

"I fought Rabid Ronni and won."

He had no idea what the hell she was talking about and was too afraid to ask. "Good on you."

"Sarcastic ass," Sammy muttered as he strode by.

With his back to her, he grinned. He doubted many people got the better of her, and he was oddly pleased he'd accomplished it. Taking an extra minute, he greeted an exuberant Tink, then proceeded through the slider to find Annie.

"You know your way around her apartment fairly well," Sammy said.

He ignored her sarcasm. If Annie wanted to fill her sister in on the details of the day they'd spent burning up the sheets, that was her option. Himself, he refused to kiss and tell—or he normally did. It grated on his last nerve that his brother had tricked him into confessing.

When Quinn found Annie, she was sprawled on a lounger, contemplating her feet, wiggling them back and forth. The sight filled him with sadness but such tenderness that his fucking chest literally ached.

She never once looked at him as he perched on the side of her chair.

He continued to stare his fill, noting her hair bun listing to one side and the smear of mascara under her eyes. And those dick-hardening, pouty lips. She seemed drained of animation, as if life had beaten her down. Where was her spark? Had he caused this?

"Just like old times," she said. "When you would visit me at the hospital. When we were friends." Her voice hitched on the word 'friends,' and his heart hiccuped right along with it.

"We're still friends, Annie."

"No. I don't want to be your friend, Quinn." She turned anguished eyes on him. "Not if you treat them so poorly."

If he were honest with himself, he'd have to admit she was right. He'd been a proper bastard in recent weeks.

"The day we were together was the day Hailey died. How is that okay?" he asked, letting her inside his tortured mind. "How do I get past not being there in her final moments? Missing the birth of my child?"

"Ty's child."

He closed his eyes and dropped his head. Yes, he mustn't forget Serena wasn't his. "I've lost everything."

"You have if you believe you have."

He frowned at the concise way she spoke. "I thought you were drunk."

"It's been a while since I've had anything to drink. Most of my buzz wore off the second you stepped through my door." She sighed and held up her shot glass. "It's a by-product of what I can do. Also, Sammy cut me off after three shots. She's the damned drink police."

Unsure what to say and where they went from there, he remained silent.

"Why are you here, Quinn?"

"You drunk-dialed me. I had to be sure you were all right."

She scrunched her nose. "I thought I dreamed that."

"Nope, you called me an asshole," he told her with forced cheer.

"Awesome." She leaned back and focused on her toes again. "Feel free to block my number."

"I *am* an asshole, Annie. Or I *can* be. I definitely was today."

"Yeah, we're in agreement about something," she muttered. "Anyway, as you can see, I'm perfectly fine."

Seconds ticked by, and neither spoke. Each lost in their own misery.

"It's been less than two weeks, and I miss you so much it hurts," he confessed, leaning forward.

Her cool expression softened a degree or two. She only hesitated a fraction of a second before she traced the planes of his face.

He'd never witnessed such abject despair from her before. The woman he'd always believed to be an open book was finally letting him see *all* the pages she contained.

"If we're being honest, I miss you, too. But we've become toxic to each other. You don't trust me, and I certainly don't trust that you aren't going to continue your Jekyll-and-Hyde routine."

He followed a lone tear as it pioneered its way down her cheek for others to follow. The desire to crush her to him, to ease all her hurts, was a living thing. But if he ever had the right before, he had forfeited it with his recent behavior.

"I trust you," he told her.

"No, you really don't." Her hand curled into a fist, and she dropped it in her lap.

Clearing the ball of emotion from his throat, he asked quietly, "Where do we go from here?"

"Block my number and forget I exist. I'll do the same for you."

Denial, hot and fierce, surged up. "Can't we remain friends?"

"No. I can't be your friend, Quinn. Please don't ask for something I can't give."

"Annie—"

"I think you should go, movie star," Sammy cut in. "She's made her decision. If you know anything about a Holt, you know we're a stubborn lot. Once we've made up our minds, that's pretty much a wrap. Cue the end credits."

He didn't bother giving Sammy's comments any consideration. Annie was carving him out of her life, and he didn't know if he could stand the loss of one more person.

"I can't lose you right now," he rasped. "I'm so sorry for what I said today. For how I've acted recently."

Her visage turned to granite, and she reached for Tink, who he'd forgotten he still held. "Goodbye, Quinn. Sammy will see you out."

His ever-present anger took over, and he dearly wanted to lash out. To verbally flay her alive for rejecting him. Her compressed lips and wary eyes checked his compulsion. He was hurting her with his erratic, explosive emotions, and it was the last thing he wanted to do. She'd paid the price for his mistakes time and time again.

He rose to pace and counted to twenty—multiple times.

Christ, it was like he was two different men. One wanted to gather her close and hold her forever. The other was a miserable sonofabitch, furious with the world and at her in particular. That incarnation wanted to rebuff her so nothing else could ever hurt him. Annie had the power to destroy him if he wasn't careful.

No wonder she was uncertain of him. He was truly embracing

Robert Louis Stevenson's main character, and lately, he portrayed Hyde as if he were born to the role.

When he finally halted and faced her, she was asleep. He shot Sammy a questioning glance. She shrugged and left the doorframe she was holding up to go inside. Was he supposed to follow? He gazed upon Annie's sleeping form. The dark-purple circles under her eyes attested to her lack of sleep. But he couldn't leave her like this. If she stayed out here all night, her back would seize up, and she'd be miserable in the morning.

With a gesture for Tink to vacate the chair, Quinn scooped Annie up. The rightness of having her in his arms struck him with the force of an oncoming freight train. If he held her a little too tightly, and if he buried his nose in her fruit-scented hair, no one other than Tink was there to bear witness.

Annie murmured words so low, he only felt them against his throat. Then she wrapped herself around him, snuggling against his chest. The gesture melted the ice wall he'd erected around his battered heart. As he walked toward her bedroom, he cradled her close. Across the distance of the living room, he met Sammy's solemn gaze.

What did she know?

His grip tightened, and Annie mewled a protest. After adjusting his hold, he dropped a kiss on her forehead.

"Would you…?" He nodded his head toward the master suite, and Sammy rushed ahead of him to open the door and draw down the covers. "Thanks. I can tuck her in if you don't mind using my phone to call a ride."

Keeping her voice low, Sammy said, "She has a pullout sofa in her office, if you want to stay."

"In case you've forgotten, I have the penthouse apartment right upstairs." He paused in stroking Annie's dark hair. "But why would you offer? I thought you wanted me to honor her wishes."

"Looks like I'm as confused as the two of you. Come have a cup of coffee. I'm sure it will take a while for a driver to get here." She paused on her way out the door. "Why do you need a ride?"

"The reception for Hailey is being held at the Newberrys' estate, and I sent the limo away." He couldn't tear his gaze from Annie's too-thin face. "I'll be out in a few."

Sammy nodded and closed the door.

Left alone with Annie, Quinn stretched out next to her on the bed to watch her sleep. It was a luxury he'd missed the day they spent making love. He toyed with the ends of her hair, wondering if walking away forever was even an option. Annie Holt had become his drug of choice, and he was an addict with no eye toward rehabilitation.

But she'd been through so much: a loser spouse, cheating boyfriends, a building collapsing on her that had nearly ended her life, the media bashing. All without any real complaint. Now, here he sat, struggling not to beg her to let him add more turmoil to her life than he'd already caused. His emotions and thoughts were a tangled mess, fluctuating back and forth like a seesaw.

She shifted to snuggle against him and released a contented sigh. The instinctive trust tore his fucking heart out. Uncounted minutes passed as he held her and stared at the ceiling. She was too precious and rare to be a part of his world, which was obvious by his tainted view of her actions. She'd never done anything other than react from the most beautiful part of her soul, and he misjudged her constantly.

He needed to let her go if he wanted her to be happy.

The decision weighed him down, and his legs felt like lead as he climbed to his feet.

"Goodbye, Annie."

Her lashes lifted, revealing dreamy blue eyes. When she focused on him, she smiled softly and opened her arms. All his good intentions flew out the window. He was damned if he could resist her invitation. Every cell of his being encouraged him to hold her. To cherish her. Tired of fighting her pull, the one that had drawn him in the moment he saw her alone in a crowded airport, he gave in.

CHAPTER 43

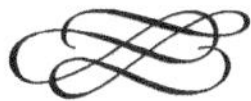

Annie shifted her neck to better feel Quinn's hot lips on her throat. She practically purred her response. If she was dreaming, she never wanted to wake. He trailed the skin down to the V of her décolletage, and she gripped the back of his head in wonder. How the hell did he make her burn this badly? Each touch of his lips to her flesh sent an internal fire blazing out of control.

Fisting her hands in his thick blond hair, she lifted his head to meet his desire-laden gaze. "Are we doing this for real? I'm not dreaming?"

His face lit with wicked intent. "I don't know about you, but you only have to move your hand a little south to know how serious I am."

Her eyes nearly rolled back in her head as his hand tunneled under the blanket to find her ready, wet, and willing.

He nuzzled her neck. "Based on your response, I'd say you are, too. But please let me know for sure. I don't want to do anything you don't want me to."

"The proof is in the pudding, buddy. I'm all for a spectacular goodbye."

He froze. Disappointment, followed closely by regret, registered on his face. Abruptly, he released her. So quickly, in fact, that her head spun, but she couldn't rule out the lingering effects of the tequila.

What had she done to cause his reaction? Wasn't she giving him what he wanted? A quick lay and an even quicker goodbye.

"I should go," he said gruffly.

"What we got here, is failure to communicate."

He laughed and flopped back on the bed. "Your imitation is spot on."

"And it definitely applies to our situation."

"It does." His tone was warm and curled around her like the loving partner she wanted him to be. "Okay, sweetheart, here goes my attempt at communication. The last time I spent the day in your bed, I tasted heaven. Being with you was like nothing I've ever experienced before. Not only did it scare the crap out of me, it made me feel I wasn't worthy of such a special gift."

"Quinn—"

"Let me finish. I can only imagine you picked up and reacted to the regret I was feeling at the time. But it wasn't for being with you." He shook his head. "I mean, it was, but only because I wasn't *free* to be." Rolling toward her, he laid his head on the pillow, level with hers. He waited until she met his eyes, so full of honesty and contrition, it didn't take someone with her talents to recognize he was telling the truth. "It was my fault you mistook the energy in the room, and I tried to stop you from rushing away, but the phone rang."

His fingers traced the arch of her brow, and he leaned in to drop a sweet, lingering kiss on her lips.

"That goddamned phone call. It was Trace, telling me the baby was in distress and they needed to operate immediately. I had to go. Dragging you with me to the hospital wasn't an option. I already felt like a complete shit for cheating on Hailey, but if we showed up together, the press was going to mob us."

She opened her mouth to remind him Hailey was the true cheater, but he beat her to the punch.

"Yes, even though I know she did it first, I felt guilty as fuck."

"Then she died," Annie concluded softly.

He nodded and closed his eyes. "She died."

With a heavy sigh, he said, "Foolishly and unfairly, I blamed you for distracting me, but no more than I blamed myself. It didn't help that every fucking time I turned around, you were with Ty." He growled his irritation. "The only thing looping through my mind was his affair with Hailey. What if he decided he wanted you, too? What if you discovered you liked him better than me?"

"That will never happen." She placed her hand along his jaw. "Never."

"No? Are you going to tell me you didn't go to dinner with him?"

Annie dropped her hand to grip the sheet. "How…?"

"How do I know? My attorney has had someone following Ty since our fight. He was looking for any reason he could find to help me gain custody of Serena." Seeing the storm clouds gathering on her face, he said, "My lawyer informed me, right before the service, that the two of you were together at the pub in Stonebrooke. If you were curious why I was so goddamned angry, it's because you walked up with him immediately after I heard that joyful bit of information."

Pissed and ready to do him bodily harm, she jackknifed into a sitting position, wincing at the warning shot her spine fired off.

"You were spying on your own brother?"

A muscle ticked in his jaw as he shifted and loosely hugged his knees. "Yes. It wasn't my idea, but when it was suggested, it made sense."

"That's deplorable, Quinn."

"Wow." He scoffed and hopped off the bed. With a shake of his head, he stalked toward the door.

"Where are you going?" she demanded. "I thought we were talking this through."

"I can't. Not without wanting to smash things." He returned to tower over her, cheeks flushed and eyes snapping. "If I'm not mistaken, you're about to defend him. Poor fucking Ty," he mocked in falsetto.

"He *loved* her."

"So did I!"

His admission hurt. Damned if it didn't. Especially when Annie wanted his love for herself. Bracing herself to deal with the rest of the ugly emotions, she continued. "I'm not saying you didn't. I'm saying he met her and fell in love. He told me the story of how he lost her to you—Mr. Popular, Mr. Movie Star."

"He *never* had her, Annie."

"Maybe not, but in his mind, that's the way it happened. I'm not saying he wasn't in the wrong, but can't you see that maybe she manipulated the situation? That she wanted you to marry her so badly she set your brother up to get her pregnant so she could turn around and con you?" Annie leaned forward, silently imploring him to understand. "Think about it, Quinn."

His indignation was palpable. *"Are you saying she didn't love me?"*

"I never met the woman! I don't know if she did or not. I assume, in her own way, she did. How could she not? But tell me this, what better way is there to convince a man the baby you're carrying is his than to get impregnated by his *twin brother*? That child would resemble you."

"Serena is *mine*."

"No, Quinn. *She isn't*. You know it. I can *feel* that you know it."

"And you're right one hundred percent of the time? You've never been wrong in your entire life?" he snapped, his questions mocking but laced with desperation.

She answered truthfully. "I have, but not about something like this. Not when it counts. Sammy also knows the truth. She's the one who confirmed it for me."

"Damn you, Annie!" he swore. "Why couldn't you have left well enough alone?"

His anger and disgust hurt. Not only in the physical sense but as someone who loved him. They'd never get past what he perceived as her betrayal. Even if, by some miracle, they managed to start a real relationship, this situation would always rest between them. Eventually, it would come back to haunt her.

The time had come for Annie to let him go.

Really let him go.

Not like the other times when she'd kept hope alive in the back of her mind and in the far reaches of her lonely heart.

The only way to release him was to get mean, to tell him in no uncertain terms they were done. Because she couldn't manage it, she said, "I was damned a long time ago. Go make your peace with your brother."

"I'm going to fight for custody."

"I wish you wouldn't, but I somehow don't doubt you will. You don't know how to lose," she said contemptuously, resting back against the headboard.

"What's that supposed to mean?"

"Come on, Quinn. You didn't love Hailey, not fully. You only thought you did, because you were worried life was passing you by. She was the perfect arm candy for your twisted world of fake people." She infused a sneer in her tone. "Maybe a part of you knew Ty wanted her for his own. A bit of sibling rivalry, perhaps?"

"You're treading on thin ice, sweetheart," he warned, taking a menacing step toward her.

"Tell me, aren't you here because you're worried about losing me to Ty? Am I another little game between the two of you?"

He reeled back as if she'd bitch-slapped him.

Essentially, she had.

"Are you serious right now?"

"Never more," she stated coldly.

"I just told you that you rocked my world. Are you really going to sit there and throw these ridiculous accusations at me?"

Shit. She hadn't counted on him fighting back.

"Come back when you have your house in order and you know what it is you want. Until then, I can't handle the conflict," she said tiredly.

He hauled her out of bed and branded her with his kiss. "I want *you*."

Knees weak and willpower even weaker, she drummed up every ounce of resistance she could. "Not enough. Not in the way that counts. *Goodbye*, Quinn."

CHAPTER 44

Quinn slammed Annie's door as he went to the living room to wait for his ride. There was nothing more to say. For reasons of her own, she was determined to push him away. Her acting ability sucked. If she thought he hadn't recognized the ploy for what it was, she was sadly mistaken.

But one thing rang true. His life was a mess.

"Come back when you have your own house in order. Until then, I can't handle the conflict."

He should've known his emotional upheaval would adversely affect her. There were a lot of issues he needed to resolve before he could pursue her. Timing was at the top of the list. If he were to start a relationship with her now, the press would tear her apart. They'd paint her with the ugly stick, as they had in the past and as they would over the next couple of days, based on his deplorable behavior at the funeral.

Fuck! Fuck! Fuck!

He was an idiot.

As hard as it would be to stay away, he had no real choice. All he'd achieved by coming here was to make it harder for both of them. But he hadn't been able to go another hour without telling her how much their time together meant to him. She'd never given him any assurances in return, but Annie was transparent. She loved him, or his name wasn't Quinn Jensen.

As he sunk down on the couch, all the mistakes he'd made to date came back to him. The heaviness draped across his shoulders, weighing him down.

"Are you okay?" Sammy asked.

His head whipped up as she dropped on the cushion beside him.

"Do you really give a shit?"

She laughed, and her resemblance to Annie couldn't have been plainer. He rubbed the place over his heart and stared out the glass slider.

"If I didn't care, I wouldn't be here asking, movie star." And for once, she seemed to be on his side.

"Yeah, I'm good."

"Hmm, somehow, I sense you're lying. But if you don't care to talk, that's your prerogative." There was no judgment in her voice.

"I don't really know you," he said by way of explanation. "I hope you're not offended when I say I have to be careful when I speak to strangers."

"Fair enough. In that case, I'll do the talking. My sister isn't a fragile flower. Not by a long shot. But she does have to be careful about emotional overload, as I'm sure you are aware." Her dark brows clashed together. "She loved Charlie. If she didn't, she wouldn't have married him. But their relationship was tame in comparison to whatever the two of you have. I've never seen her respond to anyone the way she does you. Never seen her light up. Your behavior today…" She swallowed and shook her head. Censure was inherent in her tone as she said, "Your behavior today made me want to cut off your head and spit down your windpipe. She didn't deserve it."

It was impossible not to be amused by Sammy, and he smiled as much as his weary soul would allow.

"I agree, Sammy. Annie didn't deserve it. She didn't deserve a lot of the fucking garbage I've piled on her."

"Just so we're on the same page."

"We are."

"Good. And don't let her push you away. She does that when she's been hurt." Sammy rose to her feet.

He halted her departure by gripping her wrist.

"Sammy, I'm not sure I shouldn't let her. She deserves better than me. Than what I have to offer."

She studied the hand holding her, a small smile playing about her lips. "I have confidence in you, movie star. But a word to the wise. Not everyone in your inner circle is trustworthy."

"You drop a bomb like that and intend to walk away?" he asked her retreating back.

"I've learned I can't prevent the inevitable. I can only hope to soften the fallout for those I love."

"Cryptic and unhelpful, Sammy."

Over her shoulder, she grinned and saluted. "Your car is almost here."

"Did you see it in a vision?" he asked, curious in spite of himself.

"No, he called for access to the garage a few minutes ago."

He snorted and shook his head. "Why did it take him so long to get here?"

"You needed time." Before disappearing into the kitchen, she winked, and he was taken back to the moment at the airport when he'd first met Annie. She'd winked at him in the terminal and blown his mind. These two petite sisters could rule the entire world if they ever tried.

He had the overwhelming urge to return to Annie and settle their argument. Leaving her with the strife between them went against his nature. Yet it was important to remember she was the one who'd sent *him* away. As he descended the stairs to the lobby, he'd never felt more alone in his miserable life.

"He's gone."

Annie didn't bother looking up from organizing the top of her dresser. "I know."

"He's hurting, too. Don't forget that, sissy."

"As if I could," she snapped. "As if I could ever forget how anyone else *feels*."

"Am I to be your verbal punching bag?" Sammy tilted her head, but her voice held only curiosity.

Annie's anger balloon deflated. "I'm sorry. I'm finding it difficult to handle all this. You'd think I'd be an old hand at men walking away."

"He'll be back," Sammy assured her with a hug.

"I'm not sure that's for the best." Annie changed the subject before she could reply. "When do you and Michael head home?"

"When are you okay to be alone?"

Annie shrugged. "I'm as good as I'm going to get. It's about time I get back to my old life and career."

"You do know you can do that anywhere, right? You could always head to the Keys like you planned for Christmas. Michael and I could join you for a long weekend."

"Nah. Spring is too crowded, and summer is too hot. Besides, I still have a few weeks of PT left."

"In that case, Michael and I will drive back to Florida the day after tomorrow."

"Speaking of, where *is* your husband? I haven't seen him since this morning."

"He's out, walking your property. I think we're going to take you up on that offer of land if it's still open."

Annie frowned. "Of course. But if you're only using it as a vacation home, I have plenty of room at my house. You don't need to build anything."

"I believe he has something more permanent in mind."

Annie's vision blurred, and she blinked away the moisture to see her sister's caring expression. "I would love to have you close, sissy."

"It may be a few-months-in-each-place thing to start. I don't want to be too far from Mom and Dad until Sophie is older."

After Sammy left her alone, Annie circled back to her current circumstances and the tumultuous emotions left in Quinn's wake. He might well and truly be gone this time. To accuse him of not loving Hailey had been a step too far. Yes, she'd done it on purpose to drive him away, but oh, the agony of her decision left her miserable and gave her a desire to crawl into a hole, never to come out again. Not dissimilar to a wounded beast.

Whatever fates cursed her with this awful ability had also sentenced her to a life of loneliness and heartache. For the millionth time, she told herself she was done with romantic love. The fallout was too widespread and painful to bear. She doubted anyone could come close to making her body sing as Quinn's touch had. If she closed her eyes, she could recall the feel of his lips on her hot flesh. Still feel his hands on all the right places. Feel his fingers working their magic inside her. Relive the fullness of him as he thrust into her and the explosion of their mutual release.

With a pang for what would never be, she headed for the shower.

It was time to cool down and get her head on straight.

CHAPTER 45

*O*ver the next week and a half, it seemed no matter where Annie went, she ran into Quinn. The hospital, the grocery store—*seriously, what famous actor did their own shopping?*—the pharmacy. She did her best to ignore him, but each time was a shock to her system. Each sighting made her want to abandon her idiotic reasoning and fling herself into his arms. But he never approached her. Never asked how she was doing or smiled her way. His simple nod or blank stare was all she ever received.

Today was no different. Today was her last therapy session, and she couldn't be happier. At the end of the week, she was scheduled to move back into her own home, and life as she knew it would go back to normal. Or a new normal. The limp was for life, and she imagined the body aches were, too. But she could bury herself in research and not bother to come up for air. Of a certainty, she shouldn't see Quinn again. And didn't that make her heart ache all the harder?

The hour she put in was grueling, and the therapist gave her a list of exercises to perform regularly at home to keep her joints limber. All that was left was for Trace to sign off on her chart, and her time in hospital hell was finished.

Trace entered his office with Quinn on his heels.

"Annie! I didn't realize you'd be here so soon. How's my favorite patient today?"

"I'm back to being a favorite? What an honor," she said dryly. He had the grace to look embarrassed. Why he'd had a change of heart when he was firmly entrenched in Camp Quinn, she would never know. "Don't be offended, but I'm looking forward to seeing the last of this place."

"Okay, just a quick exam, and you're free to go." He turned to Quinn. "I'll meet you outside in ten." To her, he said, "Follow me into the exam room."

"You two seem mighty chummy."

His head came around to test her seriousness. When he saw her smile, he laughed. "He's trying to integrate himself into Stephen's poker night. I decided to throw him a bone since you refused to join."

"The man's a card sharp. You're going to lose your shirt." They both thought back to the game she'd won months before. Trace grew serious when she grew flushed.

"What happened between you two, Annie?" he asked quietly as he manipulated her hip joint. "I've never seen two people more compatible."

Her eyes ached, and her throat closed with unshed tears. All she could manage was a shake of her head.

"Sorry. I know it's none of my business."

"No, it's okay. If it's anyone's business, it's yours. You've had front-row seats to the main event."

He helped her sit and lifted her shirt to exam the scar on her back. "Do you still love him?"

"Who said I loved him? Oh, that's right, *me*. Silly, Annie," she scoffed. At his serious stare, she relented. "I don't know. Maybe I never did. Maybe I was caught up in the whole movie-star-paying-attention-to-me situation."

He straightened her shirt and sat in front of his computer screen to type his notes. "You don't believe that."

"Isn't the psych eval Stephen's gig, Doc?"

Trace rolled his stool to face her. Without a word and only a raised brow, he conveyed his disappointment in her snark.

"Yeah, sorry. I'm a little sensitive today. Will you forgive me for being bitchy?"

"Are you sleeping?"

"Not great."

"Because of Quinn or from pain?"

"The pain." She refused to admit memories of Quinn were replaying in her head every time it touched the pillow.

"Mm-hmm. Okay, I can prescribe you a sleep aid if you'd like. But don't drive in the mornings until the last of the brain fog has cleared away."

"No. I don't want to take anything I don't have to. I have tea and a few pills left for nights the pain is too great."

"Do you need a refill?"

"Not yet. I can call your office if I do."

He sighed heavily and patted her leg. "Don't be a martyr, Annie. If you need the medication, take it."

"I don't like how it makes me feel."

Trace snorted and helped her stand. "You're the only one. Most times, I have to deny refills."

She grinned. "What can I say? I'm stubborn that way."

After he escorted her into the hall, sentimentality struck. This was the last time she'd see him.

"Thank you for everything, Doc." They hugged, and Annie wondered why she couldn't fall for someone as amazing as him. "Give Stephen my love and tell him not to be a stranger, okay?"

"Will do. I'll have my office call you with a few good doctors in your area for future follow-ups."

She cast him a cheeky grin. "I'll only have you feeling up my back, Doc."

"Don't let your mouth write checks your ass can't cash, sweetheart."

Quinn's soft growl made her jump. She'd felt the current, known he wasn't far, but she hadn't expected him to be resting on the wall behind her.

She refused to respond to him and gave Trace a second brief hug. She made it halfway to the exit when a different voice called her name.

"Annie?"

She halted her forward momentum and slowly spun to face the man she least wanted to see in the world.

"Charlie."

"What are you doing here?"

Her brows shot up. Her ex had to be the most clueless individual on the planet. "I had a building fall on me around Christmas."

"Oh, yes, I knew that, but I thought you'd be recovered by now. It's been months."

She bit her lip to hold back the sarcasm. "I am, for the most part. There was some physical therapy required to walk properly."

"I didn't know."

"Of course you didn't," she said dryly. And unwilling to hold back the snark any longer, she said, "That would mean you cared enough to call or think about something other than your own personal wants."

"There's no need to be bitchy about it," he said with a sullen expression.

That was Charlie, surly to the end.

A harsh laugh escaped her. How could it not? He still believed the sun only shone for him. "I need to go."

"Aren't you curious why I'm here?"

Not really.

"With my luck, you moved to town to torture me, but no, I'm not curious in the least." She sighed her impatience. "I'm sure if you were dying of cancer or some other dreaded disease, you'd have already told me."

A sly, almost ugly look flashed across his face before smugness took its place. "We moved here because my wife wanted to be closer to her family. She's pregnant. Today's the ultrasound appointment."

Wife.

Pregnant.

The information was a roundhouse kick to her head.

Bitterness filled every crack and cranny of Annie's being. He had always put their discussion about children off with one excuse or another. Until, in a temper, he'd revealed he feared any kids of theirs would be cursed—*like her.*

"Well, let's hope you are a better father than you were a husband." Although she hadn't meant to say it aloud, his gasp of outrage made her mood marginally better.

"You're nothing but a washed-up, past-her-prime woman nobody wants," he sneered. "One who's turned into a celebrity stalker by all accounts. The media made that much perfectly clear."

His face looked so fucking punchable, and in her mind, she struck him a hundred times, with big, gaudy rings on her balled-up fingers. Bottling up all the hateful comments she could hammer him with, she turned to leave.

But Charlie wasn't done.

"Is that why you're really here? To continue stalking that poor bastard, Quinn Jensen?" He followed her as she tried to exit the main doors. "I saw him down the hall. It's pathetic, Annie. You're acting like a desperate whore, chasing a guy who wants nothing to do with you."

He was only saying what the press had posted, but he'd scraped open a slow-healing wound. One everyone seemed to be picking to the point of bleeding. She wanted to scream at the injustice of it all.

As if drawn by a magnet, her eyes looked to where she'd last seen Quinn. He was speaking to Trace but staring in her direction, a deep frown of concern on his face.

The dam broke on the tears she didn't know were building.

Once started, she couldn't stop.

There she was, crying for a guy who'd probably only ever viewed her as mildly entertaining. And yet, she missed him. Missed the teasing and the easy camaraderie she'd never known with any other man.

Christ, she really *was* pathetic.

With a smothered sob, she rushed for the door as fast as her body allowed. With any luck, she could get to the waiting driver before she ran into anyone else who would delight in her misery.

"Annie!" Though it was Quinn's worried voice calling to her, she refused to stop. "Annie, wait!"

She couldn't outrace him—she knew that—but she gave it her best shot. The jolt that came with his touch was expected, but her emotions were too exposed to prevent the impact to her system. A mental barrier was harder to erect after the fact.

To get relief from the barrage of their joined force, she jerked her arm free from his hold and swiped at the tears on her cheeks.

"Are you all right?"

Her mouth dropped open. "Really?"

The man had lost his pea brain.

"Dumb question. Sorry." His face softened with gentle humor.

She nodded her acceptance of his apology. "I need to go."

"I… who was that man?" His gaze darted to the entryway of the hospital. "The one pretending to be a trout and who's now heading this way."

She didn't need to look. She pointedly turned her back more fully as Charlie moved within hearing distance.

"He's no one," she stated coldly.

Quinn grinned his appreciation of her nasty attitude. Belatedly, he recognized her ex-husband from the encounter with James. But even if he hadn't, it would've only taken an educated guess.

At roughly five-foot-nine with an unhealthy build and average looks, the guy was nondescript. Even his hair was plain. Not blond, not brown, just *blah*. If one placed Annie and her ex side by side, they'd realize the two were never meant for each other.

She was alive and vital, where Charlie was lifeless and dull.

Polar opposites.

"Annie?" Charlie asked. "Are you okay?"

At her incredulous gasp, Quinn laughed in anticipation. His Annie was about to tear Cheatin' Charlie a brand new asshole.

"Am I okay?" she snarled, spinning and nailing the fool with the most frigid expression Quinn had ever witnessed. "Are you dim-witted, Charlie? Does it fucking *look* like I'm okay?"

"I... uh... you..."

Prepared to enjoy the show, Quinn stood back and crossed his arms, watching as the dweeb stuttered and stumbled through the surprise attack. Although, the bastard should've seen it coming. He'd been married to her for years and knew nothing about her, yet Quinn recognized the volcano brewing beneath her surface.

"A plane impacted the building I was in. I was crushed under hundreds of pounds of rubble, breaking bones, tearing muscles, and collapsing a goddamned *lung!*" She drew herself up and, with a hand on her hip, perfected the universal bitch-about-to-tell-it-like-it-was pose. Quinn had never seen her more fierce or beautiful. "I was in a body cast from a *fractured* spine. And while dealing with all that *bullshit*, I have to deal with the press on my ass because *apparently* it was leaked that I'm a freak of nature by sources *close* to me." She tapped a finger to her chin as if in deep thought, but her eyes were pure violence. "I'm sure *you* had nothing to do with *that*."

Charlie sputtered, but she wasn't done. She swung her cane in his direction. "Hospital staff are asking me to read their fucking futures like I'm some two-bit storefront psychic. And, as you so rudely pointed out, the press has also reported I'm a *celebrity stalker*, pathetically chasing after Quinn." She inhaled deeply, and her expression returned to arctic. "You want to know what the cherry is on top of my shit sundae? *You* moving here, then proceeding to snipe at me and rub it in my face that you and your scrawny ho-bag are getting ready to have a child."

Her voice had turned ragged, and Quinn straightened, ready to face another assault charge on her behalf.

"You denied me a child for our entire marriage, and I hate you so fucking much right now." She exhaled a shaky breath as she clung to her fading fury. "So no, Charlie, you *fuckwit*, I am not okay. I'm *far* from okay."

That she'd wanted a child was news to Quinn, and unexpected longing clogged his throat. She'd make an incredible mother, given the opportunity.

Her tirade ended on a choked sob, and the anguish in the wounded eyes she turned on him cut Quinn in two.

"I'd appreciate it if you both left me alone. I'm going home to drink my lunch. Peace out."

She tapped her chest with a fist and held up the peace sign before she spun on her heel and limped toward her cab.

All he wanted to do was sweep her into his embrace, bury his head in her sweet-scented hair, and apologize for all the wrongs he'd done to her. All the grief he'd caused. He longed to offer her the baby she desperately wanted.

"She must be PMS-ing," Charlie said.

And wasn't that the fallback line for all Neanderthal men at large?

Annie, only ten feet away at best, stopped. Quinn could literally feel her outrage in the nerves just below the surface of his skin. Or perhaps it was his own. Without pausing to think of the consequences, he hauled back and decked the pissant, then strode to where Annie stood frozen in shock, with her mouth hanging open.

"You're a dick," Charlie screamed at his back.

"Better than a fucking asshole," Quinn returned.

He put his hands on Annie's shoulders and gave her a light squeeze. Her imitation of a marble statue was making him uneasy. "Sweetheart, look at me. Please."

But her gaze remained on her ex-husband, who was picking himself off the ground.

"That's gonna leave a mark," she said with a snort.

Quinn laughed and hauled her close.

"Maybe he'll think before he insults you next time."

"You defended me." She turned her stunned face up to his.

"Is it so surprising?" When her mouth formed the word yes, he pressed his fingers to her lips. "Don't answer that. I can see it is. I'm sorry, Annie."

"Thank you." She nodded her forgiveness.

"Can I see you home?"

Annie eased from within the circle of his arms. "It's not a good idea, Quinn. As it is, this is likely to create another media wave." She gestured toward the retreating Charlie. "And you should call a lawyer. He'll press charges. Trust me when I say, he's a spiteful prick."

"Let him. It's why I keep an attorney on my payroll."

Her mouth quirked. "Oh? You go around punching people a lot, do you?"

"No, but it felt good, so perhaps I'll start a new trend."

She smiled and shifted to go.

"Annie?" He swallowed his sadness, despising this new distance between them. "If you need anything, anything at all, call me."

Her smile died. "Goodbye, Quinn."

A tingling panic started in his gut and worked its way up to numb his face. He couldn't take it if she walked away and casually dismissed him from her life. He wanted her to continue to love him. To feel for him what he felt for her. What he could finally admit he'd felt for a long time. Fear paralyzed his actions, preventing him from running after her until it was too late and the driver was speeding away.

He was a thousand kinds of fool.

He'd effectively destroyed any chance they could have. She'd never allow herself to be the open and bright woman he'd first met, not with him anyway. Grief for what he'd killed with venomous words and dismissive actions weighed him down, and he rubbed his gut with a shaking hand as if it would stem his sudden, violent urge to be sick.

When he left her place the night of the funeral, he'd thought perhaps she would eventually forgive him and allow him the opportunity to make it right. To build the spectacular loving relationship he'd caught glimpses of whenever they were together. One with a light, easy affection and boatloads of passion. That's what they could've had if only he'd seen her for the truly genuine person he now knew her to be.

Quinn checked his watch. There was no time to follow her. To confess to everything he was feeling and beg her to give him a chance to make it right. He had to get to the children's ward for a storybook reading Trace had set up on his behalf. As he strode toward the building, he shook his head. Was it a coincidence the exact date his friend had scheduled for story time was the same day Annie had therapy? Doubtful. Which meant he had an ally on his side. He'd have to probe Trace's brain and get an idea of what the other man had planned to foster Quinn's relationship with Annie.

CHAPTER 46

That night, as Annie checked each room of her apartment, she thought about her move back home tomorrow. She'd missed the woods and her spa on the patio deck, overlooking the lake. Trying to maintain a hot temperature in her apartment bathtub was impossible. The water never quite stayed at the proper warmth.

She wondered if she could make arrangements with the management to use the facilities at the complex after hours. Back when they thought she was a hero, they were overly courteous. What would it be like now she was seen as a stalking psycho after their resident movie star?

Taking a chance they might be accommodating, she made a quick call. Coincidentally, the property manager's wife happened to be one of the people Annie's warning had saved back in December. He offered her a keycard for use of the hot tub, and the invitation was open-ended.

She wished she'd known beforehand. She'd have taken advantage weeks ago.

For once, it felt like the planets and stars were lining up in her favor.

Or so she thought until the elevator doors opened and Quinn stood inside, the sole occupant.

"I thought you moved back to your estate," she said by way of greeting.

"Mostly. My lease expires at the end of this month."

"Mine, too." Two days. After two days, the chances of running into him again would be slim to none.

"I guess that means we won't be running into each other in the elevator anymore." He'd plucked her thoughts and voiced them, and his smile seemed as sad as she felt.

The new, improved hard-hearted Annie nodded and faced forward with her back to him.

He shifted closer and toyed with the edge of her towel. "Where are you headed this late? It's almost ten."

"The hot tub off the gym."

"Won't it be locked?"

"Membership has its privileges." Annie held up the keycard the management had sent up.

As they passed the second floor and the bell dinged to indicate her destination, she couldn't contain her own curiosity. "What about you? Where are you off to?"

"Chinese run. I was in the middle of trying to memorize last-minute script changes and realized I was starving."

Her stomach's growl filled the small space, reminding her that she'd skipped dinner.

"I can bring back enough for two," he offered.

"No, that's okay. I'm sure eating in the hot tub is frowned upon. Can't have rice floating around and clogging the filter."

"I won't tell if you don't." Deep and tempting, his voice filled her with a rush of heat, sweeping through her body with the speed of an F5 tornado, followed by a desperate longing.

Their eyes connected in the mirrored panels.

His tempting grin had her breasts tightening and her stomach flipping.

Damn him!

One mischievous look, and she was done in.

The strength it took to say no was a divine act of God. No mere mortal could resist him.

"I don't think it's a good idea, Quinn."

His disappointment was a physical thing. It lived and breathed in the air around them.

"No problem. I just thought I'd offer up a decent meal, for old time's sake."

Biting the inside of her cheek as she fought the urge to leap on him, Annie was relieved when the doors opened and she could make good her escape. The pressure of his eyes on her back followed her down the hall until she could close him out with the gym door.

Fifteen minutes into her designated half-hour soak, the overhead lights cut out. Her heart increased its speed and added a heaping side helping of adrenaline.

"Hello?"

Off to her left, she heard a heavy, shuffling footfall.

"Who's there?"

She silently chided herself on her ludicrous question.

Metal scraped along metal, raising goose bumps along the flesh of her arms and plunging her stomach to the bottom of the tub.

Fuck.

This was worse than any horror movie she'd had the misfortune to watch. The scene was set: a vulnerable woman alone in the dark, no weapon of her own, unable to move fast enough to save her own hide, and not a soul around to hear her scream. Additionally, the menacing energy filling the space was enough to smother her.

"Your scare tactics aren't working," she called out.

Oh, yes, they fucking were!

"When I get out of this tub, I'm going to kick your ass," she hollered. Nothing like a little anger to shoot her laughable courage to the surface.

A chill coursed along her spine.

That would be the Holt ancestors telling her to get the hell out of Dodge, she was sure.

For a fraction of a second, she thought maybe Quinn was toying with her, but she dismissed the idea immediately. He wouldn't risk her injuring herself.

Why hadn't she taken him up on dinner?

She'd never be in this predicament if she had.

The trembling started. Despite the hundred-and-three-degree water, she was freezing. Terror did that to a person. Her lips started to chatter, and she clamped her jaw tight to hear movement over her knocking teeth.

Did she dare leave the safety of the tub and feel along the darkened room? Tomorrow the kindly maintenance man would find her stabbed, electrocuted by a toaster thrown in the tub, or drowned and bloated beyond recognition. The fourth option was a slip and fall, cracking her head on the concrete floor.

She'd never wanted Quinn to disregard her wishes more than this second.

"Look, your little game is pissing me off," she said. She could hear the fury in her own voice, but it also contained fear, and she hoped like hell whoever was out there didn't hear it, too. "Leave now, and I won't tell the management."

She nearly snorted at her own stupidity. Like anyone was going to buy that. Chances were they'd conk her over the damned head, murder her, and secure a clean escape.

As she was reaching for her towel, a hand came out of the dark. A bloodcurdling scream was ripped from her soul as she flailed, fell backward, and hit her damaged hip on the tub wall, then slipped under the water.

Arms reached for her.

Scratching at the hands trying to drown her, she surfaced and screamed again.

"*Annie!* It's me! It's Quinn!"

Quinn?

Why was he trying to drown her?

She scooted back and pressed to the side of the tub, frantically scanning the area for help.

"Annie," he called her name again, this time less sharply and more soothingly. "Look at me, sweetheart. Feel me. I'm safe. You know I'm safe."

His words did what touching her hadn't and penetrated her hysteria. Thigh deep in the water with her, he held out a hand, palm up. "Let me help you."

"Quinn?"

"Yes. It's me. Come on, let's get you out of here."

"S-someone was in the room with m-me," she sobbed, wrapping her hands around her stomach and hugging herself. "I think they were t-trying to scare me. They c-c-could still be here."

"I'll have security check into it, okay? We'll figure out who managed to get in." He glanced around the dimly lit room, and she followed his line of sight. A faint light filtered through the hallway door, but it was enough for Annie to see the shadows and get a good look at Quinn's worried expression. "Come on, let's get you upstairs."

"Do you b-believe me?" she asked tentatively, registering he'd entered the tub fully clothed to help her.

He cupped her face between his palms. "I do. The lights were out when I arrived. I thought I heard something, or someone, in addition to you." He eased further down into the water and pulled her into his lap, uncaring that he was ruining his expensive clothing. "I didn't mean to touch you without asking. I was consumed with getting to you."

She didn't protest when he put his arm under her legs and lifted her. He elevated himself to superhero status for hauling her out of the water and down the steps without assistance. After he set her on her feet, he wrapped her towel around her and rubbed her exposed limbs with another from a nearby table. He took another one for himself.

"The staff isn't going to like the mess we're leaving for them," he tried to joke.

"I g-guess it's b-better than a floating b-b-body."

Why wouldn't her teeth stop chattering?

"Christ! Don't kid about that." He gathered her close again and rested his cheek on top of her head.

"Who's k-kidding?" She swallowed hard and let her senses feel the energy surrounding them. Whoever had been there was gone, and with him, he took her adrenaline dump.

"Quinn, the hate… it was awful."

His arms tightened. "Did you see or hear anyone? Did they speak?"

"No. I thought I heard something scrape along one of the outer rails. If I had to guess, I would say a flashlight or knife. It had a metallic sound. They were definitely going for the scare tactic."

"Okay, we should call Frick and Frack." He drew back and smiled when she snorted a laugh. "Can't help it. Since you called them that, it's stuck. Where's your cellphone? I'm afraid mine took a bath."

She picked up her phone from beside the VIP keycard and handed it to him.

"What made you stop in here?" she asked as she rubbed her arms.

"I'm not exactly sure. I was walking into the lobby with the food and felt cold. Like deathly." He pulled away to gaze into her face. "If I didn't know any better, I'd say I had one of your premonitions."

"That's about what they're like, and that's exactly what I was feeling."

QUINN FOUND IT DIFFICULT TO KEEP HIS HANDS OFF ANNIE AS THEY gathered her belongings and the food to head upstairs. He needed to keep reassuring himself she was okay. It didn't sit well that she might've been attacked had he not gone looking for her.

Anger born of his fear boiled his insides.

He paused by the security phone next to the exit. "I'm going to call the front desk to see if they gave a key to anyone else. No one should've been able to get in here."

"How did you?"

Startled by the question, he frowned and thought back. "The door was cracked a little. I just shoved it open when I heard you scream."

After he'd been assured staff would secure the room until the police arrived, Quinn escorted Annie to her apartment. "Get changed, grab Tink, and let's go. You're staying with me tonight."

"You don't think this was a prank?"

"Woman, have you lost your damned mind?" He could no more help the loud, incredulous exclamation than he could stop from hauling her back into his arms. Absently, he noted her standard tangerine scent was cloaked by a heavy chlorine smell. "I'm sorry. No, I don't think it was a prank. Neither do you." He rubbed his hands up and down her chilled arms. "Do you want me to call Sammy or Michael?"

"No. It's late, and it's too long a drive." She pulled away, and he fought the desire to drag her back. "I need a shower, Quinn."

"Hold on." He dead-bolted her door. "Wait here. I want to check out the rest of the apartment."

"No one's here. I would feel it, and Tink wouldn't be calm."

He glanced down. Tink's tongue lolled to the side as she happily waited for a spec of his affection.

"Right. Okay."

"My hero." Annie patted the area of his chest over his heart.

But residual fear was still in her eyes, making her blue irises brighter.

"God, Annie." He gathered her close again, unable to resist. He'd hugged her more in the last five minutes than in all their acquaintance. "Tonight scared ten years off my life." He inhaled deeply and confessed, "I love you so damned much."

She froze.

"I have to get a shower," she blurted.

Her response wasn't the one he'd been expecting, and his stomach muscles clenched. Unreasonably, he wanted to demand she acknowledge and return his feelings. Say *something*, at least. But it was clear she didn't intend to. Her eyes darted everywhere but him, and she escaped as fast as she was able.

Had he not been soaking wet, he'd have collapsed on the couch to relieve the pressure on his trembling knees that tried their damnedest to buckle.

Annie had all but rejected him. For the first time in his life, he'd actually confessed his love to a woman outright, and her response had been, *I have to get a shower.* Hailey hadn't required pretty words, and looking back, he knew he'd never loved her to the extent he loved Annie. Not with this all-consuming intensity coupled with the endless need to touch and taste or to take care of her and make sure she had everything she could ever want. Not with the desire to hear her laughter and be her best friend—as she was his. She'd wormed her way into his life and was the first person he wanted to talk to every morning and the last at night.

Inside, his heart was shriveling to the size of a walnut.

Fuck it.

He sat down, uncaring that he might ruin her furniture. She deserved a wet couch for her cold indifference. The longer he sat, the longer his mood soured, and he stared at his soggy shoes, wondering where the hell they went from here.

What about her confession of love? He'd heard her bare her soul. Did those feelings just go away? His need to know propelled him into the bathroom.

Finding Annie sobbing on the floor wasn't what he'd expected, and the sight sent his stomach plummeting. He dropped to his knees in front of her.

"Annie! What is it, sweetheart?"

She raised tortured gaze to his. "I love you, too."

He closed his eyes in relief seconds before he collapsed next to her with his back against the vanity. He probably should have hugged and kissed the hell out of her, but the shock held him prisoner.

"But… why are you crying?" he finally managed.

"Because I feel like a jerk. I didn't know how to react after all this time."

He shook his head and embraced her. "Aw, sweetheart. I experienced the same thing mere minutes ago. It was the worst five minutes of my life when you didn't respond the way I'd hoped."

A sound suspiciously like a giggle escaped her.

"Are you laughing at me?" he demanded in mock outrage. In truth, jubilance was building inside him, shoving aside the temporary devastation he'd felt.

Annie slowly shifted to straddle him.

"*With* you, not *at* you," she assured him. Holding his head, she kissed him. The aggressive passion behind the kiss had him calculating how long they had before the police arrived, because he sure as hell wanted to take full advantage of her amorous mood.

The doorbell answered his unspoken question.

Quinn swore under his breath. "Do we do rock, paper, scissors to see who gets the door? You in the towel or me with a raging hard-on?"

She laughed, and it was the sweetest sound he'd heard in a long while.

"I have a robe hanging behind the door. I'll go," she offered.

He helped her stand, and if his hands copped a feel of her breasts and ass as he kissed her again, well, it couldn't be helped.

The bell sounded two more times before Annie laughingly escaped.

Tink was barking her excitement and dancing around when Quinn joined the small group.

Fields and Reynolds. They were beginning to be very familiar with these two.

The officers took their statements, and Fields assured Annie they'd already searched the area and reviewed the tapes. Nothing they'd seen corroborated Annie's or Quinn's stories other than the lights being extinguished and Quinn charging into the tub to assist a hysterical Annie.

Reynolds pulled Quinn into the kitchen and lowered his voice. "I don't want to be indelicate here, but we stopped by your apartment first. Is it possible your other girlfriend might've gotten wind you were down with Ms. Holt?"

Both of them were turned with their backs to the main room and hadn't heard Annie's approach.

"Other girlfriend?"

Quinn spun to face five-foot-nothing of outraged female. "I have no other girlfriend, Annie. I swear to God."

Fields and Reynolds exchanged a speaking glance.

"What?" Quinn snapped. "Please, tell me what you *think* you know?"

The older officer was the first to reply. "There was a tall blonde, all made-up, in your apartment. *Scantily clad.*"

"That's not possible," he retorted, reaching for Annie's hand. When she wove her fingers through his, he kissed her temple. "You're enough for me. You always will be," he said.

She nodded and squeezed his hand.

Relieved, he hugged her. Now that his touchy-feely dam had cracked, he couldn't get enough of holding her. Quinn didn't know what he would've done had she not believed him. He didn't want any more misunderstandings getting in the way of their relationship.

He addressed Fields. "If there's truly a woman in my apartment, she's trespassing. No one should even have a key."

The officer studied him for all of five seconds before he spoke into his radio. He signaled Reynolds, and they ran for the door.

"Fields!"

The man paused in his exit. Quinn whipped the keycard at him. Fields nodded his thanks and was once again on the move.

"Thank God we didn't go straight there from downstairs," he said.

Annie released him and moved away.

"Annie? What's wrong?" He grasped her chin and inched her face up. "Do you think I'm lying?"

"No, I believe you. I'm trying to figure out who the woman could be."

"A crazed fan? Who the hell knows?"

"Does this happen to you often?"

He studied her face, looking for any sign this might put her off. Seeing none, he said, "I admit some fans have had boundary issues. But nothing to this extent."

She gave him a soft smile. "I'm going to get that shower now."

"Do you want me to heat up the food?"

"Give me ten minutes."

CHAPTER 47

Annie picked up her phone from the counter when she headed for her bedroom. A quick check over her shoulder showed Quinn's attention was on the skyline outside her kitchen window. In the bathroom, she shut the door and turned the water on before dialing Sammy.

Her sister's sleepy voice answered on the second ring.

"Sammy? It's Annie. Don't freak out..." She went on to explain the situation. "You saw something months ago at the hospital. Was this it?"

"No. I saw you with Quinn being mobbed on your way out of the airport."

"Jesus!" she screeched and paused to listen in case Quinn came running. "You didn't think it was important for us to know?" she whispered harshly, with one eye on the door.

She heard Sammy speaking to Michael, but the words were indistinguishable. After a minute, Sammy said, "We're coming over."

"No. We're okay for tonight. Frick and Frack are here. We'll talk in the morning. I'm moving home soon."

"Annie—"

"Sammy, I've got to go. I'll call you tomorrow to fill you in, okay?"

She disconnected and climbed under the deluge of hot water. In the distance, she heard the doorbell. Figuring Quinn would handle whoever it was, she went back to washing her hair.

A few minutes later, the bathroom door opened, and a tall figure appeared on the other side of the steamed glass. Even his outline sparked her lust. God, the man was divine.

He stripped and joined her, massaging her scalp and rinsing the last of the conditioner from her hair. Odd, but for the first time, she didn't feel self-conscious in his presence.

"What did Frick and Frack say?"

"No one was in my apartment when they went back. Most of my things have been smashed or damaged. They have another officer en route to fingerprint the place. Once that's done, they'll come speak to us again."

The underlying irritation in his voice caught her attention, and she faced him. "I'm sorry."

"It's not your fault, Annie."

Yet she felt as if it was.

"I called Sammy."

"I expected as much when I saw you grab your phone."

"Here I thought I was being sneaky."

He chuckled and turned her toward the stone wall so he could scrub her back. He took great care around the lower lumbar, gently massaging the tight muscles. Her grateful groan bounced off the tiled surround.

"When should we be expecting her?" he asked against the shell of her ear.

"Tomorrow morning."

"Perfect."

His soapy fingers slid over her shoulders and down the slope of her breasts. His large hands cupped her and pulled her back against him. His arousal was evident against her bottom.

Annie practically moaned his name. "Should we be doing this right now? They could come back at any time."

"I have the feeling they'll be tied up for a bit."

But they hadn't done more than kiss before the doorbell rang again.

Quinn swore, and Annie groaned her frustration. "I'll go." Glancing down, she stroked him once. "You might want to switch the water to cold."

With a smirk, she left to dry off and answer the door.

"Do you have a washer and dryer in the apartment?"

Annie glanced up from where she sat removing the tangles from her hair. She gestured with the comb toward a nearby closet. "There's a stackable in there. Do you want me to throw in a load for you?"

"I can do it. Relax." Quinn kissed the top of her head.

"Michael may have left a few things here. Do you want me to check?"

"Sure."

Annie took the extra time to admire his bare ass as he walked away. With a happy sigh, she fished out a t-shirt and sweats.

"We never did get around to eating," he said when he returned. "Our dinner might've been left out a little too long."

"I'll make us grilled cheese sandwiches." Annie smiled and rose to her feet. "When can you get back into your place?"

"Reynolds said they'd stop down when they're done collecting evidence. I'm supposed to do a run-through to see if I notice anything missing."

As she sliced the cheese, he joined her in the kitchen. "Tell me you have beer or something with at least the slightest bit of alcohol in it."

She laughed. "Beer is in the fridge. Tequila and whiskey are in the cabinet above the stove."

He opened the cabinet and paused. A trip to the pantry was his next stop. She suspected what would come next. But he surprised her when he said nothing and returned to grab the whiskey.

"You're not going to poke fun of me for alphabetizing my pantry?" she asked curiously.

He downed a shot and shuddered at the taste. "Nah. I think it's cute."

Ducking her head, she smiled. Charlie had been an absolute ass about her need to organize. His passive-aggressive behavior had led to not returning things where he got them or purposely putting them in the wrong places to annoy her. If she happened to say anything, he'd pick a fight.

"Am I pouring you a shot?" Quinn asked, prodding her out of her musings.

"No, I'm good." And surprisingly, she was. Having him here, making himself comfortable, was like a balm to her battered soul. When he buried his nose in her hair, she sighed, content. She wasn't ready to address the future, but she could damn well appreciate the present.

The doorbell rang again, disrupting their moment.

"It's like Grand Central Station," he quipped as he headed to answer.

When Quinn returned with Reynolds, they both gave the air an appreciative sniff.

"Something smells good." Reynolds's hopeful expression had Annie passing a grilled sandwich across the granite counter.

"Here. I'll make another one."

"Thanks, Annie."

When she'd become Annie instead of Ms. Holt, she'd never know, but she suspected it was about the time she'd started feeding him.

"What's your first name?" she asked as she sliced the cheese for a third and fourth sandwich. The probability was high that if Reynolds was hungry, so was his partner.

A slight flush crept up his neck. "Ryan."

"Ryan Reynolds? That's brilliant!" She laughed.

He smiled good-naturedly and dug into his meal.

"Ryan, can you describe the woman you talked to in Quinn's apartment?"

Both men froze.

"I think I have an idea who it might've been. Humor me?" she asked prettily, adding potato chips to his plate.

Quinn's expression darkened as she charmed the officer. It didn't lighten any when he heard the detailed description of the woman who'd been hanging around his place.

"Does that sound like Paige to you?" she asked him.

"It does."

"Did she think you were out of town?"

"She no longer works for me, Annie. I fired her after the funeral."

Reynolds's head came up, and he set the last bite of his sandwich on the plate. With a wipe of his fingers on the paper towel beside his plate, he opened his notebook. "When did this happen?"

"The day after Hailey's funeral. I didn't care for the way she treated Annie."

Annie snorted, and Quinn shot her a sharp glance before his expression turned sheepish. He knew exactly why she'd scoffed. His treatment of her was no better.

"Yeah, sorry, sweetheart." He ran his fingers down her spine, causing her to squirm inside. With those magical fingertips, the man could get away with murder. Quinn smirked, as if he knew precisely what she was thinking.

Addressing Ryan, he said, "I tried to offer Paige another position with Jensen holdings, but she threw a tantrum, and I'd had enough. I told her that her services were no longer required."

"How did she take it?"

"Well, she wasn't happy about it..." He paused as if trying to remember the conversation. "Now that you mention it, she behaved oddly. She said I would regret my decision, but she'd eventually forgive me." Quinn shook his head. "Honestly, I had a lot going on and didn't give her comment much credit."

Reynolds asked a few more questions and stood when Fields knocked.

"She dated my brother-in-law about eight years ago," Annie told him. "Could've been nine. I don't remember the exact dates. She didn't take the breakup well. For a while afterward, she kept showing up wherever Michael was. Work, dinner, the dates with Sammy. He was ready to file a restraining order, but she eventually moved on. I'm sure if Sammy had had a vision at the time, they would've taken her behavior more seriously."

"At the time?" Fields asked. "You make it sound as if she's had one recently."

Annie opened her mouth, but closed it, pissed she'd blundered. Her gaze snapped to Quinn, and she shrugged at his concerned look.

"Annie? Did she?"

"Yes." She glanced at Fields. "On the phone tonight, she told me she saw Quinn and me mobbed at the airport."

"*For fuck's sake!* You didn't think that was worth mentioning earlier?" Quinn's voice rose loud enough to make her wince.

"It has nothing to do with this situation. Usually, her visions come to fruition much sooner than this. Always within a week or two. Never months." She gave him an apologetic glance. "We had a falling out, Quinn. Sammy saw no reason to elaborate because she didn't believe we were an item."

He wasn't appeased. "You could've told me in the shower."

"We were... uh... busy," she reminded him as heat flooded her face.

A matching blush tinged his cheeks. He cleared his throat. "Point taken."

She couldn't help it. Laughter gripped her and refused to let go.

"Is she okay?" Fields asked.

"She's had a stressful day." Quinn rubbed her back, placed a freshly grilled sandwich in front of the detective, and ushered her from the room under the pretext of putting her to bed.

"Point taken," she giggled. "It almost was!"

"I'm offended. It's thicker than a mere point."

Fits of laughter overcame them, and they fell on the bed. As suddenly as their humor started, it disappeared. They laid on their backs, heads turned toward one another.

"I'm afraid, Quinn. Paige isn't stable. Not if that was her downstairs earlier." She shuddered. "The intent was there, and hate resonated all around me. If you hadn't come in when you did…"

He rolled on his side to face her. With his thumb, he traced the fullness of her lower lip. Quinn remained quiet and contemplative for an inordinate amount of time before he lifted worried eyes to hers.

"I won't let anything happen to you," he assured her. "Tell me you believe me."

She did, and so she nodded.

***

Fields and Reynolds were making themselves at home in Annie's kitchen when Quinn returned.

"Can I get a change of clothes yet?"

"I'll call ahead," Ryan said. When he received the okay, he escorted Quinn upstairs.

The apartment was in shambles. Everywhere he looked lay destruction. Quinn swore under his breath as he went room to room. "That crazy bitch!"

"Yeah, this is going to cost a pretty penny to clean up."

"I'll hire someone after I get back to my estate tomorr—"

Shit!

Paige used to have access to his house. She knew the access and alarm codes even if she didn't have a key. Odds were, if she was as disturbed as he was beginning to believe, she'd probably be on her way there. "Can you send an officer to my other home? Close to Lake Lure. If she made a copy of the key for this place, as you suspect, then she probably made a copy of the other set."

"I'll call it in."

Quinn was fit to be tied. There were few articles of clothing that hadn't been ruined with either bleach or a knife. It amounted to two t-shirts, a pair of shorts, and a pair of jeans.

"How did she have time to do all this?" he wondered aloud.

"Never underestimate an infuriated woman," a female detective told him with a grimace. "I speak from experience."

"Or a psycho," Reynolds added.

"God save me from both," Quinn returned.

Twenty minutes later, after a locksmith was called and the police had finished their investigation, he returned to Annie's place. Fields opened the door with a finger to his lips and a gesture toward Annie asleep on the sofa. Tink's head rested atop her owner's neck, and Quinn was reminded of the day they'd been reunited at the hospital.

"Do you want one of us to stay?" Reynolds asked.

Quinn glanced at his smartwatch. It was well past two a.m.

"I'm not sure you need to. It must've been a long night for you guys. Annie has a dead bolt and an alarm. I'm certain Paige doesn't have a way in." When Fields didn't look convinced, he added, "I'll call Logan. He runs the security company I use from time to time."

He saw the two officers to the door, shook hands, and secured the locks behind them. Annie was sitting up when he returned to the living room.

"What are you still doing up? I thought you'd have gone to sleep a while ago," he asked.

"I wanted to make sure you were okay."

His heart spasmed before picking up its pace.

"Let's go to bed. I'll tell you about everything in the morning." He sighed when he noticed she had a difficult time straightening completely. "How badly did you injure yourself when you fell against the side of the tub tonight?"

"Not bad."

"Tomorrow, you can arrange an appointment with Trace, and I'll take you," he said as he moved to her side to scoop her up.

"I can walk."

"I know, but I'm carrying you, all the same." After setting her on her feet, he caressed her cheek. "Do you need help undressing?"

"No, thank you."

Wordlessly, they climbed in bed, and before plugging his phone into the charger, he sent a text to Logan. Twenty minutes later, they had security in place at the front door. Quinn drew Annie against him and surrendered to sleep.

CHAPTER 48

After playing the night's events over in his mind, one too many times to count, Quinn ended up with painfully little sleep. He'd finally dozed off when a pounding started on the apartment door. Unfamiliar with Annie's place, he stubbed his toe while exiting the bed.

"Sonofa—!" Sleep deprived and out of sorts, he stalked to the alarm, punched in the code, and whipped open the door. *"What is it?"*

"Holymotherofgod! Good morning to me!" Sammy's eyes were huge and focused squarely on his junk. "If you always answer the door like that, I'm coming over *every* morning."

Michael covered her eyes with one hand and made an absent gesture toward Quinn's crotch with the other. "Dude. Morning wood."

Logan's man never looked their way, but the grin on his face said he'd heard every word.

Quinn slammed the door and rested his head against the panel. A giggle sounded to his right. *"Not. A. Word.* Not one solitary word, Annie, or I swear to Christ, I'll murder someone."

She mimed zipping her lips, and the single dimple in her cheek deepened with her struggle not to laugh. The knocking resumed, and he shoved away from the wall to find his pants.

As he hurried into the bathroom, Annie greeted her guests. Shared laughter echoed from the entry. Sammy, being her usual self, must've made a comment about Quinn's member, because Michael's irate voice drifted to him. *"You're not supposed to be ogling other men's packages, Sammy."*

The absurdity of the situation struck, and Quinn bit back a chuckle. When he returned to the living room, he shot Sammy a wink as her sparkling blue gaze met his.

"Planning to stick this time, movie star?" Sammy asked with a glance between Annie and him.

"Yep, if she'll have me." He kissed Annie on the temple.

"Oh, I really hope so," Sammy cooed. "How am I supposed to hold the whole naked-twinker thing over your head for life if you don't?"

"Anyone ever tell you that you've got bats in your belfry?" he asked.

"Pfft. Spend eight months in a looney bin. You'll see what cray-cray *really* looks like."

"Shit, Sammy. I'm sorry." Annie had told him the story, and with all the drama happening, he'd forgotten about Sammy's stint in Brookhaven. Now, he felt like a complete ass for his teasing.

"Water under the bridge." She waved away his apology with a forced grin and wove her arm through his. "Come on. Michael brought donuts from that quaint bakery in Stonebrooke. Has Annie told you about their donuts? I swear the owner sold her soul to the devil to bake like she does."

Quinn was quick to pick up on her cue to change the subject. "My mouth is watering as we speak."

When he entered the kitchen, he saw Annie was moving gingerly, and he swept her off her feet to the counter, taking special care to be gentle with her.

"Hey!" Her objection wasn't as fierce as he'd expected it would be if she were truly mad.

"I know you like to be independent, but your fall last night wasn't a small thing. I can make coffee. Do you want a hot chocolate?" Maybe he should've asked before manhandling her, but his main goal was to ease her discomfort as best he could as quickly as he could.

"Coffee, please."

He shifted closer, lifted her chin, and kissed her properly. "I never got to say good morning."

Her expression softened. "Good morning. And feel free to say it that way every day."

He tucked an escaped strand of her hair behind her ear, then leaned forward to brush her nose with his.

"This could be a scene from one of your movies, Quinn," Sammy sighed. "Although, it would be better viewing for your audience if you took your shirt off."

"Sammy!" Annie and Michael scolded in unison.

Quinn laughed. As much as Sammy teased, he knew it was only that. The love in her eyes when she looked at her husband was enviable. Or it would've been had Annie not entered his life and fallen for him as hard as he'd fallen for her.

Sammy shot them all a cheeky grin and bit into a powdered donut.

"Toss me one of those, will ya?" Annie gestured.

Everyone froze, mouths agape.

"*What?*" she asked.

Sammy was the first to recover. "You want someone to *throw* you a powdered donut? *You*, Miss Can't-have-a-spot-on-her-counters?"

"Why does everyone insist on labeling me with OCD?"

"You said it. I didn't," Sammy quipped.

As Quinn handed Annie a donut on a plate, he tried his damnedest not to laugh. "How do you take your coffee, sweetheart?"

Sammy paused with the donut halfway to her mouth. "This is something you should know after all this time, don't you think?"

"What I *know*, you busybody, is that she *normally* prefers hot chocolate. Coffee is a recent development," he retorted. Why he felt the need to defend himself, he couldn't say.

"Score one for the movie star." Michael raised his donut in salute.

"You're supposed to be on your wife's side," Annie countered with a laugh.

"If you'd have just said you loved her weeks ago, movie star, you wouldn't have gone through half the drama." Sammy laughed at his putout expression. "But I guess some people are just a little slower than others in the smarts department."

Quinn groaned and shook his head. "I'm going to murder your sister, Annie. I'm sorry, but it has to be done."

"Not if I beat you to it," Annie said on a laugh.

"Famous people get acquitted much easier than the average Joe— or in your case, Jill."

She crossed her arms over her chest and huffed out a breath. "Fine. But I don't understand why you get to have all the fun."

"Hello, gang! I'm right here." Sammy scowled. "You'd think *some* people would have developed a thicker skin by now and be able to take a joke."

He ignored her and toyed with a lock of Annie's dark hair. "On a more serious note, I have baby duty this morning. Will you be okay here with your sister and Michael?"

"We need to leave for Florida within the hour," Michael injected apologetically. "Sophie has a follow-up appointment tomorrow afternoon."

"I can reschedule if you want me to stay, sissy," Sammy said.

"Don't you dare. I have an alarm and the guy Logan sent over."

"But seriously, we need to get on the road," Michael stated and kissed his wife's temple. "Now, give your sister a hug and let's go."

Quinn lifted Annie and steadied her as she settled on her feet. The sisters shared a tearful embrace before Michael picked up the baby carrier and shuffled his wife toward the door.

"Why do I always feel like I've been in the center of a whirlwind whenever your sister's around?" Quinn asked Annie after they'd left.

She giggled and patted his ass. "I don't know, *movie star*."

"Don't *you* start." In truth, he didn't mind the moniker.

"You have to say one thing for my sister…"

"What's that?"

"She calls it like it is." Annie laughed and ran her hands along his abs, beneath his shirt. His stomach muscles contracted at her touch, and his desire caught fire. Blood surged to his groin, waking his mini-me. She grinned at the evidence of his arousal. "This is definitely better than the big screen."

"Mmm." He toyed with the top button of her top. "When do you have to be out of here? Today? Tomorrow?"

"End of today. But I hate to break it to you. Sex needs to wait until after I get my hip and back checked." Her hand strayed to the button of his jeans in direct contrast with her words.

He groaned loud enough to make the dog bark.

"But…" Her voice took on a teasing note.

He perked up. "But what?"

"I have another skill I can utilize."

He swallowed hard. "Are you saying what I think you're saying?"

She sat on the couch and unzipped his jeans, freeing him.

"Well, *hello*, Mr. Movie Star," she said in a breathy Marilyn Monroe voice, sending whatever blood was left in his brain straight to his dick. Then she ran her tongue the length of his staff. "Sammy was right. You're sexy as fuck."

"Don't mention your sister, or my balls will shrivel."

"I don't think there's any danger of that happening." She laughed and fondled the anatomy in question.

"Hush, sweetheart. It's time to put that mouth of yours to good use."

SINCE QUINN HAD ALWAYS INTENDED TO SHUTTLE ANNIE BACK AND forth for her appointment with Trace, he waited at the back of the hospital to take her home. He steamrolled her objections, insisting he wasn't going to leave her alone until Paige was found. Who knew what she'd do to Annie at this point? Every time he thought of the destruction of his place, he grew clammy.

But Annie refused to cower. Not to Paige, not to the media, not to anyone.

He admired the hell out of her and wished the world knew her as he did, knew how truly amazing she was. Though their timing was crap. For a while longer, they needed to pretend to be estranged. But he wanted everyone to see what he saw every time he looked into her arresting face, every time her brilliant eyes lit up with humor or love.

And she *did* love him.

Quinn smiled from his soul as he held her hand in the elevator of their building. It stopped on her floor, and Annie went two steps before she jerked to a halt and gasped.

Written on the door in red spray paint, the words *"DIE BITCH!"* glared back at them.

Quinn's adrenaline kicked into overdrive. Acting on instinct, he shuffled her back into the elevator and placed his body protectively in front of hers, jabbing the close-door button as he searched the hallway for the threat.

"Where the hell is the fucking guard?"

"Tink! Tink's in there!" Annie cried, frantically shoving at his back. She fought him like a woman possessed.

"Annie, *stop*! The door looks secure, but we need to make sure no one is lingering. Logan's man is missing."

Before he finished talking, he had his phone in hand and Reynolds on speakerphone. He briefed him on the situation, and they were ordered to wait in the lobby.

"No fucking way. I'm getting my dog."

Of all the obstinate people on the planet, Quinn had to find their queen. The stubborn set of her jaw told him she wasn't budging without her pup. Knowing how important Tink was to her—hell, to them *both*—he pressed the open-door button and checked the hallway again. He ushered her forward, and back to the wall, he wiggled the lock. Tink's excited bark greeted him.

"Enter the key code." He kept a lookout while she did as she was told. "Feel any intruders?"

"No."

Not particularly fond of relying on her early-warning system, he trusted her abilities all the same. "Good. Grab Tink and let's go. We're not staying here."

"I need clothes—"

"We'll figure something out."

"Quinn, stop! I won't be chased out of my own apartment," she argued, stepping farther into her place. Grinding his teeth, he shut and locked the door behind them.

"Annie, you're really starting to piss me off. This is the second time in less than twenty-four hours someone has targeted you. Whoever is doing this not only knows *where* you live, but they have access to our entire fucking building. Stop being foolish."

"I don't feel I am, and I resent you saying so."

"When the police tell you not to go into your apartment and you *still* don't listen, yeah, you're being foolish."

She shoved his chest. "Then leave."

"Like hell!" Quinn inhaled a calming breath and stretched his neck from side to side. The woman was an infuriating pain in the ass, but he'd be damned if he was leaving her to manage this mess. "Look, I'm sorry. I know this must be frightening for you. Hell, it's frightening for me. But the thought of you being targeted because of my fame makes me ill."

"We don't know it's because of you."

"Seriously? Why else would someone write 'die bitch' on your door? Do you have a boyfriend I don't know about?"

She reared back as if slapped.

Dread pounded through his veins. "Do you?"

"Of course not!"

"Then what did I say to cause such a visceral reaction?"

"Charlie. You don't think it's possible he's behind this, do you?"

she asked, snuggling Tink closer to her chest, as if her fur ball could replace Annie's fear with comfort. "I mean, the first incident was yesterday, after we ran into him."

"Why would Charlie do this? It makes no sense."

The doorbell interrupted them.

Quinn only had two seconds to wonder what she intended to say before the insistent knocking required attention.

"I thought Reynolds told you two to wait downstairs," Fields grumbled. One hand rested on the hilt of his gun, and Quinn had a moment's pause. The guy looked ready to shoot Annie for all the aggravation she'd caused him.

"I had to check on my dog." His defensive attitude put her back up.

Quinn opened his mouth to defuse the situation, but Fields beat him to it.

"You and that silly dog." Fields may have sounded gruff, but the officer reached out a hand and scrubbed Tink behind her ear. She gifted him with puppy kisses on the back of his fingers, causing the grizzly old officer to grin. Who knew the curmudgeon had a soft spot for dogs?

"Anything inside seem disturbed?"

"We haven't had a chance to check," Quinn replied. "But the alarm was armed when we walked in."

"All right. Let me check it out, and if it's clear, I'll have you do a walk-through. Stay put."

Within minutes, it was determined Annie's stalker hadn't made it past the front door.

"Are you planning on remaining here, or do you have somewhere safe you can go?"

"I'm trying to talk her into going back to her lake house," Quinn injected with a meaningful glare in her direction.

"Let me guess, she thinks she's perfectly safe where she is? No one is going to frighten her off?"

"How did you guess?" Quinn asked dryly.

Fields gave her a significant look. "Every victim thinks the same thing, right before they're attacked, raped, or murdered. You should listen to your boyfriend."

"He's not… he's…"

Both men lifted their brows and stared.

"Yeah, okay, maybe he is," she conceded. "But as for leaving, you're just trying to scare me."

"Is it working?" Quinn asked, hopeful.

Annie eased down on the edge of the sofa. "Maybe a little."

He squatted in front of her and rubbed his hands on the outside of her knees. "If you don't want to go home, I can fly you somewhere else. We can go anywhere in the country, find a gated community, and hire the best security money can buy. Paige won't be able to get to us. And Charlie has no idea where we are. I think it's the safest bet right now." When she would've protested, he groaned. "Sweetheart, please. You can't stay here, and I'll go out of my mind with worry if you're at your house alone. Didn't you tell me it was a wooded area away from other homes?"

She sighed and touched his cheek.

Turning his head, he kissed her palm, cradling it against his skin.

"Please, Annie," he implored softly.

"Okay. Let me pack a few things."

Relief surged through him, and he closed his eyes.

"Thank you." The light kiss he'd intended turned deeper. Had Fields not cleared his throat, Quinn felt certain it would've morphed into something that would make the guy seriously uncomfortable.

Color crept up his neck. His standard steely control was missing where Annie was concerned.

CHAPTER 49

*I*n the end, they compromised. Quinn extended the lease on the penthouse for a month and had the locks changed, so Annie could stay over when she needed follow-up appointments with Trace, from her latest injury. Mostly, she resided at her lake home, confident she'd be okay after Fields assured her that Charlie had an airtight alibi. And much to Quinn's relief, she'd allow him to hire round-the-clock security for her.

He spent all his spare time at the hospital, arranging to be in the natal-care unit when Ty wasn't so he could visit Serena. A month after her entry into the world, it was time for her to go home with Ty. Her true father.

And the day Quinn said goodbye, it broke his fucking heart.

Annie soothed his hurt as best she could, but she couldn't touch the aching loss. Over the months Hailey had been in a coma, he'd built up the connection to Serena in his mind, and to have it severed so completely was a kick in the teeth.

He left Annie long enough to return to the penthouse, pack what few things he had, and clear out the refrigerator. Then he texted his new assistant to arrange for a cleaning service to scrub everything down. After one last look around, he headed downstairs to talk to the doorman.

"Hey, Harry. It's good to see you looking so well."

"Thanks to Miss Annie," Harold said with a wide smile. "She saved my life. She's a real hero, that gal."

"She is, but don't tell her that. She'll just play it off." Quinn passed him an envelope full of cash, along with the penthouse keys, then shook his hand. "Thanks for everything, Harry. If you ever need anything, give me a call. I put my new assistant's business card inside. He should be contacting you after he sets up a cleaning company."

"It's been my honor, sir. And if I might add, maybe don't let Miss Annie be the one who got away."

Quinn grinned. "I'll do my absolute best to keep her, Harry. You can count on that."

"Quite right, sir." Harold returned his grin, but sobered again to say, "I'm sorry about the mess with your fiancée and baby. You didn't deserve that. Just like Miss Annie didn't deserve what they've been saying in the papers."

Stomach acid in his throat, Quinn stared. "Something new, or more of the vitriol from before?"

"New, sir. Ugly things from her ex-husband."

"That fuck—" Shaking his head, he thanked Harold again and ran for the door.

"Sir! Wait! Don't—"

But he'd walked into a shitstorm of reporters, all hollering his name, all shoving lenses in his face. What the fuck was going on? The sea of press parted for Logan and Mac, and they escorted him to the waiting SUV.

After they were secure, he glanced at Mac. "What the fuck is happening?"

"Annie's husband—"

"Ex," he bit out.

"Ex-husband gave an interview and said he was attacked," Mac replied calmly. "By you."

Of course, he couldn't deny the charges, but Quinn was pissed he hadn't gotten ahead of this when it happened. "What about your guy watching Annie? Is she okay?"

"Yes, sir."

"And the employee you have at her place, he's not going to ghost her like the last one?"

"No, sir. Tony no longer works for us," Logan called over his shoulder as he got on the highway.

"Take me to Annie, please."

Logan never shifted his bald head, but his wary gaze met Mac's in the mirror.

"What?"

"There have been pictures circulating of you and another woman, Quinn," Logan said. "Recent pictures."

"I haven't…"

But he had.

Dinner with an executive producer for his upcoming shoot. Rubbing his forehead, he thought about how the quaint, low-lit restaurant could look like a romantic setting.

"Fuck."

"Leo said the press is camped out at Annie's place, and when we last talked to him, she was packing to go to her mother's." She must've seen the news about his outing with the producer. Although it was innocent enough at the time, the press must've spun it to look like more.

Quinn had his phone out and was dialing her before Mac finished speaking.

She answered on the second ring.

"I can explain."

"No need," she replied in a tight voice. "You told me beforehand you were meeting with Jessica. It's all good."

He sighed. "Annie, nothing happened. She flew out that same night. Logan was there and can—"

"I'm not upset about that," she snapped. "Jesus, Quinn!"

"Then what, sweetheart?"

"Since that goddamned accident, my life has been spiraling out of control. My business is suffering, people are digging stuff up about me, and extremists are camped at the end of my driveway with signs telling me I'm going to hell for consorting with the devil."

"Wait, what? Extremists?"

"Yeah. Sammy told me the media painted us as devil worshippers who sold our souls for our psychic powers."

Quinn bit down to muffle his incredulous laugh.

"You can laugh," she said with a gloomy-sounding sigh. "She thought it was hilarious, too, and said she was buying a goth wardrobe for the occasion."

"Sounds like you and your sister are now famous in your own right," he replied. They had his sympathies because he knew exactly what it was like in the spotlight.

"Infamous, more like it."

"But that's not all, is it?" he asked softly, detecting the underlying stress.

"I hate this, Quinn." Her voice was small and filled with pain.

"I know," he said quietly. "I hate it for you."

"Did you read what Charlie said?"

"No. I just found out he'd talked to the press, and I called you first."

"Quinn, it's bad. He's feeding into the religious fervor, saying he witnessed me performing a ceremony."

Although Quinn had been raised Christian, he didn't actively practice any religion and only attended church around Christmas or Easter when forced to by his mom.

Frowning at the horror of his mother buying into the reports of Annie's walk on the dark side, he asked, "Did you?"

It came out more sharply than intended, and he heard her quick intake of breath.

"Jesus! Not you, too! I don't have time for this. I've got a flight to catch."

It took him all of ten seconds to realize she'd hung up on him, and he redialed her number immediately. The call dropped.

Shooting an accusatory look at the towering trees lining the winding roadway to her home, he threw the phone on the seat between him and Mac.

"Devil worship, huh?" Mac was the first to laugh, having been close enough to overhear their conversation.

Fighting his amusement at first, Quinn finally gave in and laughed.

"She's never going to catch a break with the media, Quinn," Logan said seriously. "You're America's golden boy. You weren't even tainted in their eyes by the beatdown you gave Ty."

"So what? Why should my image affect her?" Quinn grew annoyed on Annie's behalf.

"She doesn't measure up to what the world thinks your perfect mate should be." With a regretful expression, Logan shrugged. "You can't say you haven't seen it with other megastars."

The truth was, Quinn had. "What do I do?"

"If you were kind, you'd let her go and pray the vultures leave her alone soon."

"I can't," he confessed. "She's my entire world."

"Then maybe set the stage for everyone else."

"How?"

"The two of you need to convince people you're not together. Sneak around."

The idea had merit. Quinn would do anything within his power to keep her safe and happy. *Anything but leave her.*

"You want to hide the fact we're in a relationship?" Annie felt sick at the suggestion.

She was leaving for the airport in ten minutes, and Quinn was scheduled to fly to California to start shooting *Hope's Promise* the next day. The role was a small-character bit he told her he'd agreed to last fall in order to start showing his diversity as an actor.

There was no time to discuss his proposition, but it wasn't

something she wanted in the least. She'd look like she ran off and left him, or even worse, like his pathetic castoff. And he would look, well, like Quinn. Sexy, available, and temptation personified. If the world saw him as a bereaved, single male, the wave of propositions he'd receive would be a fucking tsunami of epic proportions.

"The press might back off if we do," he said as she threw the last of her toiletries into her bag.

Pausing to meet his worried gaze, she asked, "Is that what you really want?"

"I think it's for the best."

"Do we have to do this now?" Why did this feel like a brush-off? Couldn't she have one more fucking day of pretend?

"It would appear better if we staged a public fight. Made it seem like we are enemies and have parted ways for good." He must've seen something in her telltale expression because he wrapped his arms around her and held tight. "It's only until we can figure something more permanent out, sweetheart. The last thing we need is the press hounding you to death. Literally and figuratively."

His concern was a living, breathing animal, and she sensed it through his tension. For him, she'd do it.

"Okay. Do we tell those closest to us that we're in a secret relationship?"

"I don't think that's wise. If someone slips, the jig is up."

"Why we have to do any of this is questionable. I doubt they know about us."

"But they'll keep fishing until it's clear there's nothing between us."

Dread built, and her heart hammered. She hated games like the one he was proposing. The one she'd just agreed to. Shifting away, she did a last-minute check of her suitcase's contents. "What are we going to fight about?"

"You pick." He sat down on the bed and smiled at her. "There's Charlie's claim of witchcraft, there's the dinner with Jessica, or we can make something else up."

"No to the first two. I'm not painting a bigger target on my back for the extremists, and I refuse to look like a jealous stalker."

"Fair enough. How about I pick the fight and you storm away? It'll look like you're the injured party."

"Stephen might come running to check my sanity, but okay."

Quinn laughed and drew her down onto his lap. Burying his face against her throat, he gave her a love bite. "I'm going to miss you."

"Ditto."

"I'm also going to apologize to Ty."

She gasped her shock. "When did you decide that?"

"At the hospital yesterday. When I…"

"When you were forced to say goodbye?" she asked softly, witnessing his hard swallow and feeling his residual grief.

"If I can have some small part of Serena's life, favorite uncle maybe, I'll take it."

Ignoring the crack in Quinn's voice, for his sake, Annie brushed his hair back from his forehead. "I think it's an excellent idea. Do you think he'll forgive you?"

"Yeah. He's Ty. If I make the overture, I think his guilt will prompt him to forgive."

"He needs your forgiveness as well. Remember that, okay? You were both hurt by all this."

"I'll remember."

She kissed him, slow and lingering, sighing with regret when she had to go. "Ready for our epic scene?"

"Believe you can pull it off? I don't think you can act that well, myself," he teased, a wicked sparkle lighting in his mossy-green eyes.

"I think we found the reason for our fight."

PART IV

CHAPTER 50

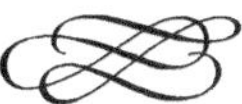

5 MONTHS LATER...

Rain had swept in overnight, beating a low, continuous drum on the roof and gutters, and made perfect their time in bed. Because Quinn's primary bedroom was on the third floor, they'd left the windows open overnight to allow for a cool breeze. Autumn was here, and Quinn sniffed the early morning air appreciatively, grateful for their first night back together after a monthlong break.

So much had happened in the interim. His brother had fallen head over heels in love. Annie had discovered a long lost half sister in Ty's new nanny-turned-fiancée, Lana Martell. And Serena was the apple of everyone's eye.

During that time, Quinn's sneaking around with Annie had presented some serious challenges he'd expected and a major fight he hadn't. But they were back to a good place since their split over a harebrained idea he'd had to test Lana's trustworthiness by offering to sleep with her.

But for whatever reason, Annie had miraculously believed him as he swore he'd never have gone through with his proposition and he'd only wanted to test her reaction to the offer. Of course, what had damned him to his time in purgatory was that he never told

Annie he'd done it, knowing she wouldn't have condoned his tactics. The day she found out, he'd known his goose was cooked.

It had taken her exactly five weeks and a day to forgive him. It had helped that Lana adored Ty and Annie adored Lana. And Quinn thanked his lucky stars every day since they'd made up. Especially ones like today when she was naked and snuggled against him to stay warm.

He heaved a regretful sigh.

"I have to go, sweetheart. My flight is in two hours, and I still need to pack."

Annie ignored him and burrowed closer. And damned if the full-body wiggling against him didn't stir his juices.

"I'll try to get back for a little bit at the end of this week, but there's supposed to be a wrap party for the crew. I should be there." He trailed one lazy finger across her shoulder. "You could always fly out to join me. The bad press has died down, and it would be an easy matter for us to say we started dating."

A kiss on his pec was all the answer he received.

He shoved away his irritation at her hesitancy to tell the world to fuck itself so they could be together openly.

Four months had passed since the filming of *Hope's Promise* started, and with the exception of their break, they had fallen into a routine of sorts. Most Friday afternoons, he flew home and drove straight to Annie's place. They would spend a lazy Saturday in bed, and Sunday evening, he'd hop a flight back to LA to resume filming.

She'd surprised him this weekend by making plans to join him at his Lake Lure house, stating it was about time she saw the place in person rather than from pictures in an architectural magazine. Somehow, his home fit her. Perhaps not as much as hers, and maybe it was just that he wanted her to move in with him so badly, but it all seemed right.

Starting three weeks from Monday, his movie career would be on pause as he explored the world of television. If everything lined up, next month he'd start shooting the second episode of his new TV drama, *Infinite Justice*.

Excitement swirled within him.

When the studio initially called to say they wanted to make the movie into a show, he'd jumped at the chance. The pilot was created and put in the can, then began the wait to hear if it would be picked up by a major network. Because Quinn had contracted to be the lead, the project received an immediate green light.

Since the original movie was set here on the East Coast, the show's producers wanted to recreate the setting. He'd be home most evenings after the shoot, and Annie was ecstatic at the idea of him working closer. She hadn't complained, but if their long-distance relationship bothered her as much as it did him, she couldn't be completely happy.

Disquiet filled him. He hated sneaking. It wasn't in either of their natures.

Quinn eased her aside and rose to gather a few clothing items. Most of his stuff he'd left in LA, but everyone had their favorites, and he was no exception.

"It's been months, Annie. I'd like to introduce you to the world as my girlfriend. Put all the other crap behind us."

"Do we have to decide right now, Quinn? My family is scheduled to arrive later this afternoon, and I have a deadline for the Pearson project. I don't know if I can get away." Annie drew on a fluffy blue robe.

Her request to delay the conversation was reasonable, yet Quinn desired an immediate answer. He wanted her to see what he did for work. Wanted her to experience what a set was like and how everyone became part of a bigger family. If she delayed, she'd miss what went into filming a movie.

"I want you to come out to California," he persisted.

The firm line of her jaw was set into what he called its stubborn, unbudging position. Sensing she was about to dig her heels in and not wanting to end their weekend on an angry note, he disappeared to shower. She could've knocked him over with a feather when she followed him.

"Quinn, please don't be mad. Traveling comes with people. You know I avoid them at all costs." She tried to soften her explanation with a smile.

"I'm not mad, Annie. I'm disappointed you won't make an effort or even *consider* making an effort." He shook his head and looked up at the ceiling as if he'd find the perfect thing to say written over the expanse of marble. "I understand it's easier for you to stay home. If being in public causes you that much distress, I don't want you to go out. But I suspect part of your reasoning is what's been reported. I think you're embarrassed to be seen with me."

Admitting his own insecurities was difficult, but Quinn needed her to view the situation from his perspective.

Her mouth tightened with displeasure, and he knew he'd struck a chord. "I'm right, aren't I? You have a hang-up about being in public with me," he accused.

"Don't start this now," she pleaded. "I don't want to fight before you leave."

He had a choice to make. Either push her and risk a major blowup, or let go of his ire and enjoy their remaining time before his flight. There was no contest. He wanted to spend his last minutes pleasing her—as always.

"Okay. But this will be your last chance to see what I do. Once we wrap this final time, I'll be done out west."

When she bit her lip, he gripped the material of her scoop neckline and tugged her closer. Bending his knees so they were face-to-face, he rubbed his nose lightly against hers. "All I ask is that you think about it, all right?"

She nodded, and he exhaled a relieved breath.

"Will you be kind enough to make me a cup of coffee while I shower?"

"I could shower with you." Her smile was jam-packed full of suggestion. An answering smile pulled the corners of his own mouth.

"You *could*, but then I'd never make it to the airport on time, you lusty wench."

"True. I guess you would need to take a later flight," she teased.

"Oh, Annie, my love, you are too tempting by far."

Quinn dipped his head and nuzzled the delicate skin below her ear. Her low moan of pleasure could be felt against his lips. Maybe he *could* take a later flight.

As he was about to take things to the next level, she surprised him by pushing away with a heartfelt sigh. "If you really are limited on time, you should be going."

He pointed to the erection straining in her direction. "I'm going to look awfully funny walking through the airport with this."

"Oh, I don't know. You'd be fighting off women left and right. That's a pretty impressive stiffy you have there, babe." She trailed her fingers from its base to the tip. "But I can take care of that for you."

"You'd have my eternal gratitude."

"You'd owe me one," she countered, dropping to the edge of the tub and running her hands up his thighs.

"It isn't enough you already get two orgasms to my one?"

"Meh." She laughed and licked his length. "Maybe."

"You're a glutton."

"You have no idea!"

Hours after Quinn had left, her boisterous family arrived. She'd invited Lana and Ty, and they made it a party.

"I have news."

All eyes turned to their newly discovered sister.

"I'm pregnant. Ty and I are going to be having a baby in about eight months."

Sammy snorted.

"That's putting the cart before the horse." To ensure Lana understood she was teasing, Sammy hugged her. "Congratulations, sis. I'm excited Sophie will have someone to play with."

"This calls for a toast!" James called.

Milk was passed to the mother-to-be, while James, Michael, Ty, and Annie each picked up a beer.

"To our lovely sister, Lana, and the next member of the Holt family. May he—or she—be bright, courageous, and full of life like his mother. And may he have his father's patience," James said.

"Hey!" Lana scowled amid their laughter.

The party spilled out on the deck, and Ty brought Annie another beer where she sat in her favorite lounger.

"Hey, pretty lady."

"Hi. Congratulations on your pregnancy. Are you going to go insane with two babies in the house at one time?" she asked.

"Probably not since we have Liam," he laughed. "I'm going to have to hire another nanny, though."

"Just don't fall in love and impregnate that one," Lana said in passing, with a swat to his butt, referring to how they'd met.

"Never!" he hollered after her.

Annie observed how Ty's gaze followed his fiancée wherever she flitted. His happiness was a pleasure to experience. The one perk of her gift.

"I'm so thrilled for you both, Ty. I'm glad you worked through your differences."

"Yeah, finding out about Quinn's proposition after the fact was a kick to the balls, but she's as genuine as they come. And I love her." He smiled. "I never thought it would be possible to care about someone as much as I do Lana. Well, other than immediate family and Serena, that is. But you know what I mean."

"I do," she agreed. "I feel the exact same way about your brother."

His green gaze sharpened on her. It was as if he'd been waiting for the perfect opening. "Then why won't you fly out to California?"

"Not you too! Did he put you up to this?" Holding back her disgusted groan was impossible. The pressure these two Jensens were putting on her for a trip to LA was relentless.

"No. But I know he wants you to see the set. He told me as much."

"I suppose I've been trying to take your initial advice to keep the two separate. I don't fit in with that crowd, Ty. And it's only been three months since that last shit was printed about me. This feels like a reprieve."

How did she explain how much she hated to have her privacy disrupted? She wanted to be more than a hanger-on. If she had to be reported about, she wanted the world to see her as more than some cow-eyed woman panting after Quinn. She needed to be seen as an individual. Smart, independent, and business savvy.

"I keep expecting the other shoe to drop," she admitted.

"What should any of that matter? You love him, and he loves you. Life's too short for all the other garbage."

"You're right. I *know* you are." She sighed and gazed out over the tree line at the back of her property. Coming to a decision, she nodded. "All right. I'll go. But it's under protest, and you have to make the arrangements. I want to surprise him."

Ty grinned and hugged her. "He's going to love it."

A flash of light in the trees drew Annie's notice. "What was that?"

"What?"

He drew back, and his nose collided with hers.

"Ouch!" they cried in unison. Their laughter echoed over the deck, capturing the attention of the rest of their party.

"Time to crank this bitch up!" Sammy shouted. "Where's your Bluetooth speaker?"

"My office desk."

"Be right back."

CHAPTER 51

Two days later, Annie woke with a sense of anticipation. She was flying to California!

Her first trip to the Golden State. Last night, she'd kept it to herself as she video chatted with Quinn. For the first time in weeks, he hadn't mentioned her joining him. He'd seemed distracted and tired.

"You all right, babe?" she'd asked.

"Yeah. I've a lot on my mind. They changed the script again. What a pain in the ass! I have ten new pages to memorize by tomorrow morning. When do they expect me to fucking sleep?"

"I'm sorry. Want to email me the pages, and we can run lines?"

He had gifted her with a weary smile but shook his head. "I love you for offering, but I can handle it. I do need to cut our call short, though."

"No problem. I love you."

"Love you too, sweetheart. Talk soon."

She'd wanted to tell him then and there that she'd be joining him, but as much as she had wanted to brighten his evening, she couldn't risk adding to his stress.

Seeing his surprise in person would be enough.

A ding indicated an incoming text from Lana.

Did you see the morning news?

No.

You need to check it out.

Annie opened her laptop, scared something might've happened to Quinn since they spoke last. Pictures of Ty and her in what appeared as an intimate embrace were unexpected. With his nose and forehead pressed to hers and their shared laughter from the nose bump the day of the party, the images suggested the two of them were sharing *much* more than a joke. Next to those were more recent ones of her and Quinn kissing in her hot tub.

The headlines were the worst. The one she saw was completely provoking.

HAS QUINN JENSEN LOST ANOTHER GIRLFRIEND TO HIS TWIN BROTHER?

Annie didn't bother reading the remainder of the article. What was the point? The damaging headline was enough.

Nausea churned in her gut, and she barely held back from sacrificing her morning coffee to the porcelain god. Had Quinn seen these yet? Was he even awake? A check of the clock showed he'd be waking about now. Would it be better to call and head this off, or should she catch the next flight and arrive sooner than she'd planned? Would he accept her explanation when she got there?

As Annie sat on the edge of her bathtub, she trembled in her anger. How could she ever live like this? The constant digs and insults to her person were too much.

But as she recalled Quinn's face, full of love and passion, she knew he was worth it. Worth anything she needed to go through. He made her feel alive like nothing and no one else ever had. During those gloomy weeks in the hospital, he'd been her ray of light.

No, she would firm her resolve and be the woman he deserved. He knew what the paparazzi were like. He'd laugh this off, and they'd each be grateful for the other's understanding.

All the way to the airport, she felt the driver's eyes touch upon her. The question was in the air between them, and she refused to acknowledge his overtures at conversation. At the airport, she fared no different. Worse, in fact. The glares from Quinn's angry fans were accompanied by blasts of negative energy and snarky comments. Annie kept her walls in place and buried her head in her laptop as if none of them existed.

One particularly ballsy older woman told her she should be ashamed of herself, throwing herself at both Quinn and his brother. Why, she was nothing but a cheap floozy!

Who said floozy anymore?

Annie smiled politely and told the woman she shouldn't believe everything she read in the media.

She checked her phone multiple times, but her standard good-morning text from Quinn hadn't arrived. God, she hoped he didn't believe this garbage. She shot him a message, wishing him luck today with a heart emoji, too much of a coward to address the media article. Surely, if she pretended it didn't exist, it would go by way of the others, right?

Her plane arrived in LA with no mishaps—if one didn't count the drink upended in her lap by the flight attendant or the hatred and disgust pouring off her fellow passengers, all directed at her. An hour into the flight, she'd wanted to stand up and scream that she was innocent. But what would've been the point? People believed the twisted truth from celebrity news stations as if it were the gospel.

The ride Ty had ordered for her was on time, and the driver kindly. Either he knew the hype was bullshit, or he lived in a bubble.

Annie settled in the back of the limo with a relieved sigh. The respite from the unrelenting derision of earlier today allowed her to regain her equilibrium. During the drive to the hotel, she centered herself with deep breathing and a chocolate candy bar. She experienced residual concern because she still hadn't heard from Quinn, and it wasn't like him. On the off chance he hadn't gotten her first text from that morning, she shot him another.

> "Hey, babe, I have a big surprise for you!
> You'll never guess what it is."

When she still hadn't received a response an hour later, she became truly concerned. They'd just pulled up to the hotel when she noticed Quinn escorting an impossibly tall blonde toward the elevators.

Dread settled in the pit of her belly.

"Excuse me one second," she told the driver. "I'll be right back for my things."

She ran to catch Quinn and inserted her hand between the elevator doors just as he bent his head to kiss the woman he was with. Her gasp alerted the couple to her presence. Neither appeared surprised to see her, and if she had to guess, Annie would've said the kiss was staged for her benefit. When she met Quinn's cold eyes, she was positive.

Wordlessly, she dropped her hand and allowed the doors to close. He would eventually sort the truth out with Ty. There was no point in her pleading her case. Not if the second he was angry he turned to another woman for a revenge fuck. Annie was too old and tired for that type of game-playing. Although his brother hadn't given him a lot of reason to trust him in the past, Annie had no such record of betrayal. Not to mention, Ty was madly in love with Lana. That logic should've been the first Quinn reached for if he'd read the false gossip.

Heartbroken and resigned, she retraced her steps back to the limo.

"My plans have changed," she managed to calmly say. Where her cool composure came from was anyone's guess. "Could you take me back to the airport, please?"

The older man watched her for a moment before offering her a kind smile and returning her bag to the trunk of his car. "Of course, Ms. Holt."

On the hour-long trip back, Annie changed her return flight to a one-way trip to Cancun. She'd worry about an end date later. Better a few weeks away than languishing at home, heartsick. Sammy would continue to watch Tink, and Annie was long overdue for a vacation. She needed to disappear for a while and get her head on straight. Hot, sunny days full of sand and sea were the key to retaining her sanity, if not restoring her heart.

***

"WANT TO TELL ME WHAT THAT WAS ABOUT?" SONJA MALCOM ASKED.

"Nothing." Quinn stared at the closing doors of the elevator and fought the urge to chase after Annie. The disillusionment on her lovely face made him uneasy.

"Sure, and I'm the Queen of England."

"Let it go, Sonja," he bit out.

But to his dismay, she wouldn't. "I actually watched the media report today. Based on that woman's expression just now, I have to say, I don't believe a word of it. And sooner or later, she's going to find out I'm a lesbian, so your game of pretend will come to light."

The muscles in his lower jaw ached from his effort to remain silent and not tell her to shut the fuck up.

"She was devastated, Quinn. No cheating girlfriend reacts that way. She is in love with you." Sonja shrugged one elegant shoulder. "Or she was before that kiss."

He was going to be sick. What the hell had he done? If Annie had made the effort to fly all the way here... Dropping his head against the wall of the elevator, he groaned.

"I'm a hot-headed ass!"

"Mmm. You said it, not me."

Jabbing a finger on the lobby button, he cursed himself for a fool. The fucking lift was taking too long, and he jumped off at the next floor to jog down the steps. Why he'd given in to the impulse to kiss Sonja when he caught Annie's reflection in the mirrors along the lobby wall, he'd never know. He only wanted her to experience a fraction of the pain she'd caused him by kissing Ty.

But had he stopped long enough to clear the barrage of false reports from his sleep-deprived mind, he'd have been able to acknowledge two universal truths: Ty was crazy about Lana, and Annie loved *him*. Instead of letting his unreasonable jealousy take over, he should've realized the photos were misleading. That there had to be a logical explanation for the two of them to have embraced. Didn't he know better than to rush to judgment?

By the time he reached the lobby, Annie was nowhere to be seen. He ran for the front desk.

"Did a small, dark-haired woman, about this tall"—he held up his hand at shoulder level—"check in within the last few minutes?"

"No, Mr. Jensen. If she's who I think she was, she returned to a limo waiting in the valet area."

"Thank you," he replied, hiding how crushed he was to find out she'd fled. But what the hell had he expected?

"Should I arrange a car for you, sir? Is there somewhere you'd like to go?"

"I… no. Thank you, Mr. Jeffries." As much as he wanted to give chase, he had no way of knowing where she might've gone. He suspected the airport, but finding her would be a needle in a haystack. Not to mention, he and Sonja had two more days before filming wrapped. He couldn't leave without costing the production company thousands of dollars and potentially facing legal action for violating his contract.

Quinn pulled his cell from his pocket and dialed Annie's number. He wasn't surprised it went straight to voicemail.

"Annie, I was a jackass. Please, call me back. Don't leave." His voice broke on the last word. "I love you."

She didn't return his multiple calls. Not that hour. Not that night. Not that week. When he flew home, it was to discover she'd never returned.

"Where is she?" he asked, frantic with worry. David was still at large.

"None of your business." Sammy's hostility was matched by Michael's. In him, Quinn had poked the sleeping bear. He wouldn't be surprised if the guy took a swing at him.

With one eye trained on Michael, he addressed her. "Sammy, please. For once, can you not give me a hard time?" His heart was on his sleeve, bruised and battered, but there, nonetheless. "I was tired, not thinking straight, and did something extremely stupid. But I love your sister more than my own life."

They remained unmoved.

"If she's here, please, ask her to grant me five minutes to explain."

"That's five more than you gave her in California," she snapped and slammed the door in his face.

He deserved her scorn, but he needed to make it right between Annie and him. The evening after he'd chased her away, he called Ty and explained. Surprisingly, his brother was understanding. Lana, not so much. If she knew where Annie had gone, she didn't intend to reveal any more than Sammy had. The Holt family had circled their wagons.

With nothing left to do but wait for her to come home, he returned to his own estate. About two weeks into his endless calls to Annie, she changed her number. Not to be outdone, for the next four, he called her business line at the same time every night before going to bed.

When the answering machine started to record, he would relay the high points of his day—which were few—and tell her how much he missed her. Loved her. Wanted her back. His calls went unanswered. But because the device always had room for his messages, he assumed *someone* was listening. He could only hope it was her and not her sister deleting everything he'd said.

He continually drove by her house, but the only vehicle in the drive belonged to Sammy. The few times he summoned the nerve to approach Lana, she treated him to a cold shoulder. He wasn't getting through their closed ranks.

Filming started on his new series.

He tried to dive into the role and lose himself to the job, but his days were achingly long, and the nights were longer and absolutely endless without Annie. More often than not, he found himself stopping at McAdams Pub for a drink before heading home. Some nights, he sat alone, and others, the cast or crew joined him.

"Hey Quinn, are you heading to the pub tonight?"

His head whipped around. His costar, Michelle Ghilardi, sidled up next to him, the invitation as plain as the nose on his face. He felt not one inkling of desire. Still, any company was better than being alone with his maudlin self-recriminations. "Yeah."

CHAPTER 52

*A*nnie walked into McAdams Pub, feeling conspicuous and a bit like an idiot now that her online date had bailed. Perhaps she should've rethought her decision to go to the local watering hole alone, but she was sick of her own company since her family had gone back home. She had the feeling Tink was in agreement that she needed to go out and have fun, for a change. Of course, she might have imagined the look of approval the dog had cast her way. After all, at the time, she did have a treat in her hand for her bestie.

She scoped out a place to sit and picked a secluded spot toward the far end of the bar. She was debating her decision to be in a crowd this large when a tall, black-haired bartender shot her a friendly smile and asked for her order.

"Surprise me," Annie said with a smile.

The other woman had great energy. Bubbly and happy, with a huge side of sass. Annie watched her go through the steps of making the drink and noticed the reason for her happiness brush a hand across her shapely butt. The long look the lovers shared nearly had Annie fanning herself.

In hopes of a distraction, she surveyed her surroundings. The place was filling up fast. Music blared, and she could scarcely hear the pretty bartender as she leaned in to tell Annie a man a few seats down wanted to buy her a drink.

"His name's Todd," she hollered over the noise. "But I'd use caution if he hits on you. He's got a mutant schlong." The woman spread her hands about a foot or so apart, then pressed her fingers and thumbs together to form an enormous circle. "Mutant!"

Annie, having just taken a sip, spewed out her cocktail. *"Jesus!"*

"Just sayin'. Poundtown with him will rearrange your internal organs forever."

As the bartender sashayed away, Annie met Todd's gaze and tamped down a giggle. His scowl was laughable, and she crossed him off her list of potential lays. There was history there. If she hadn't already read the situation from their vibes, the middle finger the woman shot Todd's way would have told her.

Without warning, the air shifted around her. Goose bumps started at her neck and traveled down her arms. Only one person had that effect on her.

Quinn.

Frantic, she whipped around to face the door. There he stood, halted by the entrance—*with a another woman.* Not the one from the elevator five weeks ago, but gorgeous, nonetheless. An invisible fist struck Annie in the gut, and sweat beaded on her upper lip. As she fought the urge to vomit, she frantically searched for a diversion. Her gaze swept the occupants of the room and lit on a guy with a rowdy group of friends. They were all staring in her direction.

Perfect.

A horny twenty-something was the ticket. He'd scratch her itch and help take her mind off Quinn at the same time.

She pasted on a flirty smile and looked away. Putting on a casual air, she took a chug of her drink. Liquid courage.

"I'm Mina, by the way," her bartender said when she returned. "You made quick work of that. Another?"

"Annie, and yes, please."

"Annie, can I give you some advice?" At her nod, Mina continued, "You don't seem like the standard cougar who hangs out in bars, trying to fill the void. Don't let your loneliness make you do something stupid."

Shock had Annie's mouth dropping open. "Why would you say that?"

"I've been where you are. Not that long ago. Luckily, I drew Todd the Mutant for my one-night stand. Once he whipped out that Godzilla cock, I almost died of fright. It cured me of looking for love in all the wrong places."

Laughter welled. The image was clear in her mind, just as Mina had intended. With a wink and a wave, she went to serve another, leaving Annie mulling over her words. Her second drink was delivered in short order.

"Hi."

She turned to see Mr. Twenty-Something standing beside her.

"Hi."

"You here alone?"

"Seems like."

"I'm Sean."

And like that, she knew she had to make a decision. If she gave the kid encouragement, he'd be expecting more by closing time. Still, she didn't want to turn him down. She needed the barrier of his youthful arrogance to block out Quinn, whose larger-than-life force continually hit her in waves.

Debating an escape, she checked the mirror and saw Quinn tucked in a booth far enough away from the door that she could sneak out without him noticing.

"So you're going for mysterious?" Sean asked after she'd taken too long to introduce herself.

"Sorry." She gave a half-hearted smile. "I'm Annie."

God, did anyone within hearing distance think this conversation was as awkward as she did? She finished her second drink and signaled for a third.

"Want to get out of here?"

She froze in place.

Had he really just asked that? *So soon?*

"Does that normally work for you? 'Hi, I'm Sean. Want to get out of here?'" she asked, curious despite herself.

His laughter had an endearing quality to it. "Sometimes."

"What percentage of the time? Ten? Twenty? Thirty?"

"You'd be surprised."

"Try me."

"At least sixty-five or seventy," he said with a self-assured grin.

"No shit?"

"No shit."

"It has to be your eyes. You look all sweet and innocent. Like a boy-next-door type," Annie concluded. His cocky grin confirmed her suspicion.

Sean reached out and fondled one of her curls. "What about it?"

"You're going to have to work a little harder than that, Hal."

"Hal? No, *Sean*. My name's Sean."

"Yeah, I know." But in her mind, she'd already dubbed him Shallow Hal. However, telling him that might provoke an adverse reaction, so she kept it to herself.

"Can I buy you a drink?" he asked.

"Now we're talking. I can see you're a fast learner."

Rather than be offended by her sarcasm, he seemed to find her funny.

Mina popped back to deliver Annie's latest round and put a beer on the counter for Annie's companion. She didn't offer any additional comments. She didn't have to. The censure in her expression relayed her thoughts on the matter.

A tightening of Annie's scalp put her on alert and prompted her to cast another sidelong look toward Quinn's table.

Shit.

He'd spotted her.

Pretending she hadn't seen him, she leaned into Sean, smiling up at him like he carried the moon on his shoulders. Her blatant admiring look captured the guy's interest, and he rested his hand on her lower back, overly confident that he'd score. Impulsively, she cut another side glance toward the man who continually haunted her dreams. Quinn glowered, and she could feel his heightened focus from across the room.

She gave an excuse to Shallow Hal and rushed off to the ladies' room. Quinn's black look had done her in. What right did that sonofabitch have to judge her? There he sat with some bimbo hanging all over him, and *he* had the nerve to glare at *her*? Especially after he'd done the same damned thing and kissed another woman in Los Angeles.

The longer Annie stared at her reflection in the bathroom mirror, the angrier she became.

"He's an asshole!"

"Thassh right! All men are ash-holes!" shouted a slurred voice from behind a stall door.

Annie didn't know whether to laugh or cry.

Christ, she hoped that wasn't going to be her in a few more years. Disillusioned and pissed at the world. Possibly drunk and cheering on other women who cursed men.

Whipping out her brightest gloss, Annie coated her lips as she contemplated her next move.

No, she wouldn't go home with Shallow Hal, but she intended to enjoy herself anyway. Another drink and a few dances should do it.

Before opening the door, she gave herself the once-over in the long mirror. The tight jeans flattered her hips and ass. Her shimmery top plunged just enough to show a deep hollow of cleavage and her unrestrained girls to their best advantage. Yeah, she looked good. Maybe not as hot as the redhead with Quinn, but sexy enough to not hate herself. Or at least she might've been tempting without the ever-present limp she was now stuck with from saving his bacon.

Fuck him.

She had to stop obsessing.

Moisture burned her eyes, and she waved her hands in front of her face to dry them. She abhorred the insecurity, the over-whelming sense of loss. A couple of deep, cleansing breaths helped restore her composure. It was time to get back out there, or Shallow Hal would find another victim.

Crumbling crackers!

Had she really just labeled herself a victim of the young player's advances?

Jerking open the door, she charged out, scarcely aware of her surroundings. She should've been. If she had, she would've noticed Quinn waiting for her in the darkened hallway. As it was, she yelped when he gripped her arm.

"What the fuck do you think you're doing?" he growled.

"Well, I *was* taking a piss," she lied. "Now, I'm rejoining my new friend to have some fun. But I'm pretty sure none of it's any of *your* damned business."

They stood toe-to-toe, glaring at each other. Frustration rolled off Quinn. But really, what the hell did he have to be upset about? He had no right.

His gaze dipped to her ruby lips, then lower. His hot gaze seared the skin it caressed. When next their eyes met, his irritation still simmered below the surface, but a very different emotion had taken over.

Desire.

Her nipples tightened in response.

Damned body parts with a mind of their own!

As if he were a wild beast, he sensed her mood swing. Those gleaming green eyes swept downward again and focused on her breasts. Her nips were poking out, bold as you please, fighting for his attention. If she didn't already know he wanted her, she'd have been completely mortified.

He shifted closer, crowding her against the wall. One hand on either side trapped her in place. Focused on her lips, he pressed his full length against her.

"God, Annie. You are driving me fucking crazy."

Not necessarily what a woman wanted to hear.

She shoved him with all the strength she possessed. The reason she was able to move him was because she'd caught him by surprise. She doubted it would've worked otherwise.

She'd made it four steps before he cut in front of her.

"Seriously? You're going to walk away? Just like that?" he demanded.

"Seriously, you are going to hit on me when you're here with another woman?" she countered. "You treat me like a goddamned bone to be chewed on or guarded when another mongrel comes sniffing around. But otherwise, I'm dispensable and beneath contempt. Fuck you, Quinn!" She punched his chest. "Doormat Annie has left the building."

CHAPTER 53

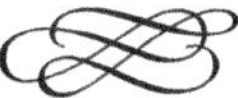

Quinn reared back, shocked by her outburst. He could see why she would question his actions to date. However, that wasn't the case. Not by a long shot. But she was right about one thing: he did have a woman waiting in the booth. Not by choice. He worked with Michelle and wouldn't dream of shitting where he ate.

But Annie didn't know that.

She also hadn't realized their lovemaking had been spectacular and had killed any desire for him to be with another woman. She was an enchantress who kept him enthralled and coming back for more. It would take ten lifetimes to tire of her, if he ever could. And he was more convinced than ever their souls had been together in a previous incarnation, just like her siblings.

"You said you loved me, Annie."

Where the fuck had that come from?

She had to be wondering the same thing because disbelief flashed across her face.

"So, what? That gets me another pity fuck from the Great Quinn Jensen?"

Her voice was shrill, and he surveyed the area to ensure no one had overheard. The kid who'd been hitting on her was heading down the hall toward them.

"Annie, you know it wasn't pity. *Far from it.* And keep your voice down," he warned.

"Oh, that's right. God forbid you get recognized by someone in your hometown. For fuck's sake, do you think they don't already know you live here?" Scorn dripped from each word.

Her every action told him she wanted nothing more to do with him, and yet, a kernel of hope popped. She hadn't denied loving him. The hammering in his heart picked up its pace.

"You said you loved me," he said again. This time, he stepped closer, crowding her against the wall again, trailing a hand down her throat, and placing his finger against her neck to feel her rapid pulse. Her quick intake of breath made clear she wasn't immune to his advances. He lowered his voice to whisper in her ear, "Did you mean it?"

He lifted his head to try and see the truth reflected in her tortured eyes. His throat grew thick with the words he wanted to say. The apology he needed to make. But the timing was all wrong. *Again.*

"Annie? Is this guy bothering you?"

The two of them remained unmoving, ignoring the young man. Each hypnotized by the emotion reflected in the other's eyes.

"Annie?" Quinn asked softly.

"No," she said, voice soft. Her half-hearted push urged him to back away. "No."

Both Quinn and her boy toy were unsure which of them she answered. The kid seemed to think it was in response to his question. Quinn suspected she'd answered his own, and his heart spasmed uncontrollably as his hope lay dying.

"I need a drink," she muttered.

He helplessly watched as she spun on her heel and limped toward the bar. From the corner of his eye, he detected the guy lingering in the hall.

"What?" he snapped.

"Are you really Quinn Jensen?"

Quinn grunted and strode past him. He was more likely to punch the dumbass in the throat than answer.

"I didn't think so," the guy said with a snigger.

Jesus, if Quinn could get through tonight without killing someone, he'd count himself lucky.

Over the next hour, he watched as the boy toy got handsy with Annie. Anger, fueled by jealousy, simmered just below the surface, waiting for the right moment to boil over. One look from her to indicate she didn't care for the guy's attention, and Quinn intended to make sure the kid took a hike.

Michelle had long since given up trying to make conversation. He'd tuned her out within the first fifteen minutes because all her sentences began with "I" and it was annoying as fuck.

"Isn't that the stalker from the funeral?" she said.

Another *I*, but this one caught his attention. He whipped his head around from where he'd been staring at Annie slow dancing with the boy toy. *"What?"*

"The woman you're staring at. I think her name is Ann or Anna something."

"Annie," he ground out. "And she isn't a stalker. Why the hell does everyone keep calling her that?"

She shrugged as if it were no concern of hers. "So do you want to get out of here and fuck or what?"

"No. I don't want to fuck. I don't *fuck* costars. But I'll be happy to call you a ride."

"Don't bother. I can manage," she snapped. In a flash, she was gone. For that, he was profoundly glad. Her persistent come-ons were wearisome. The set would likely be a tense place for a while, but whatever.

As he nursed his beer, his eyes locked on the hand touching Annie's ass. With a shake of his head, he stormed their way. Her back was to him, but he saw her tense when he was only a few feet away.

Good!

"Excuse me. I believe this dance is mine." He practically shoved the kid away as he dragged Annie against him. When the boy toy would've protested, he snarled, *"Piss off!"*

Annie didn't argue and allowed him to tuck her close for the slow song blaring over the sound system.

He nuzzled her dark curls. "I miss you."

"The redhead turn you down tonight?" she asked disdainfully.

"Did you get any of my messages?" he countered, looking down at her stormy visage.

"Yep. Every single one. I deleted them before they played out."

A flicker in her expression indicated she'd lied. He tucked her head to his chest and grinned.

"I guess it's a plus your sister didn't delete them before you had a chance to hear them."

She shrugged as much as she could. "Michael forbid it. He thought it was important I listen to what you had to say."

"Remind me to thank him."

"Why? It doesn't make a difference."

"It should." He wove the fingers of his left hand into her loose hair and tilted her head back. "I was tired the day you arrived. If I'd have had two brain cells working in unison that day, I'd have realized all the coverage was sensationalized. When I saw you there, I was hurt and angry. Feeling played. Again."

Annie's expression softened, but she remained mute.

"Sonja—who is gay, by the way—happened to rideshare back to the hotel where the production company had booked our rooms. There was nothing more to it. She gave me hell for the kiss and essentially called me a dumbass for not seeing the truth immediately."

"Do you think I don't know you were trying to hurt me? I'm not stupid." Her irritability dissipated as fast as it had formed. "What happened to the easy friendship we had in the beginning? How long can we continue on this path of distrust before we hate each other?" she asked. Sadness clung to her, and the hurt he was experiencing for causing her pain overwhelmed him.

His arms tightened.

"I trust you, or I wouldn't be here," he informed her gruffly.

"But I don't trust *you*. I don't trust you not to freak out or make horrible accusations any given day. I don't trust you not to kiss other women as punishment for whatever wrong your twisted mind creates."

The very real fear that she was telling him goodbye consumed him.

"Is it your intent to sleep with Mr. Handsy as revenge?" The question came out harsh with a raw edge.

"No. I intended to sleep with Shallow Hal to drive you away for good, but he's an annoying twat and lost his chance."

He bit back a laugh. The label fit. Her response surprised him, though.

"Why would that drive me away?" he asked, but deep inside, he suspected he knew.

She confirmed his suspicion when she said, "To you, cheating is unforgivable. It doesn't matter that you did it first."

The accusation pissed him off. He drew back and glared.

"I've never cheated on you. *Not once.* Since the day we met, I've never been with another woman."

"You don't think kissing another woman in an elevator is cheating?"

"Not when it was an act, and the woman is gay," he replied stubbornly. "Don't lay infidelity at my door, Annie, because it isn't true."

Another delicate shrug of her shoulders said she didn't believe him.

"You can tell if I'm lying or not."

"That would mean taking down my wall. I'm not doing that with you anymore. At this point, I'm better off alone." She extracted herself from his embrace. "Goodbye, Quinn."

Disbelief kept him rooted to the spot.

CHAPTER 54

The second Annie stepped through her front door, weepy exhaustion struck and she sagged back against the wall.

"Want to talk about it?"

She jumped, not expecting or feeling the additional presence. Her gaze shot to the tall, lean man resting his shoulder against the foyer opening. With his gray eyes and messy-haired appearance, he looked like he'd tumbled out of bed. The loose pajama pants and form-fitting tee shirt added to the effect.

As hot as he was, rock star Gordon James did nothing for her.

She wanted to cry harder.

Instead, she swiped at the evidence of her heartache and said, "I thought you weren't arriving until tomorrow."

"Sorry, I assumed a day early wouldn't matter since I had a set of keys."

"No, it's fine. I told Margie and Gabe you're welcome to stay as long as you need to."

Gordon was Gabriel's youngest brother, and he'd required an out-of-the-way place to hide out from a media shitstorm. Understanding the need, she'd readily agreed when her sister asked.

She tilted her chin to indicate the windows. "You may want to keep the blinds closed and avoid the deck while you're here, though. The paparazzi like to hide in the tree line from time to time."

"Yeah, I caught that online."

She shut her eyes and groaned.

"Of course, you did. The whole fucking world did."

"No judgment here, babe. I've been a victim of their creative reporting myself."

"You don't believe them?" she asked.

His lips curved up at the corners, and a twinkle lit his eyes. "I've known you for a few years, Annie. You're as true and trustworthy as they come."

"How come we never fell in love? You're obviously perfect."

He laughed and straightened.

"Timing, but give us a chance." Gordon wrapped an arm around her shoulders, giving her a glimpse into his tortured soul. He hid it well, only pouring his pain into the songs he wrote. "I was about to have dinner. Interested in sharing?"

"You cooked?"

"No. I ordered Mexican."

She let him steer her toward the dining room. "I didn't know they delivered."

"It's amazing what money can do."

As they sat across the table from each other, Annie realized with a shock that being with this man was effortless. How was it possible?

"How are you so easygoing?"

He paused in taking a sip of his beer. "Excuse me?"

"You must have the most mellow energy on the planet. How is that possible?"

"Ah, yes. I forgot about your little ability."

"Not so little. It's a huge pain in the ass most days," she grumbled and dipped her chips into the bowl of *queso*.

"I can imagine it would be. As for mellow, I pour myself into my music. It's draining—in a good way—but it doesn't leave me with a lot of excess emotions."

"I've been choosing wrong all this time. I need to marry a musician."

Gordon choked on his drink. "Uh, I'm... I..."

For the first time in weeks, she laughed. "You're safe from me, but if you have any nice friends. Let me know."

"Nope. You're all mine."

She liked that he'd caught on to her teasing.

"Or you would be if you weren't Quinn's," he added.

"Shut up."

They ate the rest of the meal in silence, each savoring the flavor of the food.

"Now that you're full and happy, or happier than you were, do you want to talk about what upset you tonight? I have my suspicions since Quinn Jensen is back in town, but I'll leave it to you to tell me."

"I don't want to burden you with my problems, Gordie."

"You aren't. Besides, I'm burdening you with mine by hiding out here."

"You guessed correctly. I was at a local bar." She chugged the remainder of her second beer and enjoyed the resulting buzz. "Quinn happened to stroll in with some hot actress. It really hurts to see him with someone else."

His brows dipped. "To make sure I have all this straight, why don't you fill me in from the beginning?"

Talking through the night, Annie relayed the whole story without leaving anything out. Not her mistakes, not the arguments, not the most recent confrontation at the bar. Gordon remained quiet and thoughtful through the retelling.

"And you're wondering if your love is worth the drama?"

"Yes. Because from where I'm sitting, I don't feel it is." She blinked back the building moisture. "The constant turmoil is too much, Gordie."

"Then you have your answer."

She nodded, miserable.

"But…"

Her head came up, and she met his silver gaze.

"If you think there's a chance for the both of you to be happy, I say grab it with both hands, babe." He shrugged and gathered the remains of their meal before walking into the kitchen. "True love only comes once in a lifetime, but no one wants to work at making a relationship last. There are adjustments and compromises in every aspect of life, Annie. Remember that."

"When did you get to be so wise?"

"I was born wise as well as gorgeous."

A shout of laughter exploded from her for the second time. "And arrogant?"

"Only slightly. It comes with the talent." He narrowed his eyes and opened his mouth before closing it again.

Annie waited, but he seemed to have changed his mind. "Say what you were going to say. I'm a big girl."

He got them both another beer and straddled the bench seat next to her.

"I know Quinn well. We met a few years back. And while a bit of arrogance *does* come with talent, deep down, he's one of the good ones. The world he lives in, it's a lonely one."

"How is that possible?"

"Most of us have an extremely small circle of friends we hold close. Trusting anyone else is foolish and leads to betrayal. Conversations, pictures, schedules… it all becomes public. We tend to be secretive and distrusting because we have to be. If he's told you he trusts you, that's everything."

Gordon had given her a lot to think about. And as she reclined on her bed that night, she thought back over all the mistakes she'd made. Perhaps not as many as Quinn, but they were plentiful. And maybe people in glass houses didn't need to be throwing stones.

The most difficult memory for her to get past was his kissing Sonja. Could she trust him not to sleep with another woman after the next fight? Or the one after that? What was the alternative?

Spending the remainder of her days alone, living a half life? Was part of her worry from her actual experience? Her husband and other boyfriends had done a number on her ability to accept men at face value. Could she dig deep for the wherewithal to put her faith in Quinn again?

At precisely ten p.m., her business phone rang. She rose and listened to the nightly message from Quinn.

"Hey, sweetheart. It's me." He sounded tipsy and discouraged. Annie rubbed the spot over her aching heart. "I needed to tell you the highlight of my day today. It was seeing you, Annie. Touching you, even if it was only for a moment in the hallway and then again on the dance floor. For a few minutes, I felt whole again."

She inched closer to the desk.

"I'm not mad about Shallow Hal. I understand your reasoning." He paused. "That's a lie. I *am* mad. Mad as hell. But not at you. Or maybe a little at you. Couldn't you pick anyone better than that wannabe player?"

He groaned, and she smiled.

"Do you want me to leave you alone for real?"

Her heart lurched and started beating double time.

"Because I don't know that I can."

She sagged against the desk and hung her head. Relief? Why was she torturing herself this way?

"But if you're willing, we can try again. I know living in a fishbowl can be a bitch, Annie. Having to wade through all the garbage..." His sigh was loud and heavy.

"You should put that poor bastard out of his misery, babe," Gordon said from behind her.

"Funny, because my sister thinks I should make him suffer."

"I've met both your sisters, and you must be referring to Sammy. No offense, but she's a bit of a hard ass."

Annie laughed.

"But listen to him ramble on. He's waiting for you to pick up."

"Yeah," she agreed, somber now. She ran her hand over the

receiver and pulled it back as Quinn's one-sided conversation suddenly ended.

"I'm going to bed," she said.

"You can't run forever, Annie."

"Maybe not, but I can walk fast for a while."

His laughter echoed around her tiny office.

CHAPTER 55

For the next week, Quinn continued to leave messages for Annie. In each, he poured his heart out, drawing out the conversation in hopes she'd find it in her heart to forgive him. Finally, when he'd had enough of his own miserable company, he grabbed his keys and drove to her place.

It took him exactly one minute to realize she'd changed the locks.

He repeatedly banged on the door until she jerked it open with a dark scowl. "What the hell, Quinn? It's six in the morning! I didn't get to sleep until one a.m."

Shit. He forgot about her late-night tendencies.

"I..." All the pretty speeches he'd rehearsed abandoned him. Mute, he shrugged.

Infusing indifference and a bit of chill into her tone, Annie asked, "What do you want, Quinn?"

You, he wanted to blurt, but realized he no longer could. He scrambled for something, anything, to say. He didn't have the right.

"I need to apologize."

Apologize, at six a.m.?

What the hell was wrong with him?

Like she was going to buy that.

He mentally scoffed at himself, almost snorting aloud in the process. Had some deadly ameba infected his brain?

Her stoney silence told him how ignorant his excuse sounded.

What was it about this tiny woman that set him off-kilter?

"May I come in?"

Turning on her heel, she led the way to the kitchen. Annie stepped behind the counter and gestured for Quinn to sit on the bar stool across from her.

"Would you like a cup of coffee?"

Her stiff politeness hurt like hell.

"I'll take a hot chocolate, if it isn't too much trouble." He'd been unable to hide the thickness in his throat, and his voice came out huskier than intended.

Annie froze in her tracks, half turned away from him. Inching back around, she glared. "I don't have hot chocolate. Would you prefer tea if you don't want coffee?"

"What? *You* don't have hot chocolate? Is there a world shortage?" His joke fell flat.

"I don't drink it anymore."

"Why, Annie?" he asked, genuinely puzzled.

She ignored his question and countered with one of her own. "If you don't want anything to drink, Quinn, how about you get to the point of your visit? I have a busy schedule today."

"Why, Annie?" he asked again, disregarding her attitude. He knew the answer but needed to hear her say it. To hear her acknowledge that she still felt something for him. He sought an opening to build on.

"Because chocolate gives me hives now."

There it was.

He grinned.

"You're a terrible liar, Annie Holt." With a laugh, he leaned forward to rest on his elbows. "Hives? Really? That is what you are going with? I would have thought a better excuse would be to say you'd drank it all and ran out."

"If your intent was some awkward conversation, you achieved it. So, you came to apologize. Great. Apology accepted for whatever you felt you needed to say you're sorry for. You can go."

Quinn struggled not to wince. Everything about her radiated coldness. The leave-me-the-hell-alone vibe was strong. Still, he could no longer walk away than he could cease to draw breath. He'd waited too long. He knew that. But seeing her again, being this close, made him realize exactly what he wanted.

"I am sorry, Annie. More than you will ever know. I've done nothing but reflect on our relationship, from the beginning until the night at the pub. I've been a horse's ass for at least half of it. We've had a rough go of it. In huge part because of me." He scrubbed his hands up and down his cheeks.

She nodded and uncrossed her arms to grip the counter behind her.

He took hope from her continued silence.

"Initially, facing up to the truth of how I felt about you wasn't something I was prepared to do. Not while Hailey was alive. I heard your words, but the fear she wouldn't pull through was more than I could handle. You were trying to tell me she had given up, and I needed her to fight." He shook his head. "Not for me, but for Serena. As it turned out, a baby that wasn't even mine."

Quinn met her eyes and shot her a self-deprecating smile.

Injecting all the sincerity he could into his voice, he said, "As for you claiming to love me, I didn't think I could trust it. So many women cross my path, and they all declare feelings for me. They don't even know who I am as a person. And at the time, I had too much on my plate to appreciate the gift of your love."

"It was one more thing you couldn't take at that moment," she replied softly.

"Yes. There I was, believing we were friends. You were providing me a refuge from the world, a place where I could forget what was happening, if only for a few minutes. Then suddenly, you changed the rules without telling me."

Quinn paused to take a deep breath. "I was just starting to trust you, to tell you things, when I overheard you talking with Trace. It took the relationship I'd compartmentalized and demolished the walls holding it in place."

"That's old news. I'm not mad about any of that, Quinn," she said, not unkindly. "I understand how it went down. I was there. But what I can't wrap my head around is why you would think I would screw your brother behind your back."

He flinched. "I left here, floating on cloud nine, secure in how we felt about each other. Then one morning, I went for a coffee and to prepare for a day of shooting. The next thing I knew, there we were, once again front-page news plastered all over the internet. The only thing was, that time, there was a picture of you and Ty embracing." Shaking his head, he gave her an imploring look. "Did you see the pictures, Annie? They looked pretty damning."

"Why didn't you ask me? Let me explain? In all the time you've known me, why couldn't you give me the benefit of the doubt?" Her lack of emotion disturbed him. Made him itchy.

"Because in my business, I can't do that. Everyone wants something. And how long had I really known you? Ten months? It wasn't like we'd been friends for years. I could have misread the situation."

"When I showed up at the hotel, you treated me like I was the dirt beneath your feet. You kissed…" Annie paused, exhaling a ragged breath. When she continued, her tone was frigid. "You couldn't even look at me with anything but contempt. I've never been so embarrassed or humiliated in my life." She closed her eyes. "You deliberately set out to hurt me."

"And you didn't purposely hurt me? Picking up that boy toy in the bar?" he argued.

Annie charged forward, her outrage vibrating off her. "Because you showed up with yet another woman, you dumbass!"

"She tagged along, Annie! I didn't invite her."

All the fight left him. He didn't want to argue. All he wanted was to have her back in his arms. To convince her that he loved her and that this time he would put her above all else. Trust her above everyone. He struggled to find the words to bring back his friend.

In the end, all he could say was, "I miss you."

TRUTH.

Annie had to give him credit. To date, he hadn't lied or concocted excuses for his actions. He'd simply stated the truth as he knew it. And he'd been acting when he kissed Sonja. Even she knew that.

Her own truth was that she missed him, too, or the Quinn she'd thought she knew in the weeks they spent bonding at the hospital. The man she'd believed him to be during the months they spent building on their relationship.

However, the man who'd said the horrible things and treated her like crap wasn't one she wanted to know or have in her life. She had a deep understanding of feelings and how people used words to wound when they themselves were wounded. But she wanted someone stronger than that, someone who, although experiencing pain, didn't react like a wounded beast and eviscerate everyone in striking distance. And she certainly didn't believe in setting herself up for heartache if it could be avoided.

Her deliberation of whether to accept his comment at face value or reject him outright was taking forever, but all she could do was stare. Helpless. Words would decide her fate one way or another. They would either send him out of her life for good, or they would mend the gap. Frozen as she was with indecision, she waited too long, and the hope dimmed from his eyes. The fear of the unknown churned in her stomach, making it ache.

The gut reaction she'd thought she had so firmly in check triggered a confession. "I miss you, too."

A light flared to life inside him, sparking an answering one within her. He rushed to her and dragged her close, burying his face in her hair. They stood there for what seemed like an eternity, each lost in the other's embrace. Quinn inched back to gaze down at her. Whatever he saw, whatever truth he sought, chased the tension from his body.

"I'm constantly apologizing, aren't I?"

"Seems like," she replied with a sad smile.

"Are we good?"

"I don't know. I just don't want to fight anymore. Ever."

"Me, either. We've had enough misunderstandings to last a lifetime."

He shifted his hands from her shoulders to her waist, adjusting his grip to lift her and place her on the granite countertop. From there, his hands played with the knot of her robe. Glancing up, he cast her a sweet smile. The last of her pique faded, and she nodded in answer to his unspoken question.

Slowly, he untied the sash and spread the edges apart, never breaking eye contact, giving her every chance to tell him no. Their breathing rasped in sync, quickening with the desire that instantaneously raged between them. Her hair clip was next to go. Using his fingers, he combed her dark curls and rested over one breast. He never said a word as he touched her, as if he feared ruining the moment.

For herself, she sat silently, not wanting to break the spell holding them in place. She couldn't speak for him, but he appeared as dazed as she was. Breathless, she leaned forward, ready for his kiss.

As he inched in, she thought she heard a voice growl, "What the hell do you think you're doing with my woman?"

CHAPTER 56

Quinn pulled back a fraction, unsure if he was hearing things, and seeing the matching want in her eyes, he shrugged it off. His imagination, then. His lips brushed hers.

The voice interrupted again. "You're seriously going to stand there making time with my girl?"

His hands never leaving Annie's hair, Quinn shifted his head back slightly to note the befuddlement in her blue eyes. Those same eyes darted to the right, and with a gasp, she shoved him back. Hard. He stumbled a few steps before righting his balance.

The haze of desire quickly dispensed. He followed her line of vision to the man lounging against the bedroom door, wearing nothing but pajama bottoms.

Gordon James.

Looking like he'd tumbled out of bed. In fairness, he always looked like that.

Both men eyed one another. Gordon seemingly casual but with an underlying smug air.

Quinn looked at Annie and read the trepidation in her expression.

She believed he was going to lose his shit.

He laughed.

"So this is where you're hiding, you sonofabitch." Shaking his head, Quinn dropped a quick kiss on Annie's mouth. Some would call it staking his claim, but he wasn't going another second without kissing her. He lifted her with a hand behind her back and another under her legs.

"And she's *my* woman, Gordie. Forever mine."

"Dammit." Gordon shrugged a shoulder. "I tried, Annie, my love. I had a small window, and now it's gone."

"Maybe if you didn't text me updates, she'd believe you," Quinn retorted with a grin.

"Let me down," Annie said softly. "I have to let Tink out."

"I'll do it."

With a pat of his chest, she crossed to an espresso machine.

He frowned. "Where did that come from?"

Gordon snorted and shoved off the wall. "I may have to hide in the backwoods, but there are some things that are a necessity."

"Fair enough."

Trailing him to the pool deck, Gordon cast a glance at the tree line.

"What you saw was all about the camera angle. You know that, right?"

"Yeah. It's not a well-known fact, but actors can be insecure." Quinn glanced through the window and saw Annie prepping three mugs. "I was a fucking asshole."

"She made up her mind to forgive you last week after she saw you at the bar. I think it was the message you left on her machine."

"You've been here this whole time?" He winced at his accusatory tone.

Gordon's dark brows shot skyward, and he shook his head. "Dude, are you mentally challenged or what? *She loves you.*"

Quinn released a self-disgusted groan. "I've not been sleeping since LA. My emotions are all over the place when it comes to her.

Is this truly what love is? I don't think I'm capable of handling the massive mood swings."

"She isn't either, so get your shit together."

"How long have you known her?" A thought occurred. "And how the hell is she able to tolerate you in her house? You're moody as fuck."

"Actually, I'm not." When Quinn snorted his disbelief, Gordon laughed. "No, really. I'm moody when I'm drinking, but that's about it. Except for the occasional beer, I haven't had any booze here."

Quinn grunted as he let Tink back inside. "Why didn't you stay at my place or Ty's?"

"Ty has the new baby, and your place is watched by the media twenty-four-seven."

"And Annie's isn't?" he snorted.

"There may be the stray reporter here, but not like the cluster-fuck at your place. Besides, I came under the cover of night and haven't gone out." Gordon grinned. "Until now. Can't wait to see tomorrow's headline."

Quinn glanced toward Annie.

"Don't hurt her again, Quinn, or I'll have to kill you. She's practically family."

"I'm going to grovel until the day I die."

"Perfect. Now, I'm going to take my coffee and disappear for a bit."

They joined Annie at the kitchen table, and Quinn straddled the bench beside her, cradling her between his thighs. Gordon stopped only long enough to pick up a mug and toast her with a warm smile.

"What are your plans for the day?" he asked her after Gordon left.

"They *were* to sleep. But I have an appointment with Stephen later this afternoon."

"Stephen? As in Montgomery?"

"I've been seeing him for about a week now." She let him sweat a minute, then said, "Professionally."

"It's strictly your business, but if you want to share, I'm happy to listen."

He wove his fingers into the dark curls resting along the pale column of her throat. His fingertips passed a whisper of a caress along her soft skin. God, he loved her neck. He wanted to plant his lips on her silky flesh and spend the next hour or day or week savoring her taste.

"Okay," she sighed.

Quinn paused to kiss her shoulder. "I love you, Annie. I was never expecting this… this feeling you evoke in me. No matter how many times I fuck up, big or small, I need you to keep saying we can start over. I don't want it to ever be too late."

THERE HE SAT, RAW AND VULNERABLE. THEY WERE A PERFECT matching pair. Annie was tired of punishing him, because she was punishing herself, too.

But she had to be honest. Had to tell him where she stood.

"You have the power to destroy me, babe. I'm not afraid to admit it. But what I *am* afraid of is losing control of my well-ordered life. We're from two different worlds, and I'm so afraid we won't work."

He gripped the nape of her neck and pulled her into him. Her shoulder was pressed to his chest, forehead resting on forehead, not even air stood between them.

"Don't do this. Please," he whispered achingly. "Don't tell me we can't make it. We *can*. I promise."

Because his pain resonated with her, Annie placed her palm over the area of his heart. He reciprocated with his on her. The rapid drumming matched his own racing beat. They were two halves of the same whole. And she desperately wanted to be whole again.

"I didn't intend to. I think it can." She cupped his cheek and leaned back to meet his wary eyes. "I think we'll make it work."

With a small smile, she took the lead and pulled his mouth to hers, fastening her lips on his. Absorbing all that was him.

He reached down to grip her waist, twisting her to face him and pulling her against him. Like a koala on a eucalyptus trunk, she wrapped herself around him.

"I love you, too, Quinn. The once-in-a-lifetime love that's all-consuming. I need you to trust in that. Please."

"I do. I will. Forever, Annie."

The sincerity of his promise made her heart sing, and she grinned. "Forever."

QUINN WASTED NO TIME GETTING HER TO BED, AND TOGETHER, THEY tumbled down on the mattress, sending Tink skittering away to avoid being squished. He fastened his mouth on the part of her delicate neck he'd been dreaming about for weeks. With his lips, he registered her rapid pulse and quirked those same lips in satisfaction.

Ah, his Annie. So quick to respond. So receptive to his every touch.

His love for her was real, profound. What a fool he'd been to not see it before. Hope and desire fueled him on, and Quinn was dedicated to rocking her world, and in doing so, rocking his own. At least, that is what he intended.

"Seriously? You two are like rabbits. Am I to take it you've kissed and made up, so to speak?" Gordon's voice, when it came, was like a bucket of cold water. They both gasped, and Annie made an attempt to scramble away.

Quinn held her down. Firstly, because he had a raging hard-on and releasing her meant his dick wouldn't receive the satisfaction it desperately craved. And secondly, he feared if he let her escape now, she would revert to denying they could have anything more.

Yeah, he had trust issues.

"What the fuck, Gordie?" Quinn yelled over his shoulder.

His indignation didn't faze Gordon one bit.

Gordon stood there, unrepentant, with a shit-eating grin on his face. Devilry danced in his wicked gray eyes.

"I know the timing is bad, but Annie's client is early. Also, you might not want to leave the bedroom door open if you don't intend to show the whole world the business end of your relationship, if you know what I mean."

Annie erupted in giggles, and because her sense of the outrageous was tickled, there was no stopping her hilarity. Tears of mirth ran down from the corner of her eyes into her hairline.

Quinn enjoyed watching her animated face. He gazed down at her, memorizing the moment, storing it up for the times he needed to be on location. Grinning, he swooped in for a quick, hard kiss, then stood and pulled her up with him.

Merry blue eyes met his amused gaze.

They stood that way long enough to make Gordon uncomfortable.

He cleared his throat. "The appointment? Should I reschedule for you?"

"No, Gordie. Please tell her I'll be right out." Annie cleared her throat as well. "I just need to change. Give me five minutes."

Quinn thought of all the things he could do to her in five minutes and offered up a wolfish smile.

Seeing said smile, Gordon told her she had three minutes tops before he exited the doorway.

"I think you'd better go, Quinn."

"Can I wait until you've finished your appointment?"

"It might take a while. She's a new client. They like to tell stories when they show you all their pictures and documents. My one-hour appointment can turn into two or three hours."

"I've got nowhere to be."

"Good." After giving him a sugar-sweet, lingering kiss, she walked away.

CHAPTER 57

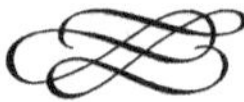

uch later, after Annie's client left, the three of them
gorged on pizza, and she realized she was happy.
She'd never known such peace. Smiling, she watched as Quinn
snuck little bits of sausage to Tink under the table. Probably in an
attempt to get back into her pup's good graces after being gone so
long.

A frisson of disquiet hit, and she shot an inquiring glance across
the table. Surprised to find Gordon studying her, she frowned in
question. For once, he wore a somber expression.

With a slight nod in Quinn's direction, he shook his head.

Getting the message he wanted to speak to her about Quinn at a
different time, she offered up a quick nod and let it go. Or at least
tried to. Apprehension drifted off him. Was he worried for her? Did
he know something she didn't? It remained to be seen.

"Are you staying today?" she asked Quinn quietly.

"I'd like to. Will it bother you if I creep out in the early morning
hours? I have to be on set by six."

She thought about it, and deep down, she wanted him to stay. If
only to chase away all her misgivings. The needy feeling pissed her
off. Annie massaged the back of her neck to dispel the tension and

said, "You have a change of clothes here from last time. I never got around to sending them back to you through Ty."

She didn't mention how she'd kept from washing his shirt for the first two weeks or that she'd hugged it to her at night to sleep. If he found out, he might actually believe she was pathetic.

"Will I disturb your research if I stay over?"

Didn't she indicate it was okay? His overt concern was annoying her. "No. I have to organize my notes before jumping into Gertie's project."

"In that case, I'd like to."

Gordon rose and took his plate to the sink.

"You two are making me sick with all the solicitousness." He pretended to gag.

"I swear to God—"

"You can't kill him, Quinn," Annie said. After leaning in to kiss his cheek, she stood. "We'd be stuck inside with the decomposing corpse, and the smell would be awful."

His laughter brought her back to a time when their friendship was uncomplicated and fun.

"Why can't we bury him in the backyard?" Quinn countered, a twinkle in his eye.

"I still get the occasional photographer lurking back there." And with her comment, they were all back to serious.

"First thing tomorrow, I'm sending my security company over to put up a fence and silent alarms."

"You don't need to do that," she protested.

Surprisingly, Gordon agreed. "Let him. You deserve your privacy as much as the next person, Annie. Also, a crazed fan could target you."

She felt the blood drain from her face. Why had she never thought some disillusioned fan could come after her here? The situation the night in the hot tub was proof enough.

Quinn glared at Gordon and attempted to reassure her. "This isn't like the apartment complex, Annie. You're safe. I could hire a bodyguard if things get worse."

Anxiety took hold. "They never caught Paige or the guy from my hospital room."

"Have either bothered you again?" he asked sharply.

"No, but I've had hang-ups on my personal phone and work line. It's why I changed my cell number."

His warm hand, resting on her hip, shifted to rub small circles on her lower back. "A few of those could've been me."

"No, I know your number and noted those." She went to her office. When she returned, she held a small notebook. "Here."

Quinn's brows collided. "I called that many times, huh?"

Warmed by his care and the fact he'd never given up on her after LA, she wrapped her arms around him from behind, resting her head on his shoulder.

"Confession? I loved that you kept trying." She kissed his ear.

His relief came in the form of sagging shoulders and a tightening of his hand over hers.

"Yeah, the rest of these, definitely not me." A few jotted notes, along with a check of his smartphone, and he had a timeline. "These were all when I was on set or traveling. I think we need to make a list and call the police."

"Why can't my life be simple for one damned day," she grumbled as she collected their plates.

Quinn rose, took the dishes from her to place on the table, and pulled her close. In the reflection of the sliding doors on the other side of her island, she observed their intertwined forms. His cheek rested on top of her head while hers was against his chest, over his heart. They resembled a marble recreation of two star-crossed lovers.

Annie lifted her head in time to witness a troubled expression flash across Gordon's countenance. When their eyes connected across the distance, all concern abruptly disappeared.

"What?" she mouthed.

"Nothing," he mouthed back with a wry smile. Aloud, he said, "I purchased lunch. You two lovebirds are on KP duty."

"I'm always on KP duty," she replied dryly. "Because *you* don't know how to wipe a counter properly."

"Here we go," he laughed. "Quinn, I hope you're taking notes. She's about to lecture you for the next twenty minutes on how to wipe from right to left and swipe crumbs into your palm."

She could hear the answering amusement rumble in Quinn's chest. "You forget, Gordie, I practically lived with her for months. I know all about her quirks."

"And he's not as messy as *you*," she informed Gordon smugly.

"Wow, a man you can live with actually exists! Better snap him up," Gordon teased.

"That's my hope," Quinn inserted.

***

A PHONE CONVERSATION WITH FIELDS AND REYNOLDS PROVED frustrating. They were convinced Paige had moved on, but Quinn wasn't quite so sure. In his experience, stalking escalated. It didn't usually go away until someone was arrested or other legal actions were taken.

"How do you explain the hang-ups?" he argued.

"Press? Scare tactics from your fans? It could be anything, Mr. Jensen," Fields said.

"Doesn't it seem odd that neither you nor my investigator can find any trace of Paige?" Quinn had been mulling over the fact that she'd simply dropped off the face of the earth. One day she was in his apartment, slashing his clothes, and the next, nothing.

"I'll admit it's strange that she hasn't been active on social media and we haven't been able to trace her phone, but perhaps she took a trip to Europe or knows we intend to bring her in for questioning." Fields sighed, and Quinn practically felt his weariness through the line. "It doesn't mean we've stopped looking. But after all this time, it's not our Lieutenant's priority. Keep your security team and PI on the payroll. That's my off-the-record recommendation."

"Thanks."

After he hung up, he had a quick conference call with Logan and Mac, then he went to tell Annie and Gordon the plan. Quinn found them by the pool, sipping margaritas.

"Have I ever told you how much I love these fucking chairs?" he asked as he settled on the end of Annie's. "I mean, who would've thought to get a double-wide lounger?"

She laughed. "Me, because Tink is attached to my hip twenty-four-seven."

"Fair point."

With a quick glance toward the tree line, he pulled her legs onto his lap to massage her feet.

"You're purposely giving them something to report," Gordon said with a light laugh.

"I am."

"But not because you care about our relationship getting out." Annie cocked her head and studied him thoughtfully. "You want to draw Paige or David out. Possibly both."

"I do. Logan and Mac think it's the best way to move forward. We can't live in limbo anymore."

"It's foolish to provoke either of them, Quinn," she warned.

"They've put you through enough, sweetheart. Let's end this."

With a quick glance in Gordon's direction, she nodded.

"Good. Now that's decided, how about you tell me why you've been trying to warn her off, Gordie?" Quinn caught them both by surprise.

"I wasn't." Gordon grimaced and ran a hand through his hair. "I simply wanted her to know what she was signing up for. My girl-friends in the past didn't."

"She knows," he said.

"I know," Annie agreed. With a soft smile for Quinn, she addressed Gordon. "I've been dealing with this on and off for three-quarters of the year. Yes, I need to grow a thicker skin, and I'm working on that, but I love him." Glancing back at Quinn, she said, "I'm sticking."

He grinned his happiness. "We're superglued now."

She laughed.

"Honestly, on paper, you wouldn't match at all. In person, I've never seen a more perfect fit." Gordon lifted his margarita in a toast. "I hope you always find a way to make it work, because I've never seen either of you look happier than you do when you're together."

Annie's eyes were shining. Whether with tears of gratitude or love, Quinn wasn't certain, but he'd always make sure her joy and well-being were his number one priority.

"Gordie, will you take a hike, please?"

With a chuckle, his friend disappeared into the house.

"What was so important that he couldn't hear?" Annie asked softly.

"This."

Quinn withdrew a ring from his pocket and held it up between them. Prior to their break, he'd picked it out and had been holding it ever since. Even when he had a moment of insanity and believed she'd strayed, he still hung on to it, praying for a misunderstanding but too afraid to discover the truth. Yes, he'd gone crazy once he saw the image of Annie and Ty. Yes, he'd behaved badly. However, he'd learned his lesson and realized what he should've known all along; Annie would never seek an extramarital affair. She didn't play games, and she didn't seek strife. And she was the best thing that had happened to him. His one true sanctuary when the world became too much.

"If it's too soon, I understand. But I love you, Annie, and I believe we want the same thing."

"And what's that?" Her sweet smile said she wasn't rejecting him, nor was she being coy. She simply sought clarification.

"A true soulmate. Someone to remain faithful until our dying day. A family for us and for Tink. She's going to need sisters and brothers."

Annie laughed, but as it tapered off, her smile was bittersweet. "And if I can't have children?"

His stomach flipped. It never occurred to him that her injuries might've affected her ability to conceive or birth a child. When her smile dimmed, he leaned forward to tip her chin up.

"Then we'll find another way," he promised. "If you want kids, that is. Do you?"

"I do."

"And you know I do. Is adoption an option for us?"

"It is." Her smile returned, brighter than the sun.

"I'm thrilled if it's just us, and I'm thrilled if we can have children together, through adoption or naturally. I just want to spend the rest of my life with you, Annie, however long that may be."

"You're an active person, Quinn. Have you thought about my limitations and how they can curtail your life?"

"Not once. Because I don't care. If all we can do as a couple is sit in a hospital room and read scripts together or enjoy the light of a Christmas tree as we gorge on crab rangoon together, then so be it. I'm happy to be wherever you are," he said honestly. "Please say you agree."

"I agree."

With a loud whoop, he climbed the length of the lounge chair until they were nose to nose.

Annie laughed as she cradled his face between her palms. "I love you, too."

"Are you okay with this ring? It's not too big or gaudy?" he asked as she shifted to make room for him to sit next to her.

For a long moment, she examined the unique gemstones with their beautiful Caribbean color. They alternated with pavé diamonds of the same size and encircled a four-carat, emerald-cut diamond.

"That's Larimar. It's found in the Dominican Republic, and it's rumored to have healing properties. The color matches your eyes," he said huskily, stroking his thumb across her lower lip. "The diamonds are conflict-free, but if you hate it, I'll take you to pick out whatever you want."

"I love it." She lifted her face to his, and the excitement shimmering in her eyes stole his breath. "It's perfect. I'm not sure what made you consider healing stones, but it's the most thoughtful gift ever." Tucking her hand in his, she asked, "Will you put it on me?"

As he slid the ring over her slender finger, he smiled at the rightness of the moment. The rightness of the woman next to him. The rightness of Annie being his forever love.

"This feels right," she said in a low voice, almost to herself, echoing his sentiment. "Perfect, somehow."

"I was thinking the same. Not to bring up my previous engagement, but it never felt like a coming together of two halves, like it does with you. It was always as if we were trying too hard to make the perfect couple." He lifted her hand to admire the ring's design. "Hailey would've hated this. Only the most expensive jewelry would do. She was a diamonds-all-the-way girl." After kissing Annie's hand, he wove his fingers through hers.

"Yes. My relationship with Charlie was similar. He was sweet in the beginning, and maybe I thought my abilities didn't allow for anything better. Any*one* better. So I settled." Annie shrugged. "Maybe that's why it eventually went wrong."

"It sounds trite, but his loss is my gain."

"I never told you, but I was truly sorry about Hailey and Serena." With her free hand, she caressed his jaw. "I know it was a bone of contention, but I never wanted you to be unhappy or lose out."

"Deep down, I think I knew that, though it was hard to see while I was in the thick of things. If you'd been truly spiteful, you wouldn't be the woman I love. And I do love you, Annie. More than I ever thought it was possible to love another."

She appeared too overwhelmed to respond, but he didn't mind. There was no denying the soft glow of emotion in her Larimar-colored eyes.

CHAPTER 58

The media storm surrounding their engagement was unreal. No matter where they went, reporters were three-people deep, surrounding them.

Annie hated every fucking second of it.

Twice—once when she went to the set to watch Quinn film and now when they were returning from a weeklong trip at his St. Martin home—she experienced a wave of ill intent. However, picking anyone in particular from the crowd was a joke. She was a head shorter than most, and her entire visual field consisted of camera lenses and Quinn's back as he pulled her along.

Shouts of "Quinn" or "Annie" made it difficult to be heard over the crowd, and as the suffocating sense of danger encroached on her psyche, she tugged Quinn to a stop and froze in place.

"He's here," she mouthed.

From nowhere, a palm-sized rock slammed into Quinn's temple, and he barely had time to look surprised as he fell to his knees. A nearby reporter grabbed for him as the other jostled Annie to get pictures of Quinn's fall. Fighting like a madwoman, she shoved, hit, and even bit someone's arm to get to him.

"Back the fuck off!" Logan shouted, throwing the occasional punch to make room for her and Mac to get to Quinn.

Her heart nearly stopped when she saw the blood gushing from his head wound.

"Quinn! Ohmygod, Quinn!" Searching for anything to stem the flow, she was about to rip her t-shirt off when Mac handed her one from out of nowhere. She balled it and pressed it to the wound as she knelt behind Quinn to support his back. "Talk to me, babe," she said urgently. "Are you okay?"

He grunted a "yes" as he tried to shift and stand. Had Mac not been there, Quinn would've dropped like the stone that had hit him.

"We have to get him to the hospital, Mac," she cried over the noise of cameras and press. "Help me get him to the car."

Together, Logan and Mac supported Quinn between them as they walked him to one of two waiting SUVs. Once Annie and Quinn were situated, Mac told her they'd meet her at the emergency room, then slammed the door to jog to the vehicle in front of theirs.

Though the ride was only five minutes at most, by the time they pulled up to the entrance doors, it was dark outside. The glowing red ER sign was over bright to Quinn's sensitive eyes, and he hissed like a vampire faced with sunlight as he raised his hand to block out the light.

"It's okay, babe," she said soothingly. "Keep your eyes closed if you have to and trust Logan and Mac to get you inside."

Trace was there to meet them.

"I saw it on the news. Holy hell!" He began barking orders for orderlies and staff to get Quinn to CT since he still couldn't seem to stand on his own. After giving Annie a quick hug and pointing her in the direction of a waiting area, Trace hurried after the wheelchair carrying Quinn.

"Start scanning any footage you can find, Mac," Logan ordered. "Get Riggs and Bosco on it, too. I want to know who the fuck did this and why. Then I want charges pressed."

"It was David Rice," Annie said in a shaky voice. "I felt him right before I stopped. It's my fault Quinn was struck."

They both stared at her for the length it took to process what she'd said. Logan closed his eyes and shook his head.

"Of course. That fucking rock would've hit you if you'd continued walking," he concluded. Wrapping her in a bear hug, he said, "Don't worry. If David's close, we're going to find him. He won't get to either of you again."

"But he will," she replied softly. Glancing out the window, she absently noted the drizzle and the sheen from the water on the ground. It would be tonight. Her nightmarish vision was about to become a reality. "Soon."

"What do you know, Annie?" Mac asked urgently.

"David is going to attack me in the parking lot tonight, or tomorrow morning, at the latest."

"We won't let that happen."

"Yes, you will. Or at least let him get close enough for Frick and Frack to catch." Her resolve was stronger than their protests, and she intended to force them to come up with a plan of action—with her as the bait.

"And what about Quinn? He's going to fire us, and that's *after* he roasts our balls over an open flame." Logan looked none too thrilled with her idea.

"This isn't about him. Or not directly," she amended when Logan's black brows shot so far up his forehead it looked like he had hair. "He was the one who said he wanted this resolved. Catching David in the act is the only way to do that, and with as many witnesses as there will be, preferably with cameras running, we are bound to get a conviction this time."

"Annie…"

"I fucking hate this," Mac muttered at the same time Logan groaned her name.

"Please, guys? I can't live like this anymore. With or without you there, he's going to come after me, and what happens if he succeeds?"

Looking resigned, Logan had a silent communication with his colleague. After a long moment, they nodded their agreement.

Trace returned to bring her to Quinn's room, and before she left the waiting area, she said, "You two come up with a foolproof plan. Whatever it is, I'll agree. But it has to be tonight. We can't risk David going back into hiding for another six months."

"Stupid, stupid, stupid! Why are you so stupid?" Annie muttered to herself for the millionth time that night as she walked to her vehicle on some pretext or another.

Mac was hiding in the backseat of the car she'd parked toward the rear of the lot earlier, when the entire place was full. Just inside the lobby entrance—eerily absent of visitors—the reporter from whom Quinn had purchased David's file waited with his camera. Jason had been all kinds of helpful for this exclusive. Logan was parked in a blacked-out SUV halfway between Annie's car and the hospital, ready to come to her aid at a second's notice.

Even knowing they were there and that Frick and Frack were somewhere close by, listening through her earpiece and monitoring the scene with their tech gadgets, Annie couldn't stop shaking.

"It's okay, Annie. Stay calm and keep your hand on the taser in your purse." Logan's voice was soothing and irritating at the same time.

How the hell was she supposed to stay calm? A psycho was out for her blood, and if they weren't quick enough, she'd get a shank to the kidney or some other vital organ.

About thirty feet from her car, she heard the telltale sound of David's shuffling walk. Spinning toward Logan's SUV, she gauged the distance.

He was the closest.

Picking up her pace, she limped toward his vehicle. And it might've been her imagination, but she could almost feel David breathing down her neck. In her dreams, she'd seen this event a thousand times. All it would take was one misstep, one ill-timed move, and she was toast.

She was almost parallel with the light post, where she was to be stabbed. With her heart thudding painfully in her head, she could barely hear Logan's voice.

"Now, Annie! *Now!*"

Ducking the arm intended to choke hold her, she feigned left and hit him with the taser right where his jacket and shirt rode up to expose his belly. She wasn't playing earlier when she'd set it to stun an elephant, and thank Christ for that, because David was larger than she remembered. A true grizzly bear of a guy.

And like an enraged bear, he swung his massive paws, knocking her to the ground. Her trusty taser flew from her hand, and the sound of the plastic casing skidding along the pavement triggered her fear.

"I was going to make it quick, bitch, but now I think I'll take my time." There was promised retribution in his voice, and Annie's knees quaked despite knowing help was imminent.

She held up a hand. "Wait!"

And weirdly, he paused. Maybe it was because she wasn't pleading for her life or screaming for help, but he appeared confused.

"Why?" she asked as she shifted to a kneeling position. "Why me? What have I ever done to you?"

"You could've saved my brother." David pointed the knife at her and shook it. "He was just a kid, and because you chose to save your precious movie-star boyfriend, Benny died."

She didn't remember seeing any small children left alone, but her memories of that day were skewed after nearly a year.

"I shouted a warning. Why didn't your parents help him get to safety?"

"He was traveling alone." The knife dropped a fraction.

The truth dawned. The boy with the earbuds who had been next to her. He wouldn't have heard her, and he'd been absorbed in his game.

"Yeah, I see you remember him, bitch. And don't try to deny it,"

David shouted. "You were sitting next to him. *You could've warned him!*"

"I'm so sorry, David. I didn't know he didn't make it," she said, agonized that she hadn't thought to make sure Benny heard her warning. "I assumed everyone saw the commotion. Heard me yelling. I'm so sorry."

"That's not going to save you, you fucking bitch!" he screamed, incensed by her apology. Only one foot into his charge, shots rang out, and his raised knife clattered to the pavement as his enraged expression morphed into one of surprise. As if in slow motion, he shifted his eyes from hers to his chest. "Benny."

It was a plea for forgiveness for not avenging his death, and the wash of regret filled Annie's heart as bullets ripped through his lungs. David's brief agony was hers as he dropped to the ground, struggling in vain to breathe.

As his life force ebbed, Annie ignored Logan's and Fields's shouts, and she scrambled over to David. Placing her hands over the wounds, she applied pressure.

"I'm sorry, David. I'm so sorry. Tell Benny I'm sorry," she cried. Her sobs weren't for David—he was unredeemable—but through the physical connection, she could see Benny through his brother's eyes, and he'd been a good kid. One undeserving of so young and tragic a death. "Please tell Benny I'm sorry," she whispered raggedly as David closed his eyes for a final time.

CHAPTER 59

"I should wring your neck and fire the lot of them!" Quinn's shout echoed around the closet-sized interview room at the local precinct, and the reverb increased the aching in his head.

"But you won't," Annie said quietly, her face buried against her folded arms.

"But I won't," he agreed in a gruff voice, squatting beside her and touching her knee. "I'm sorry I wasn't there, sweetheart. I should've been there."

"You were never meant to be there." She turned toward him. "The night was always going to play out this way. Or in some semblance of it anyway."

The sorrowful gaze she lifted to meet his was filled with pain and regret.

"He was just a kid, Quinn. Benny." Her inhale was ragged, and her eyes locked on her hands as if David's blood still stained them. "I could've saved him."

There was no point in lying or trying to ease her guilt. Annie would always feel responsible now that she knew the boy had died that day.

"Maybe," he agreed. "But if you did, Serena wouldn't be here. I, for one, am selfishly glad you made the decision you did."

Her head came up, and a small fraction of her grief disappeared. With a nod, she accepted the hand he offered her as he stood.

"Come on, sweetheart. Let's go home."

"Am I done here? Do they have everything they need for their report?" She touched his bandaged head. "I forgot to ask... Are you okay?"

"Hunky-dory."

"The 80's called, babe. They want their cheesy phrase back," she said dryly, some of her standard humor peeking through.

He smiled and drew her into his arms. "Tell that to the writers of my current show."

"It's going to flop," she predicted. "There will be endless reruns on crappy-old-movie TV."

"Thanks a lot!" Pulling back, he looked at her tear-ravaged face. "Did you have a vision of my show failing?"

An amused smile transformed her poignant visage. "No."

"Whew."

"Can we go home, now?"

As Quinn's hand contacted the knob, it turned and the door swung inward. Fields hobbled in with Reynolds on his heels.

"When are you going to get that damned knee replaced, Byron?" Annie asked, exasperation in her tone.

"Next week, you nag," Fields replied with a hint of a smile. "But have a seat. I've got news."

Quinn pulled out the chair for Annie and pressed his palms to her shoulders as she reached up to clasp his.

"What's this news?" he asked.

Reynolds passed a black-and-white picture across the table. "Recognize this woman?"

Though she looked familiar, Quinn couldn't immediately recall who she was, but Annie nodded.

"That's Daisy Jo. Charlie's new wife."

"Right. Her maiden name is Daisy Jo Rice."

It only took a second for it to sink in. "A relation of David's?" Quinn asked.

"Sister," Fields confirmed. "And the person responsible for working David into a frenzy."

"Jesus!"

"It gets better. When we were questioning her, she broke. It seems your obsessed ex-assistant paid Daisy Jo to rile her brother."

"Paige?" Annie squeaked, gripping his hands hard enough to cut off his circulation. "How would she even know to do that?"

"Apparently, she intended to go to your ex-husband, hoping he'd distract you from Quinn. But she encountered a very bitter Daisy Jo instead," Fields explained.

"Let me guess. Daisy Jo was heartbroken over the loss of Benny, and Paige used it to her advantage," Quinn said.

"Yep. She also hates your new fiancée almost as much as Paige. Because of Benny and jealousy over Charlie," Reynolds added.

Annie scoffed. "Her jealousy makes zero sense. She essentially stole him from me, and good riddance."

"I'm not sure she sees it that way when you're all her husband talks about." Fields cast her a sympathetic look. "Having met them both, I'm offering up my apologies that you had to suffer either of them as long as you did."

Quinn grinned when Annie laughed.

"I like you more each day, Byron," she told him.

"Feeling's mutual, my dear." His expression turned to one of concern, and it was disturbing on his craggy face. "But Paige is still in the wind. We have nothing more to go on."

"What happens to Daisy Jo now?" Annie asked.

"Jail time."

In a crazy way, Quinn felt sorry for her. As an accessory to attempted murder, she was likely to serve a long sentence, maybe life, and miss seeing her baby grow up. Although, with her moral code, perhaps Daisy Jo's child would be better off if she wasn't the one parenting her.

"The profile of the woman in the picture with David seemed familiar when I initially looked at it," Quinn said. "Now, I know why. I only saw Daisy Jo in passing, so I didn't make the connection at first."

"Do I have to worry about any other Rice siblings or their parents?" Annie asked Fields.

"Doubtful. They were raised in the foster-care system. No immediate family."

Well, that was one thing to be grateful for.

On the table, Annie's cellphone vibrated, and Quinn glanced at the screen.

Cheatin' Charlie.

It occurred to Quinn that Charlie might be a future problem. "What's to prevent Paige from using someone else to stir up trouble?"

"Nothing, but we hope to find her first," Reynolds said with a warm glance at Annie.

It seemed she was racking up admirers left and right. Maybe that's why Charlie's new bride was jealous. Perhaps he'd never gotten over Annie despite his new life. If the guy had two brain cells to rub together, he'd have realized his mistake immediately. He'd traded down.

"Do you need anything else from us? Is Annie free to go?"

"All free. But keep that security team in place a while longer, all right? At least until Paige is found."

ANNIE COCKED HER HEAD AND STARED AT FIELDS. "FOUND? NOT arrested or in custody? Do you not expect her to be found?"

"I should've known I couldn't get anything by you." He sighed and shook his head. "It's rare for someone to drop off the grid completely and even rarer for someone like her. She might move to another state or country to avoid extradition, but for there to be no trail..."

Understanding where he was going, Annie nodded slowly. "Do you believe David killed her?"

"Maybe. Or Daisy Jo in a fit of hormonal rage. We're working every angle. But the truth stands that David knew how to make his victims disappear for good."

A chill raced along Annie's body. Although she was hesitant to volunteer James's services, she knew he was capable of discovering the truth. If Paige had died at the hands of either of the Rice siblings, he only needed to talk to her spirit to get answers.

"What are you thinking, sweetheart?" Quinn asked with a light squeeze of her shoulders.

"James might be able to help."

Fields was skeptical, and his incredulous tone backed up his indignant energy when he said, "Your hothead brother? You've got to be kidding me."

"He's helped the police with things like this in the past." Annie grinned, knowing the officer was going to scoff. But Fields looked intrigued, and she was surprised by how quickly he'd converted to a believer. "You've come a long way since I first told you what I could do."

"What can I say? You've provided irrefutable facts, Annie. And you delivered a killer into our laps." The older man smiled, and it transformed his worn face to handsome. At one point in his life, Byron Fields had been a looker. "If your brother has an ability like yours, then I'd like to speak to him."

Crinkling her nose, she weighed her next words.

"Out with it," he ordered.

"Jamie's gift is a little different from mine. But between him and my sister, I think they may be able to help you if you have something of Paige's to work with."

"Are they psychic?"

"Sammy is, yes. Jamie is a medium, able to talk to the departed."

Fields grunted, and Ryan appeared intrigued. As the younger officer opened his mouth to speak, Fields cut him off. "Not now, Reynolds."

"I don't mind answering his questions," Annie said. "But I'd like for it to stay in this room."

For the next fifteen minutes, they asked and she told them what she knew. When they were convinced, she called her brother.

"Jamie? No, I'm fine. Why?" A glance at the clock showed it was past midnight, and she cringed. "Oh, sorry." Making a face at the officers, she shrugged. "Look, here's the deal. I need you to come and assist the Sagefield police."

His "no way in hell" forced her to hold the phone away from her ear.

"Jamie," she said softly. "Please."

"Goddammit, Annie. What do they know?" All signs of sleepiness had disappeared with his irritation.

"Everything. And we need to put the attack to rest. They caught the guy tonight, but they think he had another victim recently."

"You sound odd. Who do they think it is?" he asked gruffly.

"Paige. Michael's old girlfriend."

"The one who worked for Quinn?"

"Yeah."

James sighed heavily. "When do they need me there?"

"As soon as you can come."

"I'll be there tomorrow afternoon. Tell them to have something important to Paige handy."

"Will you bring Sammy if you can?"

"Yeah."

In the end, he didn't need to convince their sister to visit. She was already at Annie's house when they arrived home.

"Hey, sissy."

"Hey, Sammy."

They hugged, then Michael volunteered to make hot chocolates for them all as Quinn and Annie collapsed onto the couch.

After the mugs were passed around, Annie relayed the story as concisely as she could. Concluding with, "Frick and Frack would like you and James to help find Paige if you can."

Sammy's eyes locked with Michael's.

"You already know something," Quinn concluded.

"She had a dream last night." Michael perched on the arm of Sammy's chair. "About Paige. They won't find her intact. David and Daisy Jo were pretty thorough."

"Fuck," Annie whispered.

Quinn's emotions were sorrow mixed with regret, but she suspected that came from working with Paige for a while and believing he might've saved her in some small way. Or maybe the regret was because the connection they'd formed sent Paige over the edge of reason.

"I'll call Fields," he said.

"Should we tell Jamie to stay home?" Sammy asked.

"No. Maybe Paige's spirit can lead him to clues. Daisy Jo needs to spend life behind bars."

But what Annie wouldn't voice was that Paige had gotten no more than she deserved. In trying to have David murder *her*, Paige had signed her own death warrant. A hardened murderer like David Rice was never going to let her live and hold power over him.

"Go to bed, gang. Tomorrow will be here soon enough," Gordie said from the kitchen peninsula.

"Have you been there the entire time?" Quinn asked with a deep frown and a glance at Annie.

"Yep."

Laughing, Annie climbed to her feet and wrapped an arm around Quinn's waist. "Before you ask, no, I didn't sense him. But maybe you should take Zen lessons from him. It might benefit our marriage."

EPILOGUE

ONE MONTH LATER...

With James's and Sammy's assistance, traces of Paige's body were located along with the evidence needed to convict Daisy Jo. As promised, Fields kept their names from the media and claimed the police department had received an anonymous tip.

Daisy Jo was sentenced to life without parole, and Charlie was quick to divorce her.

At Quinn's suggestion, Annie blocked her ex-husband's number, and she honestly couldn't figure out why she'd never done it earlier.

Life with Quinn, though not perfect, was damned near close.

"We should get married."

Glancing up from a census report, she raised her brows. "You don't like long engagements?" she teased.

"Nope. I want to tie the knot so tight you never leave."

She laughed as he drew her to her feet, took her seat, then pulled her down onto his lap. His lips brushed the hollow of her throat, and Annie shivered her appreciation.

"You need to work out the prenup contract," she reminded him.

"Fuck that. I trust you."

She sat straighter, breaking contact with his mind-altering lips. "Quinn, that's not wise."

With a loving smile, he traced the line of her jaw with his thumb. "Did you take Charlie for everything when you left?"

"Of course not!"

"And he was a cheating asshat. So why would I think you'd try to screw me over?"

"You need to protect your assets, babe. Any decent lawyer will tell you that."

"The fact that you're arguing in my favor tells me you have a deep sense of right and wrong, sweetheart." He shifted her to straddle his lap. "All good?"

Knowing he was questioning the state of her hip and back, she nodded absently.

"So…" Unbuttoning the top of her blouse, he kissed the exposed valley between her breasts. "Annie Holt, will you marry me as soon as it can be arranged?"

"We haven't written vows," she hedged.

He halted his lovemaking to look at her face. "Are you afraid?"

Was she?

Taking down her wall, she absorbed his feelings, awash with a multitude of sensations: hope, love, certainty, determination… *lust.*

A current of awareness shot through her. From the beginning, she'd known Quinn would be important in her life.

"No," she finally replied. "I'm not afraid at all." Leaning in, she kissed him, savoring the taste of mint and coffee, his admitted addictions. "If you're sure this is what you want, that my gift is one you can live with, then I'll marry you, Quinn."

Joy flooded him and, through their connection, her.

"I've never been more certain of anything in my life, sweetheart. And, on the off chance you said yes, I reserved a jet."

"Oh?" Annie grinned as she toyed with his thick mane, mussing it with her fingers as she relished the silky feel. "You were that sure of yourself, huh?"

"No. I was scared shitless that you'd tell me no or that this was all a bizarre dream. That maybe I was the one in a coma in the hospital."

Sobering, she tugged his head back and met his solemn moss-green eyes. "I love you, Quinn. Now and always. The forever love that follows souls through every plane of existence. Every incarnation of those souls."

"So I'm not dreaming?"

"If you are, then I am, too. And I don't ever want to wake up."

When he drew her head down, his mouth covered hers in one of his soul-branding kisses. And that was why she'd love him for eternity.

Thank you for taking the time to read **AFTER YOU**! *I hope you enjoyed reading Annie and Quinn's story as much as I enjoyed writing it.*

If you're looking for James's story, please be patient. It's still a ways down the road. After You took me close to 2 years to write. However, I hope to be able to devote spare time to the project in the coming years.

Be sure to subscribe to my mailing list to learn about new releases.

For fans who like to interact, my Facebook group entitles readers to "fan only" contests, as well as an exclusive first look at covers, excerpts and more. **Cromer's Carousers** *is the most fun way to follow yet. Facebook.com/groups/cromerscarousers*

I hope to see you there!

Love & Lemon Drops,
T.M. Cromer
www.tmcromer.com

T.M. CROMER

Books in The Holt Family Series:
FINDING YOU
THIS TIME YOU
INCLUDING YOU
AFTER YOU
THE GHOST OF YOU (TBD)

Books in The Thorne Witches Series:
SUMMER MAGIC
AUTUMN MAGIC
WINTER MAGIC
SPRING MAGIC
REKINDLED MAGIC
LONG LOST MAGIC
FOREVER MAGIC
ESSENTIAL MAGIC
MOONLIT MAGIC
ENCHANTED MAGIC
CELESTIAL MAGIC
EVERLASTING MAGIC
CAPTIVATING MAGIC (10.2024)

Books in The Unlucky Charms Series:
PINTS & POTIONS
WHISKEY & WITCHES
BEER & BROOMSTICKS
COCKTAILS & CAULDRONS
WINE & WARLOCKS
HIGHBALLS & HEXES (06.2024)

Books in Sentinels of Magic Series:
THE AETHER (11.2023)
THE DEATH DEALER (05.2024)
THE SEER (TBD)